THE
GIRLS
IN THE
ATTIC

ALSO BY MARIUS GABRIEL

THE
GIRLS
IN THE
ATTIC

MARIUS
GABRIEL

LAKE UNION
PUBLISHING

Text copyright © 2021 by Marius Gabriel

Published by Lake Union Publishing, Seattle

www.apub.com

Amazon, the Amazon logo, and Lake Union Publishing are trademarks of Amazon.com, Inc., or its affiliates.

ISBN-13: 9781542028059
ISBN-10: 1542028051

Cover design by The Brewster Project

Printed in the United States of America

For Mervat

Prologue

It had been a fine memorial service, the family agreed. They'd given Dad a good send-off. The cemetery, in rural Connecticut, was tranquil. The magnificent show of autumn leaves lent additional poignance to an occasion that was melancholy without being tragic. Dad had died in the summer, three months earlier, at ninety-four, burdened by ailments, tired and ready to rest.

The service, held in the ecumenical chapel, had been well organised. The kids had all said something. Voices from different religions had spoken. There had been funny anecdotes, tears and smiles, a release of emotions, all the ingredients of a good ceremony. After the service, flowers had been laid at the grave.

The focus had been on Mom. She hadn't spoken at the service. But that didn't surprise the people who knew her well. Mom didn't do speeches or displays of feeling. She'd worn an exquisite dove-grey suit. Everyone had commented on it. She'd been graceful and gracious, as always.

Someone had remarked that over the past months she had 'settled into widowhood', and the phrase seemed to fit. She'd been dignified and restrained in public. She'd done any crying in private. She'd thanked everyone in person, had made time for friends and relations who had travelled long distances to be here and who'd been unable to come to the funeral, which by family agreement had been a small, private affair.

It had been later, back at Mom's house, that the jarring moments had come.

Maggie hadn't paid much attention to the first incident: just a few words from an old man, whose name she didn't remember, but whose face was distantly familiar. He'd given Maggie a small, faded old photograph, which made no sense to Maggie. His memory was probably failing, and he'd got her mixed up with someone else. Maggie had just smiled and nodded her thanks. She'd put the photograph away.

The second occasion had been an hour or two later, when people were starting to leave the house. An elderly relative of Mom's, one of the few surviving Rosensteins, had taken her hands and murmured some words of sympathy. The words had startled Maggie. She'd looked into the elderly relative's eyes quickly, searching for any signs of confusion. But the gaze that met hers had been serene. She'd watched the old lady leave, ushered into her car by a uniformed chauffeur.

Between the first little incident and the second, something had developed. A crack. And when Maggie thought about it, the crack seemed to extend beyond today. It seemed to travel, whispering, all through her life.

She started to feel that the strange little photograph was something significant, after all, something momentous.

Maggie didn't say anything to Mom until close to midnight, when Mom had had a rest, and the kids and grandkids and great-grandkids had all departed, leaving the house still and empty. There was an abundance of food in the kitchen, enough to feed an army, but neither of them wanted to eat. Instead, they lit a log fire and poured themselves two glasses of Dad's favourite malt whisky.

They settled into armchairs. Maggie raised her glass. 'To Dad.'

Lola raised her own glass. 'To Dad.' After a moment, she added, 'To life.'

They drank. Maggie watched the tongues of flame lick around the bone-dry logs that Dad had cut, seasons ago, before he got so sick and weak. 'Aunt Caroline said something weird to me this afternoon.'

'I heard her,' Lola replied. She, too, was staring into the flames.

'She said it was time you stopped hiding the truth from me. At first I thought she was rambling. But she wasn't. I was really disturbed, Mom. Why would she say something like that?'

Lola didn't reply. Her mother had a way of falling silent that had always made Maggie feel as though a heavy, velvet curtain had dropped around her. You couldn't reach through it. Or you didn't dare. Mom could be formidable.

But this time, Maggie wasn't going to allow herself to be shut out. 'Why would she say something like that?' she repeated.

Lola shook her head abruptly. 'Caroline had no right to speak in that way to you. She's not your mother. I am.'

'That isn't an answer. *Have* you lied to me about anything?'

'There's no answer to that, either. Truth is never a yes or no thing.'

'Mom, don't do that. I'm really upset by this.'

'I'm sorry Caroline upset you.'

'It wasn't just Caroline. There was something else. One of the old men said something, too. I can't remember his name. He gave me this.' She passed her mother the little photograph. 'He seemed to think I'd be glad to have it. He patted my arm like he'd done a good deed. But I have no idea who the people in the photograph are. He said you would explain.'

'Everyone seems to be telling me what I should do,' Lola said dryly. She put on her glasses to look at the picture, tilting it to shed some more light on to the tarnished image. 'Ah,' she sighed.

3

'Who are those people?'

'They were long ago,' Lola said, almost to herself. 'And far from here.'

'Do they have any connection with us?'

'They are the past,' Lola said. 'Perhaps they should stay there.'

'Please don't do that enigmatic routine, Mom. If there's something you should tell me, now's the time.'

Lola glanced at her daughter with dark, almond-shaped eyes, which the years had not yet managed to dull. 'Is now the time? Are you certain about that?'

Maggie felt a pang of unease at her mother's expression. She knew – they all knew – that there was much in their mother's life that was never spoken of. Someone had once said that her early life was 'a closed book', and that phrase, too, seemed to fit. There were no family heirlooms, no silver-framed portraits on the piano, no photograph albums that could be pored over by later generations. There was just Mom. She never spoke of her parents or her family. She never answered questions. And, of course, everyone could imagine why that was. 'If it's too painful for you to talk about—'

'I can talk about it.'

Maggie caught the emphasis. 'You mean that I won't want to hear it?'

'Words can't be unsaid or unheard, once spoken.'

'I understand, Mom. I'm sixty-five years old. I'm not going to fall to pieces.'

Lola looked at her daughter intently, then turned her gaze back to the flames. 'Perhaps not. But I have to tell you about a time when the whole world was falling to pieces. And none of us could save it.'

Chapter 1

It was the second time Max had been wounded, and the second time he had been sent home from the front.

That first time, in 1941, he'd been a conquering hero. On his journey back to Kallenheim, people had made much of him. The girls had blushed in the presence of a glamorous young panzer commander in his black uniform, with his arm in a sling and the Iron Cross on his breast. Older people had been pleased to see one of their warrior sons home from the war. They had smiled, pressed food on him, wanted to buy him a drink. They had taken his photograph, asked him about the campaign.

Things were different now. It was 1944. He had been awarded a second Iron Cross, First Class. But there were no smiles, no offers of food or drink, no photographs. Most of the people on the crowded, blacked-out trains avoided his eyes, but then, his grim face did not invite approaches any longer. His manner was no longer boyish and warm.

If civilians did look at Max, it was with a kind of accusation, as though they blamed him for their privations.

This spring of 1944 was a bitter one. The Russian campaign had ended in catastrophe, and now Stalin's vengeful Red Army was rolling inexorably towards Germany from the East. The British and the Americans would soon be coming from the West. Germany was being devastated by huge bombing raids from the air. It was small wonder that nobody spoke to Max.

Max's head ached. The dagger of Russian shrapnel that had laid open his scalp and gouged his skull had left him with migraines and a persistent ringing in his ears. Sometimes his vision blurred, or he saw double. He had spent weeks in a military hospital in Poland. He had finally been judged recovered enough to spend Easter with his family, and had been granted a pass for the long journey back home. Huddled into his heavy leather overcoat, he tried to sleep in the dim blue light of the compartment, but the jolting of the train made it impossible.

At Dresden, to add insult to injury, two Gestapo men barged into the compartment and demanded to see his papers. Sleek and well fed, like all their kind, they interrogated him as though he was a deserter – he, who had fought on the Eastern Front, while they fed on beer and sausages, with their boots on their desks. He half expected them to ask him to unwind the bandage that still covered his head, and show his wound. They stopped short of that, and left with sneers. Perhaps that was how they treated all wounded soldiers.

At Meissen, he almost passed out while struggling along the corridor of the train to the lavatory. Nobody helped him. They probably thought he was drunk. The exhaustion finally shut his brain down, and he achieved five minutes of sleep, which transported him instantly back to the front, to snow, mud and blood. He woke shouting. Or perhaps the shouts had only been in his mind.

The line ended at Düren. He gathered his duffel bag and kit and got off the train. There was a scene on the platform: two SS storm troopers had detained a passenger and were examining his papers. The man, who was elderly and white-haired, was protesting his innocence. Casually, one of the storm troopers struck him in the face. The man fell to the ground. Equally casually, the other storm trooper put his boot on the fallen victim's neck while they held his documents up to the light. Then they hauled him to his feet and dragged him away. He was silent now, his face a mask of despair.

'A Jew,' an old woman said loudly. 'The sooner they get rid of them all, the better.'

Max was too hardened by years of war to care much about the old man's fate, except to feel a fleeting surprise that there were still any Jews left in Germany. He pushed his way through the throng, indifferent.

In the cobbled square outside the station, a military band composed of geriatrics was playing the 'Horst Wessel Song'. The all-too-familiar tune thumped jarringly on his ears. He could not bear loud noises now. The clash of a cymbal made him wince as though a shot had been fired. It was 8 a.m. but the sky was barely light. The medieval town was shrouded in mist.

There were no taxis in the street, so he walked towards the bus station. Before he reached it, however, he heard the rattle of a pony trap behind him. A voice called out, 'Young Max Wolff? Is that you?'

Max turned. The scarecrow holding the reins was muffled in rags, but Max recognised him as Heinz Jockel, the charcoal burner in Kallenheim, who had already been ancient in Max's childhood. 'Yes, it's me.'

'I'm going to Kallenheim. Get on.'

Jockel was a garrulous, rather malicious old man, and his cart was black with dust, but it was bitterly cold and it would be quicker than walking. Max climbed on to the seat beside him, tossing his duffel behind. 'Well, Jockel,' he said, 'you must be a hundred years old.'

'Eighty-seven,' Jockel replied with the toothless smile of a tortoise. 'But I always get where I'm going.' With a jolt, the trap set off. Max sat in silence, staring ahead, but the old man scrutinised him shrewdly. 'So they made you *Leutnant*?'

'Yes,' he said shortly.

Jockel grunted. 'And now you're home for Easter?'

'As you see.'

'Does your mother know you're coming?'

'No.'

'You thought you'd surprise her, eh? With a bandage round your thick head?'

Max was already starting to feel sickened by the rocking of the ramshackle cart and the rank smell of the horse. 'I've changed my mind. Set me down. I'll walk the rest of the way.'

Jockel lit the tarry stub of a cigarette. 'You never liked questions, did you? Even as a boy. If anybody spoke to you, you growled like a dog that wants to bite. You were too busy trying to be a little Hitler. Running at the heels of Maus Bauer and the rest. They turned you into a good Nazi, didn't they?' The old man chuckled sardonically and puffed at his cigarette. 'You couldn't wait to rush off to glory, could you, and get your head split open.'

'I went to do my part for the Fatherland.'

'The Fatherland,' Jockel said derisively. 'Your father tried to make a better land than Hitler. And look what they did to him.'

'Be damned to you.'

'He would be ashamed of you.'

This was too much. 'Shut up, you old fool,' Max snapped.

But Jockel was incapable of silence. He cackled all the way to Kallenheim, complaining about the rationing, the blackout, the Nazis, the air raids. Max stared out across the Westphalian landscape, so rich and lush in the summer, now bleak and misty. The line of the great Hürtgen Forest stretched to the west, primeval and dark. There was military traffic on the road, trucks full of soldiers and armoured vehicles. The soldiers in the backs of the trucks looked absurdly young, helmets too big, doll faces pale with apprehension, thin fingers clutching their rifles.

8

Kallenheim came into view, nestling in its valley, the spike of its church rising above the timbered houses with their dull slate roofs, a picturesque village. This had been the cradle of his childhood, until they had taken his father away, and he had lost his innocence.

They rattled through the ancient town gate, the cart bouncing over the cobbles. The streets were quiet. The air of quaintness was undercut by the signs of war. Shops were boarded up, windows shuttered. Military proclamations had been pasted on the walls here and there, adorned with the usual swastikas and frowning eagles.

A few elderly people were in the square. They turned to look curiously at Max in his black panzer uniform and weathered greatcoat. He saw that the windows of the thirteenth-century Catholic church had been swathed in heavy canvas, as though it were a blindfolded prisoner waiting to be shot.

St Nicholas House, where Max had been born, stood at the opposite end of the town, next to the old mill, which had long since fallen into disrepair. It was a part of Kallenheim that had an air of abandonment. Jockel halted the cart in front of the tall, narrow brick facade, and held out a grimy palm.

'You want money for talking treason all the way from Düren?' Max asked sarcastically. Nevertheless, he gave the old man a few coins, and climbed down from the cart. His head felt as though there were an axe buried in it. Jockel sat leering expectantly, waiting for him to knock at the door. 'Get out of here,' Max said. 'Go and complain about the Führer to the Gestapo. See what they say to you.'

'I know when I'm not wanted. So long.'

'Heil Hitler.'

When the cart had rattled out of sight, Max looked up at the old house.

He thought of the last time he had seen his father. It was right here, in the street, as the police led him into their van. He'd always found his father terrifying, an intimidating martinet. That day, in

Max's wide, boyish eyes, he was suddenly frail, helpless, his customary black suit crumpled, his face hollow. He'd been lost among the brown military uniforms, crushed by the strong hands that grasped his arms and hustled him along, his feet almost off the ground.

He'd turned to look at Max over his shoulder, and had called out, 'Goodbye, my son.'

That was all. They'd pushed him into the back of the van as Max had stood frozen, clinging to his bicycle. The doors had slammed shut. The van had driven off, leaving only oily, black fumes behind.

It was a memory he could never rid himself of. It was the day his life had cracked open like a dropped egg, all its promise devastated. He recalled very little that was happy in his life after that.

Max shouldered his duffel bag and took a deep breath. He knocked on the door. It was a long time before it opened. His mother, Magda, stood framed in the doorway. She still wore her widow's black dress, her hair tied back in a bun, as she had worn it since his father's death. His unexpected first thought was how young and thin she looked. As a boy, she had seemed old to him. Now that he was in his twenties, exhausted by war, and she still not forty-five, she seemed almost a girl.

Magda's face turned white, and she took a step back, as though he were a ghost. 'Max!'

'Hello, Mother.'

'You should have given me a warning!'

'I am not an air raid,' he said, smiling tiredly. 'I thought the surprise would be a pleasant one.'

She still seemed frozen, her hand pressed to her heart. 'You're wounded! What have they done to you?'

'It's nothing. A scratch. They've sent me home to rest.'

'You didn't even tell me!'

'I didn't want to worry you.'

With an effort, she stepped forward and kissed him formally on each cheek. 'Welcome home, Max.'

He followed her through the familiar front room to the kitchen, where a coal fire was burning in the stove, struggling valiantly to combat the cold of the house. She helped him take off his greatcoat. 'Do you want coffee? We have only ersatz.'

'Anything will do.' Now that he saw her more closely, there were grey streaks in her soft, brown hair, and a blurring of the lines of her eyes and chin. Her hands were reddened with work. Silently, her face grave, she put the percolator on the stove and cut him a slice of black bread and a tiny morsel of cheese. 'This is all we have.'

'I have my ration coupons. They're generous to officers. We'll be all right.'

'How long will you stay?'

'They've given me two months. Then they'll reassess me.' He met Magda's large, grey-blue eyes. 'You don't seem very pleased to see me.'

She winced. 'Don't say that.'

'You haven't smiled, yet.'

'I'm happy to see you.' But she didn't smile. She had her hand on her throat. 'I just wasn't prepared. I haven't seen you for three years, Max.'

'They've kept us busy. I wrote.'

'I know you did, and I was grateful for the letters.' She looked at the bandage on his head. 'My poor boy. How did it happen?'

'Our tanks got stuck in the mud. They were able to pick us off as we tried to get free. We lost three panzers and thirteen comrades. I had to write to their wives. God knows what I said in the letters.' He touched his head. 'With a fractured skull, I wasn't very coherent. I recommended them for decorations. We had been through—' Something caught in his throat. 'We had been through a lot together.'

'I'm so sorry.'

'I'm all right. They took the stitches out at the hospital before they discharged me.'

'You could have been killed. You won't have to go back to fight, will you?'

'They'll send me back, sooner or later.'

'How can they ask that of you?'

'I *want* to fight. It's my duty.' He was hungry, and he started eating the bread. 'Jockel brought me from Düren. He's as sour as ever.'

His mother opened a drawer in the kitchen dresser and took out a small oilskin pouch. She put it in front of him with the air of someone performing a necessary duty. 'Here are your things.' At first, he didn't recognise the contents. Then he remembered. His 'valuables', carefully stored by his mother when he'd left for the front. His father's gold signet ring and gold watch. He pushed them away from him impatiently. 'You should have sold these.'

'How could I? Your father left them to you.'

'Donate them to the war effort, then.'

'I will not do that.'

'You know that I'll never wear these things, Mother.'

Magda's face closed. She folded the pouch and put it away again. 'You're still so bitter towards him. After all these years, and what you have been through in Russia, I hoped you would begin to understand him a little.'

'I understand that he ruined our lives,' Max said grimly. 'Don't ask me to forgive him.'

'I won't ask that, because he never did any wrong, Max. He did only good in this world.'

He pushed himself to his feet. 'I need to sleep.'

'There is something I must show you, first.'

'What is it?'

She was paler than ever. 'It's better if you see for yourself.'

12

She led him upstairs. There were no changes in the house, except that it seemed smaller and darker than he remembered. The religious pictures on the walls were faded, the floorboards creaked underfoot as they had always done.

The top floor of the house was divided into four small rooms: two bedrooms, a bathroom, and a little sitting area that was called the study. It was the only room in the austere old house that had any concessions to comfort: there were armchairs upholstered in chintz, and frilly shades on the lamps. Here Max's father had studied and written the disastrous sermons attacking Hitler, which had brought catastrophe upon all their heads. His desk was still in one corner, piled with his books and papers. There was another fire burning in the grate here, and a faint, sweet smell of flowers.

'You must try to understand,' his mother said.

'Understand? Understand what?'

She pulled a chair away from the wall, and tapped on the wooden panelling behind it. Max stared, puzzled. Then, after a few moments, he heard the muffled sound of the ladder to the attic being lowered. A pale hand pushed the panelling out from the inside, and two young women emerged cautiously from the dark recess.

Max was stupefied, looking from one to the other. 'Who are they?' he demanded.

'This is Heidi,' his mother said in an unsteady voice. 'And this is her younger sister, Lola.'

The girls were staring back at Max with the large, glistening eyes of frightened deer. 'But – what are they doing in our house?'

'They are under our protection.'

Understanding struck him like a blow. 'Are they Jews?'

His mother went to stand beside the girls, who shrank silently against her. 'Yes, Max, they are Jews.'

'You must be mad!' Max said, staggered by the enormity of what was fast dawning on him. 'What have you done?' The women stared at him without speaking. Unable to find words, Max turned on his heel and went back downstairs to the kitchen. He slumped at the worn old table and put his throbbing head in his hands. Hot and cold flushes ran across his skin. He thought of the huge efforts he had made to shake off his father's treason. Enduring the bullying, the beatings, the daily insults, month after month, year after year. The fist fights he'd had to win. The Hitler Youth years, straining every sinew to be better than all the others. The army years, the almost-suicidal efforts to win those two Iron Crosses. To become what he was today.

And now *this*.

He heard his mother come in after a while. 'They're from Berlin,' she said quietly, behind him. 'Their names are Adelheid and Heloise Rosenstein, but they call themselves Heidi and Lola.'

'Wasn't what Father did enough?' he said through clenched teeth, raising his head. 'Do you have to destroy everything all over again?'

'Their family are all gone, one way or another. They have nobody to protect them—'

'I don't care a damn for them or their family! They're *Jews*, hiding like rats in our house!'

'Max—'

'What in God's name made you do this?'

'I am indeed doing it in God's name,' Magda replied gently.

He exploded. 'Spare me the cant! I'm so sick of it. I've spent ten years trying to make up for Father.' His voice was shaking. 'Trying to erase the treason.'

'Your father wasn't a traitor.'

'Then he was an arrogant fool! He chose martyrdom because he believed he was a saint. And you're the same.' He pointed upward. 'How long do you think you can keep those two Jewesses hidden?'

'Long enough for them to find a safer place to go.'

'No. We're going to hand them over to Maus Bauer now.'

Her thin face tightened. 'Max, we can't do that. I hate that man. You know what he would do to them.'

'I don't care what Bauer does to them! I can't be in the same house as them. I'm a German officer with two Iron Crosses. Don't you understand? All that will be for nothing. It will be disgrace and shame all over again.'

'For them it would be far worse.'

'They must face it.'

'If you do that,' she said in a low voice, 'then Bauer and his gang will arrest me, too. Is that what you want?'

'Oh, Jesus.' He struck his fist on the table. 'I don't understand how they came here. Who are they? Where are they from?'

'Your Uncle Anselm sent them to me.'

Max groaned. 'I might have known. *That* religious maniac.'

'They had some protection until 1941. There was a sympathetic official who tried to shelter Jews. But then he was also arrested. They had an hour to leave everything behind. They've been on the run ever since then. Three years, Max. Three years hiding in attics, buried in cellars, going from house to house, their lives always in the hands of strangers, terrified of betrayal—'

'They're enemies of the state.'

'They're delightful young women who have hardly seen the outside world in three years.'

'And what sort of life do you think *I* have had?'

'I know what sort of life you have had,' she replied in a low voice. 'But they have endured hardships of a different kind.'

15

He felt as though he had walked from one nightmare into another. 'How could you do this to me, Mother?'

'If you had told me you were coming back, I would have had time—' She stopped, looking over his shoulder. Max swung round. The girls had come down the stairs. They stood huddled together with their arms around each other's waists, their faces pale and pinched.

'We'll leave tonight,' the taller girl said. She was schoolmarmish, with lank, straight hair and a short-sighted manner.

'You can't,' Max's mother replied urgently. 'Where will you go?'

'We can hide in the forest.'

Magda shook her head. 'You would be caught in hours, Heidi.'

'Then, as your son says, we must face it. He's right. We should never have come here. We had no right to put you in danger.'

Max cut in angrily. 'You should have left Germany while you could! There were opportunities!'

The girl met his eyes with that myopic look. 'We couldn't leave. We had nowhere to go. We didn't have a penny. The government had already taken everything.'

'Jews always have money tucked away,' Max scoffed, 'and always complain they are poor.'

'Max!' Magda exclaimed. 'Be human.'

'Human?' he echoed. 'My comrades are all under the snow in Russia. I had to bury what was left of them with only their helmets to mark their graves. Don't tell me to be human.'

The younger of the two sisters had dark, almond-shaped eyes. Her clothes were smarter, and her hair glossier. She spoke hotly. 'We didn't start this war of yours. Hitler did!'

'Hush, Lola,' her sister said.

Max glared at her. He knew the type – a smart-mouthed city girl who thought everyone else was stupid. 'You'll leave tonight,' he said brusquely.

Magda took Max's arm. 'They have nowhere to go, Max. They'll be caught in a matter of hours.'

'That's not our concern.'

'It's *my* concern,' Magda said in her dignified way. 'Your father was murdered in one of Adolf Hitler's prisons. I couldn't save him, but I can try to save these young women.'

'Father died of typhus.'

'People don't die of typhus in healthy places, Max. They tried to break his faith, and when they couldn't, they murdered him.'

'Well, when they discover we've been sheltering two Jews, we'll all have a chance to find out,' Max said bleakly. His vision was blurring with the strain. He was starting to see double, the pounding in his head like the tempo of an insane orchestra. Nausea rose up in him, uncontainable. He went to the sink and retched, bringing up the bitter ersatz coffee he'd drunk.

His mother called anxiously, 'Max! You're not well. You shouldn't be upsetting yourself like this.'

Gentle hands took his arm. When he turned, he saw it was the elder of the Jewesses, Heidi. He jerked his arm away. 'Don't touch me,' he snarled. She stepped back as though she'd been burned. He was a big man, tall and strong, and his anger was frightening.

'You should lie down,' she said. She folded her arms, frowning like the nurses in the military hospital in Vienna. 'If you have a fractured skull, then any movement is dangerous for you. You could have a brain haemorrhage.'

'You are too kind,' he said savagely. He pushed past her and clambered slowly up the stairs to his old bedroom. There was nothing he could do. He needed to close his eyes, or the Jewess's prediction would come true.

He tore off his panzer jacket and lay on his narrow bed, the pain in his head almost unbearable. The house was silent except for the rustle of the women whispering downstairs. He thought of the

17

expression on his father's face when he'd been arrested, the hollow resignation. The face of a martyr.

That face had stayed in his mind for years. It was like a family curse that had now risen from its grave and returned to haunt him.

He had no doubt that his mother had committed this folly as some sort of memorial to his father. His father and uncle had belonged to a fundamentalist sect that had opposed Nazism from the start. Joachim and Anselm Wolff had criticised Hitler bitterly from the pulpit and in tracts, condemning the atheism of the Nazi state, the persecution of Jews, and the imprisonment of clergy. Max's father, Joachim, the more outspoken of the two, had called Hitler a madman, a criminal and a murderer.

He had paid the price. The full power of the enraged Nazi state had been brought to bear against him. After his arrest, Max had never seen his father again. He hadn't gone to the trial. It was held in a closed courtroom anyway, so that the terrible things his father said about the Führer couldn't be heard by anyone else.

The sentence had been eighteen years in a military prison. His father's brother Anselm had been wiser, had apologised, and had been jailed for a year. The church had been shut down and its few remaining parishioners put on a Gestapo list.

Max's father had died in prison three years later, long before the end of his term. There had been no funeral to go to. Because his father had died during the course of his sentence, his body remained the property of the Reich. It had been buried in a common prison grave, tossed into the earth with others, with no ceremony, no marker, no memorial. The man who had fathered him had become a shameful burden, which he would have to carry for the rest of his life.

And now, here he was, facing the same shame, the same fate. Who could he turn to? There was only one person: the man who had replaced his father in so many ways, the policeman Maus Bauer.

When he awoke, he was still in his uniform, shivering in a cold sweat. His mother was sitting beside his bed. She laid her hand on his brow. 'You've slept for almost twelve hours.'

'Have they gone?' he croaked.

Magda shook her head. 'They have nowhere to go, Max.'

He struggled to raise himself on one elbow. 'They can't stay here.'

She tried to soothe him. 'We'll make arrangements. Don't worry about them now. In a day or two, they'll be gone.'

'What time is it?'

'Ten o'clock at night. Do you want something to eat?'

He shook his head. 'I want them out of this house.'

'You need to sleep some more, Max. Please stop thinking about them.'

But he was too restless to be pacified. 'How are you feeding them?'

'They are sent ration cards.'

'Stolen? Forged?'

'Anselm and Ditte get them in Cologne. They post them to us.'

Max groaned. 'And you're shopping for three people, with these illegal ration cards, when everybody knows you live alone?'

'I'm careful, Max. I go to different shops. Sometimes I walk to Hürtgenwald or even Düren to buy food. And there is always the black market.'

'My God. They'll catch you and put you up against a wall!'

'We live such quiet lives,' Magda said. 'Nobody cares about us. Try to understand, Max. Their family have been exterminated. All they want is to live.'

'I want the same. And I don't want you to end up the same way as Father because you tried to help strangers who are nothing to us.'

Her voice was even quieter. 'They are not nothing to *me*. I took responsibility for them willingly, and I won't betray them.'

'That doesn't apply to me. You didn't tell me, you didn't ask me.'

'How could I? The censors read every letter.'

'How can you expect me to go along with this?'

'I don't expect you to do anything, Max. You must do what you think best.'

'What I think best is that I go to Bauer tomorrow and tell him about the Jewesses, and ask him to help us.'

'You think that man is your friend. He isn't. He loathes me. He would like nothing better than to send us all to a camp.'

He rolled on to his side with his face to the wall. 'Let me sleep. And tell the Jewesses to pack their bags.'

She didn't answer. After a while, he heard her leave the room.

Chapter 2

'Do you think he'll inform the Gestapo?' Lola asked.

'We'll soon find out,' Heidi said bleakly. 'In the meantime, we must get ready to leave.'

Lola was trembling. 'If he informs on us, Magda will be arrested, too. He surely can't want *that*.'

'Perhaps not.'

'I had that dream again last night. The one where the Allies are just about to come, and at the last minute, the Gestapo catch us, and put us up against a wall. I could feel the bullets going into my heart, Heidi. I woke up crying.'

'I heard you. But it was only a dream, darling.'

'It was a premonition of *this*.'

'Keep your nerve, darling.'

Lola was prone to these powerful flights of fancy, which had become more and more acute the longer they lived like this, in constant fear and anxiety. There had been times, after they'd first gone on the run, when she seemed almost to relish the excitement of living a clandestine life, always alert, always having to outwit the enemy. She'd kept the élan of a spirited young woman. As the older sister, Heidi sometimes had to restrain Lola from her reckless impulses. But she'd been glad that Lola's sense of adventure had protected her from being overwhelmed by her sadness. Lately, though, she'd seen Lola's spirits sinking. Sometimes Heidi even feared that Lola was losing her grip on reality. 'We must pack,' she said.

Lola grimaced. 'I can't bear the thought of moving yet again. I'm sure they'll catch us in the open this time. And we've been so happy here. I thought we were safe at last.'

They began to pack their few belongings methodically in the small leather valises that had once belonged to their parents. All their worldly possessions could fit in them now, their clothes, their little stash of money, their false papers in Aryan names, their few toiletries.

Lola tugged the worn leather strap on her valise. 'Where are we going to go?' she asked Heidi.

'Into the forest, if necessary.'

'What will we live on, acorns? And sleep up in the branches, like birds? We're not in a fairy tale.'

'After the war, this will all be a bad dream,' Heidi said.

'Don't talk about *after the war*,' Lola burst out. 'I can't bear it. There's no *after the war* for us. Only darkness. It'll never happen. They'll catch us one day, and then our sad little lives will be over.'

'We have to have hope,' Heidi said, holding her sister tight.

'I've run out of hope. I don't think about the future any more. And I can't remember the past.'

'Don't cry, Lola,' Heidi said.

'I was thinking about Mama and Papa, and then I realised I can hardly remember what they looked like,' Lola said. 'It's so awful. I try to see them in my mind, and there's just a blank.'

'Oh, Lola.' Heidi paused in her packing. 'You remember Papa's laugh, don't you? How it used to start deep down inside, and make his belly jiggle?'

Lola brightened. 'And he would snuffle through his nose, until he couldn't hold it in any longer, and he would open his mouth and honk like a goose!'

'Remember how we used to hide in the back of the theatre and listen to the audience roaring with laughter and clapping?'

'And Papa in the spotlights, with his thumbs in his waistcoat pockets, looking puzzled at all the fuss. I can see him now!'

'Yes, he'd put on that quizzical look, and the audience laughed all the harder.'

'Mama could be funny, too, couldn't she?' Lola said wistfully.

'They were at their best when they were together. They were perfect, then.'

'Oh, those days! Until *The Countess Obolensky*.'

Heidi fell silent.

The Countess Obolensky was a farce in which Mama and Papa, among the most popular comic actors in Berlin, played a chauffeur and a housemaid who were having affairs with their employers, a count and countess. The girls weren't allowed to see it, because it was too risqué. But they'd creep in and watch from the wings. The girls loved the play precisely because it *was* naughty. The sight of their parents pretending to make love to strangers sent them into paroxysms of giggles – because, of course, nothing could *really* come between Mama and Papa. They'd thrilled to the rococo sets, the steaming spotlights, the roars of laughter and applause.

But on one night, the audience had been strangely silent. There was none of the applause that usually greeted Mama and Papa when they came onstage, none of the laughs at the appropriate places, only that ominous stillness.

And then, when Papa had pretended to kiss the countess in her boudoir, a man in the front row had jumped to his feet and shouted, 'Get your paws off her, you filthy Jew!'

Pandemonium had followed. The audience suddenly seemed to be full of men wearing red swastika armbands, some in uniform. They had come prepared for a riot. They hurled rotten fruit at the stage, pelting Papa as he stood, thunderstruck, in mid-scene.

'Why are they doing this?' Lola had wailed, cowering in Heidi's arms as everything fell apart around them. The theatre – that sacred place, more sacred to them than the synagogue – had been torn apart, letting in a torrent of boiling hatred. Their mother had come upon them.

'What are you doing here?' she had demanded, her face stark under the make-up. 'Get Lola out of here, Heidi!'

Heidi had managed to get Lola safely out of the melee, terrified and crying, but that had been the last time any of them had set foot inside a theatre. Papa had exited the stage, covered in tomato pulp, never to return.

Papa hadn't said a word that night. He'd sat in the bath, eyes closed, as Mama, crying, washed the muck out of his hair and beard. It was the first time Lola had seen her father with his vest off. He always wore a bushy beard, and somehow, she'd assumed he was furry all over, like a bear. But she saw that he wasn't a bear, he was just a little fat man. And his face seemed to have aged twenty years. She'd felt so sorry for him that she'd gone to cry under the bed with Heidi.

Later, Lola had learned that the rage was because Papa was a Jew, and the actress who played the countess an Aryan, and that even a humorous reference to relations between them was forbidden under the new Nuremberg Laws. She'd heard people talk about 'the Nuremberg Laws', which had come into force the year she'd turned twelve. Hitler had been in power for three years already, and she had been aware of the public excitement, the flags, the rallies that made Berlin reverberate. But she hadn't connected it to her own place in the world, partly because Mama and Papa – and also her protective older sister, Heidi – had sheltered her from it all.

But there was much more to it than that. It was much, much more serious. Mama and Papa had lost their careers that night, for the crime of being 'racially impure'. They'd had to sell their shares in the theatre, and look for other ways to earn their living.

But there were no other ways.

The waters had risen darker and deeper with terrible swiftness. Yellow 'Jewish stars' had to be sewn on every coat. The compulsory registration of all Jews accelerated the closing of Jewish businesses, one after another, a cascade of ruin among their friends and acquaintances. The smashing of the shops that tried to stay open underscored the process.

Prevented from studying at any school in Germany, the girls had to find work. Heidi had taken in sewing; Lola had cleaned for whoever would employ her. But the circle of their friends had narrowed steeply. Each week there were disappearances and absences. Each month there were fewer Jews – and fewer gentiles willing to befriend Jews, give them work, or associate with them in any way. Suddenly, they were alone.

They had soon lost their home. Bought by an Aryan for a pittance – which was never fully paid.

Lola remembered the day they had been moved to the *Judenhaus*, a Jewish tenement in a ghetto. The place was dark, smelled of drains and rot, and every room was crowded. Eyes had followed them from half-open doorways as they trudged up the stairs.

They'd walked into the squalid garret, its wallpaper peeling and its ceiling sagging with damp, and Heidi had asked innocently, 'Where are *our* bedrooms?'

'*This* is our bedroom,' Mama had said in an angry voice. 'We sleep here.'

'All four of us?' Lola had asked incredulously, looking around. 'In this awful room?'

'All four of us,' Mama had snapped, as though Lola was being particularly stupid, 'in this awful room. We all sleep in this room. We wash in this room. We cook in this room. We piss in this room. We shit in this room. And here in this room we will die.'

It was Mama's swearing, as much as anything else, that shocked the girls into silence. But Papa had put his arms around them, laughing merrily.

'Nonsense! It's romantic! We're in *La Bohème*! I'll be Rodolfo and Mama will be Mimì. I knew I should have been an opera singer instead of an actor.'

And he'd started singing nonsense Italian in a funny voice until they'd had to laugh, and somehow, the shadows had lifted.

But oh, for their lovely house, where they had been princesses, and hadn't even known how happy they were!

Lola sighed at the memory, an ache of sadness heavy on her breast. 'Why didn't they go to Hollywood, or England?' Lola asked Heidi.

'Papa said he couldn't be funny in English. He had such a thick accent when he tried! And Mama hardly spoke any English at all. People in other countries didn't want to hear German accents.'

'We could have gone to Jerusalem.'

'Yes. There were the Fishbeins who became Zionists and went to Jerusalem before the war. They told us to leave before things got worse, and join them. But Jerusalem sounded so alien. And then, Papa said, he didn't want us to be farmers! He said there were no theatres there for him to perform in. He always believed things would get better here.'

'But they never did.'

'No,' Heidi said sorrowfully, 'they never did.'

'I always want to remember them onstage, glowing in the spotlights, with the audience cheering and stamping their feet. I hate to think of what they became, Papa bent over other people's shoes, still trying to make jokes, and Mama lying in bed, coughing.'

'Those were awful times.'

'Perhaps we'll see him again,' Heidi said.

'If we do, it'll be in heaven.'

The packing was soon finished. They had very little. So much had been left behind. And they had packed in haste so many times that by now they were experts.

They fell silent, clutching their valises, waiting to hear their fate.

Max stood in the pouring rain across the square from the police station, muffled in his greatcoat. It was a wretched day, the dark clouds so low that they seemed to touch the battlements of the medieval walls that overhung the station. He had walked from Kallenheim, setting off before dawn, while the house was still silent, striding along the road with his head down, his mind whirling with angry thoughts.

The police station had been greatly enlarged since the beginning of the war, and had expanded into the buildings on either side. The swastikas hung in a row from the facades, now darkened by the drenching rain.

He had decided on his course yesterday, but now he felt as though he had been brought up short by an invisible wall. Informing Bauer about the Jewesses would inevitably bring trouble on his mother.

Could he make a deal with Bauer, somehow bargain for his mother's protection? A far greater punishment would surely come if he didn't volunteer the information, and they were caught. He couldn't understand how they hadn't been caught already, especially in a small place like Kallenheim. He didn't know how she had concealed the presence of two other people in that narrow house. Surely some neighbour must already suspect something. Betrayal could only be a matter of weeks away; and then he would not be here to protect her. She – along with the girls – would probably be shot out of hand.

No, the best way was to admit everything and beg for Bauer's help.

With that thought, he crossed the broad, stately square and walked into the entrance of the station. It smelled, as all public buildings smelled these days, of boiled cabbage, floor polish and wet leather. He was looking around when a heavy hand descended on his shoulder.

'Here's a Jew! Call Himmler!'

Max's heart jumped in his chest. He turned. A fat, jolly face was laughing at him. As he recognised Maus Bauer, his heart settled. 'Hello, Herr Bauer,' he said, clasping the older man's hand.

'Welcome home, son.' Bauer had now risen to the rank of *Hauptmann* in the *Ordnungspolizei*, the military force with which the Nazis had replaced the old regional police. 'We heard about your second Iron Cross.' He slapped Max's shoulder. 'Well done. I knew you had it in you. Come and have a beer with the lads.'

'I need to talk to you about something important.'

'It can wait. Come and tell us about Russia.'

Reluctantly, Max allowed himself to be led to a back room where three or four others were sitting around a wood-burning stove. They welcomed him as a war hero, although these had been the same men – the brutal '*Orpos*' – who had come for his father in 1934. Bottles of beer and glasses were produced. He was given a seat close to the stove, which was rumbling like a wasp's hive.

'What's it like over there?'

'How did you get your wound?'

'Are the Russkies good soldiers?'

They were the familiar questions old soldiers always asked. He tried to answer them in the expected way, knowing that he could never convey the true conditions to those who had not been there. He told them how he'd won his Iron Crosses, explained how he'd been injured, as so many panzer commanders were, by the enemy targeting the observation slits in the tank's hatch. He told them about the new, heavy Tiger tanks, which terrorised the enemy with their deadly cannon and massive armour, but which had suffered technical difficulties. They listened eagerly, the dark beer flowing freely from the crate despite the early hour. He saw their eyes begin to shine, their faces swell and redden as they relived their own fighting days. From the wall, large photographs of Adolf Hitler and Heinrich Himmler glared down on them.

The heat from the stove became oppressive. His wet greatcoat steamed. It was like being back in his panzer with the hatch locked. Bauer was beaming at him with pride.

After his father's shameful arrest, Max's life had become a hell of bullying and beatings. At thirteen, he'd been friendless, bewildered and terrified, a pariah with nowhere to hide. He'd been fair game for teachers. No infraction was too minor to escape punishment, no punishment too severe to meet the case. The kids hadn't needed an excuse to knock the shit out of him. Even the girls had delighted in pulling his hair and scratching his face. He still bore a scar next to his right eye from the nails of a girl named Barbara, who'd nearly blinded him.

Getting home from school had been a particular Calvary. He would be met every day somewhere along the road by a dozen village kids, who would corner him. He would have to fight one of them, while the others crowded in a jeering circle around him. He always lost the fight, and when he'd been knocked down, they would take turns to kick him, spit on him, and sometimes piss on him.

Picking himself up painfully after one of these beatings, he'd found a uniformed figure looming over him.

'You don't know how to fight, do you?'

Max had shrunk away from the huge hand that reached out. He couldn't face any more pain.

'I'm not going to hurt you,' the man had growled in disgust. 'Unless you *want* me to hurt you. You want me to hurt you?'

'Please, no.'

'Well, stop snivelling then. You know what you're saying when you cry? You're asking them to hurt you more. First lesson – never cry.'

The police were figures of terror for Max. He stared up at the man in dread, wiping his eyes. 'I can't help it,' he muttered.

'Yes you can. You know who I am?'

Max shook his head.

'I'm Sergeant Bauer. And I know who *you* are. The son of that idiot we arrested. I've been watching you. It's pitiful. Now, put your fists up. Like this.' Bauer's fists were like hams. 'If you're going to hit someone, make it count. Don't bother with the body. Go for the eyes, the nose, the mouth. A good one to the nose will stop the fight right there and then. Lots of blood. Understand? Hit them in the mouth, and you'll split their lips against their teeth. That hurts. Close one of their eyes, and they're your meatball. Now come on. Take a swing.'

Max never knew why Bauer had taken him under his wing. He was an old soldier, a *Frontschwein,* who had joined the police after the First World War. He taught Max how to box. With Bauer's instruction, Max had won his first fight. And the next. And the next five. The village boys had taken to retreating sullenly as he strode along.

Bauer had also protected Max from the worst of the mistreatment from the teachers. He had a way of making his wishes felt and obeyed. He was nicknamed 'Maus' because of his large size. His neck, which was shaved almost to the crown of his head, looked as thick as a tree trunk. And he was a dyed-in-the-wool Nazi, who had been a street fighter for Hitler in the early days of the struggle. He swung a lot of influence.

Bauer somehow got Max into the Hitler Youth, despite his father's disgrace. Bauer had patiently explained what National Socialism meant, and why his father had been so wrong to oppose Hitler, the greatest man who had ever lived. And Bauer had watched proudly as the boy painfully formed a new life for himself.

It was Bauer who had brought him the news, at the age of sixteen, that his father had died in a military prison, and had told him, 'It's better this way.'

It was Bauer who had led him inexorably towards the army, recounting tales of the First World War, and painting a picture of Max's glorious future in the *Wehrmacht*.

On his eighteenth birthday, Max had joined the army, with Maus Bauer's recommendation; and a year later he had found himself in a panzer, taking part in the invasion of France.

His whole life had been shaped to expiate the wrongdoing of his father, a burden that had almost crushed him at times. And now, Maus Bauer was the only man he could turn to for help.

As he was about to speak, it occurred to him to wonder what, exactly, would happen to the two girls.

As one of the *Orpo* men refilled his glass, Max asked, 'What happens to the Jews?'

There was a silence. Then Bauer retorted, 'What do you mean?'

'I mean, they've all been resettled, haven't they? Where are they?'

There was a grunt of laughter from another of the men.

31

'Never you mind where the Jews have gone. They won't cause any more trouble to the Reich, you can be sure of that.'

'But they haven't been harmed?'

'Who cares about them?'

The atmosphere in the overheated room had suddenly changed. The camaraderie had vanished. It was as though the ghost of his father had walked into the room, and they were all suddenly remembering; their eyes had become hard, their loose grins had stiffened into scowls. He shrugged. 'I was just curious.'

'Why did you come here, anyway?' Bauer demanded. 'You said you had to talk to me about something important. What?'

They were all watching him intently now. Max drained his glass of beer and wiped his mouth. Could he blurt out the terrible truth in front of them all? The words came unbidden. 'I need a permit to buy gasoline for my motorcycle.'

'For Max Wolff, no problem,' Bauer said bluffly. 'I'll write it up myself. Come.'

Max followed Bauer out, followed by the stares of the other men. As Bauer filled in the coupons, he looked at Max from under his heavy brows, a policeman's stare. 'What did you really want to talk about? Are you in trouble?'

Max shook his head. 'All I wanted was some petrol.'

Bauer kept watching him for a while. Max felt that nobody knew him better than Bauer did, not even his mother. Bauer had been protector, friend and father figure to him. But that did not mean he wasn't afraid of Bauer's strength and power.

'I'm proud of you, Max,' Bauer rumbled. 'You could have ended up on the rubbish dump, like your fool of a father. And look at you now. Two Iron Crosses and your own panzer command. A true Nazi hero.'

'I couldn't have done it without you.'

'Just don't ask questions about the Jews, okay? Forget them. Or you *will* end up like your father, for all your Iron Crosses.'

Max nodded. 'I understand.'

Bauer handed him the coupons. 'Enjoy your leave. Heil Hitler.'

'Heil Hitler.'

As he left Düren with his coupons, he realised that he was still left with the problem of the girls in the attic. Why hadn't he been able to confess the truth to Bauer? Perhaps it had been the brutish faces of the men in that room.

Max had imbibed the doctrines of Nazism from men like Bauer, including an abhorrence of Jews and other racially impure peoples who harmed the state. Like all the officers he knew, he had retained an unswerving loyalty to Adolf Hitler, to whom he had sworn an oath, while coming to despise and distrust the men around Hitler – Himmler, Göring, Goebbels and the rest – so many of whom were plainly criminal types.

And sitting in that room, with those beer-swilling *Orpos*, he'd felt profoundly uncomfortable. They were not like the comrades he'd served with in Russia, soldiers who lived by a soldier's code, and to whom truth was precious.

Why did Bauer have such thugs around him? He remembered something Bauer had once said to him: 'You cannot run Germany with priests and preachers. We need men who are not afraid to spill a little blood – or a lot.'

He reached home in the early afternoon. The weather was still bad, rain beating down from a lowering sky. He entered the house and caught at once that unfamiliar scent of flowers. It must come from the Jewish girls, perhaps some perfume they used. That alone would be enough to arouse suspicion if the Gestapo ever came in.

Thank God the house was set apart from the village, and had no immediate neighbours.

His mother was in the kitchen, peeling turnips and potatoes, which she grew in the back garden. She turned to face him with an expression of dread. 'Where did you go?'

'I told you. To the police station in Düren.'

'To do what?'

'I got petrol coupons for the motorcycle.'

'Nothing more?'

'Nothing more.' He saw the relief flood her eyes. 'But I haven't changed my mind, Mother. We have to find someone else willing to take them.'

'I was their last resort.'

'Well, we'll find somebody else,' he repeated. He looked at the pile of turnips his mother had peeled. 'Is that all we have to eat?'

'It's what we have every day. They're from the garden.'

'Well, today we have something better.' He reached into his knapsack and brought out a string of sausages. 'Look what the butcher gave me. I told you my ration coupons were worth something.'

Magda's eyes widened. 'Sausages!'

'So they tell me.'

'But – these are pork.'

'If we're lucky,' he said with a smile. 'They might be cat.'

She shook her head. 'The girls can't eat pork.'

'Why not?'

'Jews never eat pork. It's forbidden.'

'That's rather inconvenient,' Max said ironically. 'I'm not familiar with the dietary habits of Jews, but pork is a great luxury these days.'

'Perhaps they'll eat it,' she said doubtfully. 'I'll ask them.'

'We are not running a restaurant,' he retorted. 'If they won't eat sausage, then I will, and they can have my turnips.'

Upstairs, in the narrow attic space that was accessed behind the panelling, Lola pressed her ear to the boards. 'He's back,' she whispered.

Heidi nodded. 'Yes.' They could hear the man's voice down-stairs, his voice raised, his tone peremptory, angry.

'I hate him,' Lola whispered. 'How could a woman like Magda produce a son like him?'

'He has been indoctrinated, like all the others.'

'Not all, Heidi. Why do some Germans become Nazis, and others resist?'

'You know the answer, darling,' Heidi said, putting her arm around Lola. 'A few are monsters, the rest look away.'

'I think you're wrong. I think most are monsters. A few are sane. I hate all men. All of them.'

'Men are cats, and we are mice. You must behave like a mouse, darling.'

They heard footsteps on the stairs, and huddled back into the darkness silently. The tap on the panel was Magda's. They came down the ladder and peered out apprehensively. Magda looked tired and sad. 'Please come downstairs, girls. My son wants to talk to you.'

'Remember what I said,' Heidi whispered in Lola's ear as they followed Magda. 'Be a little mouse!'

Lola huddled into her cardigan without replying.

Max was waiting in the kitchen. He wore the black uniform, complete with his Luger pistol in its holster and his Iron Crosses and campaign ribbons. Lola wondered bitterly whether he was trying to impress them with his medals. She could hardly bring herself to look at his face. Under the bandage that was wrapped around his brow, it was pale and stern. He had very blue eyes, the eyes of a true Aryan. How nice to be born with those blue eyes, that straight nose and square chin, like a recruiting poster for the *Wehrmacht*. You would hardly say he was human at all. Just a steel vessel of pure German blood.

They stood in front him, like children waiting to be rebuked.

'I've decided not to inform the police of your presence yet,' he said, in his clipped way. 'This is for my mother's sake, not yours. For whatever reasons of her own, she has decided to make herself responsible for you. But I am responsible for *her*. And you can't stay here. Your presence puts her life in danger. Not to mention my own.'

Lola wanted to scream. She clenched her fists and clamped her jaw tight so as to make no sound. It was Heidi who answered him.

'We understand,' she said calmly. 'Your mother has been more kind to us than I know how to say. We'll never forget what she has done. Or the risks she took for us.'

He seemed slightly nonplussed for a moment. Maybe he had expected them to argue, or plead for compassion. 'Perhaps you know what happened to my father,' he went on curtly. 'He tried to defend the Jews, and he was arrested for it. He died in prison.'

'We know that,' Heidi said.

'The point is that there would be no mercy for my mother if she were to be caught sheltering you. Even I myself would suffer – and I have devoted my life to the Fatherland to atone for what my father did.'

Lola couldn't hold herself in. 'Don't you think your beloved Fatherland is a very strange place,' she said, oblivious to Heidi pinching her arm hard, 'if helping other human beings has become a crime?'

36

His face grew even colder. 'I am not a theologian, like my father. Nor a lawyer. I am not concerned with moral issues.'

'Of course not. Your speciality is killing.'

He frowned grimly. 'My speciality is staying alive.'

'Unfortunately, in our family, we never developed that particular speciality,' Lola retorted. 'They've taken our father and mother, our aunts and uncles. Our friends stood by and did nothing. The only ones to help us have been strangers, like your mother.'

'Which was very convenient for you.'

'Do you think we *want* to be shut away in an attic like two broken toys?' Lola shot back.

'Hush, Lola,' Heidi said. She looked Max in the face. 'We're fully aware of the terrible risk your mother is taking. You're right. We were selfish, thinking only of ourselves. As soon as we can leave, we will.'

Magda looked up. 'We'll find someone to take you, Heidi.'

'Thank you, Magda,' Heidi said.

'But we'll wait until after Easter, won't we, Max?' Magda said, looking pleadingly at Max.

'Very well.' Max folded his arms, looking down at Lola and Heidi from his considerable height advantage. 'My mother tells me you don't eat pork.'

'We eat anything,' Heidi said quickly, before Lola could produce some unwise retort.

They sat around the small pine table to eat the meal that Magda had prepared, a stew of sausage and turnips that was richer than anything they had eaten in months. Lola ate little. That they weren't being thrown to the wolves just yet was small consolation; they would soon be leaving this refuge and entering the terrors of the outside world again. Her stomach was knotted. She kept her gaze away from his face, looking instead at his hands. They were square and neat, like tools, like the rest of him. They made her want to jump up and run from the table.

Halfway through the meal, they heard the rumble of a motorcycle approaching the house, followed swiftly by a squeal of brakes and a thunderous knocking at the door. They all froze.

'Girls!' Magda whispered. 'Run upstairs!'

'No point.' Max put his knife and fork down, and calmly folded his napkin. 'The table is laid for four, and we don't have time to clear away. Stay here and keep quiet,' he said. He shut the kitchen door as he left.

The women sat staring at one another, white-faced. They heard male voices at the front door, a bark of command, and then a silence. After what seemed like an eternity, the door banged shut, and the sound of the motorcycle faded away.

Max came back into the kitchen carrying a package. 'It was a military courier. He brought this.'

'What is it?' Magda asked.

'I don't know.' He cut the package open with a knife as they all watched, and took out a small box. Inside the box was a metal disc bearing an insignia with a swastika. 'They've awarded me a Wound Badge,' he said.

'You can add it to your collection,' Lola heard herself say in a hard, shaky little voice.

'I have no desire to collect any more of these,' he replied. There was a letter with the badge, which he read in silence. 'From my company commander,' he said, folding it. 'He congratulates me and hopes I am profiting from my sick leave. I wonder what he would say if he knew who my dinner companions were.'

They ate the rest of the meal in silence. Lola was trembling. A knocking at the door always produced this effect on her. The girls helped clear the table and wash up, and then went back upstairs to read, as they did almost every afternoon.

'I think I'm going to be sick,' she said to Heidi.

'Try and keep it down. You need the nourishment.'

'I can't bear to be in the same house as him!' Lola exclaimed.

'Hush. Keep your voice down. Don't make him angry.'

'He's already angry! Didn't you see his face?'

'You were impertinent to him, Heloise.'

'Impertinent! I'd like to knock his teeth in!'

'Please, at all costs, avoid knocking his teeth in,' Heidi said dryly. 'You promised to be a little mouse, and instead you were a big rat, biting and scratching.'

'He deserves it.'

'It's not a question of what he deserves. It's a question of saving our skin.'

'Sometimes I think I'd rather be dead than live like this.' Lola went to the window and peered out, an action that was strictly forbidden.

'Come away from the window, you idiot.'

'The mist is coming down. There's nobody out there.'

Heidi pulled her back and drew the curtains. 'And don't talk about wanting to be dead. Everyone else is dead. So we have to live for them.'

'So you keep saying.' Lola turned her dark-shadowed eyes on her sister. 'But you know what? Sometimes I would just like to live for myself, for one hour. For one minute. For an instant that was mine alone.'

'Oh, Lola.'

'At least in the *Judenhaus*, horrible as it was, the space was our own.'

Heidi hugged her younger sister. 'It will be all right,' she said. 'One day the war will end, even if you don't want to believe it. And then we will be free again.'

'What if Germany wins?'

'Germany can't win. God wouldn't permit that.'

Lola drew back from Heidi. 'God permits all sorts of things. I don't think He exists at all.'

'Come, let's study a little and forget our troubles.'

'I'm not going to study any more today. My head hurts too much. Where's my Sir Walter Scott?'

Their stock of books was diverse, consisting of the late pastor's library of theological works, old novels in English and German, Romantic poetry, and history, supplemented by whatever Magda could pick up for them. The books lined every space, and were piled on the pastor's desk. Lola was currently reading *Ivanhoe*, and finding the dense English a struggle, though the story was exciting. They left the panel to their tiny, secret room open, as they always did, so they could slip into it at the first hint of danger, and curled into the armchairs. It was cold up here. The heat from the smouldering logs in the grate barely lifted the wintry chill, so they bundled into blankets.

Heidi, whose eyes were weak, always held her reading materials close to her face. Her spectacles had been lost in the last move, and until she could procure a new pair from somewhere, she had to put her nose almost to the page. This had the effect of making her literally disappear into her book, an ancient Greek lexicon, into which she was making tiny notes with a pencil.

Lola stared at her own book, trying to shake off her forebodings. But the letters seemed to swim on the page like fish. She could not follow the plot. After a while, she closed the heavy tome again.

'He isn't human at all,' she said. 'He's just a machine that has learned how to hate.'

Heidi didn't have to ask who Lola was talking about. 'I think he's just very unhappy,' she said from behind her book.

'What are we going to do?'

'I'm not going to think about it any more.' She turned the page. 'I just want to forget everything for one hour. I suggest you do the same.'

Lola stared at her elder sister for a moment. All she could see were her fingertips and the top of her head. The jotting of Heidi's pencil was like the scratching of some small animal. With a sigh, she picked up *Ivanhoe* again.

'That girl has a bitter tongue,' Max said to his mother.

'She's had a bitter life.'

'What do they do up there all day?'

'They study from your father's books. Lola is teaching herself English and Latin. Heidi learns ancient Greek and French.'

He grimaced. 'A Jewish women's college – in our house.'

'What would you suggest? A stroll through the town? They don't have much choice. And they were driven out of school. They read as many books as I can find for them. They listen to the radio, if there's a concert, or to the British station in the evenings.'

'Listening to the BBC is punishable by death.'

'Their very existence is punishable by death.'

'You have a ready answer for everything, Mother.' He picked up his Wound Badge and looked at it. He shook his head. 'You always feel sorry for the undeserving.'

'Oh, Max! Have you ever stopped to ask yourself what the Jews have done to deserve a tenth of what has been done to them?'

'Everyone knows what they've done.'

'You mean the poison they print in *Der Stürmer*? Ritual sacrifice and white slavery? Plots for world domination? You're twenty-three years old, Max. You can't believe those stories.'

He shrugged. 'If I think about the Jews at all, it's to thank God that I am not one of them. But to tell you the truth, I think less about them than about the man in the moon. I just don't want them in our house.'

Magda sat at the table and put her head in her hands. 'What am I going to do?' she said, half to herself. 'Where am I going to send them?'

Max got his old BMW motorcycle out of the shed behind the house. He hadn't touched it since he'd joined the *Wehrmacht* in 1939. Before the war, it had been his liberation, the only way he could feel truly free. He'd ridden all over Westphalia, the wind in his face, his mind empty of any thoughts except the road ahead. Without it, his sanity might have given way.

Under its tarpaulin covering, the motorcycle was dirty and forlorn-looking. But he cleaned the carburettor and put a little gas in the tank; and some energetic work with a rag brought the black enamel to a shine again, and removed the white oxidation from the aluminium motor housing. Getting it to start was another matter, but at last it kicked into life and began to thump reluctantly, emitting clouds of evil-smelling smoke.

He rode to the heavily fortified fuel depot in Düren, the motorbike coming to an undignified stop several times en route, and requiring to be coaxed back into life. But once the tank had been filled with fresh gas, using his precious coupons, the BMW cleared its throat and began to sing in its old bass voice.

It was strange to be riding around the countryside again. The scenes of his boyhood filled him with a queasy mixture of nostalgia and discomfort. The rain returned, drenching him, but he had become hardened to bad weather in Russia and he ignored it, urging the motorcycle up to ever-higher speeds, so that the raindrops beat against him like bullets – until on a sudden corner, he lost control of the bike and ploughed off the road into a muddy field.

His heavy greatcoat protected him to an extent, but the jolt to his head was horrible. He lay in the mud, his double vision returned, the pain splitting his skull. For a long while his mind was nothing but a jumble. Slowly, the kaleidoscope pieces resolved themselves. He dragged himself to his feet and somehow got the bike upright again and back on to the road. The bandage around his head had partially unravelled. With numbed fingers, he unfastened the pins, unwound the fabric, and let it flutter into the mud like a shot bird.

The bike wouldn't start again, so he ended up pushing it all the way home. He arrived exhausted and bedraggled. When he came through the door his mother cried out in alarm. 'Max! What happened to you?'

'A slight mishap with the bike.'

'But where is your bandage?'

'I took it off,' he said wearily. 'It was annoying me.'

'My God. Have you seen yourself?' She got a mirror and showed him. The livid scar snaked around his skull, escorted by the puckered dots where the stitches had been removed. Now that his head was no longer being shaved, stubble was growing around the ugly laceration. He pushed the mirror away. 'I don't need to see it.'

'You're frozen.' Magda put more logs in the stove and fussed over him, trying to remove his sodden clothing.

Lola had come down to see what the commotion was about. 'What has he done to himself?' she demanded.

'An accident on the motorcycle. Help me get his shirt off.'

Lola began unfastening the buttons of his shirt. She glanced at the scar on his scalp and grimaced. 'Is that where they removed your brain? No wonder you are such a *Dummkopf*.'

'Leave me alone. I don't want your help.'

'How lucky you are to be able to rush around the countryside,' she said bitterly. 'I wish I could have that freedom, just for one afternoon. I certainly wouldn't throw myself into the mud, I can tell you that. But you *are* a *Dummkopf*.'

'And you are a *Schweinehund*,' he muttered.

She hauled his shirt off. 'At least you haven't broken anything.' She inspected him as he sat shivering by the stove. 'So this is the Aryan *Übermensch*? I would never have known.'

'Lola, go away,' Magda said irritably.

'I was only trying to help.' She retreated, and went back upstairs.

'What's going on?' Heidi greeted her.

'He's had an accident on his motorcycle. You should see him, huddled by the fire, feeling sorry for himself. He looks like a skinned rabbit, so thin and pale!'

'I don't think that's funny,' Heidi said.

'I do!'

'Poor Magda. None of this is easy for her.'

'He called me a *Schweinehund*.'

'And what did you call him?'

'I'm not telling you.'

'You promised you wouldn't annoy him.'

'No, I didn't.' Smirking, Lola curled up in her armchair with *Ivanhoe*. After a while, she went on. 'His bandage came off. He has a huge scar on the side of his head. It's so ugly.'

'Poor man.'

'If you insist on feeling sorry for these Nazis, I will start to doubt your sanity, Heidi.'

'He's as much a victim of the Nazis as we are,' Heidi said mildly.

Lola let out an impatient snort. 'You can write him a letter of condolence from whatever concentration camp we are shortly to find ourselves in.' She felt unable to sit still. Something was boiling inside her. She jumped up and went to the window again and looked out. 'It's still raining.'

Heidi exclaimed in annoyance, 'How many times must I tell you to stay away from the windows!'

'Oh, what does it matter? Let them shoot me.'

'That's all very well for you to say, young lady, but what about *me*?'

'You're right. You're a better person than I am. So much better. You deserve to live. I don't.'

'Heloise, please. These fancies are unhealthy.'

'It's true! You're patient and good, and generous and sweet. You even feel sorry for the Nazis. I am a wicked, bitter little bloodsucking Jewess, just like in those cartoons from *Der Stürmer*. I don't forgive them. I would claw their eyes out if I could. I hate them, and I hate myself for hating them! I should run out and drown myself in that ditch down there – and then you'd have a chance to survive.'

Not sure whether she was laughing or crying, Lola sat on the floor and buried her face in her hands. Heidi came to sit beside her, and put her arms around her. 'Don't get so emotional, darling.'

'I would rather die than be caught by the Nazis,' Lola said, her voice muffled in her sister's hair. 'I'd sooner take my own life than let them take it.'

'If the worst comes to the worst, then I agree,' Heidi said. 'We have the Veronal.'

'Do you think it hurts?' Lola asked. 'Or makes you feel bad?'

'No. You just fall asleep. Remember Mama?'

'Do you think Papa was wrong to do what he did?' Lola asked in a small voice.

Heidi was silent, thinking back to that dirty, cramped room where they had been forced to live. Mama had said she would die there, and she had been right.

Mama had grown sick – whether from the misery, or from the germs, nobody knew, because no hospital would take her in for treatment. By then, the only work Papa could find was mending the broken shoes of other inhabitants of the ghetto. He'd managed to get his hands on some tools somehow, and he'd shown some skill in cobbling, piecing heels and soles and uppers from scraps of leather cut from shoes too far gone to fix.

'You see, girls?' he'd say. 'One shoe eats another!' And he would stage a little performance in which a shoe with a flapping sole would become a hungry shark, devouring smaller shoes with noisy abandon, slurping and belching, until they couldn't help laughing till their sides ached.

But Mama just lay in bed, silent and withdrawn, growing weaker every day. She was a handsome woman, who'd played lusty, racy parts onstage, making the audiences whistle and stamp; but her looks faded swiftly, her curves melted into angles – and then the pain came.

Mama would cry out with it so loudly that the neighbours would bang on the walls, but she couldn't help it. There was no way to dull the pain, and no escape for any of them. It was in the room with them, day and night, ravaging Mama.

When it got too terrible to bear, Papa had gathered up all the money they had, and had gone out. When he came back, the money had gone and all he had in return was a brown glass bottle with a pretty pink label.

'What is it?' Heidi had asked.

'The Jews' last friend,' Papa said. 'Veronal.'

The barbiturate had become a window of escape for many of their friends in those days. At first the suicides had been shocking. Later, they had envied those with the resolution – and the means – to take their own lives. Now, Veronal had become very expensive and hard to obtain. Like everything that offered Jews an escape, the Nazis had snatched it away.

When Lola had been asleep, Papa had talked quietly to Heidi.

'I'm going to give your mother a glass. There won't be any more pain. But she won't wake up, either. You understand?'

'Papa, no!' Heidi had started to cry, but Papa had taken her arms in his strong hands and gripped tight enough to make her stop.

'You can't cry any more. It doesn't help. You've got Lola to take care of. Because I won't be here much longer either.'

'Papa!'

'There'll be enough Veronal left for you and your sister, if it ever comes to that. So keep it safe.'

The girls had lost many things on their long journey, but never the Veronal. They clung to that. It was the only thing that gave them a sense of control over their destiny. They'd taken the decision to live, and had done everything they could to survive. But the lure of the little brown bottle had been increasingly powerful lately. The war seemed to have no end. People said it would last ten years longer. Ten more years of this existence was perhaps more than any soul could bear.

'No,' Heidi replied now. 'Mama was in terrible pain. She just wanted to die.'

'So it wasn't – murder?'

'Of course not!' Heidi stroked her sister's face. 'How can you ask that? It was an act of mercy. He just gave her enough to make sure she didn't wake up again.'

'He cried so much that day. His beard was wet with it.'

'We all cried,' Heidi replied. 'At least she died with dignity, in his arms. And was spared the concentration camp.'

'We'll do the same.'

'Yes. We'll do the same.'

Chapter 3

St Nicholas House was small, and it was not easy for Lola and Heidi to avoid the intruder. They stayed upstairs as much as they could, buried in their books, their ears tuned to the sounds from downstairs, like deer in a forest. They tried hard not to make any sound that might irritate him, or remind him of their presence. At the same time, they could hear almost every word that was spoken in the kitchen below.

'When I hear his voice,' Lola said, 'I want to run down and snatch up the carving knife, and plunge it into his heart.'

'That would be very bloodthirsty, my dear.'

'Oh, I know I'm a monster. When did I turn into a monster, Heidi? We used to be just ordinary girls. People thought we were pretty and sweet, didn't they?'

'Yes,' Heidi said sadly, 'they did. Our house was always full of people. Mama and Papa were celebrities. People wanted to know us. Being Jewish wasn't a "thing". Nobody mentioned it except the Nazis. We were Germans. Mama and Papa hardly even went to the synagogue – the one the Nazis burned down in the end. We were *normal*.'

'But there was something inside us,' Lola said. 'It was growing all time, like a nasty lump, waiting to take over our lives. That's what *really* killed Mama. She started to get sick the night of the play, when they threw rotten tomatoes at Papa. She'd been so brave until that happened.'

'Why not do some Latin subjunctives?' Heidi advised.

'I hate Latin subjunctives only a little less than I hate *him*.'

'Persevere, Heloise.'

Lola smiled despite herself. That was what her elder sister had always said to her when she complained about homework – while they could still go to school. 'I will,' she sighed.

Heidi peered at her own book ruefully. 'I wish I still had my spectacles. This page looks as though a spider swam in the ink-pot and then crawled across the paper.'

The intruder, for his part, barely seemed to acknowledge their existence at all. He ignored them as much as possible. It was only in the evenings, when he came up to his bed in the room next to the study, that they felt his presence nearby.

During the day, they had the use of the late pastor's study, but at night they slept in the cramped attic above. It was a tiny crawl-space, just beneath the roof tiles. Wedged in together, they were uncomfortable and airless. Lola, who was prone to nightmares, found it especially claustrophobic. But it was an excellent hiding place, since even if the access panel in the study were to be removed, there was no hint of a space overhead. You had to know there was a ladder that could be pulled down.

From their refuge, they could hear him walking round his room below, and occasionally muttering to himself. Then they would hear the thump as he took off his boots, one after the other; the squeak of the bedsprings as he got into bed; his deep sighs as he went to sleep.

'Really, it's like being married,' Heidi commented ironically. 'Without the inconvenience of conjugal relations.'

Lola rolled her dark eyes. 'You have such a way with words. I would say it's more like taking up residence in the lion's den.'

They also sometimes heard him talking in his sleep – and on occasions, crying out unhappily. 'He must have seen terrible things,' Heidi commented.

'I hope he never sleeps peacefully again,' Lola said with relish. 'I hope his evil deeds sit on his chest all night long.'

His presence in the house had further diminished their already restricted life, creating a prison within a prison. Avoiding him made Lola more tense and nervous than ever. 'God, how I hate this life. I wish we could go out, even for one hour,' she mourned. 'I would give anything to feel the wind in my hair again. Just to stand in the rain would be bliss. Plodding through the mud would be heaven.' She sighed. 'Even to be back in Berlin, working at the factory, and walking home – oh, how wonderful that would be!'

'I don't have very happy memories of the streets of Berlin,' Heidi said with a sigh. 'Especially after they made us wear the stars. Remember how we used to have to hurry along, with our heads down? You couldn't so much as look in a shop window without some Nazi starting to scream at you. As for stopping at the kiosks to look at the newspaper headlines—'

'It must be very nice for Nazis,' Lola said ironically, 'to have someone to blame for everything that goes wrong. My God, if we were responsible for all the things they say we do, we'd have our work cut out.' Her eyes gleamed with an idea. 'Do you think we could poison him with the Veronal?'

'We may need it for ourselves one day,' Heidi said gently. 'And I don't think poisoning him is any better than sticking the carving knife in his heart.'

'Life was at least bearable until *he* came along. I'm so tired of having to rummage for my things all the time.' Their few possessions were still packed in the valises, in case they had to make yet another lightning getaway. He had yet to denounce them, but they dared not unpack. 'Be patient, my darling,' Heidi said. 'He'll have to go back to the front, one day.'

'Where I hope some Russian will shoot him!' Lola gave an odd little laugh that was half a sob. 'Oh, Heidi! I feel so wretched today!'

'All right,' Heidi said, closing her book, 'let's forget the Latin subjunctives. Let's have a film.'

Lola brightened. One of their amusements was to recall plays and films they had enjoyed in their past life, reciting as many of the lines as they could remember, and singing the music. 'Which one?'

'What about *My Song for You*?'

'Oh, yes!'

They had loved the musical so much that they had seen it three times, not least because its star tenor, Jan Kiepura, was both handsome and Jewish (and now on the Nazis' banned list). Lola started crooning the sentimental title song. Heidi joined in, finding the harmony.

They kept their voices as low as they could. But as her thoughts went back to her old life, and the faces she had once known, the plaintive melody seemed too painful for Lola, and she stopped singing. 'We must have been happy, then,' she said. 'But I can't really remember what being happy feels like.'

Easter had arrived. Max took Magda to the Easter market in Düren, which was subdued, and almost bare of luxuries this year. However, the effect of his uniform, and his *Wehrmacht* ration coupons, procured them a hare, which substituted for the goose of years past, and a basket of fruit, fresh winter vegetables and other rare treats. The back garden had yielded new potatoes and beetroots. The old pear tree had given them some hard, green pears.

With these, Magda made an Easter dinner, to which they sat down together in the warmth of the kitchen at ten in the evening, to avoid the remote possibility of any neighbours dropping in. Since *Pastor* Wolff's arrest, few of the townspeople came to the house or associated with Magda, and there was not much danger of intrusion, but Magda was still wary and took all the precautions she could.

Max refused to pray, but Magda insisted they all hold hands around the table while she prayed, 'Heavenly Father, you have raised your son from the dead and made him to be lord over all things in heaven and on earth. Give us faith that in the risen Christ we can overcome the fear that death separates us from your mercy, and grant that when he comes to judge, we may see Jesus Christ our Lord, who lives and reigns with you in the unity of the Holy Spirit, forever and ever.'

At the conclusion of the prayer, Max, who had been holding Heidi's hand on the one side and Lola's on the other, muttered an 'Amen', and dropped the girls' hands as though they were hot.

Magda lit four candles on the table, and by their fluttering light they began to eat.

'I've been studying your Christian Bible,' Lola said conversationally. 'To improve my mind. It's quite the most confusing book I've ever read.'

'Give it a rest, Heloise,' Heidi sighed.

'I'm serious.' Lola speared a roast potato on her fork and considered it. 'I've learned that everything is the Jews' fault. The whole Easter catastrophe. We're to blame for it all – trial, whipping, Crucifixion, the lot. You would never know that dear Jesus was a Jew at all.'

'Jesus wasn't a real Jew,' Max retorted.

Lola arched her delicate eyebrows. 'Oh, really?'

'He rejected the Jews. So they killed him.'

'Please let's not have a religious argument,' Heidi said.

'I'm only asking for clarification,' Lola said innocently. 'Perhaps *Leutnant* Wolff can explain more. The masculine mind is so much stronger than our own.'

'I would like to enjoy my Easter dinner in peace,' he growled.

'Surely Easter dinner is the best occasion to try to understand Christianity,' she replied sweetly. 'Can you tell me, please, what were the commandments of this new manifestation of God?'

'Love thy neighbour as thyself,' Magda said.

'You see,' Lola said, dissecting her portion of braised hare, 'this is what confuses me. Jesus, formerly a Jew, instructs his followers to love their neighbours. All of whom are Jewish, of course. And yet, for two thousand years thereafter, we see nothing but Christians persecuting Jews, and inflicting every kind of suffering on them. Not to mention upon every other kind of Christian. Does it make sense?'

'Of course it doesn't make sense,' Max said impatiently.

'So it is nonsense, then?'

'All religion is nonsense. Yours as well as mine.'

'Ah. Now I have it clear. We are to believe in nothing. There are no Jews and no Christians. Very good. Thank you, *Leutnant* Wolff. My mind is greatly eased.'

The meal was followed by sweet things that had been unknown since the start of the war – marzipan, cookies, even chocolate eggs bought by Max. The confectionery seemed to sweeten Lola's mood, or perhaps it was the glass of beer, or successfully crossing swords with Max; in any case, she became quite gay. Max studied her face covertly in the candlelight. Flushed by the food and the warmth of the stove, she had lost the pinched look she often had. She had braided her hair in an old-fashioned style, and he caught that elusive scent from her. Would he have known her as a Jewess, had he passed her in the street? Probably not; he would have thought her like any other pretty girl.

'Do you use scent?' he asked her abruptly.

'Since the Brownshirts smashed our favourite shop on the Kurfürstendamm,' Lola replied tartly, 'we've given up buying perfume.'

'There is a scent,' he persisted.

'We Jews exude a special odour,' she replied. 'A good Nazi can detect it from a hundred yards.'

'Don't be absurd.'

'It's our perfume,' Heidi said. 'Our mother always bought it. We have a little left. It smells of jasmine.'

'Well, you will have to stop using it,' he said.

All the happiness drained out of Lola's rounded face. 'Is this the latest racial law from Nuremburg?' she demanded.

'The scent is pervasive. It's all over. Anybody coming in will know that there are young women in the house.'

'They will think it's *my* perfume,' Magda said, looking anxiously at Lola's expression.

'No,' he said curtly. 'You don't wear perfume. And this smell is – alien.'

'You hear that, Heidi?' Lola said, her voice tense. 'We smell alien.'

'I chose the wrong word,' Max said stiffly. 'I intended to say exotic.'

Lola put her knife and fork down with a clatter. Her almond eyes were now glistening with tears. 'So the last shred of our old lives, the last scrap of pleasure, is to be taken from us.'

'I mean only—'

'I cannot bear this any more.' Lola jumped up, the tears spilling down her cheeks, and ran up the stairs.

In the silence that followed, Heidi sighed. 'I'm sorry. I'll go to her.'

'No.' Max put his napkin down. 'I'll speak to her.'

'You will get a frosty reception,' she warned.

Max went upstairs. He reached the study to find Lola curled into a ball in one of the armchairs, her face in an angry knot.

'You're being very silly,' he said curtly. 'And you're spoiling our Easter supper. Come down to the table.'

She did not look at him. 'I don't care anything for your Easter.'

'You should care about upsetting my mother.'

'Of course I care about *her*. I just wish you had never come back here.'

'It's my home,' he retorted.

'I hate the sight of your ugly, scarred face. Leave me alone.'

'Why must you be so offensive?' he demanded angrily. 'We are risking our lives to protect you. We all have to obey the rules.'

'You people and your rules,' she said in a bitter voice. 'I loathe them.'

'Rules are made to keep order.' He tried to keep his anger in check. 'Perhaps I expressed myself badly about the perfume,' he said. 'I meant it for your own protection.'

'Oh, yes. We had to wear the yellow star for our own protection. Our family were sent to concentration camps for their own protection.' Her voice was rising. 'For our own protection, our money was stolen from us, we had to work as slaves, move to the ghetto, hide in attics like mice and never see the sun again. And now, for our own protection, we must have our perfume confiscated.'

'It's only scent!'

'Oh, yes, it's only scent,' Lola retorted. 'We bought it the last time I ever went shopping with my mother.'

He felt his anger fading somewhat, replaced by something that was almost embarrassment. 'Well, if I'd known that—'

'It came from a smart shop in the Kurfürstendamm. Egon Levinson. A Jewish shop. I remember the day we bought that perfume. I was just fifteen.' Lola was talking fast, breathlessly. 'I remember walking along the street with my mother, chattering about something, and suddenly she stopped. Her face changed. I thought I'd done something wrong. But she was staring at Levinson's. Someone had painted a big Star of David on the door. And on the window, in huge, red letters, the word "JEW". I remember the way the paint had run down the glass. There were Brownshirts standing outside, handing out leaflets, shouting at anyone who went in. But Mama just ignored them. We went in. And Herr Levinson brought out our favourite perfume and said, "Buy as much as you can afford. I will be closed tomorrow." So my mother bought three bottles. This is the last one.'

'I didn't know that, of course.'

'And as we came out,' Lola rushed on, 'the men outside spat on us and used filthy words. I had to wash my hair when we got home. And Herr Levinson was right. He closed his shop the next day. He was sent to a camp. We never saw him again.'

Max felt shamefaced. He did not know what else he could say. He looked around the room. 'I had no idea Jewish girls were so studious,' he said, in what he hoped was a conciliatory tone.

But this remark infuriated Lola further. 'Don't you know how insulting it is to assume all Jewish girls are the same?'

'I wouldn't find it insulting to be told I was like other German men.'

'That's different!'

'In what way is it different?'

'Because you *Aryans* have made a special case out of us Jews. You make us all the same – like lice – like bedbugs – so you can stamp on us.'

'I didn't say you were a louse or a bedbug. I said you were studious.'

'It was an idiotic comment.'

'I didn't mean it as an insult.'

'It's how it all begins. "You Jews" this, "you Jews" that. And when you have lumped all Jews together, you can justify anything you do to them. There are no longer good Jews, bad Jews, clever Jews, stupid Jews, old Jews, young Jews. There are just Jews. But I am a German, just like you, whether you like it or not.'

Max frowned. 'But they say that you consider yourselves Jews first, before anything else.'

She snorted. 'Did you get that from *Mein Kampf*? You Nazis would like to see us all swept away. Then you can fulfil that glorious vision of a Germany filled with rows upon rows of blond Aryans, stretching as far as the eye can see. But I will tell you one thing, *Leutnant*.' She wagged her finger in his face. 'When the last Jew has gone, you will regret it!'

'Why?'

'Because you use us to give yourselves an identity. You're not all blond-haired and blue-eyed. Look at Goebbels: he's a positive goblin. But you can pretend you are all beautiful – so long as you have inferior races to despise. I wonder what you'll do when there is nobody left to hate?'

'If it comes to that, I agree with you about Goebbels. Now, will you come back to the table?'

She hid her face away. 'No.'

Judging that this was about as far as he would get, Max went back down the stairs. He stood awkwardly at the kitchen door, very conscious of having spoiled the evening. 'I meant well,' he said resentfully.

'I know,' Heidi replied, 'and she will understand tomorrow. Tonight she is emotional. She misses our parents and – well, she misses everything that she has lost.' She turned to Max's mother. 'Thank you, Magda. It was a wonderful meal. I'll clear up.'

'Go to her, never mind the clearing up. We'll do it.'

When Heidi had gone upstairs, Max sat down with a grunt. 'What a spoiled brat that girl is.'

Magda rested her chin in her hand to look at him. 'You could be more diplomatic, Max.'

'I didn't intend to upset her. It was an issue of security for all of us.'

'Lola is young. And she is under a great strain. It would help if you could refrain from fighting with her.'

'I don't fight with her. She fights with me.'

Her eyes were wise and weary. 'You are everything she fears and hates. She thought she was protected here, a little bird safe in its nest. And now you have come to shake the tree.'

'My only concern is for you.'

'You might express your concern in a more delicate way, sometimes.'

He sighed. 'I am not used to women.'

'You should be gentler with her, Max.'

'I never thought I would miss the army. There, if you need to say something, you say it. Nobody storms off in a temper because you haven't been *delicate*.'

'But this is not the army. And even I find you a little rough at times.'

'I'm trying,' he replied. 'But she doesn't make it easy. She takes that tone with me—'

'What do you expect?'

'I wish she would understand that we're all suffering in this war.'

'She will never understand that. She didn't choose the war. You did.'

'Hardly. I just did my duty.'

She touched his cheek and smiled at him sadly. 'One day, my dear boy, you may find that you had other duties, which you neglected.'

After Max had gone to bed, Magda stayed in the kitchen, thinking.

She realised she had found herself caught in the middle again tonight. Max was her son, however wrong she believed him to be; and knowing what his teenage years had been like, she no longer tried to persuade him that his father had been a decent and honourable man. On the other hand, she had come to regard Lola and Heidi as adopted daughters, and she knew how they, too, had suffered. They were opposite sides of the same coin that had been hammered red-hot in the Nazi mint.

Her marriage to Joachim Wolff had not been an easy one. When he'd asked her to marry him, she'd been astonished. He was nearly fifteen years older than she was, an austere man, greatly admired in the small congregation of St Nicholas, but known to be extremely strict, with himself as well as with others.

Magda had never quite known why he'd chosen her to share his ascetic life. He'd seen something in her – gentleness, sweetness of nature perhaps – that he thought he could mould. But she was very young, and the prospect of becoming Frau *Pastor* Wolff had not been very appealing to a young woman just out of school. St Nicholas House did not seem like an abode of joy.

Her family had pushed her hard to accept him. She was neither beautiful nor clever, they had bluntly pointed out. Nor was there any dowry to attract a wealthier husband. She could expect no better offer to come along. The gentleness and sweetness of her nature had yielded before the pressure.

Had Joachim been disappointed in her as a wife? That she had not turned out to be filled with the Spirit, as he was? Oddly, she had become more religious since his departure, as though his presence had somehow inhibited her dialogue with God. But in the early years of the marriage, he had always made her feel that she was failing in her duties as a Christian.

In those days of the Weimar Republic, Germany had been chaotic. Fanatical right-wing parties had swarmed out of the gutters, spouting racial hatred. Joachim had seen it as his duty to be a beacon of moral guidance.

He'd spoken out against fascism even before the Nazis came to power; and once Hitler had begun to hammer the Third Reich into the oppressive system he'd set out in *Mein Kampf*, Joachim had not held back his righteous indignation.

Magda had lived in fear for so many years – fear of the brutal retribution the Nazis would exact on those who criticised them.

She'd tried to shield Max from the danger her husband's moral stance had put them in. He'd been a happy boy, blissfully ignorant of the shadow that increasingly loomed over the family.

But she knew that Max, too, had been a disappointment to Joachim. He had not been filled with the Spirit, either. Her husband had seemed unable to understand that a boy of ten or twelve would rather be out in the fresh air than listening to sermons in a gloomy church. Joachim had told her that he'd felt the ineluctable pull of God from the age of six. Max had felt the ineluctable pull of playing football and climbing trees.

And where Joachim had chosen martyrdom, Max had had martyrdom thrust upon him, unasked for.

Her heart had been broken twice over. Once for her husband, and once for her son. Joachim's fate had been terrible. Max's had been scarcely less so.

To see the boy come home day after day, with a swollen and bleeding face, his body covered in bruises, his clothes drenched in urine; to know that the teachers at his school despised and victimised him; to fear that he would be taken from her by the state: all that had been very hard to bear.

When Maus Bauer had taken an interest in the boy, she'd been torn. She distrusted Bauer's motives, knowing him to be nothing but an opportunistic thug. But he had offered protection. And even if Max had been pulled into the very system his father had died denouncing, he had found a way to survive, to escape martyrdom. That was something.

When Max had gone to war, all her terror had returned. In her heart of hearts, she hadn't expected him to come back alive. Not from Russia. Hitler's mad plan to conquer the vastness of Soviet Russia had squandered the lives of four million German soldiers. That Max had survived thus far was in itself a miracle. And the war was still not over.

After he'd left, she'd been terribly lonely. She'd become little better than a ghost in St Nicholas House, inhabiting the lives of the departed, with no life of her own, no reason to be there, no reason to even be alive.

When Joachim's brother, Anselm, had asked her to take in the two Jewish girls, Magda hadn't hesitated. She hadn't been able to protect her husband or her son, but she could protect these two innocents, who were persecuted for nothing they'd ever done.

She'd welcomed Heidi and Lola, taken them into her heart. They'd become friends from the start. At last, she had a reason for living again – and a way of undermining, in however small a way, the monstrous tyranny of the Nazi state.

But Max's arrival back from the front, wounded and filled with anger and despair, shattered the peaceful life they'd all built. There was no telling what would become of them all, now.

Chapter 4

The dream was a horrible one, of burning flesh and the screams of men in mortal agony. He could not free himself from the flames that encircled him and stripped away his skin and muscle, down to the charred bones.

A hand shook him awake, and he hauled himself upright, sucking air desperately into his lungs, his body bathed in sweat. His eyes were stretched wide, but he still saw nothing but fire. He heard a low voice calling his name.

Then the fire faded slowly, and became the glow of a candle. Lola was at his bedside, peering at him through her tumbled hair. 'Are you all right?'

He sank back on to the wet pillows, flinging his arm across his face. 'What are you doing here?' he gasped.

'I thought you were dying. You're going to wake the house, shouting like that.'

'It was a nightmare.'

She pointed at the ceiling. 'Heidi and I sleep just above. She didn't wake up. But I did. Do you want me to change your bandage?'

'No,' he snapped.

'Very well.' She turned to go.

'Wait,' he said hoarsely.

Her face was pale, almost luminous in the darkness. 'What is it?'

'I didn't mean to upset you about the perfume. I'm sorry. I meant well.'

She was silent for a long while, looking at him. At last she said, 'I have nightmares, too. Mine are memories, rather than dreams. I suppose yours are, too.'

'Yes.'

'Do you dream of battle?'

'You wouldn't understand.'

'I've been through a lot in my life,' she said grimly. 'Believe me. Do you dream of death and wounds?'

'I dream of friends I saw die. Nothing prepares you for that. A man who's been beside you through thick and thin, who you've come to rely on absolutely, who you've come to—' He stopped.

'To love,' she said.

'Yes. To love. And then you see him torn apart in front of you. You try to save his life, but you can't. All the blood, the screaming. And nothing you can do. You look into his eyes and you see him leaving, like a train pulling out of a station, turning the bend, gone. And a part of you goes with him, and never comes back. That is the worst.'

She was silent for a long while. 'I saw my mother die,' she said at last.

'How?'

'She was sick. I think she had a cancer inside her. We never found out exactly, because we couldn't take her to a hospital. Jews aren't allowed in hospitals. She was in terrible pain at the end. She couldn't bear it. And we couldn't bear to watch her. She cried and screamed and begged to die. Eventually, she did. One night she just went to sleep in my father's arms, and didn't wake up again. Everything was so quiet after that.'

'That's very sad.'

'I didn't understand much about it, then. But Heidi told me later what our father did. He'd got a bottle of Veronal from somewhere. They'd said goodbye to each other. Then he gave her a large dose, and she was released from pain.'

'You mean – he killed her?'

'Yes, *Leutnant*. He killed her.'

'My God.'

'You look shocked,' she observed dryly.

'You're very matter-of-fact about it,' he said.

'Oh, I'm heartless.'

'I don't think you are.'

'Well, let's say I've done all my crying already.'

Max tried to see her expression in the dim light of the candle. 'Your father did the right thing.'

'Of course. A very correct action. Very Nazi.'

'Why didn't you leave Germany before the war?'

'What wonderful advice! The difficulty being that, with no money, nobody wants you. The state took everything we had. And if we wanted to go, there was the Reich Flight property tax, based on an assessment of property we didn't even have, because they'd already stolen it. Naturally, we couldn't find any country willing to take a pair of penniless orphans. What other bright ideas do you have?'

'You talk as though it's all my fault.'

'Well, you're the only Nazi here right now.'

'I don't call myself a Nazi.'

'You look like a Nazi to me. Blond hair, blue eyes, teeth like a lion.'

'I wasn't allowed to join the Party. Because of my father. I joined the army instead.'

Lola snorted. 'Excuse me if I don't quite grasp the distinction. Good night.'

She straightened and went quietly out of the room. For a moment, her figure glowed in the doorway, rimmed with light from her candle. Then the darkness pushed in all around him again.

He lay thinking about her. Something had begun to dawn on him – that it was a simple thing to hate and despise people as a group – say, Jews – when you didn't know any; and quite another to maintain that contempt when you were confronted by a living, breathing human being. Especially a woman as spirited and intelligent as Lola Rosenstein.

What did she think of him? How did she see him? As a hulking brute, no doubt. Stupid but dangerous. She had no reason to feel anything but fear. He had her life in his hands. Yet she stood up to him fearlessly. Heidi was different. She was cautious, diplomatic. She took care not to upset him. But Lola—

Lola was like the injured ermine he'd once tried to adopt as a boy, twisting and biting even as he tried to be kind. She gave no quarter and expected none, argued with him to his face. Perhaps, like the ermine, she would sink her teeth into his hands one day and be gone. He wondered how he would feel if that happened. Surprisingly, he felt that something bright would go out of his life.

Women in general were a class he understood very little, having been a soldier since the age of eighteen. He knew almost nothing about them.

There had been a girl, the last summer before he joined the *Wehrmacht*. Her name had been Traudl. They'd swum in the dam, and walked in the forest. She had let him go a little further each day on the warm sand among the elderberry bushes that flowered along the banks. He'd thought about proposing to her. But he'd had to leave for the army before that moment could come. He'd heard she had since married someone else, and was already a widow, with a small child. He doubted whether he would recognise her now. He had almost forgotten her face. But not the feel of her body against his.

His sexual education, such as it was, had been completed on drunken weekend leaves by the anonymous Lili Marlenes who waited for soldiers underneath the lantern by the barrack gate, and took the money before, not after. And those women had not been interested in anything but the money.

Lola and Heidi might be Jewish, but he had become aware that they were also ladies, of a class that in any other circumstances would have commanded respect. Their current position in the Reich's hierarchy didn't alter that fact, nor did the accident of their having taken refuge under his roof. He felt confused, the hard edges of his thinking starting to blur and crumble. Since his father's arrest, he'd accepted everything that National Socialism had taught him about Jews, about their wickedness, their cruelty. But Lola had described to him a life in which it was ordinary Germans who were cruel, and the Jews the victims. Was that the Jewish cunning he had been warned about? Or was it possible that his father had seen a flaming injustice that others hadn't wanted to acknowledge?

Whatever the case, and he did not want to confront that very large issue yet, he had been brutish to Heidi and Lola, and now he felt guilty about that.

Perhaps he had forgotten how to be human. The war had done that. The necessity to kill or be killed had dominated everything. When they weren't fighting, there had been the unceasing work to repair the panzers and keep them rolling, to find food and shelter, to bury comrades. There had been no normality. It was hard to believe, sometimes, that he had spent five years in the *Wehrmacht* – five years at war, his entire adult life.

He touched the scar on the side of his head, feeling the raised weal under the stubble. Yes, she was right. It was ugly. *He* was ugly.

He was twenty-three years old, but he felt a hundred inside.

They sat around the radio upstairs while Heidi, who was the expert, searched for the stations. The radio, a brown Bakelite *Volksempfänger*, was not equipped for shortwave, but the girls had set up an ingenious aerial, using a wire coat hanger, which let them receive foreign stations after dark, especially the BBC European service, broadcast from across the Channel.

Snatches of speech and music from various countries ebbed and flowed out of the speaker as Heidi's delicate fingers turned the dial, now and then invaded by the threatening growl of the Reich's jamming stations. At last the BBC announcer's voice could be heard, reading the news.

The four of them listened to the faint voice intently. The war news tonight was mainly about the progress of the Soviet army, and the war against the Japanese in the Far East. But there was an item reporting that a transport of several hundred elderly Jews had been sent by rail to a concentration camp, and gassed on arrival, their bodies burned to ash in ovens.

Max was unconvinced, but this report had an intense effect on Lola. She burst into tears. 'We didn't ever say Kaddish for Papa. We don't even know how to say Kaddish. We never had to learn, because we were women. But now I wish we could!'

Max wanted to offer some words of comfort, but did not know how. 'What is Kaddish?' he asked.

Lola turned to him fiercely. 'Shut up! None of you will rest until everything and everyone who is not Aryan is dead. The Jews are just the start. You'll exterminate everyone in the end, and preside over an empire of bones.'

Max looked helplessly at Heidi.

'Kaddish is the prayer of mourning,' she explained.

'Why can't you try and say it?' he asked.

'Oh . . .' She made a little gesture. 'There are lots of reasons.' Her face was melancholy, but she didn't cry like Lola. It was as though Lola felt the emotions for both sisters, while Heidi was always closed and self-possessed.

Magda put her hand on Lola's. 'Perhaps we can say a prayer of our own?' she offered hesitantly.

'It's not the same,' Lola snapped through her angry tears. She pushed Magda's hand away. 'How can a Christian pray for a Jew?'

'But it can do no harm?' Magda pressed.

'Do what you want,' she said sullenly.

Magda got to her knees and clasped her hands. 'Our Father in Heaven,' she said, 'comfort the souls that have departed with divine peace, and take them unto You. Grant their bodies soft and quiet rest in the earth till the Last Day, when You will reunite body and soul and lead them into heavenly joy there.' She prayed on in silence.

Without knowing quite why, Max got to his knees beside her and locked his fingers together, closing his eyes. He tried to remember the words of prayers, so he could ask for some consolation for Lola and Heidi. It had been so long, and only disjointed fragments swam into his mind. He couldn't piece them together in any coherent way, so he groped for words of his own, words of apology, of regret, expiation. He could find none. Between his father's arrest and this spring of 1944 there lay a violent wasteland that should have been his youth, that should have been his life. How could any words take that away? How could any prayer restore to him the lost years, the lost innocence? Who would forgive him for the things he had done?

He felt a gentle touch on his shoulder, and opened his eyes. Lola was leaning forward, looking into his face with a strange expression. 'What are you doing?' she asked.

'I don't know,' he said. 'Trying to pray, I think.'

She touched his face. Her fingers came away wet. 'You're crying.'

69

'I'm sorry.' Max looked from Lola to Heidi. 'Sorry about your parents. They shouldn't have been taken from you.'

'No,' she said. 'They shouldn't. None of it should have happened.'

Magda and Heidi went down to the kitchen to make a pot of the precious cocoa that remained from Easter, leaving Lola and Max together. Lola looked at him with that puzzled expression. 'Did you really pray?' she asked in a low voice.

'I tried. But I can't remember how to. The last time I tried to pray, I was about twelve years old. My father used to make us pray ten times a day. Most of the time, I just pretended.'

'Were you pretending just now?'

'No. I really tried.'

Lola frowned. 'You really prayed for my parents?'

He glanced at her briefly. 'To tell you the truth, I think I ended up mainly praying for myself.'

She grimaced. 'At least you tell the truth.'

'I think people usually only pray for themselves.'

'That's probably true.'

'Unless they're saints. Like my father.'

She let out a snort. 'Oh, your father's a saint, now?'

'It depends on what you think the word means. I can tell you that whatever a saint is, living with one isn't easy.'

'It's never easy being the odd one out,' she commented bitterly. 'Do you believe in God?'

'I don't think so. Not in the way my mother does, anyway. And you?'

Lola shook her head. 'No. I gave up on God a long time ago. He gave up on me, didn't he?'

'He didn't. You're here, aren't you?'

'Yes. But you don't want me to be here.'

'Perhaps not at first,' he replied. 'But now—'

She raised one dark eyebrow. 'Now . . . ?'

'Now it's different.'

Lola looked amused. 'How is it different, *Leutnant*?'

Max felt the awkwardness of his position. 'Now I don't mind having you here.'

'You don't mind? My goodness. What has brought about this extraordinary turnaround?'

'It's not a turnaround.'

'Then what can it be?' she asked mockingly.

'I feel sorry for you. Now that I know more about your life.' He tried to find the right words. 'I wasn't very nice to you when I found you here.'

'That's putting it mildly.'

'I was worried for my mother. I was in a bad way. When you come back from the front – well, you're not really right in the head.'

'You probably never will be, *Dummkopf*.'

He smiled. 'Probably not.' Their eyes met briefly. 'I'm sorry.'

She dropped her gaze. 'Thank you for trying to pray for our parents, anyway.'

He shrugged. 'For all the good it did.'

'Perhaps it did more good than you know.' She rose, smoothing her skirt around her thighs. 'If someone can at least pray for himself, then there must be some good in him.'

Two days after the broadcast, he drove to Düren to see the army doctor there. After a long wait in a line of other wounded soldiers, the check-up was thorough. He underwent a cranial X-ray, a procedure he had come to dislike intensely, and was then subjected to a battery of tests by a doctor, a middle-aged SS major in full uniform.

'We will have the radiography results when the spool is developed,' the doctor told Max. The skulls and lightning bolts on his black uniform sat oddly with his position as a medical officer. 'As you can see, there are many more men to be X-rayed, so it will take time. But I can tell you now that you will not see the inside of a panzer again, Wolff.'

'What do you mean?'

'I mean that after an injury like yours, they will put you in charge of a desk. That's if you are lucky.'

'I have been in panzers for five years, a commander for three of them.'

The doctor's eyes were a pale green. He had a clipped moustache and shaven head in imitation of his master, Himmler, and was wearing several medal ribbons. 'That is all over. You were in perfect health before, give or take a few broken bones. A traumatic brain injury puts you in a different category. You also suffered from a case of diphtheria whilst in hospital, which damaged your lungs. You will never be put in charge of such a valuable piece of equipment again.' He tapped Max's file. 'The results are here. Your reactions are slower. You complain of migraines, blurred vision, depression and insomnia.'

'These are things that will pass!'

'The Reich cannot wait for your symptoms to pass. There are fitter young men eager to take your place.' The pale, icy eyes surveyed him. 'You are the son of the so-called *Pastor*, Joachim Wolff, are you not?'

'Yes.'

'Who grossly insulted the Führer and the Fatherland?'

Max stiffened. 'What does this have to do with my case?'

The man made a note in the file. 'Everything must be taken into consideration. Germany needs men it can rely upon.'

'I've been at war since 1939. How can you say I am unreliable?'

'You should have been court-martialled for what you did in Russia,' the doctor said with venom. 'Your soft-hearted company commander saved your skin. But you come from tainted stock. Your name is Jewish, is it not?'

'No, it is not. It is a good, Aryan name.'

'I note you are circumcised.'

'My father was a devout follower of the Bible. He believed it was God's wish.'

'The wish of the Hebrew god.'

'Am I to be punished for what my father did?'

'There may be a hereditary, degenerative weakness. You showed cowardice in the face of the enemy.'

'You know nothing about it,' Max said in a tight voice.

'In the cognitive tests I have given you, you have performed unevenly. Your judgement can no longer be relied upon. Your speech is hesitant, and you walk slowly.'

'What nonsense!'

'In short, you are not the man you were. You may end up sweeping floors.'

'Damn you!' he snapped.

'Also, you are prone to outbursts of anger,' the doctor added with a thin smile. 'These can be very dangerous, *Leutnant*. I advise you to restrain them. You will be contacted. Heil Hitler!'

Max wandered around Düren, his head throbbing. *Not the man you were.* The dire words echoed in his mind. A curt dismissal, after giving his all to the Fatherland. To be told by that skull-faced SS thug that he was a coward, that he would end up sweeping floors! As though he were a helpless idiot!

He glowered at the swastika flags that hung from all the buildings, brilliant in the spring sunshine. The war had chewed him up and spat him out. Twenty-three, and on the scrapheap.

The town market was busy. He could remember a time when the stalls were piled with vegetables of every colour, with hams and ropes of sausage hanging temptingly from the awnings. Now they were sparse, the vegetables small, meat non-existent. Everything else was going into the war effort. He paused by a second-hand book stall and looked through the offerings. Several copies of Hitler's *Mein Kampf* were piled up, former owners either deceased or perhaps having become disillusioned with the Führer's message. A few years ago, disposing of the holy book would have been blasphemy. Every household had a copy. The sales had made Adolf Hitler a millionaire. Now it was less in demand.

But hidden behind them was a row of more intriguing material, including a three-volume compendium of the poet Heinrich Heine. Heine had been a Jew, and his works were no longer in the bookshops, despite his status as one of the great German Romantics. Max picked them up. They were well thumbed, but clean and intact. He opened a page at random, and read, *Where men burn books, they will also in the end burn men.*

The words struck him with force. He remembered the fierce heat of a night long ago.

How old had he been? Sixteen?

The book burning had been held in a public square, organised by the Hitler Youth. It had been dramatically orchestrated, as all Nazi ceremonies were: the flare of torches illuminating the swastika flags all round the square, the rows of uniformed teenagers standing in line, their jackboots gleaming in the firelight, their arms raised high, the drums pounding out a vast, heavy heartbeat.

And he, bursting with pride at being part of it.

Sweating in the heat, he had helped shovel armfuls of volumes on to the bonfire, side by side with the older Hitler Youth boys, who were almost men and would soon be in the army, defending the Fatherland. He could still feel the flames singeing his eyelashes, could feel Maus Bauer's approving hand, heavy on his shoulder, pushing him on.

He remembered glancing at the volumes furtively to see just what made these writings so malevolent. Puzzlingly, they seemed to be solemn works of literature, science and philosophy, with jaw-breaking titles. Perhaps these very volumes of Heine had been among them. The youth next to him had been lucky enough to have a trove of racy magazines to destroy, with sexy photos of half-naked girls in abandoned poses. He remembered the boy tearing out particularly juicy photographs and stuffing them in his pockets until they bulged.

It didn't matter. It had all gone into the flames. The pyre had flared high into the night sky, embers and flaming pages whirling in the cold autumn air. He'd been exalted. Looking back now, being allowed to participate in the book burning had been an important rite of passage – a pagan ceremony, marking his acceptance into the tribe. He'd had a thrilling sense of belonging, of being absorbed into the German *Volk*, no longer an outcast, but a real German at long last. It was almost as though he had been burning everything in his life up to that moment, and beginning a new existence, forged in the furnace.

His father had been a man of books. *He* would be a man of fire.

Max thought of his comrades whom he'd witnessed burning to death in the Russian night, trapped inside their tanks. And of the BBC's claim that the bodies of murdered Jews were incinerated in huge ovens. He'd thought that was propaganda. But there was a fire burning in Germany. It had been burning for years, devouring lives, hollowing out the nation, consuming everything that was worth keeping. He stood staring into space, until the woman behind the stall spoke to him.

'I'm sorry, what did you say?' he asked.

'One Reichsmark each. They're good-quality books. They belonged to a professor of literature.'

'What happened to him?'

'He doesn't need them any more. Not where he's gone. Don't tell anyone where you bought them.'

'I won't.'

He paid the woman what she asked, and put the books in his knapsack.

Chapter 5

Max presented the books to Lola in the evening. He had intended them as a peace offering, to build on the progress they had made recently. However, when he held them out to her, Lola looked suspicious.

'What are these?'

'For you. Heinrich Heine. One of our greatest Romantic poets.' He smiled. '*And* he was Jewish.'

She didn't return his smile. 'I don't want them,' she said shortly.

He was taken aback. He'd expected enthusiasm. 'Don't you like poetry?'

'I am very fond of poetry.'

'Well, Heine is supposed to be one of the best.'

'So I hear,' Lola said acidly. 'Have you read him?'

'Actually, no.'

'Not on the Hitler Youth syllabus?'

'Well—'

'Of course not. Scorned, along with Proust, Mendelssohn and Mahler.'

'Lola,' he ventured awkwardly, 'you said there was some good in me.'

'What on earth has that got to do with anything?'

'I'm trying to be nice. Please take them.'

Lola clasped her hands firmly behind her back. 'I don't want them.'

Max sighed. 'You're being silly.'

The hot colour came and went in her face. 'Oh, I am very silly, I agree.'

'I don't mean that as an insult. I just thought that some poetry would help pass the time. It must be very tiresome to be cooped up in that room all day long.'

'Quite tiresome. The only thing that would make it more tiresome would be having to follow a reading list imposed by *you*.'

Now it was Max's turn to flush. 'I'm not imposing a reading list,' he said stiffly. 'Why do you twist everything I say?'

'Why do you say such stupid things?'

This was going from bad to worse. He put the books on the kitchen table. 'They're there, anyway.'

Afterwards, in the privacy of their quarters, Heidi was sorrowful. 'I would really have liked to have those books. I love Heine. Why can't we have them?'

'Because he came in telling me I should read Heine because Heine was Jewish! The impertinence! And of course, he's never read Heine himself.'

'I suppose it's pointless asking you to be more diplomatic with him,' Heidi said with a sigh.

'If diplomacy worked with such people, we would still be in our nice house in Berlin, and getting ready to go out to the opera tonight.'

'At least don't be horrid to him, darling.'

'Heidi, I am not going to allow myself to be courted by a Nazi.'

'Courted!'

Lola gave her sister a very dry look, and retreated into the bathroom, since it was her turn to have the luxury of a bath. Heidi was left blinking in surprise. Lola was the younger sister, but in some respects she was more aware, and saw things that Heidi didn't.

Even as children, Lola had always been the one to catch people's eyes. Heidi had been studious and clever, but that didn't really show, except on those acutely embarrassing occasions when Mama and Papa would demand that she fetch her schoolbooks to show their friends all her gold stars – or even worse, make her read out an essay she'd got a commendation for. That would produce polite applause or a pat on the head.

With Lola, it was always a gasp of delight. 'Oh, what a beautiful child! Oh, what a lovely girl! Look at that face! Look at those eyes!'

Lola was the one invited to sit on the uncles' knees. Her bottom was the right shape for avuncular knees. Heidi's wasn't. An uncle had once actually pushed Heidi off his knee with a laugh, saying, 'Ouch, what a bony little backside!'

And later, Lola was the one who had the boys around her, like bees around a rose, while Heidi brought in the *Schnecken* and the *Rugelach*. Buzz, buzz, buzz, with eyes only for Lola, even while they snatched the pastries off Heidi's plate and crammed them into their mouths.

Heidi had never been jealous. She loved her younger sister far too much to begrudge her the attention she got merely for being pretty, especially when the pleasures of life had become very few and far between, and the uncles and the boys were long gone, God rest their souls.

But she had always been conscious of being in the shade when Lola was around. She was the older, plainer sister who would become a doctor (until the Nazis put paid to *that* idea) but of whom nobody ever said, 'She'll follow her mama and papa on to the stage, mark my words!'

Who wanted to be an actress when you could be a doctor? But there was annoyance, nevertheless. Heidi might have had much to say, but she was seldom asked. People wanted to hear what Lola thought, what Lola had done. And *that* was annoying, too. When you were pretty, you were always centre stage.

Courted. Yes, that was the word. The world courted Lola, and she had the luxury of picking and choosing. It had made her spirited, impertinent. That was a luxury too, a great luxury.

One night, before she'd got so ill, Mama had spoken about Lola to Heidi. Mama had been brushing Heidi's hair, which never gleamed like Lola's, and was too thin to be tossed like Lola's, or styled like Lola's.

And Mama had said, 'Promise me you'll look after Lola when I'm gone.'

'You're not going anywhere, are you?' Heidi had demanded.

'We all have to go, some time or another. I won't always be here. Lola needs you. Even if she doesn't seem to. You'll have to watch over her. Protect her, even if she doesn't seem to need protecting. Promise me, Heidi.'

Heidi had sighed. 'I already do, Mama.'

And Papa had said the same thing, just before they'd taken him away. It was a sacred commandment.

After Mama's death, Papa barely noticed what he wore or ate, allowing the girls to care for him like he was a child. He continued to work, but repairing the shoes of the destitute was not a profitable line of business. He would sit for hours at his cobbler's last, his hands open in his lap, staring at nothing. When he did have work he earned pennies, which were soon spent. Heidi had quietly sold what remained of their mother's clothing and jewellery in order to survive.

Papa had been broken by hardship and grief. He was barely recognisable as the exuberant, confident comedian who'd held audiences in the palm of his hand. The once-glossy beard drooped in grey wraiths from his gaunt cheeks. The jiggling belly was long gone. His hollow eyes seemed to see nothing. Thin, weary, he was a man who was waiting only for the end.

When the deportation order had come, from a state agency euphemistically named the Central Office for Jewish Emigration, he had accepted it with resignation, even dignity. The order stated that he would be resettled in some undisclosed location in the East, but they all felt it for what it was, a sentence of death. He would be collected the next day for transportation.

He had put his arms around the weeping girls and drawn them close.

'We won't see each other again,' he said. 'Heidi, look after Lola. Stay together. Live.'

The night had been spent in weeping. There had been little time for farewells the next morning. The deportation order included several dozen other lodgers in the *Judenhaus*, all of them over fifty years of age. A line of trucks arrived in the street just after dawn to take them away. The soldiers tramped through the house, shouting orders, kicking open doors.

'Pack a suitcase! One suitcase each! Nothing more!'

Papa had packed his suitcase already. He sat on it, waiting, like a child going off to school, while Heidi and Lola clung to him.

A soldier thrust open the door, his machine pistol at the ready. He looked round the room and wrinkled his nose.

'You people live like rats in your own filth! It stinks in here! Disgusting! Leopold Rosenstein?'

'I am he,' Papa said wearily.

'Get up. Move!'

Heidi pleaded with the soldier. 'Please don't hurt my father! He's sick!'

'Sick? It's because of people like you that we have shortages. Jews like you are hoarding the food that decent Germans need. You sabotage the war effort while our soldiers die. Move! Move!'

He grabbed Papa's jacket and dragged him out of the room, thrusting him down the stairs. The girls tried to run after him, but the house was in turmoil, the narrow passages choked with crying tenants and shouting soldiers. An officer barred the way.

'Get back in your rooms, now!'

The window of their room looked out on to a dark well, so the girls ran to their neighbour across the hall, who had a window on to the street. Frantic with grief, they all crowded at the window. It had started to rain. Down below, the soldiers were driving elderly men and women into the trucks. Some were too feeble to clamber up, and had to be pushed or dragged.

'There's Papa!' Lola said, sobbing.

Their father shuffled in the line, his head down, his face obscured by his hat.

Lola banged on the window, which was nailed shut, to try to get his attention and wave goodbye, but he didn't hear.

The steps into the back of the truck were iron, and wet with rain. Papa slipped – he who had been so nimble, who had never missed a beat onstage – and sprawled in the road, losing his hat and his suitcase.

Heidi and Lola cried out in horror. The soldiers hauled him to his feet and thrust him into the truck. Diminished and bedraggled, he disappeared from sight. A soldier threw his suitcase after him, but his hat was left lying in the rain, where it was trampled into pulp.

They never saw him again.

Desolate and alone, the sisters had clung to one another, facing a wretched future that promised only imminent annihilation.

Weeks later, they had received a letter purporting to be from him; but it had been on a crudely printed form, and the few lines of writing were not in his hand. They announced, with ersatz cheerfulness, that he was 'happy and in excellent health', and that he had been resettled in a town named Theresienstadt. The place was a showcase for 'Jewish resettlement', touted by the Nazis as evidence of their humane approach. Everyone knew, however, that it was a tightly guarded ghetto, no better than a concentration camp.

There had been nothing more after that. And they had sensed that he was dead.

And now, was Lola being courted by Max Wolff? If Lola had noticed, then it was probably true, and Heidi thought it was not good news. He was a very handsome young man, but if he was indeed smitten with Lola then it would surely be disastrous for them all.

The roar of the trucks outside the house made the delicate china on the kitchen dresser rattle. It was followed by harsh shouts and the thud of boots on the pavement outside. Magda turned a white face to Max.

'Say nothing,' he commanded. 'Do you understand?'

She nodded.

There was a pounding on the front door. Max went to open it. There were two military lorries blocking the street. They had brought a detail of *Ordnungspolizei* in their field-grey uniforms, jackboots and steel helmets. At the head of them was Maus Bauer, his thumbs in his belt. He stuck out his arm. 'Heil Hitler!'

'Heil Hitler,' Max replied tersely.

'You don't seem very pleased to see your old friend.'

'What's this about, Herr *Hauptmann*?'

Bauer raised his eyebrows in ironic surprise. 'Herr *Hauptmann*, is it? I remember a time when I was your Uncle Maus.'

Max indicated the men standing behind Bauer. 'This looks like official business.'

'It is. We've come to search your house for Jews,' Bauer replied.

Max was astonished at how calm his own voice sounded, though his heart was pounding. 'There are no Jews in my house.'

'Except you, of course.'

Max smiled mirthlessly. 'Except me, of course.'

Bauer's small, pouchy eyes almost closed as he chuckled. 'Himmler will be delighted that we have finally caught the notorious Jew Wolff.'

'Very amusing.'

'Stand aside, Max.'

Max folded his arms. 'I have no intention of allowing your men into my house.'

'And how do you intend to stop me, son?'

Bauer was a *Hauptmann*, but Max as a military *Leutnant* effectively outranked him. 'I am a serving panzer commander on sick leave,' he said icily. 'You have no authority over me.'

Bauer made an elaborate show of looking up and down the street. 'I don't see any panzers. Only my trucks. And my men.'

At all costs, Max had to forestall a search. The most cursory exploration would reveal the girls' hiding place in minutes. 'Why are you doing this?' he asked. 'Your superiors will come down on you like a ton of bricks.'

'Not if I go back with a brace of nice, plump Jews,' Bauer retorted.

Max felt a nasty jolt. Was it possible Bauer knew about Lola and Heidi? 'There are no Jews hiding in my house. I will not have my mother upset by your thugs tearing the place apart. She has enough to deal with.'

'Well, now. It's your mother who is the problem, here.' Bauer was still grinning. 'And I'm trying to help you. You'd better let me in, Max. Before things get ugly.'

That got through to Max. Perhaps Bauer was ready to help.

'They stay in the street,' Max said, indicating the men. He let Bauer into the house, and shut the door firmly. What did Bauer know? He could only imagine the terror of the girls upstairs. He prayed that they wouldn't make a sound. They went into the kitchen, where Magda was preparing a meal. Max could see her hands shaking.

'Nice, cosy kitchen,' Bauer commented, looking around. 'Plenty of food and coal, eh?'

'Get to the point,' Max said.

'The point, my young friend, is that your mother has three ration cards.'

Max felt an icy ripple flush through his veins. It was pointless to deny the charge. 'I obtained the ration cards for her,' he said in a clipped voice. 'You know that a widow's ration card is not enough to keep body and soul together. I don't see why she should starve while I am fighting for the Reich.'

Bauer nodded. 'What a good son you are,' he said dryly. 'The fact remains that she is a criminal. And wherever we find illegal ration cards, we are bound to search for Jews in hiding. You could feed a whole nest of Jews on three ration cards.'

'That will not be possible.'

Bauer laid his hand on his pistol holster. 'And if I arrest her? Will it be possible then?'

'Take your hand off your pistol,' Max said grimly.

'You're not on the Russian front now, Max.' But Bauer dropped his hand. 'We are old friends. We must come to some other arrangement.'

'What are you talking about?'

'Ration-stamp fraud is a serious offence. If I pass this on to the SS, all your decorations and service record won't save your mother.' Bauer rubbed his finger and thumb together. 'A little sugar in my coffee, yes?'

Max was shocked as realisation dawned on him. 'You're shaking me down? After all these years?'

But Bauer showed no embarrassment. 'Times are hard, son. We all need to take care of ourselves.' He gave Max a hard smile, with hard eyes.

It had come to the crunch. Max had looked up to Bauer for so long. Now he was seeing that the idol had feet of clay. But it was far better that Bauer had come for a sweetener than that he'd intended to turn the house upside down. Max went to the drawer in the dresser and took out the oilskin pouch. He shook the contents on to the kitchen table – his father's gold signet ring and watch. The things gleamed dully. Bauer picked them up and studied them with a well-practised eye.

'Your father's?'

'The watch is Swiss,' Max said coldly. 'A Rolex.'

Bauer wound the watch up with his thick fingers, and then held it to his ear. 'Not bad,' he said. He slipped the valuables into his pocket. 'Mutual cooperation is the best policy, Max.'

'I didn't know you were this kind of man,' Max said in a quiet voice.

There was a red flash of anger in Bauer's eyes. 'The war makes us all do strange things. Including you.'

'Do us the courtesy to leave our house.'

Bauer looked into Max's face. 'Neither of us are fools, Max. Keep your nose clean. You understand me? I took you under my wing when you were a boy. But you're a man, now.' He gave Magda a mock salute. 'Heil Hitler, Frau Wolff.'

She raised her own arm shakily. 'Heil Hitler.'

In the little downstairs hallway, Bauer lifted his nose and sniffed the air. 'It smells of Jews in here. Pretty little girl-Jews with powdered faces.' He laughed at Max's arctic expression. 'For your own personal use?'

'I don't know what you're talking about.'

In the street outside, Bauer's men were lounging and smoking. Most were old soldiers, like Bauer himself, with the hardened faces of their kind. 'I've searched the house myself,' Bauer told them. 'It's clean.' He turned to Max. 'You'd be surprised at how cunning your co-religionists are. Want to see today's haul?' He led Max to one of the trucks and jerked the tarpaulin tailgate aside. Cowering inside were half a dozen men and a couple of women. Most had bloodied faces. Max saw an eye puffed closed, broken teeth. 'Those two were hidden in a barn. Bad news for the farmer. You know the penalty for concealing Jews – he gets shot, the state confiscates the whole property. His family have lost everything. And that one was masquerading as an Aryan in plain sight – imagine the insolence! We'll take them back to the station and have some fun with them for a few hours. Then hand them over to the SS.' Bauer dropped the tarpaulin again. 'Heil Hitler.'

'Heil Hitler.'

Max watched the *Orpo* men clamber into the trucks. Maus Bauer's broad back was the last to climb on board. He grinned over his shoulder at Max. But there seemed neither humour nor friendship in the grin. The motors roared, spewing out the toxic fumes of wartime diesel. They lumbered down the street. When the noise faded, he went back into the house.

Magda was leaning on the sink. She looked half dead with fear. He put his arm round her shoulders. 'They've gone.'

'He knows,' she whispered.

'He suspects something. I think he only knows about the ration cards.'

'I'm so sorry,' she said. 'I should have been more careful.'

Max was feeling nauseated, not only about the narrow escape for them all. Maus Bauer had been his Dutch uncle, for a decade or more. Now he saw Bauer as a common thug. The disillusionment was sickening. Was it the war that had changed Bauer so much?

'Will he come back?' Magda asked.

'He may. We'll have to deal with him if he does.'

'How?'

'We'll find a way.'

'Do you think he knows about Heidi and Lola?'

'He's not as stupid as he looks,' Max said obliquely. 'We must be much more careful, Mother. The girls must be frightened out of their wits. I'll have a word with them.' He went upstairs and tapped on the panel. 'You can come out,' he called.

After a pause, the board slid open. Heidi and Lola emerged. They looked very shaken. 'We heard everything,' Heidi said.

'He's gone now.'

'What if they come back?' Lola asked. She was very pale.

'We have to be prepared for that. We must make your hiding place harder to detect. We can put the desk in front of it.'

'Then how would we get out?'

'I'll think of something,' he promised.

Heidi looked as though she were about to faint. She laid her hand on her throat. 'He was in the house! I thought my heart was going to burst out of my chest.'

'Come downstairs and get warm,' he said.

They sat in the kitchen, drinking the ersatz coffee that was made of charred acorns. Lola was trying to regain her composure. 'We listened to you from upstairs. You sounded so cool. How did you manage that?'

'One learns to think straight under fire.'

'He gave them his father's watch,' Magda said.

Heidi was stricken. 'Oh, I'm so sorry!'

Max shrugged. 'Don't concern yourself. I never wanted it. And I imagine my father would have approved,' he added.

'We heard him call you a Jew,' Lola said.

'His idea of a joke. He's been making the same one since I was a boy. Because of my name – Wolff. He thinks it sounds Jewish.'

'How ironic,' Lola said. 'It does sound Jewish.'

'Well, it isn't. Wolf with one "f" is Jewish. Wolff with a double "f" is not.'

'I am very sorry to inform you,' Lola retorted, 'that we know a family in Berlin named Wolff with a double "f", and they are quite emphatically Jewish, with hooked noses and red hair, and for all I know, also cloven hoofs and horns.'

'We *knew* them,' Heidi corrected gently. 'They were deported in 1940.'

In the silence that followed, Max said, 'I'm sorry you had a fright.'

'Oh, we were prepared for the worst.' Lola took a brown bottle from her pocket and shook it gaily.

'What is that?'

'A magic potion. It eradicates Jewishness.'

'Veronal,' he said. They must have had it left over from when their father used it on their mother. He was oddly shocked. 'Don't think of using that!'

'What else could they do,' his mother asked, 'if there was no escape?'

'I've been in some tight places,' he replied, 'when there seemed no escape. I always came through to the other side.'

'You Aryan heroes,' Lola said in mock admiration. 'The gods themselves protect you. With us Jews, they are a little more careless.'

Max got to his feet. 'I'm going to see about that bookcase.'

He spent the morning trying to make the girls' secret room more secure. The desk was heavy, but not immovable. It made an effective block. He fastened a loop to the back of it, so that they could pull it up against the wainscot when they retired, and push it away when they wanted to come out. Wax under the feet made it easier to slide, and prevented telltale scratches on the floorboards. It was by no means foolproof, but it was something, at least, until he could think of a better solution. He also reinforced the catch that held the panel in place, so that it was harder to open, and nailed felt on to the inside, so that it sounded solid when it was knocked. With luck, the refuge would survive a cursory search – providing the women within didn't give themselves away.

Later in the afternoon, they met at the foot of the stairs. 'I don't want those Heine books,' Lola said, 'but my sister does. She's still labouring under the delusion that she's a German.'

'I'll give them to her.'

She paused and looked towards the window. 'Thank you for the thought. It's a strange life, ours. We live with dread. It's always there, in the pit of our stomachs. It never relaxes its grip. And our thoughts go round and round on the same treadmill, all day long. We have nothing new to think about or talk about. We just remember our friends and family who are now dead or vanished. And wonder when our turn will come.'

Wisely, he didn't try to offer consolation. He just nodded silently. She looked up at him. Her eyes were so dark that one could almost not detect the pupils, yet they sparkled like jewels, and could snap into anger or laughter in a heartbeat. He thought of the dark water of the dam where he had swum so long ago, of how one could sink into its depths.

'You don't know what it's like to wear the yellow star,' she went on. 'Once, on a tram, an old man with white hair screamed at me, "Jewish bitch! They should string you all up!" And the woman next to him said, quite calmly, "No, they give them a prussic-acid injection. Or shoot them in the back of the head." I was so upset that I jumped off at the next stop, even though it was snowing, and I had to walk two hours to get home. Another time, a group of boys followed me, shouting obscenities. They threw stones. I was so afraid that they would attack me. But it was their hatred that really frightened me. They knew nothing about me, and I knew nothing about them, but their hatred was like something black being pulled over my head. I couldn't breathe. It's not just the fear of being killed or hurt. It's being hated that makes life intolerable.'

'Why didn't you cover the star with a scarf?'

'You don't know? It has to be displayed. You can't hide it, because if the Gestapo catch you concealing it, the punishment is very severe. Once, when my hair was longer, it happened to fall across the star. A Gestapo man became enraged with me in the street. He wanted to shoot me, there and then. Nobody interfered. He was with a woman, and she calmed him down. He shouted, "Next time I see you, I will shoot you." I just stood there. I think I would have been happy to die, at that moment.'

'You may think of me as a brute,' he said, 'but I want you to know that I have never behaved like that to anyone in my life.'

She looked at him strangely for a moment, as if coming to some sort of decision about him. 'I suppose there is some good in you, after all,' she said. 'That policeman – Bauer. He's a friend of yours?'

'He was,' Max said with a grimace. 'After my father was arrested, I had a hard time. I became a punchbag for the local kids. I think they would have killed me in the end. Bauer took me under his wing, for some reason.'

'In what way?'

'He taught me how to box. So I could defend myself. Got me into the Hitler Youth.'

'Ah. Made you into a good little Nazi?'

'Something like that.'

'Why did he bother?'

'I suppose he felt sorry for me.'

'Hmmm.' Her eyes narrowed. 'You must have been a pretty boy.'

'What do you mean by that?' Max demanded.

She smirked. 'I'm just saying.'

'There was nothing like that,' he retorted indignantly.

'Take it easy. But he still came to put the squeeze on you?' She studied his face. 'How did that make you feel?'

'I suppose I shouldn't be surprised. He's a rough diamond.'

'But you must have been attached to him.'

'I was.'

'So – a disillusionment for loyal Max.'

Max shrugged. 'Russia taught me not to get too attached to anyone or anything. Everyone dies.'

'I'm sorry I said your wound is ugly. You can hardly see it, now that your hair is growing.' She paused. 'How did you get it?'

'I'm sure you don't care.'

'I didn't say I cared. I'm just curious.'

'It happened on the retreat from a town we'd held for a few weeks. We finally had to give up our position when our supply lines were cut off. We had hardly any ammunition or food left. It was almost nightfall, but we received orders to engage the enemy and hold them for a few hours while the others got away.' He paused, remembering. 'The Russians drew us into an area we didn't know. It turned out to be a marsh. Within ten minutes, three of our tanks got bogged down in heavy mud, and the rest of us were forced to get them out, somehow. We had to attach cables to the trapped machines and drag them. And then the Russians attacked from the darkness.'

'It was a trap,' she said.

'Yes. The Reds had chosen their ground cleverly. These weren't the inexperienced soldiers who ran away from us in 1941. Not any more. These were battle-hardened and well-equipped troops, fighting for their homeland to the last drop of their blood.'

'You can't blame them.'

'I didn't blame them. I just didn't want to leave my bones there. Their fire was heavy and accurate. There was no way we could counter-attack effectively. We were sitting ducks. We just had to concentrate on getting the trapped machines free. For three hours we wrestled with the marsh. We took hit after hit. The steel cables snapped under the strain, and when they did, they whistled through the air like scythes. They would take your head off if they caught you. Our fuel reserves were running almost to zero. It was only the extra-heavy armament of the Tigers that protected us. Then one of the panzers was hit in the fuel tank. You never forget the sight of a tank catching fire. Some of the crew managed to get out. But they were drenched in burning gasoline. They were human torches. They ran a few yards before collapsing. There was nothing to do but administer the coup de grâce. We had to kill our friends to end their agony. Just as your father had to kill your mother.'

'Yes,' she said in a low voice.

'A little while after that, my own Tiger took a direct hit to the cupola. It knocked me out instantly. When I came to, I was covered in my own blood, and more dead than alive. I knew it was the end. I pulled myself together enough to order a retreat. We left three of the Tigers behind, and thirteen of our comrades.

'When we reached our company, there was talk of a court martial. They put me in a forward hospital while they decided what to do with me. After a couple of days I left without telling anybody, and got some of the others together for a reconnaissance. We went back to the swamp to retrieve the bodies of our men. The Russians had taken the Tigers but left the dead. They were already starting to putrefy. Friends, comrades, men we'd laughed with and fought with, now just charred and mutilated flesh.'

She nodded silently.

'We dug field graves, and marked them with crosses cut from young birch trees and whatever stones we could find. We marked each one with the dead man's name. I suppose we were hoping that when the madness was over, somebody would find the graves and give them a proper memorial. But I think they're still there. Anyway, that last effort almost killed me. I went back to the field hospital, and they sent me to Poland to be X-rayed. They found my skull was cracked like an eggshell. They told me I had bleeding on the brain, and that it was a miracle I'd survived this long. I wasn't really conscious for a long time after that. I just knew that they did two operations. And I remember the hopeless chaos and confusion all around as the Russians got closer.'

'You were lucky to live.'

'Berlin didn't see it that way. They wanted us court-martialled and shot. Allowing three tanks to be captured by the Russians is unthinkable to men who fight the war from behind desks. Our company commander interceded, and saved us from that. And then I got diphtheria. That meant weeks more in hospital before I could be sent home. And that was when I met you. And then my troubles really started.'

'You shouldn't make a joke of it.'

He shrugged. 'It's all over now.'

'Except in your dreams. You still have them, you know. I hear you crying out in your sleep.'

'And I hear you, crying out in yours.'

They stared at one another for a moment. 'When you went off to war as a kid,' she asked, 'did you think it was going to be like that?'

'No. But then, nothing ever turns out the way you think it will, does it?'

'No.'

As if by mutual accord, they both looked away. Lola turned and went upstairs without saying anything more.

Listening to foreign radio broadcasts, particularly the BBC, had been a crime since the first weeks of the war. It hadn't mattered much to Max, since he considered most of what was reported from the Allied stations nothing more than propaganda. But of recent months, he had grown to distrust the official Reich media almost as much. The incessant harping on an imminent victory, and announcements of devastation wreaked on Germany's foes, did not square with what he himself had seen, nor with what he had heard from fellow officers.

Magda and the girls tuned in to the BBC each night. Lola, who spoke better English than he did, translated the difficult parts. The light programmes were sometimes absurd. One could imagine the broadcasters as chinless, tweed-clad caricatures. But the news reports were sobering. The casualty figures that the BBC gave differed widely from the official Nazi versions. Germany was increasingly encircled by hostile forces, the Soviets pressing in from the East, and a vast assault force was clearly being massed on the other side of the Channel.

American and British bombers in fleets of up to a thousand were systematically pulverising targets in France and Germany. It could only be the softening up before the invasion. Now that he was recovering from his injuries, Max had begun chafing to get back to his division. Germany needed him, and he had not yet been summoned back to the battlefield. Had the SS doctor destroyed his chances of getting back to the front?

After the broadcast, Heidi and Magda went down to do the dishes, leaving Max alone with Lola. He was still thinking about the news. 'I have to get back to my company,' he said, almost to himself.

'Why are you in such a hurry to be killed?' Lola asked.

'I'll be needed. The Allied invasion will start very soon.'

'That's the first thing I've heard you say which has made me happy.'

'The invasion won't be a very happy affair.'

'For us, it will.'

'You may be glad to be shut away in a cupboard.'

'Nonsense! I'll rush out and kiss the first American soldier I see.'

'And what if he's a Russian?'

'I'll say *yevreyka, yevreyka*! That's Russian for Jewess. He'll kiss me back.'

Max snorted. 'May I remind you that the Russians invented pogroms, long before there even was a Germany.'

'Heavens,' Lola said. 'Things have come to a pretty pass if a Nazi yields to anyone in anti-Semitism.'

'I don't think of you as a Jew.'

Lola grimaced. 'You say some idiotic things. Am I supposed to take that as a compliment?'

'I just mean that I wonder whether I would have known you were Jewish, if we had met before the war.'

'Of course you would – you would have seen my yellow star.'

'And your hooked nose, red hair, horns and tail.'

'Exactly.'

'When I was a boy, there was one of those *Stürmerkasten* in Düren. A noticeboard with the latest copy of *Der Stürmer* on display.'

'Yes, I know what they are.'

'I used to stand in front of it with all the other kids, gaping at the drawings – Jews as monstrous spiders, or poisonous snakes.'

'And now you're forced to live with two of these creatures under your roof. Did you ever talk to your father about things like that?' she asked curiously.

'Talk to my father? Nobody talked to my father. Least of all me. I was to be seen and not heard. My father talked, and expected others to listen. As for *Der Stürmer*, I was forbidden to look at it. If he caught me looking, he would give me a thrashing.'

'Poor little Aryan boy,' Lola said ironically.

'Maybe if he'd tried to explain, instead of getting out the whip, I'd have understood more. But he thought I was too thick-headed to understand. Or maybe he was just too busy. Anyway, he kept the explanations for church. And his sermons were very difficult. Whereas the drawings in *Der Stürmer* were easy to understand.'

'So you chose to believe them?'

'After he was arrested, I had to make sense of what had happened. Everyone said that my father had been crazy to defend the Jews.'

'Did you put the blame on the Jews for what happened?'

'I put the blame on my father,' Max replied. He hesitated. 'If I'd been closer to him, I might have stood up for him. But I wasn't close to him. I know that sounds strange to you – you loved your father. To tell you the truth, I was afraid of mine. He was aloof, what they call a disciplinarian, always ready to give me a whipping for something or other. Especially falling asleep in church. He believed in not sparing the rod. He was very stern at the best of times. Very committed to his religion. There weren't a lot of happy moments for me or my mother. As for the Jews, I didn't have any feelings either way at the age of twelve. I was just a kid.'

'You still are, if you ask me,' Lola said. 'But when you became a man? You must have been able to use your judgement! Did you think it was right?'

'There were so few Jews out here. This is not Berlin. Yes, I heard that things happened here and there. People disappeared. But from the age of eighteen, I was at war. I went to battle to protect the Fatherland, or so I believed. I never asked who started the war, and what it was all about. I just wanted to do my part, and do the best I could. I felt so honoured to be assigned to a panzer battalion. I was one of the elite. Our officers were good men. I never believed any of them capable of doing anything dishonourable or criminal.' He searched her face for a sign that she understood him. 'Do you trust that I'm telling you the truth? You know that I'm not like the SS, or anything like that.'

'When I first saw you, in your black uniform, you terrified me,' Lola said.

Max smiled wryly. 'The uniform is only black so it doesn't show the oil. Life in a panzer is filthy. Between the dust, the grease and the cannon smoke, your skin goes grey, anything you wear goes black. You scarcely look human. And you often don't get to wash for weeks at a time.'

'It doesn't sound very enjoyable.'

'No, it's not very enjoyable. On my twentieth birthday, Franz, one of my best friends, was killed. My crew caught a chicken from somewhere. They were roasting it for me in a bucket over a wood fire, making jokes and laughing, when a Russian sniper shot Franz in the stomach. He was the comedian of the tank. Everyone loved him. It didn't matter how tired or scared we were, he could always make us laugh. He was a good soldier, too. We gave him all our morphine, but it didn't seem to help. He took hours to die.'

'You were so young,' Lola said sadly.

'I remember thinking, by my next birthday, the war will be over, and we'll be drinking champagne to Franz's memory. But we were still fighting on my twenty-first birthday, a year later. And that night, we had a cold snap. The army hadn't supplied us with proper winter gear. We were in the middle of the Russian winter, with summer uniforms and lightweight tents. We had to light a fire under the panzers to get them started every morning. Before daybreak, twelve of our company froze to death. It was minus twenty. We organised a burial party, but the ground was so hard that we couldn't bury them. And we had no heavy equipment. So we poured gasoline over them, and—' He stopped, seeing her expression. 'I stopped having birthdays after that.'

'How old are you now?'

'Twenty-three. And you?'

'Twenty.'

'When is your birthday?'

'Soon. June the fifth.'

'Perhaps we'll have a party.'

'A party? You must be mad. Haven't you been cured of parties by now?'

Max walked into the garden to get some air. Reliving war memories always left his mind spinning. Or was it Lola who made him so confused?

He touched the raised weal of his scar under the bristles of hair, and wished his head did not ache so much. He tried to imagine a life so wretched that one carried a bottle of poison always. And then, to have the resolution to use it!

The girls in the attic were very different from anyone he'd ever known before. That was certain. He might not understand them very well, but they had brought something new into his life. They'd sparked new emotions and new ideas in him.

In the study, Lola was also restless. Max Wolff's account of the war had upset her. She had actually pitied him, a Nazi and an enemy.

Heidi had come upstairs from the kitchen. 'Is something wrong, darling?' she asked delicately.

'He was telling me about friends of his who were killed in the war.'

'And?'

'I ought not to feel anything when I hear about Nazis being killed,' Lola said, picking up her books, 'but he made me feel sad.'

'You should be careful of those feelings,' Heidi said.

'If I was careful of my feelings,' she replied, opening the pages, 'I wouldn't be Lola Rosenstein.'

Though Max had long accepted that the Nazi Party was riddled with corruption, and largely run by criminals, he clung to the idea that Hitler was somehow above it all. It was hard for him to shake off the image of Hitler that he had grown up with, as Germany's saviour. Lola, who was starting to hope that Max could be educated, found this infuriating.

'Don't you see? Hitler tells them all exactly what to do – and just makes sure that his name isn't connected with any of it, so people like you keep thinking he's not a monster!'

'He's not like the others, Lola.'

'Not like the people he put in office? Please, Max! Do you really think that anything is done without his approval? He's a small-time crook who gathered enough thugs around him to grab power from weak old men who couldn't hold on to it any more.'

'Hitler is more than that,' Max said stubbornly.

'Can you tell me one sensible thing that he has ever said or done?'

'He saved Germany from Bolshevism.'

'By plunging us all into an endless war? I would rather have Bolshevism, thank you!'

'You're too young to know what you're talking about.'

'Your father knew what Hitler was, and he was not afraid to say it.'

'Leave my father out of this, please,' Max said angrily.

'You need to open your eyes, Max.'

'And you need to curb your tongue.'

Heidi, wisely, stayed out of the arguments between Lola and Max. What worried her now was not that Lola was too hostile to Max, but rather that she was growing too close to him. Lola was no longer depressed. If anything, she was overexcited. Heidi decided to say something about it in the wake of one of these furious quarrels.

'Darling, I wish you wouldn't get so heated in your discussions with Max.'

'But he drives me insane!'

'It would indeed be insane,' Heidi said gently, 'to get too emotional about him.'

'Oh, Heidi! Don't you get emotional about these issues?'

'Of course I do. But what concerns me is that you get emotional about *him*.'

They were upstairs in the study, Lola deciphering Sir Walter Scott and Heidi painstakingly transcribing her spidery Greek characters. Lola marked her place in *Ivanhoe* with her finger and looked up curiously at her elder sister. 'What are you talking about?'

'I don't like to see you getting too involved with him.'

'We're at opposite ends of the spectrum, in case you hadn't noticed.'

'I had noticed. I also notice that you arouse powerful emotions in each other. And that is not desirable, considering the circumstances we all have to live under.'

'You mean that we detest one another?'

'I mean the opposite.'

That Heidi had put her finger so accurately on the sore spot made Lola all the angrier. 'My dear sister, you have the wrong idea altogether!'

'You said yourself that he was courting you.'

'I didn't mean it like that! That's offensive!'

'Yes, I know I am offensive. But I *am* older than you—'

'By two and a half years!'

'—and perhaps just a tiny bit wiser.' She got up and went to sit on the arm of Lola's chair, smoothing the rebellious curls away from Lola's brow. 'I've always been a tame bird. But you are a wild bird, Lola. You don't belong in a cage. You were only sixteen when the war began. Since then, you've grown up in a very strange environment. You've had none of the things that girls of your age usually have – parties, dances, holidays. Beaux. Young men to talk to and go to the movies with. Max is the first man you've had anything to do with since you became an adult woman.'

'And he happens to be a Nazi.'

'He excites you – I see it. I also see the effect you have on him.'

Lola laughed shortly. 'If you think I care two hoots for Max Wolff, or he for me, you couldn't be more wrong.'

'There's a tension between you and Max that we can all feel. Magda hasn't said anything to me about it, but I know it worries her, too. Too much passion between you and Max will make life intolerable for all of us in this house. It may end up endangering our safety.'

Lola raised her eyebrows. 'Endangering our safety? May I remind you that he was all for throwing us out, or handing us over to the Gestapo, a few weeks ago! It's only because of me that he's changed his mind.'

'Yes, darling,' Heidi said, even more gently. 'That's exactly my point. He has grown very interested in you. And you in him. And I suspect he has the same problem that you do – I doubt that he has known many eligible young ladies since he became a soldier. So to him, you're very exotic and fascinating, just as he is very annoying to you; and the result may be an involvement that we should all wish to avoid.'

'Even if there was any truth in what you're saying – and there isn't – what harm could it do?'

Heidi paused. 'Do you remember that man I worked for in Berlin? Herr Dietrich?'

'Max is not like that,' Lola burst out indignantly.

'The position is the same, Lola. We are very much in his power. A word from him, and our lives are over. You're like a mouse between a cat's paws. Such a mouse cannot afford to fall in love with the cat, no matter how interested the cat is in the mouse.'

'You're jealous of me!'

'I'm not jealous of you, Lola.'

'You've always been jealous of me. Just because I get a little fun out of life—'

'This isn't *fun*.'

'You're upset because he doesn't bother with you. And you project your feelings on to me!'

'That's very unfair.'

Lola was breathing quickly in her anger. 'Please don't say any more.'

She raised her *Ivanhoe* to shut Heidi out, and after a moment, Heidi went back to her own place.

Lola's words had wounded her. Of course, Lola had always been 'the pretty one', the spoiled one, but Heidi had never felt any jealousy.

She thought back to Herr Dietrich in Berlin.

A sympathetic official, once a friend of their parents, had found them work in one of the Reich's armament factories, making bullets and shells for the *Wehrmacht*. They'd had no choice but to do the work, bitter as it was to be helping Hitler to fight the very people who might save them. The only justification for their continued existence was now aiding the war effort, bent over machines for twelve hours each day. And even that had come to an end. The sympathetic official had himself vanished, his sympathy for Jews proving his undoing. And the girls had received deportation orders, telling them to pack a suitcase each and present themselves at the railway station, where the cattle trucks awaited them.

By then, nobody believed in the hoary myth of 'resettlement cities' any longer. No letters ever came from these fabled places. No Jew ever returned to tell them of the healthy air and the crystal streams. The resettlement cities were actually concentration camps, where only death awaited. The girls had known that they stood on the edge of the abyss.

They'd been scraping together their paltry wages from the armaments factory, spending almost nothing on themselves. With their savings, they had exchanged their distinctive Jewish identity cards for regular ones in 'Aryan' names. The supplier was a drunken banknote forger, and the papers weren't very convincing, but they couldn't afford anything better. They'd unpicked the yellow stars from their coats, and had slipped out of their old lives and into the maelstrom that was wartime Germany.

For six months, their luck had held. They'd found work and lodgings, and nobody had looked at them too closely. Lola had worked as a cleaner in a canteen, and Heidi had found clerical work in a stationery office.

But Heidi's boss, Herr Dietrich, had taken a fancy to her. He was a balding, smirking man of fifty, with an endless store of smutty jokes. He'd started by ogling her, bestowing unwanted compliments on her, and inventing pet names for her. His favourite was *Schneckchen*, little snail, because she shrank into her shell at these advances.

'But you are married, Herr Dietrich,' she'd exclaimed once in dismay, as he loomed over her, trying to kiss her at her desk.

'When you eat doughnuts every day,' he'd chuckled in reply, 'every now and then you want a jam tart.'

He'd moved on to cruder approaches. It was his delight to wait until she was busy with the filing cabinets, come up silently behind her, and slide his hand up between her thighs, or reach around to grab her breasts.

She was soon fighting him off daily – which only excited him more. He assumed, like all his kind, that she was 'playing hard to get'.

There was nobody to help her. She dared not complain to anyone else in the office. Her disguise was wafer-thin, and any examination of her papers would reveal the truth.

Heidi would never forget the terrible sense of helplessness she'd felt during that time. Trapped, with no way out, the pressure had made her ill. Her hair had started coming out in skeins each time she combed it, and she'd been physically sick at least once a day. To be hunted as a Jew, and tormented as a woman, was a double burden she was slowly breaking under.

Herr Dietrich had been a resourceful man, not one to take 'no' for an answer. He'd opened her purse one day when she wasn't looking, and had examined her identity card.

Flushed with triumph, he'd confronted her with it in his hand. 'This document is a forgery. You are not who you say you are. I've got you now, my little snail!' As Heidi recoiled from him, he'd advanced, his eyes gleaming behind his spectacles. 'I don't care what you are. But you won't be pushing me away any longer. You're going to meet me in the office lavatory every day for some fun – or I go to the Gestapo.'

She'd actually considered giving in to him, for Lola's sake. Protecting Lola was everything to her – and if Dietrich denounced her, Lola would be doomed, too. But to give her credit, Lola had refused to countenance the idea.

'I'm not letting you do that for me. I'll cut his throat, first!'

Cutting Herr Dietrich's throat proving unfeasible, once again they'd had to vanish in the night. They'd packed their bags and fled. And now there was an added terror: if Herr Dietrich had denounced them, the Gestapo would be hot on their heels.

Lola's turbulent relationship with Max had brought all this back to Heidi. Magda was one of the kindest people they had come across in their long flight; but Max was not like his mother. Who knew how he would behave, if Lola provoked him too much? He could become a second Herr Dietrich, or just turn them in to the Gestapo if she offended him. He was an unknown quantity.

And though she had never been jealous of Lola, Heidi was wishing that Lola was not quite so vivacious, not quite so pretty. It was not the time to shine.

Chapter 6

Summer had arrived, with longer days of sunshine, blue skies, and a flood of green leaves in the formerly bare trees. It became all the more wearisome for the young women to be indoors all day long, never emerging from St Nicholas House.

Cold in the winter, the pastor's study was hot and airless in the summer. The only way to make it bearable was to keep the windows open – and that meant extra precautions. Conversation had to be conducted in whispers, in case a passer-by heard them. There were not many of these, since the house was isolated, and conversations between Lola and Heidi had dwindled since the quarrel, but the strain of enforced silence all day told on both of them. Nor could they ever appear at the windows to enjoy the view across the fields. Any sharp-eyed observer would be sure to spot them. And the police were still combing the countryside, looking for the enemies of the state – Jews, gypsies, black marketeers, deserters and the thousands of others on the death lists.

With the invasion surely drawing ever closer, Max could not understand why his recall to arms was being delayed. He tried to place a call to his company commander, to find out more details, but the switchboard could not connect him.

He began taking long hikes through the forest, determined to get himself battle-fit. The migraines were devastating at times; he fought through them, wanting to be whole again. In quiet forest glades, he stripped off his shirt and exercised rigorously, until the sweat dripped off him. Then he would plunge into a cold stream to wash, before starting the long tramp home, where a new quarrel with Lola was sure to begin.

Finally, Max received a summons to present himself at the military clinic in Düren again. Once again, he waited for two hours with other patients, many of whom were missing limbs or eyes. Max had known some of these men from boyhood, and though he had not had many friends, there was a shared life between them.

The talk was soldiers' gossip about comrades serving in various parts of the vast battlefield that Europe had become. Some had been decorated, others wounded or captured or missing. And many had been killed. The toll of dead young men was staggering. An air of fatalism, if not defeatism, hung in the air. The unspoken theme was a longed-for end to the war which had already lasted five years, and had taken so many of their young friends and families.

When a one-legged *Feldwebel*, a fanatical Nazi, burst out with a speech praising the Führer's military genius, a silence fell, and another man spat eloquently on to the floor.

Max was depressed by the attitude of his fellow soldiers. Though he no longer believed that Germany could win the war, he was determined to defend his country. He knew what to expect from the Red Army, should they ever set foot in Germany. And there were women in his home who would need to be protected.

At last, Max was called into the consulting room. The same SS doctor was in attendance, with his shorn skull, cropped moustache and ice-green eyes. He did not ask Max to sit down, leaving him standing in front of the desk.

'I have this for you,' he said, pushing a yellow card across the blotter.

Max picked it up. It bore the red seal of the *Oberkommando*, and was signed and stamped by a *Generalmajor* he had never heard of. For a few moments he did not know what it was. Then he saw that it was a discharge from the *Wehrmacht*.

Stunned, he read the terse terms that were typed on to the card. He was entitled to disability pay, civilian food stamps for two more months, a travel allowance of a few marks, and a bar of soap. He looked at the back stupidly. A series of stamps, dates and signatures showed the progress of the discharge through the High Command. Among them was the name of his old panzer company commander.

'Why have they done this to me?' he demanded in disbelief.

The SS man leaned back in his chair. 'I warned you, young man. Your results were definitive.'

'What am I supposed to do now?' he asked tightly.

'Find work. There are fields to plough and armaments to build. As you see, you will not have military rations for long.'

'I'm a panzer commander. I can fight!'

'You mean you can run away.'

'How dare you?'

The SS doctor's eyes gleamed. 'If you raise your voice to me one more time, I will see to it that you are transported from here straight to a concentration camp.'

Max was silenced.

'There will be a Home Guard set up in the next months,' the doctor continued. He was already bent over his papers, writing. 'You will be called up for that. Your name is on the list. In the meantime, the army is over for you. You are dismissed.'

Max emerged into the brilliant sunshine, feeling dazed. He was no longer a soldier. The thing that had given him his identity, his pride, his sense of manhood, had been taken away. He felt as though he had been reduced to nothing. He set off slowly for home.

'Why such an angry face?' Lola asked him.

'I've been discharged from the *Wehrmacht*,' he told her.

'You should be glad for that,' she said. 'At least you won't be shot or blown up again.'

'I can't believe they've done this to me.' He put his aching temples in his hands. 'I feel they've kicked me in the teeth.'

'Do you really think Germany can still win the war?'

He shook his head slowly. 'No. Not any more.'

'Then what's the point of getting yourself killed now?'

'If I can do anything to protect Germany,' he said heavily, 'then my life doesn't matter.'

'A good German to the last.'

'There is such a thing as a good German,' he rejoined. 'Perhaps you have seen the worst side of life. But there is another side.'

'Oh, yes. Wagner at Bayreuth, and all that. Unfortunately, we were never invited.'

'Nor was I, come to that. We didn't get much Wagner in the panzer corps.'

'Personally, I can take Wagner or leave him. He's Hitler's favourite composer. I'm sure he would have been admitted to the Nazi Party.'

'You're very sarcastic today.'

'It comes of being an *Untermensch*. My sister and I have experienced the full flavour of Aryan culture over the past few years, believe me.'

She had gone pink in the cheeks, as she did when she was angry, and he sighed. 'I know you have. Let's not get into a fight, just this once. I'm too depressed.'

But she continued. 'It's odd. Even though we are subhuman, and touching us defiles pure-blooded Germans, there was no shortage of Aryans ready to grope our backsides, and touch our breasts, and try to get us into bed.'

'If that's true, it's disgraceful.'

'Disgraceful that good Germans could lust after an *Untermensch*?'

'Disgraceful that a woman should be treated like that by any man.'

Lola smiled grimly. 'Heidi had a boss who was like an octopus. An Aryan octopus, of course. She had to fight him off all day long. When he couldn't get his way, he checked her papers, and found they were forged. He threatened us with the Gestapo if she didn't become his mistress.'

Max shook his head. 'I'm sorry to hear that.'

'You know what was really sad? She actually considered giving in.' Her black eyes were burning. 'That's how low we sunk. And she would have done it, too – to protect me. But I wouldn't let her. I would rather die. So we had to run.'

'Where did you go?'

'After the octopus? It was very hard. There are eyes everywhere in Germany. Everyone watches everyone else, you know that. We knew that if the octopus had told the Gestapo about us, they'd be on the lookout for two women together. So we split up during the day. I've never been so lonely in my life. Just walking the streets, looking for any work I could find. Or even a crust of bread on the pavement. At night we would meet up and share whatever we'd been able to scavenge. If we were lucky, we'd get into a hostel where they didn't check our papers. If we weren't, we slept under bridges and in ditches. Or just walked the streets all night.'

'My God. Anything could have happened to you.'

'Most of it already had,' Lola said dryly. 'But it got worse. The air raids started. At first it was once or twice a week, but soon it was almost every night. There was one night that was absolutely terrifying. There were hundreds of bombers up there, circling Berlin. The whole city was shaking with the blasts. Flames shooting up into the sky. And every now and then one of the bombers got shot down, and we would see it crashing down in a fireball. We were stuck in a park, because we didn't dare go to an air-raid shelter. You couldn't just go in. You had to belong to that district. The wardens wanted to know who you were and look at your papers.'

'Lola,' he said quietly, 'I didn't know you'd been through that.'

She shrugged. 'Well, after that, we knew we couldn't sleep rough any more, and the air-raid shelters were just as dangerous. And our little bit of money had run out. We were half starved and more than half frozen that winter. It almost ended there. So we did something crazy.'

'What?'

'We walked into a shabby little church. We'd heard that there were some priests who would help Jews. There were a lot more who would turn you away – or turn you in. We just took a chance. It was our last resort. We wouldn't have lasted more than a day or two longer before we collapsed, or got caught. We had holes in our shoes. And Heidi was coughing up blood. She had pneumonia, though we didn't know it. By some miracle, the pastor was one of the good ones. He hid us in his house, gave us warm clothes and food. We slept properly for the first time in weeks. It was like having a door opened.' Lola's eyes were wet with tears at the memory. She couldn't speak for a while. 'He passed us to another family,' she went on at last. 'Religious people who were prepared to risk their own lives for strangers. They were in touch with an underground network that tried to save Jews. But it wasn't over. We were shunted from house to house, town to town, for weeks. At last we came across your uncle.'

'Anselm?'

Lola nodded. 'Yes. In Cologne. He and Ditte looked after us for a week while Heidi got her strength back. He's a wonderful man.'

'Is he?' Max asked sceptically.

'You don't like him?'

Max thought back to his teenage years. 'After he was released from prison, he visited us a few times. I think he was trying to play a bigger part in my life. He came to Kallenheim for my birthday one year, with gifts. A train set and some books. I remember him telling me not to listen to what they were saying about my father. He told me that my father was a good and honourable man, a man of God. He said he only wished he had a tenth of his courage, and a tenth of his faith. He wanted me to get on my knees and pray with him for my father.'

'And did you?' Lola asked.

'It meant nothing to me. I was still struggling to survive the beatings and the misery at school. I preferred the gospel of Maus Bauer.'

'What's that?'

'Put your fists up, hit them in the mouth, split their lips against their teeth.'

'Oh, Max.'

'I'm sorry. But it meant far more to me than Uncle Anselm's prayers. And when Bauer heard that Anselm was visiting, he lost his rag. He said that if I listened to Anselm's "trash" I'd go the same way as my father. That was enough to slam the door shut.'

'Poor Anselm.'

'He just seemed a weak, watery copy of my father. And he hadn't chosen the birthday presents very well. The train set was too young for me. The books were religious tracts about dying youths who sailed up to heaven after repenting their sins. I tore one of the books, and deliberately left the train set out in the rain. The carriages all rusted and the paint peeled off.'

'What a little bastard you were.'

'Yes. But he got the message. There were tears in his eyes. As he left, I heard him telling my mother, "The boy is lost to us, it's too late, the Nazis have got their hooks in him."'

'And they had,' Lola said in disgust.

'I'm sorry,' Max replied, 'but I don't have the milk of human kindness sloshing around inside me, like they do. Creeping along, loving your neighbour and kissing behinds wasn't for me, Lola. I learned that early on in life. If you don't stand up for yourself, you get trampled down.'

'What a charming philosophy,' she said dryly.

'If you Jews had a bit more of that philosophy, you might not be where you are today,' he retorted.

Lola reddened with anger. 'I ought to slap your face. It's a mistake to think you're human. Anselm saved our lives. And your mother opened her heart to us without asking questions. Tell me,' Lola challenged, cocking her head to one side, 'why are you such a Nazi *Dummkopf* when the rest of your family are so decent?'

She stalked off.

Despite himself, it still stung to be thought of as 'a Nazi *Dummkopf*, incapable of any finer feelings. He must show her that he was not altogether a beast.

He decided to give Lola a party, however small, on her birthday. He knew it was taking a risk. Lola's reaction to friendly approaches could be violent, as he had learned to his cost.

'Are you sure about this?' his mother asked, when he approached her for advice.

'It might cheer us all up,' he replied.

Magda knew that it was very hard to stop Max once he had an idea in his head. With much reluctance, she agreed to help.

He got back on his bike and returned to the market in Düren, and after a search, found what he was looking for: an old wind-up gramophone with a few well-worn recordings of foxtrots and waltzes. He knew that Lola was unlikely to agree to dance to the 'light music' chosen by Dr Goebbels and broadcast on the *Reichs-Rundfunk* – and he was very much hoping that she would dance with him, remote as that possibility seemed.

He was also able to stock up on some extra groceries. Anselm and Ditte had sent coupons from Cologne. So long as Anselm and Ditte were not found out, they could rely on these precious gifts. Together with what they grew in the garden, and Max's coupons, they were adequately, if not lavishly, fed. But Max's military rations would be cut soon, and they would have to make adjustments. With his privileged officer's food-and-petrol allowances, he had been able to put food on the table for his mother and the two guests. It would get a lot harder now.

Riding home with the panniers of the BMW loaded, he noted that the first harvests had begun. The early crops were being reaped, the early fruits picked. But the men and the women doing the work were slaves, grey-clad prisoners from the conquered lands in the East, who had been brought in to replace the men of the master race who were away fighting the war. They trudged sullenly through the fields, and were herded back into camps at dusk.

And the coming invasion cast a long shadow over the green-and-golden landscape. Army units were being mobilised across Westphalia to dig in. An engineer battalion had set up camp a few miles from Kallenheim and begun digging a vast network of trenches and gun emplacements across the fields and into the forest. Gangs of civilian men and women were drafted into the taskforce, lured by the promise of extra rations. The grim-faced work parties could be seen trooping along the country roads, looking no happier than the Slavic prisoners, plainly people who had already lost faith in victory.

Tank obstacles of the type known as 'dragon's teeth', pyramids of concrete set in rows, marched in undulating lines around the hills. The war had come to this most beautiful and tranquil part of the Fatherland.

Max came across a group of panzers rolling towards the front, trailing the familiar reek of diesel and hot steel. When he saw the crews looking at him in the indifferent way he used to look at civilians, he felt like shouting, 'I am a soldier, like you!' But he wasn't. The Fatherland had rejected him, now, in its hour of need. He was not considered worthy to defend it any longer. It was a bitter draught to swallow.

His discharge from the panzer corps, clearly because the SS doctor had recognised him as Joachim Wolff's son, had wrenched things loose in his mind, things that he'd thought were meshed as tightly as steel cogs.

He'd had faith in Hitler's military genius up until this year. It was a basic tenet of German belief that, whatever else he might be, Adolf Hitler was a military mastermind. That had been borne out by the extraordinary early victories of the war, some of which Max had participated in. Like Alexander the Great, Hitler seemed to have conquered half the world in a few short years.

Yet now, Max felt that the extraordinary victories had been due to the extraordinary aggression of the attacks, rather than to any great genius on Hitler's part. The world had been unprepared for the sheer viciousness of the Nazi assault on civilisation. Small and weak countries had simply been steamrollered in those ferocious early campaigns. Larger countries had reeled back, or gone under.

Now that the Allies had built up their military strength and had been joined by the Americans, however, the tide of the war had changed irrevocably, and the forces ranged against Germany were irresistible.

'What's all this?' Lola demanded suspiciously, venturing cautiously into the little front room.

There had been surreptitious noises all evening, whispers and rustlings from downstairs. Now, looking around, she saw the result.

For a moment, Lola stared, not sure what emotion she was experiencing. Then she burst into tears.

Heidi put her arms around her. 'Happy birthday, darling. Don't cry.'

'I don't want any of this!' Lola choked.

'Max and Magda arranged it all,' Heidi said, soothing her.

Through blurred eyes, Lola took in the pains that had been taken to celebrate her birthday.

Max, Heidi and Magda had put up decorations, mostly pictures cut out of magazines, strips of coloured paper, and even a few balloons (precious items now that rubber was in short supply). There were wild flowers from the hedgerows, arranged in vases, and branches of evergreens hung on the mantelpiece. The table had been set out with pastries, cookies and a *Gugelhupf*, stuck with coloured candles. There was wine. Magda's best china was out, too.

'Happy twenty-first birthday, Lola,' Max said, taking her hand.

She glared at him. 'You had no right to do this!'

'I know,' he said. 'But it's a big day. We didn't want it to pass without even a "Happy Birthday".'

'I wish Mama and Papa were here,' she burst out.

'I wish your mama and papa were here, too. They would be so proud of you.'

He probably meant it to be comforting, but the effect was only to make Lola cry even more. She hadn't marked her birthday with any kind of celebration for years. 'Oh, this is too much!'

'Have your cry,' Heidi coaxed, 'and then let's have a glass of wine.'

There were small presents: scented talc, tortoiseshell hairclips, a bar of scented soap. There was even a gramophone in the corner. Max put on a record, rather crackly selections from *The Merry Widow*, and the charming music creaked out of the speaker like a ghost from the past.

Between laughing and crying, Lola let herself be ushered to the seat of honour, and served with food and drink. After this shaky start, Lola's mood improved. Max had obtained a few bottles of a pre-war *Gewürztraminer*, and the flowery, delicate wine helped make her feel better. Sweet things to eat, which were such a rarity now, cake and pastries and smiling faces around her, all combined to make the dark present fade away, and bring back the dear past she had almost forgotten.

When they'd eaten, Max put on some dance music. The strains of foxtrots and waltzes were irresistible. Heidi made her get up and dance, while Max danced with his mother. The room was small and crowded, and they had to push all the furniture aside to be able to move around without danger of upsetting everything, but it felt magical to be whirling around the room.

'I'm so glad to see you happy,' Heidi said, smiling at Lola. 'One day soon all the bad things will be gone. I feel it in my bones.'

'I hope you're right,' Lola said. 'The bad things have lasted an awfully long time.'

'You're all grown-up. I remember when you first came into the world. I was so excited to be getting a little sister. I had planned all sorts of games for us to play. I was even prepared to share my toys with you. Imagine that!'

'Very noble!'

'Papa took me to the hospital to see you. Of course, I was expecting a dolly with golden ringlets and fluttering blue eyes. And there you were in Mama's arms – a fat, little, furious monkey with clenched fists and black eyes like two currants stuck in a bun. But I was prepared to forgive you all that. I'd brought you a present – a frog I'd caught in the garden that morning. I was sure you'd be delighted. I put it on your tummy. Well! What a performance! Mama screamed like a banshee, and you started screaming too. The nurses came running in, and when they saw the frog, they started screaming as well. Papa tried to catch the frog, but it shot off like a bullet. And the obstetrician, Dr Marx, was called. And there he was, this famous man with a bald head and a grey beard, on his hands and knees under Mama's bed, trying to catch my frog. And everyone in the room screaming.'

Lola had heard the story a dozen times, but it still made her laugh. 'You were horrible to me even then,' she said.

'Not at all. I was very fond of frogs. I still am. I could never see what all the fuss was about. But it was just as well Papa saw the funny side, or I would have been in deep trouble when we got home.'

After a couple more dances, they changed partners, and Lola found herself in Max's arms. She stiffened, then allowed herself to move freely again.

'What were you and Heidi laughing at just now?' he asked, looking down at her.

'A silly old story.'

'Tell me.'

'When I was born, she brought me a frog as a welcome present.'

Max smiled. 'Sometimes, if you kiss a frog, it turns into a prince.'

'I've never had that experience,' she retorted. 'I hope you're not talking about yourself.'

'I wasn't.'

'I never thought I would be dancing with someone like you.'

'Someone like me? I thought you didn't like oversimplifications.'

'*I'm* an individual. *You're* an oversimplification.'

'That's not fair!'

'It's my birthday. Everything I say is fair.'

They danced around the little room together, watched by Heidi and Magda, who had sat down. Max was a good dancer, his body strong, his movements sure. Lola allowed the music and the rhythm to take over her thoughts. Perhaps it was the sugar in her veins that made her feel dreamy and happy, or the *Gewürztraminer* that had gone to her head; but it was pleasurable to dance with a tall, handsome man, to forget all the sorrow and anxiety, to leave everything behind but this golden moment.

She looked up into Max's face. He wore an expression she hadn't seen before: happy and proud. The way he held her in his arms was tender. She felt protected for the first time in a long, long while. She felt cherished too.

She caught Heidi's eyes watching her. Lola knew what Heidi was thinking: that dancing with Max this way was inappropriate.

Was it wrong?

Life, she had long ago decided, was mainly sad. It was a bumpy mixture of what should have been and what actually was. Usually, *what was* differed tragically from what should have been. But if you could pretend, even for half an hour, that what should have been had become real, was there any harm in it? Was it wrong to dream, to yearn, to hope?

Max had been brutal to her at first. But he had also shown himself to be capable of surprising kindness and understanding. He was trying, in his way, to atone. It could not be easy for him.

The war had battered him, as it had battered her. Neither of them were perfect. Neither were unwounded. Perhaps there was common ground – a fellowship of the damaged? Perhaps she could warm to him a little?

The music changed, became slow and languorous. She let him draw her close, closer, until their cheeks touched. She felt his eyelashes brush her face, and knew he had closed his eyes. She closed her own eyes, losing herself in the swaying of the dance, wistful and almost asleep.

'They fight all the time,' Heidi murmured to Magda, 'but they can't stay away from each other.'

'She's changing him,' Magda replied. 'He listens to her. He's never listened to me. When his father was arrested, he suffered so much. He was beaten and ostracised at school. He felt he had to go to the opposite extreme to set things right, prove himself a good German. He wouldn't allow me to say a word in defence of his father. I've waited for years to see his mind start to clear.'

'I am not sure,' Heidi said, picking her words with care, 'that their friendship should get any deeper.'

'I am quite sure it should not,' Magda replied. 'It's not healthy for either of them. They've been thrown together in a very strange way. When the world returns to normal, both may find they've made a terrible mistake. There will be broken hearts.'

'My feelings exactly,' Heidi said. 'But what can we do about it? I tried to talk to Lola, and she was furious with me.'

'I'll try to have a word with Max,' Magda sighed, 'but I think he will get angry, too.'

The record had ended. Max and Lola stood for a while, clasped together in silence, lost in some other world – until Heidi touched Lola's arm, and said firmly, 'Lola, I think it's time you went to bed.'

'I'm sorry if I was an old killjoy,' Heidi said upstairs, as they undressed for bed. 'It was just uncomfortable to see you in his arms.'

'Don't worry, I'll get back to tormenting him again tomorrow.' Lola smiled.

'That's not very comfortable, either.'

'But I so enjoy provoking him. He starts steaming and snorting through his nose. It's most gratifying. I feel like a bullfighter in the ring.'

'As long as your bull doesn't decide to charge.'

'I'll just do a pirouette and stick my sword in him again as he thunders past. It's a blood sport without the blood. Just harmless fun.' She sighed. 'Tonight was beautiful though. I find it more and more difficult to imagine ever getting out of here. Sometimes I think it'll never happen. I know we have each other, darling. But – forgive me – I've been so lonely.'

'I know you have.'

'You're calm and rational. A real grown-up. I'm not like you. I'm stupid and trivial. I need distractions. I've longed for someone to torture, and now I've found him. It's a great consolation.'

This conversation did not do much to set Heidi's mind at ease. She felt as though they had all been frozen in a glacier for months, and now that the thaw had set in, everything was starting to change and move in unpredictable ways.

The invasion began the next day.

The news started coming in on the radio from midday, an electric crackle of reports that Allied landings had been made on the coast of northern France, supported by heavy air attacks and airborne troops. The enemy had set foot on the territories of the Reich

– and they were only a few hundred kilometres from Kallenheim. Lola was exultant.

'I couldn't have asked for a better birthday present!'

They huddled round the radio, listening to the babble of propaganda that spewed out, trying to sift the real information from the lies. Goebbels and his minions were trying to give the impression that the invasion was wonderful news for Germany. 'We have the enemy at our sword!' came the vaunt. 'He landed exactly where we knew he would land. We've got him where we want him, and now we will inflict a crushing defeat!'

'Is that true?' Lola asked Max.

He shook his head. 'No, Lola. It's the end.'

As the day wore on, the slightly hysterical tone of the broadcasts became somewhat more subdued. The German people were exhorted to hear the news of the invasion 'with deep seriousness' but also 'with the imperturbable certainty that we will emerge victorious'.

It was impossible for the girls to feel totally joyous, knowing that ferocious fighting was taking place, and that thousands of young men were being killed; but there was real hope now, where before there had been only a wish.

Max was in a sombre mood. For a long time now he had not believed that the war could be won. Goebbels' assurances of final victory were so much hot air. Listening to the radio, he had heard Winston Churchill describe the war as a threat to civilisation, which had unleashed horror for no other reason than to satisfy the wild ambitions of Adolf Hitler. That no longer seemed like enemy propaganda to him. His faith in the Führer was draining away. What he had believed was divine inspiration was increasingly looking like fanaticism.

But he knew that the end would not be swift, and would inflict yet more suffering on both Germany and the Allies. If the past years had produced a slaughter, the coming ones would drown that in blood. There would be a dreadful reckoning.

And he also knew that their geographic location was going to put them on the front line. To get into Germany from the landing sites, the Allies would come straight through Westphalia and the North Rhine. The war would soon be on their doorstep.

And as he looked at the three women, and felt how deeply he cared for them all now, he wondered how he was going to protect them from the coming storm.

He couldn't get rid of the feeling of Lola in his arms as they'd danced, her touch and her warm breath on his cheek. It had been a deeply unfamiliar sensation, yet it had somehow felt perfect. An odd combination.

There was much to admire in Lola Rosenstein. Her name suited her well. She was a rose to look at: velvety, sweet. But she was a stone in other ways, obstinate, strong. It was a mystery. He felt increasingly drawn to her, to the point of wondering what would have happened between them in other circumstances.

News of the invasion continued to come in. The BBC, normally a reliable source of war information, was tight-lipped about the progress of the battles. The German radio, led by the strident voice of Goebbels, continued to proclaim that all this had been expected and planned for, and that the *Wehrmacht* had been poised to annihilate the enemy, which it was now doing in magnificent style.

What was clear, however, was that the Allies were continuing to land men and machinery along the French coast, despite heavy losses. And as the days went by, Goebbels finally conceded that the invasion was 'the greatest onslaught of the war', and a crisis of life and death for the entire nation. It was a case of 'fight or die'.

A few weeks later, more startling news broke. An attempt had been made on Hitler's life. A bomb had been placed near him in a bunker at general headquarters, the Wolf's Lair itself. Several generals had been killed or injured. But a divine providence had saved the Führer's life.

The blame at first seemed to be laid at the door of the British Secret Service; but then an even more stunning announcement was made: the bomb had been placed by senior German officers, some of whom had been arrested and confessed. Their names were given. The ringleader, Count von Stauffenberg, had already been executed. A hunt was underway for other plotters who had escaped.

Hitler himself made a broadcast to prove that he was alive and well. This was in itself highly unusual. It had been months since Hitler had spoken on the radio or been seen in public. There had been rumours that he was sick, or had suffered a nervous collapse. But the voice they all knew so well rasped out of the speaker, as menacing as ever.

The four of them sat around the radio, listening to Hitler dismiss the assassination attempt as the work of 'a small clique of stupid officers' who had wanted to get rid of him. He ordered the army to ignore any orders given by the 'rebels'. And he transferred complete command of the *Volkssturm* to Heinrich Himmler, the chief of the SS.

Max switched the radio off, profoundly depressed.

'All of Germany must be in mourning around Hitler's coffin,' Heidi said in her dry way. 'Mourning that it's empty.'

'If only they'd succeeded!' Lola said. She was very agitated. 'The war would have ended tomorrow!'

'Perhaps. But now this has just made things worse. Hitler has handed control over to Himmler. Germany is going to become a complete SS state.'

'I thought it already was.'

'There was at least some sanity until now,' Max replied heavily. 'From now on, it will be madness. The SS are utterly ruthless killers, trained and hardened to show no pity. Hitler has decided that the only way to win the war is to let them take control. There's no chance of peace any more. There is no option but to fight to the bitter end.'

Lola's hopes, which had been raised so high, began to sink as the end of July arrived with no sign of American tanks in Kallenheim. She had cherished an image in her mind, perhaps foolishly, of being able to rush out into the streets and present flowers to the first liberators. That was clearly a dream that was not going to materialise anytime soon.

Max tried to prepare the women for what was to come. He had taken part in an invasion, on the victorious side, and he knew what to expect.

'The Siegfried Line passes close to Kallenheim,' he told them. 'We're in the direct path of the Allies. They'll inevitably enter the Reich here. It's the gateway to the North Rhine, to all our coal and steel, our dams, our heavy industry, our factories and farmland. It's all of immense strategic importance. Kallenheim is going to be at the centre of a battleground.'

'We're no strangers to a difficult life, Max.'

'This will be difficult in a way you haven't yet experienced.'

'Are you trying to frighten us?' Lola asked.

'I suppose I am, yes. I want us all to start making preparations.'

'I'm always deeply impressed when you take that authoritative tone. I feel I should snap to attention and shout, "Heil Hitler, my leader!" So tell us about these preparations.'

'We must think about leaving Kallenheim.'

'But where can we go?' Magda asked.

'To Düren.'

'The police headquarters – and Maus Bauer – are in Düren!'

'Yes,' Max agreed, 'along with thirty thousand other people. Here in Kallenheim, everyone knows us. If Maus Bauer wants us, he knows exactly where to find us. Nobody knows us in Düren. We can lose ourselves among the refugees that are pouring in. We'll say that Lola and Heidi are my cousins. Nobody will challenge it. Trust me, we'll be much safer there than here.'

'Why can't we just sit it out in Kallenheim?' Heidi asked. 'And wait for the Allies to liberate us?'

'It won't be as simple as that. The fighting is going to be intense. That means air attack, tanks, artillery, infantry, the lot. You can't imagine what it will be like. It will be hell on earth.'

'How will we find a place in Düren?' Magda asked.

'I'll start looking,' he replied.

The announcers on the German radio crowed with the news that the long-awaited secret weapon had at last been unleashed on England. Named the Vengeance Weapon, it was a scientific marvel, a pilotless flying bomb that could be launched from the Continent and would drop on London out of clear skies. It flew too fast to be shot down by either the English fighters or the anti-aircraft batteries. It carried a warhead of one thousand kilogrammes of high explosive, and it caused horrific loss of life when it landed on the crowded streets of the English capital.

It had been many months since Göring's bombers had been able to fly in safety over England, so the propaganda machine made the most of this new miracle weapon. Hundreds, the harsh voice rasped, had already been killed or injured, and the skies over London were glowing fire-red, with huge palls of smoke blotting out the sun. Terror had spread across southern England.

The reports plunged Lola into a new despair. 'I hate them so much,' she said, clenching her fists. 'They are cruel, cruel, cruel.'

'I don't understand what they intend to achieve,' Magda said wearily. 'It seems so indiscriminate to kill women and children. It won't stop the invasion.'

'No, it won't,' Max agreed. 'It's not intended to stop the invasion. It's intended to feed the bloodlust of our own people. That's why they've called it the Vengeance Weapon. It's exactly the same thing with the persecution of the Jews – throwing raw meat to the beasts to keep them from devouring their masters.'

Magda looked at him strangely. 'You sound just like your father,' she said in a quiet voice.

He had no answer to make to that.

Chapter 7

The thunderbolt came out of the blue summer sky without warning.

Max was working in the garden, stripped to the waist, when the grey trucks roared up to the house. There was no time to do anything. He stood like a statue, leaning on his spade as the *Orpo* men piled out of the lorries, carrying rifles. He was cursing inwardly that they hadn't already made the move to Düren. Here in Kallenheim, they were all too easy prey.

The last to emerge was Maus Bauer, swaggering up with his thumbs in his belt. He grinned at Max and raised his arm. 'Heil Hitler!'

Max didn't bother returning the obligatory greeting. 'What do you want?'

'So. You don't give the Hitler salute?'

'Let's not waste time. If you've come for another bribe, you can forget it.'

Bauer's smile widened, but his eyes were hard. 'We've come to search your house. Properly, this time.'

Max tried to conceal his dismay under a surly exterior. He was praying the girls were hiding themselves, but despite the precautions he had taken, a search would find them in a few minutes. 'The Americans are coming, man. You should be preparing for that, not chasing imaginary Jews round the countryside, wasting petrol and manpower.'

'You talk a lot, Max. But you don't give the orders around here. You are not even in the army any longer. They threw you out.' He sneered at Max's expression. 'You think I wouldn't hear about that? And we know the truth about your heroic exploits in Russia, too. You escaped a court martial by a whisker. Only because your sentimental company commander covered up for your cowardice. I wasted my time with you. You were just like your father, all along.'

'What do you know about it?' Max said contemptuously. 'You sit behind your desk, growing fatter every day, and you come here to accuse me of cowardice?'

Bauer flushed. 'Be careful what you say.'

'I've served the Fatherland well. That is worth something.'

The gang of *Orpo* men had clustered around Bauer now. They were all older men, but their faces were hard, their eyes fixed on Max like a pack of dogs around their quarry. Bauer spat at Max's feet. 'You handed three Tigers to the Communists! They should have shot you on the spot.'

'Take your thugs and get off my property.'

'Not until we've searched your house.'

Max stepped forward, lifting the spade. At once, with a rattle, half a dozen rifles were trained on his belly. He lowered the implement again. Bauer was no longer smiling. 'I see you for what you are, now,' he said. 'A Jew-lover and a sniveller, like your father. Disloyal officers like you tried to kill the Führer. You deserve what you've got coming. Bring him with us.'

Two of the *Orpo* men took Max's arms, and they marched him into the house.

Max's stomach was churning. He kept his face expressionless as the search began. Did Bauer really know something? Or was it the

130

common bluff that the police were so expert at? It was impossible to tell.

Magda stood like a statue at the sink, her face white as bone. The search was ruthless. It began in the kitchen. The *Orpo* men emptied cupboards, sweeping crockery and provisions on to the floor, and then trampling everything under their boots. They went from room to room, and everywhere they went was the sound of furniture being broken and fabric being torn. They ripped the curtains down, bringing the pelmets with them. Ornaments were smashed. The religious prints were pulled off the walls and broken on the floor.

Heavy boots kicked holes in the wainscot. Rough hands tore up the carpets. Drawers were emptied, their contents strewn on the floor. Max kept his jaw clamped tight. The viciousness of the search showed what this was, a punishment. He was clinging to the wafer-thin hope that they were so intent on destruction that they might miss the girls' hiding place behind the panelling upstairs.

They pushed Max up the stairs to continue the search at the top of the house. The bedrooms were torn up in the same ruthless way, his mother's mattresses stabbed with bayonets, her wardrobes opened and emptied. They took care to empty her drawers and rip her underwear. The smallest spaces, where no human being could have hidden, were broken into.

His own bedroom received special attention. They threw his uniforms on to the floor and trampled them under their boots. They found his military decorations in the bedside drawer, and made sure these were stamped on, as well. His Luger pistol was taken, and stuffed into Maus Bauer's pocket. It was pointless to protest at the pillaging. They were enjoying every moment of it.

At last, they came to his father's study.

The desk was covered in books, as always. Bauer picked up one of them. 'Hebrew, eh?'

'That is Greek,' Max said shortly. But he had noticed with horror that the pages were covered with Heidi's pencil notes.

Bauer threw it aside contemptuously, apparently not noticing the feminine handwriting. He looked around, smirking. 'Now, then. If I wanted to hide some Jewesses, this is the room I would choose to hide them in.' He sniffed the air. 'I can smell them. To work, boys.'

They began by pulling all the books off the shelves.

'This rubbish is of no relevance to Aryans,' Bauer said. 'It should all have been burned, years ago. Destroy it all.'

The men obeyed, deliberately wrenching the covers off each volume and ripping out fistfuls of the pages. They were too ignorant to know what they were tearing up; it was all one to them, French, German, English, Latin, Greek. The study was soon ankle-deep in torn books.

Max tried not to think of the girls cowering up in the attic, in case his face gave his inner anguish away. But their terror must be ghastly.

When they were done with the books, the *Orpos* slashed the armchairs and pulled out the stuffing, disembowelling the cushions. They hauled down the curtains and smashed the prints on the walls.

Then they began hammering on the wooden panelling. Max felt sick with fear. He was certain that the colour had gone from his face. The *Orpos* had started to sweat in the summer heat, their brown uniforms darkening. Their animal smell was choking. Perhaps it would mask the jasmine scent of the girls' perfume.

One of them uttered a sudden shout. 'This panel is hollow.'

Bauer bared his teeth at Max triumphantly. 'A loose panel? Really, Wolff! You couldn't think of a better place to hide your Jews? Open it.'

Max's head was swimming. He could feel the blood pounding in his brain as he watched the *Orpos* haul the desk away from the wall. Boots and fists hammered at the panel until it splintered open. They tore the planks away. One of the *Orpos* got on his knees and thrust his body into the dark space behind. There was a tense silence. Then he withdrew, wiping his red, sweaty face.

'It's empty.'

'Are you sure?' Bauer snapped.

'Look for yourself, Chief. There's nothing in there.'

Bauer bent down to inspect the hollow. Max felt that his knees might buckle. If Bauer groped around in there and located the ladder that reached the crawlspace, he would find the girls, and it would be all over for all of them. He had to distract them now. 'Bauer!' he rapped out. As Bauer straightened, Max stepped forward, and slapped the man hard across his fat face. 'You've destroyed my house for nothing, you bastard!' he rasped.

Bauer's mouth dropped open in astonishment. There was a stunned moment of silence. Then, with a roar of rage, Bauer got his hands around Max's throat and dug his thumbs into Max's windpipe. Max responded by hunching his strong shoulders and getting his own thumbs into Bauer's eyes.

Then the first rifle-butt slammed into his kidneys.

They beat him until his father's books were spattered with his blood, and they themselves were too out of breath to swear at him any more. They used the rifle-butts at first, and then their boots.

They only stopped when one of them said, 'We're going to kill him if we go on.'

'Roll him over,' Bauer commanded.

Max felt hands hauling him on to his back. Through his swollen eyelids, he saw Maus Bauer's crimson face swim into view. 'You Jew-loving bastard,' Bauer said thickly. 'You've had this coming to you for a long time. I took you under my protection, but you're rotten through and through, just like your father. And now, I've got another little present for you. I'm going to tell you how your father died.' He shook Max savagely as Max's head lolled back, and he started sinking into unconsciousness. 'Wake up, Wolff. I want you to hear this. They said your father died of a fever. Well, he didn't. He kept on preaching to the other degenerates in prison. You don't get away with insulting the Führer as easy as that. They hanged him.'

Max tried to push Bauer's face away, but he was too weak, and some of his fingers seemed broken.

'They strung him up with piano wire,' Bauer said. 'That's the very worst way to go. Personal orders from the Führer himself, direct from the Reich Chancellery. That's what Hitler does to people who insult him. That's how we'll deal with you. It's only your Iron Crosses that are saving you now. Next time we meet, they won't help you. I'll watch you choke, and spit in your face.'

He released Max at last and let him slump back among the ruined books.

Max heard their boots tramping down the stairs. He forced himself not to sink into the darkness until he heard the trucks driving away. Then he closed his eyes, and let the tears slide down his cheeks.

He awoke briefly to find Lola bending over him with a sponge.

'We know what you did,' he heard her say. He saw that she was crying. Then he went under again.

The next time he woke up, it was really bad. And the time after that, even worse. He felt broken in every part of his body. At first, it was all he could do to lean over the bed and vomit into the basin that his mother held for him. After a while, he managed to get to his feet and limp to the bathroom, with Magda supporting him.

They'd cracked the bathroom mirror, but in the remaining shards he saw a dismembered reflection of his own face in shades of red, blue and purple. He looked down at his body. The bruises had spread into one another, giving him a piebald look. His piss was stained with blood. 'Forgive me, *Mutti*,' he mumbled to Magda.

'You saved all our lives. There is nothing to forgive.'

'He told me what they did to Papa in prison.'

'Hush. Don't think about it.'

'Did you know?'

'Don't cry, Max.'

But he couldn't help it. Sobs were racking him. 'I was wrong. He was a good man. And they are monsters.'

'Come back to bed.'

She sat beside him while he wept. When he'd fallen silent at last, she said, 'The death certificate said typhus. But Anselm found out the truth, and told me. You were too young to be told about such things at the time, so I kept it from you. And then you left for the war. I thought it was better you didn't know.'

'How could you live with it all this time, *Mutti*?'

She touched his forehead. 'He suffered martyrdom, Max. And his belief in God never broke. He died in his faith. I am proud of him, and that is my consolation – as I am proud of you.'

Max turned his face to the wall. 'I have done nothing to be proud of. It's all been delusion and waste. I thought I was strong. But it's you who've been strong, not me. I've been weak, only weak.'

He stayed in bed for another two days. The girls came to bring him food, but all he wanted was water. Lola stared at him with large, stricken eyes. 'Please don't die, *Dummkopf*,' she whispered.

'I have no intention of dying, *Schweinehund*.' He tried to smile. 'I'm not so easy to kill. I'm sorry about your books.'

'We're gluing them back together. Heidi's very good. I get the paste all over my fingers. You know how clumsy I am.'

'I do.'

She took his good hand in both her own – the other, with the broken fingers, had been strapped up by the old doctor who'd visited Max the day of the beating. 'You deliberately provoked them to save us. That was very brave.'

He felt that he was broken inside – not just from the beating, but from the knowledge that he had served a false god all these years. A false and cruel god who had created a false and cruel system, in which hideous things were done to satisfy the basest of human drives: arrogance, bloodlust, naked ambition.

Bauer's savagery had been shattering. Yet it was not a betrayal. Bauer had always been Bauer. It was he, Max, who had pretended to be something he was not.

Bauer had always been a committed Nazi. He'd always made it clear who the enemies of the Reich were.

Max realised he was beginning to hate the part of himself that he had once been so proud of. He had been shaped in a forge that created only weapons. And since the age of eighteen, that was what he had been – a bludgeon to be used against those deemed less than human.

What had it been like for his mother to know that he had become a weapon of the Nazi state? He could only imagine her grief. And his father had died knowing his son had joined the Hitler Youth. How terrible that must have been.

He'd lived a life without love. He had never known his father, not properly, and his mother had become remote when Maus Bauer had come into his life. There had been mindless duty, hard work, loneliness and sacrifice. But not love.

Yet, in the depths of his darkness, love had crept into his life. His feelings for Lola had deepened, running through his heart like a river cleaving a desert, cleansing and nourishing.

Now he felt that he needed her as he had never needed another human being. He had scarcely been able to admit to himself that he was falling in love with Lola. But he had been falling in love for a long time. And now there was no way back.

If Lola Rosenstein had not been Jewish, his path would have been clear. Such a clear path, starting with the simple act of kissing her lips, and leading to the altar. Any man would be honoured to share his life with Lola Rosenstein.

But Lola Rosenstein was a Jew. And then there was the war that embroiled them all, the skull that grinned down on them at every moment, mocking every grief, every pleasure.

'I don't think you should spend so much time alone in his room,' Heidi told Lola. 'It's not sensible.'

'The war has to end one day. And then Max and I can make a life together.'

'The world can never go back to what it was,' Heidi said sadly. 'Haven't you realised that by now?'

'Then we'll make a new world,' Lola replied. 'Where there aren't any Aryans or Jews, just people.'

'A new world,' Heidi repeated, shaking her head, 'built on the graves of our murdered family? I don't think so. If we survive this, we have to leave Europe behind us.'

'And go where?'

'America. Perhaps even Palestine. Whoever will take us.'

'Then Max will come with us. He saved our lives. We owe him that.'

Heidi just shook her head again. The difficulties of surviving this year alone were crushing enough, without thinking of what would come after. She was glad that Lola had finally started thinking of the future, perhaps a sign that she was no longer quite so trapped in her sadness; but Heidi knew that the end of the war – whichever way it went – would not erase the horrors that had gone before.

But there was no point in trying to change Lola's mind now. If it helped her to cling to the dream that she and Max had a future together, then it was not sisterly to contradict her. But it was sisterly to feel a deep disquiet.

Putting the house back together again took up all their energies. Maus Bauer and his thugs had done a lot of damage. Broken glass and china simply had to be thrown away. As Max recovered from the beating, he tried to repair some of the furniture and the marred cupboards and doors, but it was a difficult task, and there was the constant fear that, at any moment, Bauer would be back for a second assault.

Heidi never seemed to have a problem finding sleep, but it eluded Lola. She lay awake in the cramped little bolthole, her mind whirling with thoughts – about the war, about Max, about the future. Paradoxically, the thought that liberation might be only a few months away filled her with a new and more acute terror. What if the Allies came too late? What if Maus Bauer and his men returned, and this time did not allow themselves to be distracted?

What if someone betrayed them? So many people had helped them, a long line going back to Berlin, three years ago. Any one of those people could be arrested by the Gestapo at any time. Everyone talked. That was well known. And if that happened, she and Heidi could be traced here to Kallenheim. The next knock on the door could be the men in the black leather coats. Then it wouldn't matter that the Allies were on their way. They would be murdered – *liquidated* – all the same.

There had been a particularly upsetting report on the BBC. The Russians had arrived at a Nazi camp in the Baltics to find that the last prisoners had been killed by the guards only hours earlier. Even as they fled, the SS had taken care to slaughter the remaining Jews in their clutches. Obsessively murdering Jews seemed to outweigh everything else with those people, even self-preservation.

'They'll be killing Jews until the last minute of the war,' she had said to Max.

The thought of being caught, with liberation so close at hand, was unbearable. After all they had suffered – to be killed at the last minute! It would have been better to have died years ago, with Mama and Papa and the others.

Though the house was completely blacked-out, so as not to show a chink of light to the outside, she knew that it was a full-moon night. A deep longing to go out and see the moon seized Lola. It had been months, almost a year, since she had been outside.

Without waking Heidi, she slipped out of her bunk and wrapped her gown around her, and made her way down through the silent house. She slipped through the kitchen, unbolted the back door, and stepped out into the garden.

The vastness of the night overwhelmed her. Her life had been lived on such a small scale for so long, with distances measured in inches, and walls all around her, that she had a sense of decompression, like an undersea explorer emerging from a diving bell.

She looked up dizzily. The moon was as brilliant as a searchlight, so intense that it cast solid shadows from the trees and the ruined mill opposite St Nicholas House. The quiet was immense, but it was different from the silence of the house. It was alive. She felt the wind on her face. The distant bark of a dog came to her. An owl was calling somewhere. There was nature all around her. She could feel the universe expanding, the earth spinning under her feet, the stars whirling through the sky.

Joy and alarm flooded her at the same time. With her heart soaring, she walked into the garden, through the rows of vegetables that Magda had planted. She was barefoot, and the freshly tilled earth was soft under her feet. She dug her toes into it and stretched her arms up to the sky. For a long while, she remained like that, anchored yet free. She almost felt that she was growing physically, as though she had become a tree, with her roots in the earth and her branches reaching high.

Then she heard a footstep behind her.

'Lola,' Max said in a low voice, 'what are you doing?'

She turned to see his tall figure. 'I couldn't bear to be inside any longer.'

She expected him to be angry with her, but he came to stand beside her. 'I couldn't sleep, either. I heard you going down the stairs and opening the door.'

'It must be the moon.'

'It must be.'

'I could never sleep when the moon was full. But it's been so long since I saw it like this.'

'Your life has been very hard,' he said, in a gentle voice she'd never heard him use before. 'No wonder you want to keep yourself in a fortress. Like those crabs which make their home in some other animal's shell.'

'I'm not familiar with the habits of crabs.'

'These ones retreat when approached. All you see are a few claws sticking out of the shell.'

'That sounds a good policy.'

'I admire your strength, Lola.'

Lola snorted. 'You needn't be ironic.'

'I'm not trying to be ironic. I've just learned what it's like to be on the other side.'

She smiled wryly. 'Yes, you have. And how do you find it, on the other side?'

'Terrifying,' he said briefly.

'A good way of putting it. The Nazis don't make good enemies.'

'No.'

'So. You're one of us, now. An enemy of the state.'

'So it seems. I keep thinking about my father. He died a terrible death.'

'Don't think about it, Max.'

'Bauer said he was killed that way on direct orders from Hitler. Those officers who took part in the plot – they were also hanged with piano wire, on Hitler's orders. The cruelty is sickening.'

She touched his arm. 'Max, stop. Just enjoy the moon.'

He looked up. 'In Russia, when the moon was full, we got no rest, because the enemy were sure to attack. It would be as bright as day, except with no colours. A black-and-white world. We would be on the move day and night, so we were always exhausted. We had to shake each other awake all night long, because we would fall asleep at our posts. That's all the moon meant to us.'

'This is a different moon.'

'Yes. A different Max.'

'And a different Lola.'

Max had the sense of having crossed a river between them that had formerly seemed unbridgeable. A distance of miles had been reduced to a few inches. She was standing so close to him that he could feel her warmth.

Lola had the same sensation, as though they inhabited different planets with remote orbits, which had suddenly swung unexpectedly – and perilously – close to one another. Her heart gave a lurch. 'Do you think,' she asked, 'that if we'd met in different circumstances – if there was no Hitler and no war – we would have been friends?'

'I think we would have been more than friends,' he said quietly. 'Much more.'

She was silent for a while, feeling something swelling in her throat. At last she said, with a catch in her voice, 'It makes me happy to hear you say that.'

'Perhaps there's some hope for us. Not to be what we could have been to each other, but to be *something*. Something better than we are now.'

'I will try, if you will.'

'I will try.'

For a moment, Max had an extraordinary impulse to take her in his arms and kiss her. He even moved involuntarily a fraction closer to her. Her expression changed, her eyes widening. Then she turned and hurried back into the dark house. The gravitational pull of that other, alien planet was frightening. She made her way up to bed, trying to catch her breath.

Max remained, while the earth and the stars spun slowly around him. He thought of what would happen to her in the hands of the Gestapo. It was too much to bear that she, who had never harmed a fly, and had wanted only to live, could be crushed in the hands of such creatures as those. He felt something change inside him, like the lurch of a tank when the gears were engaged. He would not let that happen.

The end of August brought exciting news for the girls. Paris had been liberated. De Gaulle and his Free French had paraded triumphantly down the Champs-Élysées. The girls were breathless, although for Max it was bitter to hear that German soldiers had surrendered and been captured. His sense of national pride, battered as it was, remained strong enough for him to feel shame at these defeats. And the news meant that Belgium, and the Reich itself, was in their sights.

Heidi couldn't fail to notice Lola and Max's midnight trysts, which were starting to be more and more frequent. They would go out into the garden and stay there for an hour or more before coming back to bed.

Lola simply laughed, however. 'Darling, we don't *do* anything. We just talk a little. Sometimes we just stand in the moonlight without saying a word.'

'Standing in the moonlight together isn't doing nothing, Lola. Apart from the fact that you could be seen by anyone, an air-raid warden or a neighbour taking a stroll, it simply isn't appropriate.' She raised her hands. 'And please don't tell me I'm jealous, because I'm not.'

'I know you're not. But it's hard for you to understand.'

'It's not hard at all. Do you think I haven't got a heart as well as you?'

'Well, your heart is yours. My heart is my own. Max and I have made a pact.'

'A pact?' Heidi echoed sharply. 'What kind of pact?'

'To be better to each other.'

'Lola, what would Papa say, if he were here?'

'He's *not* here,' Lola said, her voice rising. 'None of them are here. They're all gone. It's just us, all alone. You can't expect me to live my life as if Papa was looking over my shoulder – or the rabbi, or the neighbours, or anybody from our old life! I've decided to look after myself. You're not Mama. Mama's dead. And I'm grown-up.'

'I just want you to be sensible. Is that too much to ask?'

'Why should I be sensible?' Lola demanded passionately. 'Why should Max? Why should we bother? We could all be dead tomorrow! He makes me happy, Heidi. And I desperately want a little happiness before it all goes dark.'

'Oh, Lola!'

'He doesn't want to hurt me. He only wants the same as I do, just to be together. We're not doing any harm. We don't kiss, or even hold hands. We're just *together*. And when we're together, it's as if this golden bubble closes around us and holds us safe and secure. Everything goes away. All the terrors and the horrors and the crying – it's all gone. There's just happiness for a little, short while.'

Heidi was silent. Hearing this, she knew that it was pointless to argue any further. She could only pray that whatever gods were left in the universe would watch over them.

Max was recovering from the injuries inflicted by the *Orpos*. But he felt changed forever. So much had altered in him during these past weeks. The last vestiges of his faith in Adolf Hitler had been torn away. For the first time in his life, he had begun to understand why his father had behaved as he did – and for the first time, he felt awed by the sacrifices that his father and mother had made. While so many others stood back and watched evil happen, they had taken a stand against it. He had been too young to understand what they were doing, and he had rebelled against them. He understood a lot more, now.

He also understood that he, like millions of other Germans, had been deluded by a strident call to patriotism, and had become the weapon of an evil government with fearsome ambitions. He'd believed in Hitler's ranting. He'd believed the potent, endless pro-paganda spewed out by Dr Goebbels. It had blinded him to the truth. It had been persuasive, but it had been a sham, a lie. And now Germany faced a reckoning for the terrible things it had done. The Thousand Year Reich, which had lasted eleven years so far, was not going to give in without a bloodbath.

His only consolation for it all – and his only escape from it – was Lola.

At first, when he'd got back from the front, he'd hardly been able to bring himself to look at her. Now, she was everything to him. He wanted only to be with her, to lose himself in the peace she brought him.

She affected him more deeply than anyone he had known in his twenty-three years of life. Those small hands had closed tight around his heart; those midnight eyes, so innocent and wide, had captured his gaze and would not let him look away.

He had slept with soldiers' women and felt release. But with Lola, it was enough to stand in the light of the waning moon, and feel her close to him. There was no need for anything more than that. Indeed, her slightest touch sent shudders through him. The quietest words she spoke were capable of swaying him like a tree in a strong wind.

She was so young. She had endured things that no young woman should have endured. But the tragedy of her life had made her unique. It had made her – and he could find no other word – holy. He wanted to be worthy of her. He wanted to protect her, to shield her with his body if needs be. No more harm must come to her. But he trembled when he thought of what was to come. The future was too dark to look forward to, the past too dark to look back on. Lola was an eternal present, a world in herself – and the only happiness he felt was when he entered Lola's world.

Chapter 8

The first rainy week of a wet autumn brought the sounds of war ever closer. Belgium fell to the Allies and was liberated. The Russians were well into Poland by now, and the fight for northern Italy was coming to a slow end.

Max watched the measures with foreboding. Pillboxes, concrete bunkers, trenches and anti-tank obstacles were being reinforced. Minefields were being laid. The yellow skull and crossbones signs, with their ominous legend, *Achtung Minen*, were appearing among the trees and in the fields.

Log roadblocks were being erected at the entrance of the villages in the region, designed to slow down enemy tanks. They had an almost medieval appearance, and Max doubted whether they would present any real obstacle to Shermans and Churchills.

His memories of those villages in Russia were vivid. He saw in his mind the streams of people fleeing, a few pathetic possessions in their arms, their lives shattered and blazing. That was what he had inflicted on the Russians. That was what would be inflicted on him and his.

For Lola, this autumn was rich with love. She hadn't believed that she and Max could get any closer. But as the sounds of the war approached, her feelings deepened. Her longing to be with Max was an ache that never left her. Their lack of privacy was a torture;

they had agreed to try to behave 'normally' in front of Magda and Heidi, which required great self-discipline. But in the night, when they could meet in the garden under the gnarled old pear tree, which now bore sweet, golden fruit, they entered a magical world where no eyes could see them, and nothing else mattered.

She had told Heidi that they didn't even hold hands, and at first, that had been true. They had been almost too shy to touch one another at the beginning. But as the days passed, it became unbearable *not* to touch each other. They held hands as they whispered together; then he would put his arm around her waist, and she would feel his mouth touch her hair; and then he would hold her with both arms, and she would lay her cheek against his chest, and feel his heart beating, and his voice would be just a deep rumble, the words he spoke of no consequence, his tone saying everything that needed to be said.

The nights were so silent. Even the rumble of military traffic faded away at midnight. When it rained, the pear tree sheltered them, not that they would have cared about getting wet.

One night, as they whispered together, the sound of heavy footsteps in the garden made Lola cling to him in fright. They waited in silence, until a loud grunt identified the intruder as a wild boar that had wandered out of the Hürtgen Forest to root for Magda's turnips. Max chased it off, and it fled noisily.

Lola couldn't stop giggling, until Max bent down and silenced her with a kiss on the mouth.

'Sorry,' he whispered. 'But you were making too much noise.'

It was the first time they had kissed, and she was too startled to say anything. Her lips felt as though they had been burned. She pressed her hot face to his chest.

'Are you angry with me?' he asked.

'No,' she mumbled.

'Then why are you hiding your face?'

It was too embarrassing to tell him that it was the first time she had been kissed on the mouth – that it was, indeed, the first time she had been kissed by anybody outside her family. A woman of her age should have had at least one beau, if only for self-respect. But her heart was bounding like a doe, and she wanted to laugh out loud with joy. 'You surprised me, that's all.'

'I surprised myself. I haven't kissed a girl since I was seventeen years old.'

'And who was that?' she demanded, instantly jealous.

'Just a village girl. Nothing like you.'

'An Aryan maiden,' she guessed, 'with blonde braids and bosoms like a Valkyrie.'

'I can hardly remember,' he said tactfully.

'How can you lie to me?'

'Then I don't want to remember. I have never cared for anybody except you.'

'There's no need to tell even bigger lies!'

He took her hand and laid it on his breast. 'Do you think I am lying?'

Lola could feel his heart beating hard and urgently under her palm. Her knees felt unsteady. She put his hand on her own breast. 'I have the same phenomenon.'

'Perhaps we're coming down with something.'

She laughed breathlessly. 'We will have to go to bed.' She clapped her hand to her mouth in mortification. 'Oh, goodness! I didn't mean it like that!'

Max put his arms around her and laid his forehead against hers. 'Are you really mine?' he whispered.

'I suppose so, if nobody else will have me.' She felt her head spinning with joy.

The night sky suddenly lit up. They both turned. A cold, white beam of light had stabbed up into the sky from the anti-aircraft batteries a mile or so away. It traced a path through the clouds, then was joined by another, and then two more. The searchlights reached up high into the darkness, losing themselves in space, swaying, intersecting, making dazzling arcs.

'Is it a raid?' Lola asked in alarm.

'No. Just a drill.'

More beams were soaring up now. The cloudscape was revealed in silver draperies, the reflected glow bathing their faces. They looked at one another, as though seeing each other for the first time. Now the rumble of the generators was clearly audible, drifting across the fields to them.

'It's beautiful,' Lola said, pressing close against Max.

It would not be so beautiful soon, Max thought, but didn't say the words. 'We have to get back in the house,' he commanded. 'It's as bright as day out here.'

Under the shelter of the kitchen porch, Lola stopped him, and lifted her face to him. 'One more.'

He bent and kissed her again. This time, his lips lingered on hers, warm and firm. Lola's eyes filled with tears. Not wanting him to see that she was crying, she tore herself away from him and hurried into the house.

'What's the matter?' he called after her.

'Nothing,' she said. 'I'm just happy – so happy!'

She slipped back into her bed and lay there, wide awake. Her life had changed so unexpectedly. In the depths of her unhappiness, she had longed for comfort, for consolation; and some divine providence had sent it to her in a form she could never have dreamed of.

She imagined the touch of his lips on hers again, warm and tender, and she shivered with delight. She had found a treasure in the darkest of places, and she wrapped her whole being around it, possessing it and being possessed by it. She had been through so much in her short life – tragedy, terror and heartbreak – but this was the one thing that had been absent. It was utterly new to her; and yet she felt it with some deep, primal sense of recognition, and knew it was right. She couldn't wait to see Max again. But she also needed time to absorb what was happening to her, to savour it and feel how it was transforming her. Sleep would be a long time coming.

In his own bed, just a few feet below Lola, Max also lay awake. He thought of Lola's soft mouth, like a rose pressed against his lips, and the sweet scent of jasmine on her skin. Those searchlights had brought home to him that Kallenheim would soon find itself on the front line.

There was not much time.

Lola slept very little, perhaps an hour or so before dawn. Heidi woke with a groan. 'My God. We do nothing all day, and yet I feel exhausted when I wake up.'

'I feel wonderful,' Lola replied gaily.

Heidi gave her a very old-fashioned look as she rose.

But when they went down to the kitchen, Max had already left the house. He had gone out on the bike again, Magda told them, on some mysterious errand.

The house was cold and empty without him. Lola felt that, in his absence, she was undefended, a maiden in the tower without her knight protector. She prowled nervously around the house all morning, getting on Heidi's nerves.

'You're like a cat on hot bricks,' Heidi complained. 'Settle down. You haven't touched your Latin verbs.'

'Damn the Latin verbs,' Lola retorted. 'I hate the sight of them.'

'He'll be back, by and by,' Heidi said dryly. 'You might as well help Magda in the kitchen, if you won't study.'

Lola went down to the kitchen to do as Heidi had suggested. Magda had pulled up some onions, and Lola got the task of chopping them up for onion soup. Their fumes made her eyes burn; but the tears were a kind of release for the bottled-up tensions in her heart.

'What's he doing?' she asked Magda. 'Why is he taking so long?'

Magda put some more onions in front of Lola. 'This is what we women do, my dear. We wait for them.'

Lola turned her teary eyes on Magda. 'At least you don't scold me, like Heidi does.'

'Does she scold you? What for?'

'For feeling as I do about Max.' A stinging tear rolled down her cheek as she sliced through the milky onion layers. 'I know you don't approve.'

'It doesn't matter whether I approve or not.' Magda smiled a little sadly. 'In these questions, the opinions of others don't matter at all. The heart always finds a way.'

'Oh, Magda!' Lola wiped her eyes with her wrists. 'I can't help my feelings, though Heidi seems to think I can.'

'I was concerned at first. I didn't want either of you to be wounded by the other. But now I see that he is good for you. And you are good for him. You both need to be healed. Come, my dear. Wash your eyes.' She took over the onion-chopping, apparently resistant to the fumes. 'For a long time,' she said, as Lola rinsed her smarting eyes, 'I've thought of you and Heidi as my daughters. And for an even longer time, I have felt that Max was lost to me as a son. You've brought him back to me. And for that I will always love you.'

Lola was crying in earnest now, and not from the onions. 'I only want to make him happy.'

'I hope you make each other happy. There's very little happiness to go around, these days.'

They laid the table, and waited for Max. But he didn't return, so they had the soup, with the black loaf that was the only bread available nowadays, named pumpernickel because it filled one with wind.

Lola had started to worry. Had something happened to Max? Had her own behaviour last night disgusted him, and was he staying away because she had been too forward? She told herself not to be silly; but without him, she now felt unhappy and incomplete.

Max did not return until dark; and when he did, he had news for them. He gathered them all around the kitchen table and spoke seriously.

'We can't stay in Kallenheim any longer,' he said bluntly. 'We have to leave very soon. The *Wehrmacht* will soon start billeting troops in Kallenheim. If they put a couple of soldiers in our house, there is no way we could prevent the girls being found. We don't have any option but to leave St Nicholas House. I've found us a place in Düren. An apartment on the fourth floor, in Oberstrasse, a quiet back street. The landlady, Frau Haussmann, is the mother of Lorenz Haussmann, one of my old schoolmates. He served as an infantryman in the Russian campaign, and was captured in 1943. He's in a POW camp in the USSR. She's happy to rent it to us. She doesn't want strangers there. I've got a bond with her, and I trust her not to ask questions. And she needs the money.'

'Max, I'm afraid of going there,' his mother said. 'To Düren. To someone else's house.'

He put his hand over hers. 'We don't have any choice, *Mutti*. We can't stay here. There's more space there, too. The girls will have proper beds. They won't have to cram themselves into the attic every night.'

Lola turned to her sister. 'Heidi, imagine! A real bed!'

'It sounds too good to be true,' Heidi said with a wistful expression.

'But how will we all get there?' Magda asked. 'You only have the motorbike.'

'Jockel,' Max said. 'He's always around at night. He can take the girls in his trap. We'll shut up St Nicholas House, and leave everything here. It's all broken, anyway – and the apartment is furnished.'

'Can we trust Jockel?'

'He's eighty-seven, and in any case, he detests the Nazis. He won't say anything to anyone.'

'What about our books?' Heidi demanded.

'We can take a few books with us. But the rest will have to stay behind.'

'I'm not leaving my novels!' Lola exclaimed. 'I don't care about the Latin textbook, but I can't do without Sir Walter Scott.'

'We'll take Sir Walter Scott with us,' he promised.

He sat back while the women began discussing his proposal. He had made it all sound easy, and had glossed over the obstacles; but in reality, it was going to be difficult. It would need luck for them to reach Düren with their hides intact. And once they were there, they would need a great deal of luck to remain undetected until the British and Americans arrived. It was only the prospect of finding themselves in the middle of a huge battlefield that had driven him to contemplate the move.

There was the possibility that Düren might be bombed. Every major city in the Reich had been bombed already, some of them apparently devastated, although most of the details were kept from the wider public like themselves. But Düren was far from a major city. It was a beautiful old town dating back to the time of Charlemagne, peaceful and of no military importance. With any luck, it would be spared, as other small towns had been spared, and its civilian population protected from the worst of the fighting.

They might even be able to live a more open life there. They would appear to be an ordinary family, seeking refuge in the town, as so many families currently were.

The women had all reached an agreement. Magda spoke for them. 'All right. We go.'

It was by now raining heavily almost every day. The trenches and fortifications that were being dug around the area turned into lagoons of mud. Vehicles bogged down, improvised ramparts collapsed on the hapless excavators. Max saw that all kinds of odd contraptions were being devised – old tank turrets were being mounted on wooden stockades, cannons from earlier campaigns were being salvaged and shoehorned into bunkers. The whole performance had an air of desperation about it, the last resort of a nation that had exhausted its resources.

They prepared for their move to Düren. It had to be done quickly and without any fuss. Max went to see Jockel in the house in the Hürtgen Forest – little better than a hovel – where he had lived for almost ninety years. The old man was making charcoal. He had piled wood into a large mound, covered it with turf, and was now burning it down. The dense clouds of smoke hung in the damp air among the dark trees.

He was leaning pensively on his rake, surrounded by sacks of charcoal, when Max arrived. 'So,' he said, without turning his head, 'last time you saw me, you cursed me, and threatened to call the Gestapo. Now you want something from me.'

'Yes,' Max replied.

'I heard what they did to you. They taught you a lesson, eh?'

'I learned a lesson,' Max agreed. 'And you were right about my father. He did want a better Germany. I was too young to understand.'

The old man spat a gob of sooty phlegm. 'You're still too young to understand.'

'Maybe so.'

'And now? You want me to take those Jewish girls of yours away from here?'

Max was startled. 'How do you know about them?'

At last, Jockel turned his red-rimmed eyes on Max. 'I may be old, but I know things. Where are you sending them?'

'We are all moving to Düren. I need you to take the girls in your cart.'

'If they catch us, they'll put us all up against the wall.'

'I know that. I'll pay you.'

'You can't pay me enough, son.' Jockel pointed a gnarled finger into the forest. 'You see what they're doing in there?'

'Yes.'

'Digging holes, like badgers. They think they can stop the *Amis* and the *Tommies*. They don't know they're already beaten.'

'How much do you want?' Max pressed.

'I don't want your money. I'll do it for nothing, just for the satisfaction. But tell your girls they're going to get dirty.'

Max felt a surge of relief. He reached into his pocket and took out the hip flask. It was silver, engraved with his name. It had been presented to him by his company when he'd won his Iron Cross, First Class. 'Take it.'

'I told you. I don't want payment.'

Max shook it. 'It's full of schnapps.'

'Oh, well, in that case . . .' Jockel pocketed the flask. He pointed at the sacks of charcoal. 'I'll hide them under those when I deliver to Düren. It's not going to be very nice for them. But better than the Gestapo, eh?'

'When do you deliver?'

'Friday evening.'

'Friday evening it is, then.'

As Lola folded her few clothes into her valise, she was glowing with excitement.

'Somewhere new!' she said to Heidi. 'I can hardly wait! It feels like we've been here forever.'

'I just hope we're going to be safe.'

'I trust Max with my life,' Lola replied.

'We don't have much choice,' Heidi said dryly. The prospect of leaving Kallenheim was not as appealing to her as it was to Lola. They had been safe here – until the arrival of Max. And though Lola regarded Max as a saviour, it had been Max who had disrupted the peace of St Nicholas House, and it had been Max who had attracted danger in the form of the *Ordnungspolizei*. However, it was clear they couldn't stay here any longer, so it was best to put a brave face on things.

Magda, too, was anxious about leaving St Nicholas House. She had lived here since her wedding day, twenty-five years ago. The thought that she might never see it again, with all its mixed memories of her marriage, and Joachim, and the life they had had, was distressing. They would also have to somehow make up for the vegetables that she grew in the garden, and which played such an important part in their diet. Like Heidi, she hid her feelings as best she could.

Magda would go with Max on the motorcycle to Düren. But the girls could not easily be extracted from the village without arousing suspicion, which was why Heinz Jockel had been the solution.

He arrived as promised on Friday evening, as it was getting dark, and stopped his horse behind the garden wall. Heidi and Lola climbed quickly over the wall. They had wrapped themselves in their coats to keep the black dust off their clothes. With Max's help, the girls were lifted into the back of the trap. They curled up in the straw. Max and Jockel covered them with a tarpaulin and then carefully arranged the bags of charcoal around and on top of them. The idea had sounded disagreeable, but it was far worse in practice. The bags were heavier than they had expected, and Jockel had not been exaggerating when he'd said they would get dirty. The black charcoal dust penetrated their nest, acrid and choking. Lola began to cough at once.

'If you do that, young lady,' they heard the old man say, 'we'll never get past the checkpoints.' Lola pressed her handkerchief to her face and tried with all her might to stop.

The journey to Düren was hideously uncomfortable. They were stopped twice, and heard the voices of soldiers talking to the old man each time. Lola felt she might choke to death, stopping herself from coughing and sneezing. But there was no attempt to search the cart.

Half an hour later, Jockel stopped the cart a third time. The girls felt the bags being pulled off them. Lola sat up to find they were on a quiet country road outside the town – and Max was there. She threw herself into his arms, and they embraced tightly.

The girls got themselves dusted off as best they could, and then they all walked into Düren.

Lola was dizzy with excitement. The town was serene in the black-out. Few people were on the streets, and not a chink of light showed from any windows; but by the light of a quarter-moon, they could see wide boulevards, elegant old buildings. It was like a dream to walk free in the night, with Max on one arm and Heidi on the other.

The building was in a quiet back street, as Max had said, but not far from shops and a small park. Max had a key. They went into the foyer and up winding flights of stairs to the fourth floor.

Magda was waiting for them there. Lola walked in and looked around. It was a charming apartment, furnished in Biedermeier style, with gleaming furniture and darkened oil paintings on the walls. The girls took off their dirty coats and went from room to room, exclaiming in delight. 'It's so big!' Lola said. 'And warm!'

'There's a coal boiler in the basement for heating. And an air-raid shelter for the building, too. And this is your bedroom.'

It was a plain little room, evidently unused for some time. But it had bedside cabinets, a dressing table, and – best of all – two proper beds for the girls. Lola lay back on one and stretched out her arms. 'I feel I'll be able to sleep properly here, for the first time since Berlin.'

Max sat beside her and stroked her cheek. 'You look like an angel. A rather sooty angel.'

'I'll wash my face.' She kissed his hand. 'Thank you for bringing us here.'

'I hope it was the right decision,' he said, his tender smile fading.

'I have faith in you, Max.'

Before they all went to sleep, they had a meeting around the table where they would from now on eat their meals. 'We'll have to see the rest of the war out here,' Max said. 'It may not be more than a few weeks. It may be months, yet. There's no way of telling.

But we have no place to hide you two girls any more. If anyone challenges you, you're going to have to show your fake papers and simply lie. My guess is that the authorities will soon have more important things to worry about than looking for Jews. Let's hope so, anyway.'

There was a soft tapping at the apartment door, early the next morning. Lola, who was the first to wake, went cautiously to open it, and encountered their landlady, Frau Haussmann. She was a little, thin, grey-haired woman with dark circles under her eyes. 'I don't wish to disturb. I just came to see if you were all comfortable.'

'Oh, very comfortable, thank you. It's a lovely apartment. Would you like to come in and have coffee?'

'Thank you, I have already had my coffee. I will not intrude on you.' Frau Haussmann took Lola's hands in her own and looked into her face earnestly. 'You are Jewish, are you not?'

'Oh, no!' Lola said, alarmed. 'I am Frau Wolff's niece, from Berlin!'

The woman waved away her denial. 'It's all right. You are safe with me. I have always believed that we are all God's children. There is no room for hate in the world.'

'I'm very sorry to hear about your son.'

'He is better off in a prison camp, though the Red Cross tell me their conditions are very harsh.'

'I hope you see him again soon.'

'It will be years,' the older woman said. She lowered her voice. 'He deserted, and went over to the Russians. He could not stand it.'

'Couldn't stand the war?'

Frau Haussmann raised a finger, her eyes flashing. 'No! He was a brave soldier. It was the SS. They made them do horrible things. Civilians, shot and buried in the woods.'

Lola felt sick. 'Is that true?'

'My son was not a liar. He told me on his last leave. They made the men drunk to be able to do it, but the drink did not take away the memories. Some of them committed suicide rather than have to keep doing it. Lorenz told me he would go over to the enemy when he had the chance. I thank God that he made it.'

'That is terrible!'

The other woman dabbed her watering eyes. 'Lorenz is a good, Christian boy. He wouldn't let them turn him into a murderer. The others did what they were told. But he had a conscience.'

When Frau Haussmann had left, Lola stood trembling in the living room. She could not rid her mind of the images that had formed.

Max came into the room and laid his hands on her shoulders. 'Who was at the door?'

Lola backed away from him. 'Don't touch me.'

He was startled. 'What's the matter?'

She could hardly speak at first. 'Frau Haussmann told me her son was forced to do terrible things in Russia. Murder civilians. Did you do those things?'

'Lola—'

'Did you do those things?'

'No,' he said. 'I swear to you.'

'Did you know they were being done?'

Max grimaced. 'We were always the spearhead, on the front line – first in Poland, then in Russia. We heard that there were SS units, *Einsatzgruppen*, that followed behind us, "mopping up". We heard that they committed massacres. We also heard that some infantry battalions were involved. We didn't want to know the details.'

'So you knew!'

'We knew something, Lola. But remember, we had a war to fight. We didn't give much thought to anything else. We had no time to stop and massacre innocent people. We tried to fight a clean war. We never deliberately harmed civilians. We never shot enemy prisoners or wounded. And we tried to keep as far as possible from the SS. In December 1942, we were told that our company was going to be incorporated into the SS because they needed experienced panzer men. But thank God, our generals fought Himmler, and it never came to that.'

She heard him out. But he could see in her eyes that the doubt remained. 'You must have done wicked things, sometimes.'

'We fought to a code, whether you believe me or not.'

Lola's face was melancholy, her mouth turned down. 'I don't know what I believe, Max.'

'Whatever you believe, I am no longer the man I was. I only care about protecting you, Heidi and my mother, now.'

She nodded and turned away. But Max felt that something had changed between them. She saw him as she had done when they first met: an enemy. He did not know how he was going to win her back, but it made his heart ache.

And there were more pressing worries facing them now. It was some weeks since a package of food coupons had arrived from Ditte in Cologne. The city had been heavily bombed, everybody knew that. Whether Anselm and Ditte had been killed in an air raid, or were unable to obtain the precious coupons any longer, was uncertain; Magda had tried to telephone Anselm, but the lines to the city were damaged, and she had not been able to get through.

If they were to feed themselves, they would have to find an alternative source of coupons. And that was not going to be easy.

Chapter 9

Life in Düren was very different for all of them. Lola, in particular, felt the change greatly. After a couple of days of looking wistfully out of the window, she dared herself to go out in public. She didn't tell Heidi or Max, but quietly slipped out of the apartment alone.

The town was prosperous. Its handsome streets and handsome architecture spoke of an ancient history. There was almost a pre-war feeling about Düren, apart from the swastika flags that were draped on public buildings. A kind of peace lay over the town, despite the threat that pervaded everyday life in the Third Reich – that mixture of war, hunger and the Gestapo. But the worst fear of all, for Lola, was the Gestapo.

Going out without the yellow star sewn to her jacket was still a harrowing experience. As she wandered through the streets of Düren, with her heart beating fast, she had to stop her fingers from constantly straying to the place on her breast where it had been. Her body seemed to burn exactly there, as though the star, invisible now, was red-hot. She put her hands in her pockets to stop them from betraying her.

There was no mercy for a Jew who appeared in public without the star. The punishment was death. She could not help the feeling that people were staring at her, detecting some Jewish lineaments in her face, seeing the guilt in her eyes, or guessing her shocking secret from her Berlin clothes and accent.

She hurried along, trying not to meet anyone's eyes, not speaking to anyone, half terrified of discovery, half entranced by the joy of being outside during the daytime for the first time in years. She felt as though some umbilical cord linking her to Heidi, Max and Magda had been severed. To be alone was frightening and exhilarating.

She had a little money in her purse, if only she dared spend it. But the one thing they needed was food, and without coupons, bread, potatoes and meat were unobtainable. Perhaps she could find some vegetables or fruit. To return with something edible would be a coup. She was tired of being so dependent on others. She especially wanted to show Max that she could stand on her own feet.

There was a market at the end of the street, with stalls set up under a stone arcade. It was crowded with women shopping for their families. She slipped among the throng, looking hungrily at the goods on offer. Much of it was bric-a-brac. People were selling anything they had – ornaments, bits of silver cutlery, prints. A pair of horn-rimmed reading glasses caught her eye.

'How much are these?' she asked in a timid voice.

'Ten pfennigs,' the man said, yawning.

Lola picked them up and put them on. Her surroundings loomed large and bright through them. She handed over the coins and pocketed her prize.

Jubilation surged in her heart. It was the most normal thing she had done since she had left Berlin!

She looked around for more trophies. A tray of apples glowed red in the grey light. They were small, but they looked so crisp and sweet. Her fingers closed around the remaining coins in her coat pocket. She edged closer to the stall. When it was her turn, she bought the last four. She felt even more jubilant. And her mouth was watering already. She imagined herself triumphantly presenting her bounty to Max and the women.

Something tugged at her coat. Lola looked down. A little girl was looking up at her. A pretty child, with red hair and green eyes. But the freckled face was pale, dirty and thin, and the clothes were shabby – as were those of the mother, who was trying to bargain for a few mouldy-looking potatoes. Refugees, two of the hundreds who were crowding into Düren.

Instinctively, Lola held out one of the apples she had just bought. The little girl took it hesitantly, her eyes wide.

Suddenly, Lola heard a man's voice behind her say loudly, 'Jewish bitch!'

Lola was paralysed with fear. She had betrayed herself somehow. The Gestapo cells were only a moment away. Should she run, and risk a bullet?

She turned in dread. The man who had spoken was elderly, with a pointed white beard. But he was not looking at her. He was staring at an older woman, who was hurrying away with a basket over her arm. Lola glimpsed the yellow star on her coat as the woman turned to look back for a moment.

'They should gas them all, like rats,' someone else said.

Lola was trembling from head to foot. She left the stall, and on an inexplicable impulse, followed the Jewish woman.

She caught up with her down a deserted alley, and called out, 'Wait!'

The woman turned with a hunted air. Seeing Lola, she backed against the wall, holding her basket defensively in front of her. 'What do you want?' she asked in a weary voice. She was in her sixties, sallow-faced, with lank, grey hair.

Lola didn't know what she wanted. 'I am a Jew, like you,' she said in a low voice.

The other woman's eyes dropped to the place where the star should have been sewn. 'Where is your star?'

'I cut it off.'

'You're mad,' the woman hissed. 'They'll hang you if they catch you!!'

'I know that.'

'What do you want with me?'

'You are the first Jew I've spoken to in three years,' Lola said. 'Except my sister.'

The woman stared. 'You're from Berlin.'

'Yes. We ran away in 1941. We've been in hiding ever since.'

The woman looked around, frightened. 'I was married to an Aryan. I was privileged. But my husband died, and they make me wear the star, now. I think they will deport me soon.'

'You should take it off! Hide!'

'Where would I go? Everybody knows me. And my daughters are here. We had them baptised as Catholics, but they're *Mischlinge*. They will be deported, too. They're only nineteen and twenty.'

'I would like to meet them,' Lola said eagerly.

'That's impossible,' the woman snapped. 'Someone might come. You mustn't be seen talking to me. I'm going, now.'

'Wait,' Lola pleaded as the woman turned to leave. 'Perhaps we can see each other again?'

The woman shook her head and hurried away.

Lola was shaken by the incident. All her excitement had evaporated, and her pleasure in the stately old town had been made bitter by the man with the white goatee and the woman who wanted to gas all the Jews. She walked back to the apartment with her three apples. Max was waiting for her there.

'Where have you been?' he demanded, frowning.

'I went out for a walk.'

'A walk! Are you mad?'

'Quite sane,' she said tartly. 'Though everybody seems to think otherwise.'

'You should not have set foot out of doors!'

'You don't own me,' Lola snapped. 'Leave me alone!' She thrust the apples into his hands and pushed past him. He looked after her in astonishment as she went to her room. She knew she was being bad-tempered with Max, but there was something new in their relationship. The sweetness of those nights under the old pear tree had given way to something more complex. She was growing up with the swiftness of a butterfly emerging from its cocoon after a long sleep.

'I met a Jewish woman in the market,' she told Heidi in their room. 'But she didn't want to talk to me.'

'You didn't approach her, did you?'

'Yes.'

'Lola! That was madness!'

'She has two daughters about our age. I wish I could meet them.'

'That's impossible!'

'She's afraid they're all going to be deported.'

'A good reason not to go near them. The Gestapo will be watching them.' Heidi took Lola's arms and shook her. 'You shouldn't have spoken to her. Be sensible! You can't trust anybody.'

'She's a Jew, like us!'

'Did you tell her where we live?'

'No.'

'Good. Because if she's arrested, they will get everything out of her.'

Lola digested this. 'All right. I'll be sensible in future. Oh! And I got you a present!'

Heidi looked dubious. 'Really? What?'

'Guess!'

'A golden cow to worship.'

'No. These!' She held out the spectacles.

Heidi blinked, then put them on. She took up her book and looked at the page. 'Oh, Lola! You're an angel!'

'Are they right for you?'

'They're wonderful! I can read again!' Heidi hugged her younger sister. 'Thank you, Lola!'

Lola glowed with pride. 'And they suit you, too. You look very intellectual.'

'I heard you snapping at Max,' Heidi said.

Lola frowned. 'He got on my nerves. He's very domineering. Sometimes I wonder if he's done bad things.'

'This is the Third Reich,' Heidi said in her dry way. 'We've all done bad things.'

'He says he never did anything really terrible. I'm not sure if I believe him.'

'I thought you were in love with him.'

'Perhaps I am,' Lola said thoughtfully. 'But you can be in love with someone and not quite trust them, can't you?'

'Never having suffered from that particular complaint, I can't say.' Heidi smiled. 'But I would guess that the one thing goes with the other. I don't see how you can have love without trust.'

'Well . . . he did save our lives.'

'Yes. More than once.'

'He just annoys me.' She laughed a little angrily. 'You know me. I'm not very good at being obedient.'

'I have noticed that,' Heidi said gravely.

There was a knock at the front door. At once, Lola's heart was palpitating again. Had she been observed, and followed home?

But it was only Frau Haussmann, the landlady. 'I came to tell you that there is a soup kitchen in Düren for the hardship cases.' She smiled wanly. 'That means many people. It comes from the public welfare. It is thirty pfennigs with a coupon, or fifty pfennigs without. Only noodles. They serve it in a bucket, not very elegant, I am afraid, but—' She spread her thin hands. '—it keeps body and soul together for the poor.'

'If it comes to that,' Magda replied for all of them, 'we'll be very glad of it.'

Max was in a state of puzzlement. His little Lola had become sharp-tempered and prickly. He seemed not to be able to say anything that didn't annoy her. Baffled, like a bull confronted by a matador, he didn't know whether to retreat or charge. He longed for the tender moments under the old pear tree, but they seemed to have gone forever. Did she really believe that he had committed atrocities in Russia? Or was she simply asserting herself now that she was no longer so much under his control?

He longed to hear her call him *Dummkopf,* and to see that mischievous smile on her lips. But it was gone.

Yet again, he had that impression that he knew very little about women or their ways. He'd felt full of confidence when he'd been her protector. Now that she was showing independence, going out into Düren on her own and talking to strangers, she seemed not to need him so much, and that made him uncertain.

He felt that he would like to sweep her up in his arms and crush her to his chest, kiss her passionately on the mouth, and tell her she was his alone, and must obey him in all things.

But somehow, he doubted that would ever work. He would most likely get his nose bitten off.

When she prepared to go out again the next day, he tried to be more diplomatic.

'It's not a good idea to go out every day, Lola. If the *Orpos* stop you, your papers will make them suspicious.'

Heidi and Magda joined in his entreaties, but Lola wouldn't listen.

'I've been locked up for years,' she retorted. 'Nothing happened to me yesterday. I'm going, and you can't stop me!'

'Then I'm coming with you,' Max said.

'I don't *want* you to come with me!'

'Nevertheless,' he said, 'you can't stop me – just as I can't stop you.'

Her face went pink. 'I don't need a chaperone, Max.'

'I'm not a chaperone. Just a friend.'

'Let him go with you,' Heidi begged. 'I'd feel much better.'

Lola shrugged with bad grace, and pulled on her coat.

They walked out into the day, which was grey and damp. The main streets were busy. The influx of refugees, mainly drab-looking women with small children, desperate to get away from the fighting, had swollen the population of the town.

Max felt that people were looking at them, and was acutely uncomfortable. Most people in the Third Reich assumed that one in ten was a Gestapo informer or agent. One never knew who was watching, who was putting two and two together. He kept close to Lola, though it was obvious she was trying to get away from him. Luckily, he was so much taller than her that it was easy for him to stay beside her without appearing to be pursuing her.

They walked through the crowded streets, not speaking to one another, until Max eventually broke the silence.

'Have I done something to offend you?' he asked in a quiet voice.

'No,' she replied shortly.

'You seem angry with me.'

'I'm just tired of being cooped up. So tired!'

'I understand,' he said.

'No, you don't!' Lola shot back. 'You don't! You can't!'

'I've been a soldier,' he said. 'I do understand what it feels like not to be free.'

'But you don't understand what it feels like to be a Jew,' she retorted.

'Hush, Lola!' he said in alarm, looking around to see if anyone had heard.

'You don't,' she hissed. 'Not to be able to trust anybody.'

'You can trust *me*, Lola.'

She just shook her head, too angry and upset to reply.

Max sighed. 'I thought it would be easier for you, coming to Düren. I didn't want to make it even harder.'

'Sometimes it's easier to renounce something you love, rather than try to be satisfied with a tiny amount. That just makes it worse.'

Max was about to reply when a shadow fell over them. They stopped dead, confronted by two men who had stepped in front of them. They were in civilian clothes, but their expensive leather coats and arrogant manner identified them immediately as Gestapo, even before they showed their bronze badges. Had they heard something that Lola had just said? Or been attracted by the obvious passion she showed?

'You,' the elder said to Max, hard-eyed. 'You are of military age. Why are you not with your unit?'

'I have been discharged.' Max produced his discharge papers. The two men examined them carefully. Max was trying to appear calm, but his heart was racing. He dared not look at Lola.

'So. You're a holder of the Iron Cross, First Class.'

'Yes.'

Max could see by the man's badge that he was a senior Gestapo officer, a major. 'Russia, eh?'

'Yes, Herr Major.'

'My brother commanded an SS panzer division on the Eastern Front. General Paul Horstman.'

Max nodded. He knew that Horstman's command was associated with atrocities against civilians and prisoners of war, but he kept his expression neutral. 'He fell at Kursk last winter, I believe. My condolences.'

Horstman's expression became less intimidating as he handed Max's papers back. 'You should be serving in the *Volkssturm*.'

'I'm waiting to be called up.'

Horstman nodded, then turned to Lola. 'What about your little friend here?'

'We're just taking a breath of fresh air,' Max said.

The major smiled, and seemed inclined to leave. But then his companion held out his hand to Lola. 'Papers, Fräulein.' He snapped his fingers.

Lola's hands were trembling as she fumbled for her papers. All might yet have gone well, but she took a long time to retrieve them from her bag, too long. Max felt the atmosphere change. The bonhomie went out of the older Gestapo man's face. The younger one snapped his fingers again. That was one snap too many.

Like herd animals sensing a predator, the people on the pavement were now giving them a wide berth. Max could sense the aura of danger, just as he had been able to on the Russian front, the cold tap of death on his shoulder.

Lola finally got her *Kennkarte* out. The younger Gestapo man snatched it from her shaking fingers and examined it. Then he gave Lola an icy glance. Without a word, he handed the document to his older companion.

'This document is a forgery,' the older man said in a clipped voice. There was nothing warm about him now. A Luger pistol had materialised in his hand, pointing straight at Lola's heart. Her face was white and blank. She swayed, and Max instinctively took her arm to stop her from falling. 'You will come with us to headquarters.'

'Herr Major—'

There was a second Luger now, pointing at Max. The younger officer jerked his head. 'Move.'

There was no possibility of resisting here in the street. His only hope lay in talking their way out of it somehow at Gestapo head-quarters. But that was almost impossible. He was not even a serving panzer commander any longer. And if Maus Bauer and his men got involved – as they surely would – it would be all over for them both. Lola could expect to be shot out of hand, and he would be lucky to spend the rest of his days in Dachau.

They marched down the street, which had emptied, as if swept by a huge, invisible broom. Max felt sick to his heart. Unless he could somehow get a message to his mother and Heidi, they too would shortly be arrested. All four of them were doomed. He kept a tight hold of Lola's arm. He could feel her trembling uncontrollably.

They walked across the square into the police station. The last time Max had been here he'd been a war hero, full of self-righteous indignation, prepared to denounce Heidi and Lola. Today he was being marched in at gunpoint, a criminal and an enemy of the state.

The irony did not escape him.

They were taken to a charge office where they were made to sit on a bench while a woman secretary began to type out the arrest form.

Lola felt that everything around her was a terrible dream, from which she would awaken, to find she was safe in bed. But she knew it wasn't a dream. Her body was icy, her heart a lump of lead that had forgotten how to beat. She stared at the handcuffs clamped around her wrists. Her life had seemed unbearable. But there was nothing in it that could not be borne, compared to *this*. Why had she been so mad?

The interrogation would start soon. She had heard what they did. The beating. The face pulped. Then the fingernails torn out with pliers. Electricity. Bones broken, teeth smashed.

One always talked. She knew she would talk. And there would be a long, long line of arrests, going all the way back to Berlin. Every person who had helped them. Every person who had sheltered them. They would all be rounded up and suffer the same fate.

She huddled close to Max, who was looking straight ahead. She wanted to tell him she was sorry, but there were no words.

Max was watching the secretary clatter at her typewriter as the Gestapo major dictated. The formality was due to Max's former rank. Otherwise there would have been no need for anything but a swift journey to the interrogation room. That would come soon enough. With the Gestapo, there was no recourse to a judicial process. Once they had been booked, no lawyers were allowed, no appeals. Held under 'preventive arrest', they would simply disappear from the world as if they had been swallowed into the earth.

He could feel Lola quivering against his side. He longed to comfort her, but any such attempt would bring further disaster upon them. He did not want to think what they would do to her in the cells. He shut his mind to those images. Instead, he focused on the Luger in the holster worn by the guard beside him. If he could snatch it away somehow, despite the handcuffs, he could put a bullet through Lola's head, and spare her what was to come.

And if he was lucky, he could do the same for himself.

His grim thoughts were interrupted by a bustle at the door and a familiar, coarse voice. Maus Bauer had arrived. He swaggered up to Max and Lola, and stood with his legs apart, his thumbs in his belt, grinning down at them.

'What a pretty little Jew-sow. Is this what you've been hiding all this time, Wolff? I knew we would catch you at last. I could smell her.' He leaned forward and sucked air in through his large nostrils. 'Unmistakeable, that Jewess odour. Sickly sweet. Oh, we're going to have some fun, I can promise you!' He guffawed. 'A *lot* of fun.'

If Max could have torn out Bauer's throat in that moment, he would have done.

The Gestapo major came across to them. 'On your feet.'

Max helped Lola rise. Her legs seemed barely able to support her. Horstman looked at Max with a mixture of disgust and pity. 'You've thrown it all away. A distinguished military career, gone. And what for? A roll in the hay with a Jew? There's nothing I can do for you, son. You must pay the price, now.'

As he was making this speech, Max felt the ground beneath his feet shaking. He had assumed that the heavy thudding was his own heartbeat. Now he realised that it was something else.

'Air raid,' he said tersely.

Conversation in the room stopped for a few seconds. The thudding had grown louder and heavier. The ground was quaking under their feet, rattling the desks. The groan of an air-raid siren began. Suddenly, a row of windows above their heads blasted in, showering everyone in the hall with blades of glass. The place erupted into pandemonium, people fighting each other to get to the exits. Maus Bauer fled like the rest of them. Only the Gestapo officer stayed where he was.

Max held out his wrists. 'Please.'

Horstman looked into Max's eyes. Swiftly, he unlocked their handcuffs. 'Get out of here.'

Max did not pause. He grabbed Lola's hand and they made for the door.

As they ran, he thought it was inconceivable that the Allies would mount an air raid at ten o'clock in the morning, but daylight raids had become increasingly common – and of course, there was little air-raid protection for Düren, a most unlikely target.

They emerged into the street to find it in chaos. People were fleeing in all directions. The backdrop to the city had become a pall of black smoke. The drone of aircraft was everywhere. They looked up. A formation of heavy, four-engined bombers was emerging from the clouds of smoke, no more than ten thousand feet up. With no anti-aircraft batteries to bother them, they could take their time.

'We have to get to the apartment!' Lola said. Max nodded. They began to run towards that part of town. But at the other end of the square, a huge fountain of cobblestones, earth and human bodies surged up a hundred feet in the air. The blast wave hurled the two of them off their feet. They staggered upright again, dazed. With his head ringing, Max groped for Lola's hand and they crawled under a Gestapo truck that was parked down the street from the police station.

They clung together there as the stick of bombs fell along the street towards them, growing closer and closer, until their eardrums felt as though they were bursting with each blast. The truck that sheltered them rocked and bounced like a toy. Smoke and debris blasted around them, blinding them and filling their eyes, noses and mouths.

They could barely think. The air was filled with the whistle of falling bombs and the violent concussions that followed. Max counted twelve, fifteen, twenty bomb blasts, the last few so close that he felt a numbed surprise that they had survived and not been torn to pieces.

The cobblestones of the square rained down, lethal projectiles of granite. There was a pause in the hellish onslaught. They crawled out from under the truck to find the square utterly changed. Barely a building around it remained intact. Some of the bombs had been incendiaries, and fires were already blazing from the ruined walls and roofs. The large church opposite had been torn in half, its steeple miraculously still upright, but all its windows blown out. Other structures were no more than heaps of rubble. The square, which had once been stately and calm, was now scattered with human bodies and the debris of bricks, tiles and earth.

'We can't get back to the apartment that way,' Lola said. Her face was coated with dust so that only her eyes seemed human, familiar. Max realised he must look the same.

They could already hear the drone of more aircraft. 'We need to go round the back streets,' he said. The next formation of ten or fifteen bombers came into view over the rooftops, geometrically spaced, calm and implacable. Max felt a spasm of rage as he stared upwards. Hadn't they already done enough? He wished he could reach up and claw them out of the sky like a giant. His head was splitting, and he felt he couldn't move.

Lola dragged at his arm. 'Max! Move!'

He nodded dumbly, and they set off. But more huge spouts of dirt and brick were now rearing up at the other end of the square, where the street to the air-raid shelter lay. They were going to be trapped in the square very shortly.

They found an alley between tall houses and ran down it. As the explosions marched closer towards them, they took shelter in a brick portico. The ground under their feet trembled as though made of jelly instead of ancient stone slabs. When the bombs were falling close, it was impossible to do anything but hold each other tight. There were no thoughts or emotions, just an animal desperation to survive.

The last bomb in that stick landed close to the end of the alley. The blast tore down the narrow street, plucking doors and windows out of the buildings and smashing them into matchwood. Broken glass rained down around them, strewing the street with blades. In the breathless pause that followed, they realised they couldn't shelter there any longer.

They picked their way through the debris to the other end of the alley. They emerged to see that the quarter of the town where they had lived was now in flames.

'*Heidi*,' Lola screamed. Max thought of his mother. If the two women hadn't got out of the apartment in the first few minutes, they were now in the midst of that conflagration. But he could feel no emotion now. His and Lola's only chance of escape was to get out of Düren. And the next formation of bombers was already approaching, the hum of their engines filling the sky. No more than a minute or two seemed to separate each wave. They had little time.

But the pavements were already full of debris, making it hard to tell where they were. A hot wind was blowing through the streets in search of fire to feed.

This next wave of bombers was higher than the last. Their cargoes of bombs could already be seen, dotting the sky in regular rows, growing swiftly larger, their whistling growing louder. They ran as far as they dared, and then took shelter in a doorway.

This time, the bombs were descending with parachutes. They began exploding with huge, blinding flashes in the air, over the oldest quarter of the town, producing an extraordinary sight: the ancient medieval roofs were smashed and then instantly sucked into the sky, beams and tiles and slates and chimneys flying up like chaff being threshed, leaving the buildings defenceless for the high explosive that would surely follow.

Max grabbed Lola's hand, and they stumbled a few streets further on, avoiding piles of rubble before the next wave of bombers approached, their engines droning pitilessly in the darkening sky. People ran in confusion, screaming in terror, or whimpered as they cowered in doorways.

'Why are they doing this?' Lola sobbed.

'I don't know,' Max replied, his voice hoarse from the dust. He felt a weight of despair. Perhaps it was preparation for the invasion of the Rhineland. Perhaps it was punishment for the V2 rockets. At this point in the war, it was no longer possible to say who was taking vengeance on whom for what. There was nothing left but destruction and carnage.

He felt something he had never felt in all his years of war: an utter helplessness in the face of this monstrous violence. He and Lola were like people torn from a ship that had seemed so strong and safe, and were now pitched in a raging sea.

They threw themselves on to the ground, pressing their faces together and grasping each other's clothes as the blasts shocked the town, making the earth beneath them tremble, again and again.

Between each assault, they staggered to their feet and tried to get further out of the town. They were now among a crowd of several hundred people fleeing the destruction, making for the countryside.

Around the corner, they were met with a vast crater, its bottom already filled with rushing water from a burst main. They had to clamber down the steep sides, wade through the stream, and then claw their way up the other side, using an overturned telephone kiosk for purchase.

Buildings were burning everywhere. Through the hum of the bombers and the thudding of their bombs came the constant crash of falling masonry and splintering glass. A clock tower was starting to lean perilously over the street. They had just managed to get past it when they heard it slump down in a mighty cascade.

Bodies lay everywhere, some small, some no more than bundles of cloth, some burning like effigies. Scattered around them were the casings of incendiaries, which had released phosphorous sticks. These had set small fires everywhere, but the fires would soon take hold, spread, and join up to make an inferno. It would become horribly dangerous for anyone to get in or out of the old town centre.

There was no sense of time, only the constant flight to the fields. At last they reached the shore of a small lake. They huddled at the water's edge, with a full view of the destruction of the city. Many people, Lola included, couldn't bear to watch or listen, and covered their heads. But Max couldn't tear his eyes away, though his brain was split in two and his heart breaking.

Still, wave after wave of bombers roared over the town, unopposed by air defences of any kind, pouring down devastation. It was an apocalyptic vision. Towers tumbled, venerable buildings vanished in paroxysms of black dust. The sky grew dark with smoke and dust, yet it was as bright as day beneath the shroud, because the bombers were now dropping heavy liquid incendiaries, creating terrifying pillars of flame that soared up into the black skies, shedding a lurid light on the inferno.

Even those who had reached cellars and basements might be incinerated where they sheltered. Anguished, Max knew that this bombing technique, highly effective and incredibly destructive, had been perfected over years of war. It was designed to destroy towns and cities and kill as many human beings as could possibly be achieved.

But even in the most violent battles on the Eastern Front, Max had seen nothing like this. It was literally soul-destroying. He held on to Lola, trying to offer comfort.

At around midday, the last flight of bombers droned away into the distance. Düren was burning from one end of the town to the other. The group by the lake, exhausted and mentally shattered, could only watch as the fires raged through the afternoon. The blaze was so intense that fierce winds rushed in to feed them further, creating waves on the lake and feeding more oxygen into the blaze.

At last the fires started to die down. As soon as they dared, they made their way back into the ruins of the town to search for Magda and Heidi, holding each other's hands as tightly as possible, for fear that in letting go they might lose each other.

Chapter 10

It was like walking into a vast oven. The heat that radiated from the burning buildings of Düren was so intense that Lola had to shield her face with her arm. The tar of the roads had melted, and it stuck to the soles of her shoes, threatening to pull them off, scorching her feet. Blackened timber was smoking among the wreckage, choking the air. She clung to Max's arm as they entered the nightmarish landscape.

The thoroughfares were choked with rubble. The steeple of a church had come down almost intact, and now lay across a street, its bronze bell spilling out like the tongue of a slaughtered animal. Electricity cables hung everywhere. Pipes wrenched from the fabric of the town like disembowelled entrails spewed water or flared with blue and yellow gas flames. Parts of the town were still burning fiercely. Elsewhere, the fires had died down. But in any case, there did not seem to be a single building that had not suffered catastrophic damage.

And the dead were everywhere. They lay in their hundreds, caught before they could find shelter or flee the town. Some were battered or mutilated beyond recognition. Others appeared peacefully asleep. Some were still burning, their flesh consumed with white phosphorous or thermite. Blackened faces and limbs smoked at every corner.

They came across a truck neatly parked in the middle of the road, all four of its tyres blazing, the incinerated bodies of its passengers smouldering where they had fallen. Max thought he recognised the humped shape of Maus Bauer, but it was impossible to be sure.

Lola could barely take in the horror. She kept seeing the dead bodies, realising that most were women and children who must have been caught in the open while shopping. These were the people Lola had seen in the market, many of whom had fled the war in other areas, hoping to find sanctuary in the peaceful old town – only to be slaughtered here.

The street back to the apartment was obstructed. There was no way Lola and Max could clear the way barehanded.

But men of an SS panzer regiment had arrived with all their available vehicles, and the soldiers were now picking their way through Düren, trying to rescue those trapped in the ruins. Max recognised the slim figure of their commander, Jochen Peiper, whose reputation for brilliance and ruthlessness – not to mention his close relationship with Heinrich Himmler – had made him notorious. Max clambered over the smashed brickwork to him and called out. 'Herr *Sturmbannführer*!'

Peiper turned and glanced at Max. His boyish face was pale with emotion. 'I know you.'

'*Leutnant* Max Wolff. We served together in Russia.'

Peiper nodded. 'I remember. The one who lost three Tigers.'

'Yes.'

'Could happen to anyone. And you fought well. Why aren't you in uniform?'

'I was discharged. A fractured skull. My mother and sister were sheltering in a house two streets away,' he said urgently. 'We can't get to them. I need help.'

'Those American and English swine,' Peiper said grimly. 'Wait until we come face to face with them. I will make them pay for this. I can give you two of my men, no more.'

Max saluted. 'Thank you.'

With the men Peiper had given them, they began hauling the charred beams and masonry out of the way. The soldiers had pickaxes and shovels. Lola and Max used their bare hands. Lola found herself working shoulder to shoulder with two members of the SS. All that mattered to her was finding Heidi and Magda. And finding them, if God willed it, alive.

As they picked their way through the rubble it was impossible not to see the mangled children and their mothers, buried under the weight of the wreckage. None were alive. They laid the bodies in rows to be taken away. Lola felt numb, too numb for grief or anger. That would come later. She had thought of the Allies as liberators until today. It had not occurred to her, somehow, that from thousands of feet up in the air, she was just another German, just another enemy.

It was growing dark by the time, with aching bodies and bleeding fingers, they reached what was left of the apartment house. The entire building had slumped to one side and the roof was gone. It looked like a house made of toy bricks that a spoiled child had kicked over.

The entrance to the basement was in the side alley, and was blocked with an avalanche of bricks that had come down from a neighbouring building. Once again, they began the task of hauling away the wreckage, their nails tearing down to the quick, their lungs choking in the dust.

At last they cleared the door. The men smashed it open with their pickaxes. Clouds of dust poured out. They shouted, but there was no reply, just an ominous silence.

Max took a flashlight from one of the soldiers and clambered down the dark stairs, closely followed by Lola. They kept calling, but only silence greeted them.

In the darkness at the bottom of the stairs, Max's torch beam flickered over a figure lying on the floor. It was Frau Haussmann, their landlady. She was dead, though she looked merely asleep, her eyes closed and her mouth half open. The next body was that of the building's caretaker, Herr Schmidt. He, too, was dead, his fingers still trying to wrench his shirt collar open.

'Suffocated,' the SS man who was with them said tersely. 'The oxygen burned up and they couldn't breathe.'

Max felt an overwhelming sense of dread. Could his mother and Heidi possibly have survived?

Lola called out wildly, 'Heidi! Where are you?'

There was no reply. In the dim light, they tried frantically to locate the people who had taken shelter here. There were dozens, huddled in corners or sprawled on the floor.

The next bodies they came across were all women of various ages, surely tenants in the building. They must have run down here in a group during the first minutes of the raid. None were alive. Some had their children in their arms.

Heidi and Magda were lying together in the far corner. They had died together, suffocated like the rest, Magda's head resting on Heidi's shoulder as though both were asleep.

Lola uttered a broken cry and fell to her knees, putting her arms around her sister. She rocked the lifeless body to and fro, moaning, 'Heidi, Heidi, Heidi! Come back to me!'

Max knelt down beside her, exhausted and despairing. He didn't have any words.

'You can't bring her back,' the SS man said curtly. 'She's gone. At least it was quick.'

After her first agony of grief, Lola began crying quietly, with a strange dignity, pressing her sister's face to her breast as though trying to comfort her. 'I wasn't here,' she said through her sobs. 'She died without me. We should have been here!'

'We couldn't have done anything,' Max said.

'He's right,' the SS man said. 'You would have died along with them.'

Lola looked up at them. 'You brought us to this,' she said, her face wet with tears. 'You, and people like you.'

The SS man turned away without replying.

Max had no tears yet. He gazed at his mother's face in the wan light of the soldier's flashlight, thinking how little he had known this woman who had borne him, raised him, and formed him. They had spent years at opposite ends of the world, in every sense. It was only in the last few weeks that he had begun to see what she was, and to understand her deep, quiet strength.

It was too late to say how sorry he was, to kiss her hands or try to explain, or make any amends. All that was done, now. He felt as though everything that had protected him and nourished him had been stripped away. Only Lola was left.

While they were carrying the bodies up to the street, Jochen Peiper arrived.

'You found them?' he asked Max.

Max nodded. 'They did not survive,' he said heavily.

Peiper laid a gloved hand on Max's shoulder. 'We will avenge them,' he said.

'Yes,' Max nodded, though vengeance was the last thing on his mind.

Peiper looked at Lola, who was crying inconsolably over Heidi's body. 'Your sister?'

'Yes, *Sturmbannführer*.'

'What is her name?'

'Heloise.'

'Give her my condolences. Have you somewhere to go?'

'My mother's house in Kallenheim.'

Peiper shook his head. 'Sorry, *Kamerad*. Kallenheim is gone. The bastards hit it with fighter bombers at the same time as Düren. Some fool of a local commander put tank traps around the town. The English thought it must be important. Just ruins now. They bombed several other towns nearby, too.'

'Then we have nowhere,' Max said flatly.

'Think about it tomorrow. You will need somewhere to sleep tonight. My men are making a bivouac outside the town. We'll start work burying the dead at dawn. You two will eat and sleep with us.'

Max nodded dumbly. There was no way he could refuse the invitation – more like a command – without arousing suspicion.

The bivouac was a simple affair of a few tents and a cauldron of potato soup. They sat in the cold, damp night, sheltered under awnings, watching the red glow of Düren in the distance. The heat from the destroyed town could still be felt on their faces.

Peiper's men were exhausted, and there was little conversation, except for exclamations of hatred against the Allies, who had inflicted this carnage on women and children. Nobody mentioned the fact that the Reich had inflicted – and continued to inflict with its rockets daily – exactly the same carnage on British women and children.

Jochen Peiper sat with Max and Lola. As always, Peiper was alert, despite the terrible day that had passed.

'What do you think of my crews?' he asked Max.

'They look very young.'

'They are all young since Normandy,' Peiper said dryly. 'I've been training them. Working them hard. The Führer has asked us to perform a miracle with these youngsters. Most of them have never fired a shot in anger. I wish I had the men we had in Russia. But they're all dead or captured. Nothing to be done. We will do our best.'

'You're ready to face the Americans?'

'Better than that.' Peiper rinsed his mouth out with coffee and spat. 'We're going to mount a counteroffensive through the Ardennes. What do you think of that, Wolff?'

'You'll be cut to pieces,' Max said.

Peiper laughed shortly. 'That remains to be seen. We SS know how to fight.'

'Yes.'

'Sorry about your mother and sister. War is a terrible thing when it sweeps up the women.' He gestured at the burning ruins of the town. 'This bombing is not war. This is murder. Even on the Eastern Front, we saw nothing as bad as this.'

Max thought of the Russian villages he had seen burn, and said nothing.

'Of course,' Peiper went on, 'it's the Jews who order these terror raids. They laugh at the slaughter. They are to blame for the entire war. They benefit from it all. They're behind Roosevelt, behind Stalin, behind Bolshevism and capitalism, and they have only one goal – Jewish world domination. But even the enemy are starting to see this, now. The victory of our ideas is certain.'

Lola sat huddled in the blanket that one of the panzer men had draped over her shoulders. She felt utterly numbed. She could not accept that Heidi was dead. It seemed as unreal an event as the fact that she was now sitting among a couple of hundred SS fanatics, and being shown kindness by them. A young officer brought her a cup of hot chocolate, an unimaginable luxury, and patted her arm consolingly. Were she to betray her Jewishness by a word, neither he nor a single one of his comrades would hesitate to put a bullet through her head. How strange it was. She poured the hot chocolate into the ground, untasted.

She listened to their voices, talking in regional accents from all across Germany – Bavarian, Saxon, Swabian, Berlinisch – comfortable with each other, united. This was what it was like to be Aryan, to be one of them, not a hated outsider. But she had never been one of them, and never would be one of them.

And Heidi lay in the ruins of Düren, and Lola would never hear her sister's laugh, or feel her comforting touch again. She was the last of her family, now. All the rest were gone. Men like the officer who had given her hot chocolate had destroyed every last one.

Was there any point in living? Even the bottle of Veronal had been lost now, but there were other ways of resigning from the job of life. She could walk into the river, and let herself sink down to the oozy bottom. She could jump up now and cry out, 'I am a Jew! I am responsible for the war!' and let them shoot her.

She would think of something.

Peiper gave Lola and Max a tent to themselves and a sleeping bag each, apologising for the spartan accommodation. They lay huddled together in the dark, their minds full of the frightful images of the day.

'We have lost everything,' Max said in the darkness, 'except each other. But we must go on.'

'Why?' she asked in a dead voice. 'There's no point.'

'The point is that we have been given life. We have to use it until it is taken away from us.'

'Like this? With nobody and nothing?'

'I have you. You have me.'

'It's not enough.'

'It is more than many people have.'

Lola was lost in tears. Her eyes burned agonisingly. 'What are we going to do, Max? Where are we going to go?'

'Kallenheim was destroyed today. So were other towns. All this bombing means the Allies will be here soon. The battle will be all around us. We must leave as soon as we can. We'll go to Anselm and Ditte in Cologne.'

'What if they're dead?'

'Then we will think of something else.'

During the night, Lola crept out of her sleeping bag and into Max's. They lay wrapped in each other's arms, battered, stinking of smoke, unable to sleep despite their exhaustion.

True to his word, Jochen Peiper got his crew up at dawn to begin the work of burying the dead. By now help had arrived from outside. Ambulancemen with stretchers were carrying the wounded away, and the NSV, the National Socialist People's Welfare organisation, had set up a canteen, making potato soup for the hungry.

The burial was a stark affair. There were no coffins. The bodies of the dead, including Heidi and Magda, were wrapped in curtains, bedsheets and whatever materials could be scavenged from the ruins, and then laid side by side in a trench dug by a tractor. Max saw some of the SS men throwing severed limbs into the trench, including, in one case, a woman's pale leg, still wearing a shoe, looking like a dummy from a modiste's window. Even the burials of his comrades at the front had been carried out with more tenderness, with flowers and markers.

Among the weeping and sobbing all around him, Max was stony-faced and silent. He did not feel he was worthy to shed a son's tears for his mother. He had not been a good son. A bad son had no right to cry. His grief had to take the form of actions from now on, not empty gestures.

An official came to hastily write down the names and addresses of the dead. Heidi had to be buried under a false name, and out of her religion, things that grieved Lola terribly. They were the last things the Third Reich had stolen from her.

'At least she lies beside a friend,' Max said, trying to comfort her.

But Lola was beyond consolation. They had endured so much together, she and Heidi. And now she was gone, killed by the very people from whom they'd hoped for salvation. It made no sense. The world had become a hideous place where the innocent were tormented and the wicked thrived. Of all the horrors that they had endured, this was the worst. There could be no day more terrible than this one. She wondered numbly whether she would survive it, or whether her heart would split in two with the pain, and kill her.

Max's feelings for Lola had changed in these last days. He'd thought of what he'd experienced under the old pear tree in Kallenheim as love. He now knew that emotion had been something as light and fragile as spun sugar.

Love was something different, something deeper and far more painful. Love was this overwhelming need to protect Lola from more harm, because if anything happened to her, it would tear his heart out.

Love was the fear he felt when he looked at her, so young and pure, in this dreadful world that he had helped to create, where innocence was seared, and goodness shattered.

Love seized him by the throat and made him gasp for air. Love made him want to lay down his life for her. Love told him there was nothing more important in the world than Lola – not country, not honour, not family. She was everything to him.

He did not even require her to love him in return. He just didn't want to imagine a life without her. He had made a mistake with his mother, and he had lost her. He would not lose Lola.

'That sister of yours doesn't look much like you,' Jochen Peiper commented after the brief ceremony.

'We have different fathers.'

'Are you certain she is racially pure?'

Max straightened. 'What are you suggesting?' he snapped.

Peiper's eyes were hard in his clean-cut face. 'No need to lose your temper, Wolff. One sees many strange things these days.'

'There is nothing strange here.'

Peiper shrugged and turned away. But Max's hackles were raised. Peiper was a fanatic, but not a fool; and it would take only a few casual enquiries to expose his lies. They had to move on from here quickly.

Buses and trucks were being laid on to transport the homeless – effectively the whole town – to other sites. Many of the inhabitants of Düren had lost their *Kennkarten* and other identification papers in the raid. It was an opportunity for Lola to acquire a new identity.

'You must use my name from now on,' Max told her. 'You're Heloise Wolff. My younger sister. As soon as we can, we'll get you an identity card to match.'

Lola grimaced. 'One of these days I shall forget what I am really called.'

'I hope one day that will be your real name,' Max said.

Lola's eyes were swollen with crying, but she looked at him angrily. 'What are you saying?'

He realised he had said something stupid. 'Nothing. Just don't forget.'

He went to find transport for them.

The crowds of people needing a ticket out of Düren numbered in their thousands. Max queued for two hours at one of the desks and obtained tickets for them both. Somewhat ruefully, he found they had been allocated to a Luftwaffe base near Münster. It did not sound a particularly safe location, but there was no arguing with the authorities. The base was equipped to house and feed a large group of people, and that was what mattered now.

Max tried to avoid encountering Jochen Peiper again during the rest of the day. Rescue attempts had now given way to locating and disposing of the dead. Max joined in this grim task. The devastation was overwhelming. Something like five hundred bombers had dropped three thousand tons or more of high explosive on the ancient town. There was not a single street left intact, and if Düren was ever to be inhabited again, it would need to be rebuilt from the ground up.

The pitiful remains of the dead had to be gathered with shovels in some cases. Even the supposedly tough, young SS crews were affected by it; for many, it was their first real experience of war. Max wondered whether attacks like this would really hasten the end of the war – or simply harden the spirit of ordinary Germans to resist to the end.

Lola had joined a group of women tending to the surviving children, a lot of them orphans. Dazed and in many cases seriously injured, the little ones were apathetic. They called for their mothers, or for milk; but the milk had run out, even for the most serious cases. So had bandages, medicines and beds. And mothers.

Lola, who'd had little to do with children in her life, at first had no idea what to do. But she soon found that comfort could be given with a gentle touch or word, or by holding those children able to be held.

It was a strange experience to hold someone else's child and be called *Mutti* or Mama. Oddly, she was able to find comfort by giving comfort. It helped her to think about Heidi, and Magda, and all the other women who had gone before, without breaking down in helpless tears.

The long day wore on. The only food available was the same thin soup from yesterday. It grew dark. A drizzle had started to fall, hissing among the embers of the town, helping to put out the last fires.

Max returned from the burial work, looking pale and exhausted, complaining of his migraine. She was worried about him. Big and strong as he was, he had not recovered from either the fractured skull he'd sustained on the Eastern Front, or the beating that the *Orpos* had given him. There was something about him that reminded her of the hurt children she'd been nursing all day, something fragile.

They sat together, sharing the same spoon and the same bowl of soup, without speaking.

At ten in the evening, the first buses and trucks began to leave. Theirs was called close to midnight.

The wounded were put on first, some on stretchers. Lola and Max sat together in the back seat of the bus, huddled into each other's body for warmth. The windows of the bus were louvred, but as they set off for Münster, they could see the ruins and flames of the town, and hear the drone of enemy aircraft in the night sky as the bombing raids continued.

It was strange that she now thought of them as *enemy* aircraft.

Chapter 11

They arrived at the airbase early the next morning. As their bus drove along the perimeter, they peered out of the window at their new home. It did not present a very reassuring aspect. It had obviously been bombed more than once. Although it bristled with anti-aircraft batteries, its runways were dotted with deep craters, some in the process of being filled. Several hangars had burned to skeletons, and a large group of fighter planes, evidently destroyed on the ground, had been bulldozed into a scrapheap.

They had slept intermittently on the bus, Lola's head on Max's shoulder, and now they were starting to feel the battering they had received over the past days. Burns and bruises were aching all over their bodies.

The bus stopped at a large dormitory block. As they left the bus, their names were taken, and they signed a reception list. Lola did not stumble over giving her surname as Wolff. Max took it as a good omen. He had made up his mind, at some stage over these past weeks, that Lola would be his wife one day, and call herself Lola Wolff ever after.

He prayed it would come true. But there was the war to be survived, first.

They were greeted with yet more soup. This time it was even less appetising, and each bowl had a lump of stale bread floating in it; but they were grateful to have anything to eat at all.

Their quarters were to be a large communal dormitory, with white-painted steel beds spaced out at two-metre intervals. There was no separation of the sexes, or any other refinement. However, on arrival, everyone was allowed three minutes in the shower, and Lola took advantage of this to wash the grime and stink of smoke away with a bar of shared soap. She had to pick other women's hairs off it before she could bring herself to use it.

They'd made the journey without baggage of any kind, just the clothes they stood up in. These were now taken away to be washed and an assortment of second-hand clothing was given out by Nazi Welfare 'sisters' in white aprons and caps. Lola received an ankle-length mauve dress that her grandmother might have worn. Max was given a set of dungarees that had clearly belonged to some factory worker.

They were also given rather threadbare overcoats, and wearing these, they went outside, despite the cold and damp, to escape the smells and sights of the dormitory.

The dormitory blocks were separated from the airfield by a mesh fence. They stood together at the fence, looking at the Junkers 88s taking off and landing, the deafening roar of their engines like the snarling of cornered lions.

'Do you think it will end soon?' Lola asked.

'I don't know,' he admitted. 'Sometimes I think it can't possibly last much longer. Other times I think the Reich will have to be destroyed yard by yard before it ends.'

'Then there will be nothing left.'

'They've tried to kill Hitler once. Perhaps they will succeed next time.'

Lola looked down at the old-fashioned shoes she'd been given, with their blocky heels and tarnished buckles. 'I wonder where they got these clothes from?'

'I heard someone say they were taken from prisoners in the concentration camps,' he said without thinking.

Lola grimaced. 'God.'

He cursed himself silently. 'I'm sorry.'

'We can't get away from it, can we?'

'One day we will.'

'I don't think so. I think it will always be with us. Heidi was right.' She looked at him with her dark, haunted eyes. 'That's my deepest fear. That the war will end, and we will still be prisoners of what they did to us. Until the day we also die.'

'Please don't talk like that, Lola,' he pleaded. 'I want to make you happy. I want us to have a life together, not just when this is all over, but now, here.'

'What happiness can we have?' she asked. 'Heidi is dead. Your mother is dead. We stand here wearing dead people's clothes, in this factory of death. How can you talk about any kind of future?'

'I don't know how it can be,' he said slowly, looking into her face, 'but my love for you takes all that away. It fills me completely. There's no room for anything else.'

She turned away wearily. 'You talk like a fool sometimes, Max.'

'I know I'm a fool,' he said. 'You're the brains of the outfit.'

'I feel so old,' she said in a heavy voice. 'I feel like my life is already over.'

He put his arms around her. She allowed him to hold her for a while, while the war planes screamed into the air. Then she pushed him away.

They remained in a kind of limbo for the next few days. They were seen by Luftwaffe doctors – both had inflamed lungs from the smoke, which required treatment – and slowly recovered from their injuries.

Grief over the deaths of Magda and Heidi was harder to deal with. Lola sank deeper into depression each day, and Max found it almost impossible to lift her out of it. His own approach was to try not to think about his mother. They sat together in silence for hours on end, or wandered around the perimeter of the airbase, watching the planes land and take off. Sometimes the night fighters would return trailing smoke, with their fuselages shot full of holes, to be greeted by wailing ambulances and fire engines.

More civilian refugees were crowding into the base all the time, filling up all available beds. With no radio to listen to, except the *Reichs-Rundfunk* broadcast in the dormitory, they were cut off from reliable war news. All they heard was the incessant exhortations to fight, assuring Germans that victory was inevitable. One of the new arrivals, a young woman, climbed up and tore the wires off the loudspeaker. There was a chorus of disapproval.

'I've heard enough Führer speeches,' she said as she got down again. She was a country girl with a pink, snub-nosed face. Her two children crowded under her arms like chicks under the wing of a belligerent hen. 'They can all go to hell. My husband is dead, and my brother is missing in action, and now they've bombed our village. And I'm left with two kids! I don't want to hear any more.'

The grumbling continued. But nobody bothered to reconnect the speaker.

There was no indication as to when they would be moved off the base. Most of the civilians billeted here were like Lola and Max, bombed out, with no homes to go to. Max was still determined to make for Cologne and try to find Anselm and Ditte. But they were now further from Cologne than they had been at Düren, and he wanted Lola to recover a little before they faced the uncertain journey, which was likely to involve hardships. She was still in a fragile state, both physically and emotionally.

One afternoon, they were put back on the bus and driven into Münster to register for new documents and food coupons. Lola felt a rising panic in her breast at being confronted with Nazi officialdom once again.

Max tried to reassure her. 'Düren was burned to the ground. All their lists have been destroyed. The town hall is in ruins. Nobody will be able to trace you.'

'The Nazis can trace anybody anywhere,' Lola said bitterly.

'In this chaos? I doubt it. And even if they eventually get around to asking any questions, we will be long gone, or the war will be over. Keep your nerve,' Max said, squeezing her hand.

Münster had been heavily bombed, but was still functioning as the regional capital, and was busy with traffic. The civic offices were crowded. Lola and Max were soon separated, men to one side, women to the other. As if in a bad dream, Lola shuffled along, listening to the women around her talking, bewailing the loss of their homes and possessions, complaining about the soup and the accommodation at the airbase, cursing the Allied bombers.

At last she was pushed into a room where an official sat behind a desk piled with papers. He had a shaven head and plump face, lined with folds of good living. He picked up his pen.

'Name?'

'Heloise Wolff.'

The man's pen stopped an inch over the paper. 'Wolff?'

'Yes.'

He studied Lola with colourless eyes. 'Are you of Jewish descent?' he demanded.

Men like this had stripped Lola and her family of everything – pasty bureaucrats who blandly ordered death and deportation, who destroyed the lives of others without a qualm. She was suddenly filled with rage. It boiled up in her, heating her ice-cold veins and setting her failing heart pounding. 'How dare you!' she said sharply, straightening her back. 'I am German through and through.'

The man blinked, taken aback. 'Of mixed race?' he enquired.

'I have just told you that I have no Jewish ancestry. Why do you insist with these offensive questions?'

'Excuse me. The name—'

'How *dare* you? The name is Aryan! Wolf with one "f" is Jewish. Wolff with a double "f" is not. You should know this before you make such accusations!'

The man's doughy cheeks flushed. 'We have to ask certain questions.'

'If I was a Jew, would I be standing here before you?' she demanded.

'Excuse me,' he muttered. He wrote the name down. 'Date of birth?'

'June fifth, 1923.'

'Address?'

'I lived at number three hundred Oberstrasse, but it no longer exists. It was destroyed in the bombing. I have lost everything – my clothing, my ration cards, my identification papers, all my money.' She tapped the desk with her finger. 'I require assistance!'

She emerged from the office half an hour later, and found Max waiting for her anxiously in the hallway.

'Let's get out of here,' she said.

'How did it go?' he asked her as they made their way out to the street.

She opened the folder she was carrying, and showed him her haul. 'Temporary identity document – you note I am now an Aryan. Food coupons for six weeks – bread, meat, margarine, vegetables. Clothing coupons for dress, shoes, coat and hat. Soap

198

coupons for four months. Assistance papers, twenty Reichsmarks in cash, and two months' tobacco coupons.'

'Tobacco coupons? You don't even smoke!'

'We can trade them for food and clothing coupons with people who do,' Lola said.

'How on earth did you get all that?'

'The official was helpful,' she said.

Max threw back his head and laughed. 'My heart was in my mouth all this while, and you have been conquering everything before you.'

'I have become a *Nazifresser*,' she replied.

'How did you do it?'

'I thought of everything those people have taken from me, and I decided I was entitled to at least a few coupons.'

But on the way back to the airbase she thought back to the interview, knowing she had been as close to death in there as during the bombing of Düren.

Max had been right. Life was given out to be used. It could be taken away at any moment. But while she had it, she had to use it. Death had been her constant companion for so many years that she had almost forgotten how to live. Real life had been a dream, a mythical place outside and beyond the four walls where she had been imprisoned with Heidi. Now that she was alive again, no matter how dreadful the circumstances, she must face it.

How much she wanted to be able to discuss these issues with Heidi. They had talked so much. So much! Surely no two sisters in the history of Germany had ever talked to one another so much, about so many things, for so long!

And now the companion of her confinement was gone.

Only Max remained.

She looked back on the nights under the old pear tree and thought how sweet they had been. A fairy tale, in which she had been the princess in the tower, and Max the brave knight who had come to rescue her.

Things had changed since then. She was not a princess, and Max not a fairy-tale knight. They had been thrown together, however. They had been given each other, in the same way that they had been given life, by a random destiny.

Did that mean they belonged to each other now? They certainly belonged to no one else. Her life was in his hands. His was in hers. There was nothing to do but get on with it. They would have to learn to live together.

They would have to learn to live.

The Münster airbase was surrounded by wooded areas where they could freely walk, offering them the only form of recreation they could take. The roads were crowded with military vehicles, but once some distance from the base, they could take paths into the wood, and soon be surrounded by trees.

In this winter month, there were few birds singing, and the only trees left in leaf were the rows of dark pines and firs. But getting away from their fellow evacuees was a great relief.

'I can't stand to hear them complaining,' Lola said as they walked through the dead leaves. 'They're lucky to be alive, but all they do is moan about the food and the beds and the nice furniture they've lost. I wish they could see the world through my eyes.'

'It's hard for them,' Max said. 'For ten years, the Nazis promised glory. Nobody told them it would be like this.'

'They were happy enough to dish it out,' Lola retorted.

'That's human nature.'

They had reached a little brook. Overhead, through the gaps in the conifers, the sky was a leaden grey. It was very cold, and ice was starting to glaze the rocks and crystallise on the leaves of the ferns that hung over the water. Their breath clouded in the still air of the forest. Lola huddled against Max, trying to find additional warmth in his big body. He put his arms around her.

'We stood like this under the old pear tree,' he said.

'That feels like a hundred years ago. It's so strange to think that Magda and Heidi were alive, then. I keep wanting to talk to them. I turn as though I'm expecting them to be there. But they'll never be there again.' She laughed. 'Sorry. I'm talking like an idiot.'

'No, you're not.'

'After the bombing, I kept wishing that I'd died then, too.'

'Lola, please don't say that.'

'If I hadn't insisted on going out that morning, we would both have been in that shelter. We'd both be dead, now. I feel so guilty, Max. I feel like we shouldn't be alive!'

'But we are alive,' he said gently. 'It's not something to be guilty about. It was just fate.'

'If I'd had the bottle of Veronal, I'd have taken it.'

'And where would I be, then?'

Lola shook her head. 'You would be much better off without me.'

'No, I wouldn't. You're everything to me.'

'I've been nothing but trouble.'

'Lola, darling, don't talk like this.'

'You were the first man ever to kiss me.' Lola pressed her cheek against his chest. 'Did you know that?' she asked.

'I hoped I was the first. I didn't know.'

'You must have been able to tell.' She raised her face to his. 'I wish we could still kiss each other, Max. But something has gone out of me.'

'I'm just grateful that you're alive,' he said, looking down into her face. The grief that she had been through had left its mark.

There were dark shadows under her eyes and her skin was dry and pale. Their breath mingled in white clouds. 'I wouldn't want to live without you.'

'Don't worry, I've decided not to die,' she said wryly. 'You're stuck with me.'

'And you're stuck with me.'

She burrowed into his coat. 'What's going to happen to us?'

'I want to leave for Cologne as soon as you're strong enough.'

'How far is it?'

'A hundred miles or so. The problem will be finding a train – and getting tickets on it.'

'I'll be well soon, Max. I promise.'

They walked back to the base, to find their dormitory in confusion. Someone had complained that the radio loudspeaker had been disconnected, and two Gestapo officials had arrived to investigate. The snub-nosed young woman had been identified.

'She said the Führer can go to hell,' a man shouted from across the room. 'She said she wished the Führer was dead!'

'It's true,' a woman said, nodding vehemently. 'She said she wished the Americans would get here and string him up. She is a traitor!'

The Gestapo men had seized the woman's plump arms. She was struggling, her face redder than ever. Her children were wailing in fright. 'Let me go, you bastards!'

Instinctively, Max strode over and confronted the Gestapo men. 'She's already given her husband and brother to the Reich,' he barked. 'She doesn't know what she's saying. Let her go.'

The men glared at him. 'You want to come with her to headquarters?' one said grimly.

'She's a war widow, damn you! She has two children!'

'She can explain it in the cells. Stand aside.'

One of the Welfare officers had arrived in his khaki uniform with a swastika armband. Max turned to him. 'Are you going to allow this?' Max demanded. 'The Gestapo have no right to come in here and arrest civilians who have lost their homes!'

The man shrugged, plainly frightened. 'What can I do? I'm sure they will release her when the matter has been cleared up.'

Max clenched his fists. He couldn't afford to get mixed up in this, and expose Lola to the risk of discovery. He was forced to back down, boiling inside.

The woman was hustled out of the dormitory, still arguing furiously. Her screaming children were dragged along behind her. Nobody else attempted to intervene.

'What will they do to them?' Lola asked in a low voice.

'Whatever they want,' he replied bitterly. 'Germany has gone mad. She's right. The sooner they string Hitler up, the better for everybody.'

The air-raid siren began to wail at eight the next morning, while they were all eating their meagre breakfast of ersatz coffee and dry bread. There was a general rush for the shelter, all the dormitories emptying. But the heavy thud of bombs had already begun, accompanied by the pulsing blast waves that they knew so well.

Outside the building was a maelstrom of noise and terror. They were just in time to see the silvery shark shape of an American fighter roar low over the runway, its machine guns blazing. As it soared back up into the sky, an explosion of aviation fuel lit up the morning. A searing blast of air swept them off their feet, followed by billowing, evil black clouds that blossomed upwards. Flaming debris, trailing smoke, arched down around them.

The sky was full of Allied planes weaving in and out of the smoke. They picked themselves up and ran to the civilian shelter, a somewhat inadequate structure half buried in the trees, and pushed their way in among the crowds. The raid was in full progress now, a symphony of howling, snarling aero engines, punctuated by blasts that shook the ground and made the flimsy protective sheeting of the shelter sway.

'They do this when the heavy bomber fleets are coming,' an older man, who had been there longer than the others, told them as he hunched under a shower of dust. 'They try to pin down our interceptors so we can't defend our cities.'

There were already some wounded being dragged in, bleeding and dazed. One man, with a severe chest injury, died on the floor at their feet.

Lola felt a strange detachment. She had seen so much death. It no longer shocked her. People were alive one moment, and gone the next, leaving these empty shells that had to be disposed of. It was not callousness; it was just an acceptance that the same thing could happen to you at any moment, and there was nothing to be done about it.

She sat huddled against Max as the attack raged. She felt more at peace since their talk in the forest; closer to Max. She knew he loved her. For some reason, he had taken her to his heart, and she was grateful for that.

She had hated her own powerlessness. For years, she had been forced to depend on others to shelter her, feed her, keep her safe. She had been reduced to the role of a child in an adult world.

But now the adults were all gone. Heidi, Magda, all her relations – they were all gone. She and Max were all that remained of her world. Grieving over Heidi and Magda was as futile as grieving over the dead man who lay, still warm, at her feet. It served no purpose. She had to gird her loins and get on with life as an adult.

Her twenty-first birthday had come and gone, and she no longer had an excuse for being passive.

When the all-clear sounded, after an hour of strafing and bombing, she turned to Max.

'We can't stay here,' she said. 'It's not safe. We need to leave for Cologne as soon as possible.'

He glanced at her. 'Are you feeling well enough?'

'Yes,' Lola said. 'I'm as well as I'll ever be. Let's go.'

Chapter 12

It took them two days to get travel permits, and then two more to get tickets to Cologne. Rail services throughout the Reich had been thrown into chaos by the constant air attacks, and the few trains still running were crowded to capacity.

They had tried to telephone Anselm several times before setting off, but getting through was impossible. They had decided to simply arrive, and take their chances on his being still alive, and then being willing to help them.

The train journey was slow. They had little luggage, just the few clothes they had managed to acquire in Münster, packed into a couple of carpet bags. The train was crammed full with refugees and evacuees, mainly women and children, and the two of them stood for the five-hour journey, which was extended with frequent stops and periods of moving at a snail's pace, the train's iron wheels squealing.

The journey took them through a number of Westphalian towns, and gave them a wider glimpse of the war: several of the districts they passed through had been bombed into ruins, just like Düren. The stations had been hit in many places, too, the lines uprooted in twisted tangles of rail and timber, the platforms wrecked. Passage through them had been reduced to one line, accounting for the endless delays.

At one station, a locomotive had been flipped like a toy on to its end, and stood stark against the bleak sky. At another, a neat row of corpses was laid out beside the tracks, victims of a strafing run that morning.

This had not been shown to them. The Reich's radio reports had always minimised the destruction, and there had been no photographs in newspapers to illustrate what months of carpet bombing had done to Germany. Both Max and Lola were shocked.

'I didn't know it was like this,' Lola said in a hushed voice, peering out of the steamy window.

'Nor did I,' Max confessed.

'Things can't go on like this. The country is being destroyed.'

The land looked deserted. Nobody was in the fields, which were often cratered where bombs had either missed their mark, or been jettisoned. It was a dark day, and snow began to fall, blurring the harsh black edges of things with a fragile white dusting.

They arrived at Köln-Deutz station in the early afternoon. The snow was still falling lightly but persistently, the sky a strange, greyish yellow. They had to cross the Rhine to get to the city, walking across the huge Hohenzollern Bridge, which was as yet untouched by the bombing.

But long before they reached the other side, they could see that what they had reached was not so much a city as the ghost of one.

The great cathedral, with its twin spires, still stood as it had done for seven hundred years. But all around it was devastation. The empty windows of the bombed buildings, roofless, and in many cases reduced to no more than a few walls, stared blindly down at pavements lined with rubble. Rows upon rows of streets, all in the same shattered condition, receded into the darkness that seemed to have swallowed Cologne.

Next to the main station, they entered a street where a number of military vehicles were parked. There was a small crowd loitering around a wooden framework. As they approached, Max realised with a shock that it was a gallows. A Gestapo detachment was busy taking down the bodies of the men they had publicly hanged. 'Don't look,' he muttered to Lola.

But Lola had already seen the horrible sight. 'Some of them were just boys,' she said in a shaky voice. She grasped the sleeve of one of the bystanders. 'Were they Jews?' she asked.

The man shook his head. 'Antisocial elements,' he said laconically. 'They strung them up this morning. Man, you should have seen them kick. Like a football team, I can tell you. They've been hanging up there all day, to encourage their mates. Now they're carting them off to be buried.'

Silent and stunned, Max and Lola walked on through the desolation. The cruel images had brought back to him the manner of his own father's death, and he felt sick to his stomach.

Here and there, homeless families were grouped in the streets, some trying to cook meals on open fires among the ruins of their dwellings, others sitting listlessly, without speaking or looking up. A few women and children were pushing handcarts laden with a few pathetic sticks of furniture, or a bathtub, a metal fireplace, a rolled-up carpet – anything that could be retrieved from the ruins of their own or other people's houses.

Some were now living in their basements, below street level, in imminent danger of being buried alive should the damaged structures above them collapse.

This once-beautiful city had been reduced to the Stone Age. To achieve this vast ruin must have required thousands of heavy bombers, thousands of tons of high explosive, thousands of terrible deaths.

Occasionally, Lola and Max encountered groups of Asiatic-looking soldiers, recruited to defend the Reich from the conquered nations, some riding little Mongolian ponies, or marching out of step in undisciplined groups, talking in unintelligible languages, led by weary German officers.

Other than these wraiths, the broad streets of Cologne were largely empty.

The air was toxic, poisoned by smashed sewage mains, or made acrid by the smoke from blackened beams protruding from the heaps of wreckage. There were worse smells, too, where putrefying human bodies had yet to be recovered from the rubble or from basements.

They walked down boulevard after boulevard, where not a single structure remained intact, where rows of trees had been reduced to charred stumps, where in place of city blocks, only mounds of raw earth were heaped up. Strange glimpses of a former life appeared now and then: family rooms exposed by the shearing-away of an entire facade, a staircase leading nowhere, the iron skeletons of domes and arches.

The snow kept falling. At a crossroads, they had to pause for a line of refugees plodding slowly along, carrying children or supporting the elderly. Escorting them was a group of men in *Volkssturm* uniforms. A young woman holding an infant stopped to look at Max and Lola.

'Have you got food?' she asked in a hoarse voice, holding out her hand.

Lola dug in her bag and pulled out one of the loaves she had been keeping for later. The woman took it silently. She stared at them for a moment longer, her face blank. Then she turned and walked on, gnawing the bread.

Max saw that the *Volkssturm* soldiers were boys of no more than sixteen, their thin faces peering warily from under the brims of forage caps too big for them, hauling rifles too long for them.

Max had not been in Cologne since his own boyhood, on family visits to Anselm. Then, of course, the city had looked very different. Now he seemed to be in a place he had no knowledge of. He kept checking the map he had brought, but there were no longer any street signs except those that had been chalked up on the ruined walls by various military units.

'I don't really know where we are,' he confessed to Lola. They had been walking for hours, and were exhausted. They sat on the steps of what had once been a handsome apartment block, before incendiaries had burned it to a husk. He put his head in his hands. 'This is terrible. We shouldn't have come.'

Lola put her arms around him. 'We didn't know. They hid the truth from us.' She saw the tears seeping from between his fingers. 'I've never seen you cry before.'

'I'm sorry,' he said, his throat choked, 'sorry for everything, Lola.'

She pulled his head on to her bosom and stroked his hair, rocking him gently to and fro. 'It's not your fault,' she whispered, 'not your fault, my darling.'

A few streets further on, they met an old man muffled in a greatcoat, who gave them directions.

'But that street is like all the others,' he said, peering at them from reddened, rheumy eyes. 'You won't find anybody there.'

With sinking hearts, they walked on, shivering with the bitter cold that was starting to gather as darkness fell. The snow blew into their faces, stinging their lips and eyes, muffling the sound of their footfalls. The streets of bombed-out buildings had a special silence: they absorbed every sound without an echo. The empty windows did not reflect, the doorways were empty. The only sound was the wind that moaned through the ruins.

There were no lights. The streetlamps had all been obliterated. More by luck than anything else, they finally found themselves on the right street, just as the last gleam of evening was leaving the sky.

But the old man had been right. The block where Anselm and Ditte Wolff had lived had been bombed, like all the rest. The night sky showed through the roof beams and the vacant windows. They stood on the steps. Despair filled Max.

'Maybe there's somebody sheltering in the basement,' Lola said. 'Let's go and take a look.'

Max looked up dubiously at the pockmarked facade. 'The place could collapse at any moment.'

'We've come all this way,' Lola pointed out.

They went cautiously into the building. What had once been the hallway was a maze of shattered masonry and debris that had fallen from above. They had to clamber over piles of it in the almost dark. The stairs down to the basement were right at the back. They stood peering down into the blackness, and caught a whiff of woodsmoke.

'Listen!' Lola whispered. 'There's somebody down there.'

Max cocked his head. He could hear something from below. They picked their way gingerly down the stairs, feeling their way along the walls. As he reached the bottom, he heard the muffled sound of voices.

'Wait here,' Max said to Lola. He pushed open the door of the basement cautiously. The room was smoky, lit by a few candles and an open fire on which a pot was cooking. Some two dozen figures were squatting around the fire, huddled in blankets, talking in low voices. At the creak of the basement door, they all stopped and turned to look at Max.

'Hullo?' he said.

The reply was a warning shout – and a shot. Max ducked instinctively as the bullet struck the brickwork next to him, showering him with fragments. He grabbed Lola and began groping his way back upstairs. Hands seized them and dragged them down. He tried to struggle, but there were too many of them. He and Lola were thrown on to the ground. Several knees slammed into his chest and belly, pinning him on his back. In the dazzle of a flashlight, he saw that a pistol was pointed at his face.

'Don't shoot!' he shouted. 'I'm just looking for my uncle. Dr Anselm Wolff. He lived in this block.'

'He's lying,' a voice said. 'They're Gestapo. Shoot them now.'

'We're not Gestapo!' Max protested.

'Cut their throats, they're Nazis.'

'Wait,' he heard a voice say. 'This one's a woman.'

'A woman?' the voice behind the pistol demanded, in a strange, rasping whisper. 'Who the hell are you?'

'Lola, from Berlin. This is Max, my friend. We don't want any trouble. And we're not Gestapo!'

The flashlight shone full on their faces. There was a muttered conversation in the darkness, which Max couldn't hear over the pounding of his own heart. 'Get them over to the fire,' the rasping whisper behind the pistol commanded. 'A red-hot fork in the eyeball will get the truth out of them.'

Hands grasped them both and hauled them over to the fire. A shadowy face loomed into Lola's. 'Who did you say you were?'

'Lola. Lola Schmidt,' she said, picking the first name she could pluck out of the air.

'And who is this big lunk?'

'I told you,' Lola said. 'He takes care of me. His name is Max.'

'He looks like a soldier. Are you a soldier, Max-who-takes-care-of-Lola?'

'I was a panzer commander,' Max growled.

'Cool,' a young voice said from the darkness.

'It's not cool,' the whisperer retorted. 'He's an enemy. Where's your panzer now?'

'I was discharged from the *Wehrmacht*.'

'Why?'

'A head injury,' Max said tersely. He was starting to realise that some of their captors were teenagers of sixteen or less. He could just make out their slight figures in the red glow of the fire. The one holding the pistol and the flashlight, however, was an adult of thirty or so.

'Your brain must be mush to come to Cologne,' the whisperer said. 'Everybody's left or leaving. Except us. And we're going to have to shoot you.'

'You can't shoot him,' Lola said. 'Who'll look after me?'

'We'll look after you,' an adolescent voice piped up.

'No! He's my fiancé!'

'Put the gun away,' Max said. 'We don't mean you any harm.'

'But maybe we mean *you* harm,' the man with the hoarse voice said. 'We kill Nazi officers.'

'He's not an officer any more,' Lola said, 'and he's not a Nazi.'

'Who are you people?' Max demanded.

There was a chorus of answers. 'We're the Navajos!'

'What's left of us.'

'They hanged thirteen of us this morning at the railway station.'

'Strung them up.'

One of the young people started crying. Max had assumed it was a boy, but he now saw that it was a girl of sixteen or seventeen, with her reddish hair cropped close to her skull. Others were sobbing or wiping their eyes.

'They killed our comrades,' the whisperer said. 'It's only justice if we kill you, *Panzersoldat*.'

'We saw them taking down the bodies as we arrived,' Max said, watching the pistol carefully. 'Were they members of your gang?'

'We're not a gang!' somebody said angrily. 'We're anti-fascists!'

'We're the resistance. We beat up the Hitler Youth and sabotage the war effort.'

'We're free fighters.'

'You're very brave,' Lola said. 'And we're so sorry about your friends. It was terrible. I cried when I saw how they died.'

There was another silence. 'Put the gun away, Florentin,' someone said. 'They're okay.'

To Max's relief, the pistol was lowered at last. Its owner tucked it into the back of his waistband. He had a hard-bitten face with a broken nose, and several teeth missing. 'Maybe we shoot you later,' he said to Max. 'For now, we eat.'

They sat around the fire, drinking soup doled out in tin mugs. Max shared out the second loaf of bread they had brought from Münster. The leader of the motley group, Florentin Polanski, was a Pole who told them proudly how he had escaped from a concentration camp. 'But they gave me some souvenirs to take with me,' he said with a gap-toothed grin, indicating his broken nose and his throat. 'They tried to hang me, and I nearly croaked. I kicked like fury, and the rope snapped. They were laughing so hard, they didn't bother to try again. I broke out when the Russians bombed our camp. But my vocal cords are gone. That's why I talk like this.'

He was reticent about the reason for his having ended up in a camp. He boasted of his anti-Nazi exploits, but some of what he said sounded to Max more like the behaviour of a habitual criminal than the deeds of a resistance hero. The younger ones seemed to half admire, half fear him.

They had been 'Edelweiss Pirates', part of a much larger group of rebellious young people, who detested the Hitler Youth and the restrictions imposed by the state. After brutal persecution, there were only a few scattered local chapters left. This one, the Navajos, had been active in Cologne until they had incurred the wrath of the Gestapo. After a running battle with the police, a group had been arrested. Himmler had ordered the hangings they had seen that morning.

Lola told them about the bombing on Düren. When she told them about Heidi, the girl with the cropped red hair came to sit next to her. 'I lost my sister, too,' she whispered. 'I lost all my family. I'm the only one left. My name is Angelika.'

None of them knew anything about Anselm, or any of the other former tenants of the block.

'We'll ask around,' the crop-haired girl promised. 'Somebody may know something.'

Most of the inhabitants of Cologne had fled weeks earlier, they said, after the last devastating air raid, leaving it a ghost city. The population had shrunk to a quarter, and life was almost impossible for these remnants. There was no longer gas or electricity in most of the city. The only water came from hydrants in the streets. There was no public transport, no law and order – apart from the Gestapo – and no food.

The Welfare 'sisters' distributed rations each day, but the Navajos scorned these. Trying to claim them, in any case, would expose them to the risk of arrest. They preferred to scavenge what they could from the rubble.

It was hard to believe that in the middle of the twentieth century, Germans had been reduced to living like this. Max studied the Navajos squatting around the fire. They were a mixed group. Some were foreign forced labourers who had escaped, some just local teenagers who had lost or been separated from their parents. At least two, who kept in the shadows, looked like deserters from the *Wehrmacht*. A few, like Florentin, came somewhere between resistance fighters and hardened criminals.

He didn't feel especially safe in this company, especially with Lola, but there was nothing to be done about it now.

After their spartan meal, the Navajos produced a guitar and an accordion, and began to sing. Some were youth songs about wandering free in the mountains, others more political:

Hitler's power makes us small, we are still in chains.

But once we are released, we will break free,

Our fists are clenched, and our knives are drawn,

We Navajos fight for the freedom of youth.

As the songs grew dreamier and sadder, the younger Navajos fell asleep one by one, huddling together. The girl with the short hair, who had said her name was Angelika, brought Max and Lola blankets. The three of them huddled together in a corner, Max keeping a watchful eye on the older men until they, too, went to sleep in their different places.

Then he at last closed his eyes.

Despite all that he had been through, all the places he had slept during his time in the army, this was one of the strangest nights of all, after one of the strangest and most disconcerting of days. He was drifting in nightmares about the grey figures dangling from the gallows, the desolate streets of Cologne, when something woke him. He opened his eyes to see the shape of Florentin Polanski hunched over their carpet bags, rooting inside.

He could make out the butt of Florentin's pistol, protruding from the back of his belt. He reached over and yanked it out. Florentin grew very still as Max clicked off the safety and put the gun to the Pole's ear.

'If you want to see morning,' Max said in a low voice, 'go back to your kennel.'

Florentin raised his hands. 'Sorry, *Kamerad*,' he muttered, 'I got confused.'

'I'll hang on to the gun,' Max replied, 'in case you get confused again.'

Florentin crawled back to his place by the fire. Max knew he would have a knife as well, but he doubted whether there would be any more trouble.

The exchange had disturbed some of the sleepers, who rolled over or groaned. After five minutes, there was a silence that lasted till morning.

The next day, they emerged from the basement to find that it had snowed again during the night. The white covering made the devastation eerier than ever. They went in search of anyone who might know anything about Anselm, accompanied by two of the younger Navajos, including the girl, Angelika.

The Navajos boasted cheerfully about their exploits under Florentin's guidance, which seemed to consist mainly of stealing butter to be resold at ten times the price on the black market. The prospect of being hanged by the Gestapo didn't appear to deter them.

Max hadn't held out much hope of finding any neighbours, given the destruction of the neighbourhood, but a few families had remained, living in their basements. One couple, four doors down, had news.

'The Herr *Doktor* Wolff?' the elderly woman said, peering up at them from her area window. 'Oh, yes, he survived the bombing, although they lost everything. I spoke to him the day he left.'

'Do you know where he went?' Max asked eagerly.

'He and his wife went to their country home, near Dresden. He gave me the address in case anybody asked for him. Wait there, young man, I will get it for you.'

Max's hopes, which had just been raised, now sank again. Dresden was a good three hundred and fifty miles away to the east, in Saxony. The old lady hobbled into her house to get the address and came back with a slip of paper. She handed it up to Max.

'Thank you,' he said, taking it.

The wrinkled face peered at him. 'I know you. You are the nephew from Kallenheim.'

'Maximilian, yes.'

'They told us you fought in Russia.'

'Yes.'

'How is your mother?'

Max shook his head. 'I'm afraid she is no longer with us. An air raid.'

The old woman sighed. 'I am sorry, young man.'

'Thank you.'

'Dresden has been lucky,' she said. 'No bombs there. Yet. Go to Dresden. Be safe.'

He thanked the old lady for her help, and they walked back. He showed Lola the address. 'It's a long journey. It's going to be difficult to get there. It means getting our papers checked at every point.'

'What choice do we have?' she asked. 'We can't stay here, and we have nowhere else to go.'

'Very well, then.'

Angelika had been listening to them intently, looking from Max to Lola with the quick, hazel eyes of a young vixen. 'Take me with you!' she begged.

'We can't take you, Angelika,' Max said firmly.

'Please!' She grabbed Max's sleeve. 'Take me!'

'Where are your mother and father?'

'They died in the bombing, months ago. I have nobody here.'

'Then you must go to the Welfare.'

'I can't.' She pointed to her hair, which had been cut so short that her pale scalp was visible through it. 'The Gestapo shaved my head to show I was one of the Edelweiss Pirates. The Welfare won't help me.' She lowered her voice. 'And I'm frightened of Florentin. He makes us all work for him. He tries to get into my bed at night. One of these days he will rape me.'

Lola looked at Max pleadingly. 'Max, we can't leave her here.'

'She's not our responsibility,' Max replied.

'What will you do in Dresden?' Lola asked the girl.

'At least I'll be away from this horrible place. I have papers. Proper papers! Once my hair grows a little, I can get a job in Dresden. I won't be any trouble to you, I swear.'

Max was not so sure about that. He took Lola aside. 'With that shaved head, she'll just draw attention to us, Lola. She's a juvenile delinquent. Everywhere we go, the Gestapo will notice her.'

'We can get her a hat.'

'She's trouble.'

'I know what you are,' the girl whispered, sidling up to them.

'What do you mean?' Max demanded.

Angelika cocked her head at Lola. 'She's a Jewess. Isn't she?'

'You've got your wires crossed, kid,' Max growled.

'I know that look,' Angelika retorted. 'I know a Jew when I see one. Don't worry. I won't say anything. *If* you take me with you.'

'I could break your neck right now,' Max said grimly. 'Nobody would miss you.'

'I can help you!' Angelika said. 'I can be very useful! You'll see!'

Lola took Max's hand, and looked up at him with her large, dark eyes. 'If we leave her here, she'll end up being put on the streets by Florentin. Or hanging from a gallows. I couldn't bear that. Please, Max.'

Max had long since learned that he could deny Lola nothing when she'd set her heart on a course of action, whatever misgivings he might have. 'All right,' he sighed. 'But you keep your big mouth shut, understand?'

Angelika was jubilant. She tried to kiss Max's hand. 'Thank you, thank you!'

Florentin, however, was less pleased. 'You've got a woman,' he hissed when they informed him. 'Why do you want mine?'

'She's not your woman,' Max retorted. 'She's barely an adult.'

'Oh, that one's adult all right. You'll see. At least give me my gun.'

'So you can shoot me in the back? No chance. I'm keeping it.'

'I tried to help you,' Florentin said indignantly, 'and this is how you repay me?'

'Help us? The way you're helping those kids?'

'I put food in their bellies and a roof over their heads.'

'You're a real saint. I should put a bullet in you now,' Max said.

Florentin raised his hands, showing his missing teeth in a placatory grin. 'Okay, *Kamerad*. Keep the gun. And the girl. I have plenty more of both.'

Max was strongly tempted to carry out his threat, but they gathered Angelika's few possessions and set off once again.

Chapter 13

Their luck held at Cologne station, at least insofar as their papers went. There were so many people jostling to get in that the three of them were pushed through with only a cursory inspection of their documents. Trains from Cologne had only just started running again after the last huge raid, and people were still leaving the city in their thousands.

Inside, the station was chaotic, a sea of large groups milling from one platform to another. Much of the huge structure had been damaged by bombing, with areas of rubble cordoned off, which made the congestion worse.

There was the usual assortment of evacuees, especially long lines of bewildered children being shepherded by NSV officials, each child with its name on a placard tied round its neck on a piece of string. Many of the children were in lederhosen or short dresses, despite the freezing weather. Their legs were mottled with the cold. Lola wondered where there would be a safe place for these waifs, whose lives had been shattered through no fault of their own.

Equally pathetic, in a different way, were the lines of war-wounded soldiers being transferred from the Western Front to hospitals. Some were missing more than one limb, or had faces masked with bandages. The worst cases lay motionless on stretchers on the ground, showing no signs of life.

There was also a group of Jews, under Gestapo guard, headed for a KZ-Lager.

At first shocked by the vision, Lola couldn't take her eyes off them. They were mainly women with children. The women wore yellow stars on their coats. In addition, some official hand had painted a huge cross on each of their backs in whitewash, so there was no chance of any of them slipping away in the melee.

Where would they flee, in any case? They had the haggard faces of doomed souls, their heads wrapped in scarfs, their eyes already contemplating death. The children looked exhausted and gaunt, pinched with hunger.

Lola ached to rush forward and snatch a child, any child, just one child – and run as far as she could with the precious life in her arms. To save one life, to save one child, how overwhelmingly important that seemed!

But as though guessing her impulse, Max's strong fingers closed around her arm, pulling her away. She looked over her shoulder despairingly. The line of Jews was already being herded towards a platform, the white Xs disappearing in the crowds.

She couldn't help crying after that. Tight-faced, Max went to find tickets, leaving her with Angelika.

'That could have been you, eh?' the girl said to Lola with the callous directness of youth. Lola made no reply. Angelika shrugged. She was wearing a felt hat that they had found for her, which covered her shaved scalp, and was carrying her few possessions in a small cardboard suitcase. 'Don't cry. Just thank your lucky stars it wasn't you. I'll be back.' She wandered away among the crowds.

Lola tried to control her tears. The roar of the station rose around her, sucking her down into a dark whirlpool. She felt terribly alone. She had been uprooted so many times, had lost so much and so many, that there was almost nothing of her left. The crowds milled around her, each face tense with anxiety, each body thrusting forward urgently, each uniform or badge determining a fate.

What point had this war served? Had anybody really benefited from it? Even the men who commanded the armies from distant places – had they prospered from all this death, all this displacement and destruction?

It was hard to imagine that they had. To conquer other people's countries might bring wealth, a better standard of living for the victors; but it would soon have to be paid for in blood. Before long, everything that had been stolen was worthless, and you lost what was your own before, lost it forever.

Standing alone in this station gave Lola a vision of the vastness of the suffering, the meaninglessness. It was overwhelming. It could not be comprehended. She simply rolled in it, like a pebble tossed by breakers on a beach, one of millions of pebbles that were thrown together, jostled for a while, then were torn apart and sucked down into the waters again.

Max returned at last. 'There are no tickets to Dresden. But I managed to get three tickets to Osnabrück.'

'Osnabrück?'

'It's about a third of the way there. They said that from Osnabrück we might be able to get tickets to Dresden. We'll have to take our chances. Our train leaves at eight o'clock tonight.'

Lola nodded wearily. 'All right.'

'Where's Angelika?'

'She went off, I don't know where.'

'You have to keep an eye on her, Lola,' Max snapped.

'Don't shout at me,' Lola shot back at him, her eyes filling with tears again.

'I'm not shouting. But you're the one who insisted she came with us.'

'She's your responsibility, too.'

223

'I went to buy tickets! And I didn't want to be responsible for her. I have enough to do, looking after *you*!'

'I don't need you to look after me!' Lola's fraught emotions were surging out of control.

'Yes, you do. How would you manage without me?'

'You can go to hell, Max. I would manage just fine.'

'Don't be ridiculous.'

'I hate the way you talk to me,' she said in a trembling voice. 'I hate the way you assume you're some kind of Aryan superman, condescending to the *Untermensch*. It's men like you who have destroyed the world.'

'I'm always in the wrong, aren't I?' he said savagely.

'Yes! You are!'

'Here I am,' Angelika said gaily. She had arrived back, beaming. 'And look what I got you.' She held the bar of chocolate out to Lola.

Max was astonished. 'Where did you get that?'

'From a man.'

'What the hell do you mean, "from a man"? What man?'

Angelika's eyes sparkled. 'He wasn't paying enough attention. He was too busy reading the timetable.'

'You stole it!'

'I liberated it. Lola was crying. I thought it would cheer her up.'

Max snatched the chocolate bar out of her hand. 'This is military chocolate. You stole it from a soldier! You little rat. Do you know what would happen to you if they caught you? To Lola? To me?'

Angelika's foxy face was wary now. 'I never get caught,' she said.

'Then why did they shave your head?'

Her face closed. 'That was once.'

'What else did you steal?'

'Nothing.'

Max grabbed her chin and jerked her face up to look into her eyes. 'What else?'

Sullenly, Angelika produced a wallet. It had a swastika emblazoned on the front, and was stuffed with Reichsmarks.

Max snatched that away, too. 'My God. From the same man?'

'No. From another man.'

Max looked around quickly. 'We need to get out of here before the police come looking. Move!'

Angelika's pale, thin cheeks bore the red marks of Max's fingers, but she was smirking as they hurried away from the spot. As soon as he found a rubbish bin, Max pulled the money out and dropped the wallet into the trash.

They eventually found a corner in the waiting room where they could sit, obscured from view by a stack of broken doors. Max tried to keep his eye on Angelika, but it wasn't easy. He was certain she had managed to pillage more than a wallet and a bar of chocolate on her foray – especially when she nonchalantly produced a packet of cigarettes and lit one up. It was easy to see why Florentin had regarded her as such an asset.

The Reichsmarks she had brought in – not to mention the chocolate – were very welcome. But the risk she had taken was hair-raising. Were she to be arrested, they would all be headed to a KZ-Lager.

And Max could see the SS and Gestapo men moving through the packed station, checking papers, interrogating anyone who aroused their suspicion. Even as the Reich crumbled about their ears, the Nazi apparatus was tightening its oppressive, relentless grip. It occurred to Max that if Himmler, Goebbels and Göring hadn't allocated so many able-bodied men to the persecution of Jews and other imaginary enemies of state, Germany might have had a chance of winning this war. He prayed that none of these vampires would come over to demand their papers. Sheltered by the wreckage, their luck still seemed to be holding.

Lola, who was exhausted, fell asleep with her head on his shoulder. He turned to Angelika. 'Don't you ever do that again.' He scowled.

'I was just trying to help. I told you I would.'

'This is *not* what I had in mind. Where did you learn to steal like that?'

'We all have to survive somehow, boss. If I hadn't learned how to pick a pocket, I'd have starved.'

'And if you get caught, you'll be hanged.'

'I told you, I never get caught.' Her hazel eyes sparkled playfully. 'I stole the wallet off a Gestapo man.'

He stared at her, appalled. 'Jesus.'

'They're my favourite marks. They're so arrogant. They think nobody would dare steal from them. I saw it sticking out of his back pocket. His backside was so fat, it practically popped out into my hand.'

'You know what would happen to Lola if she was arrested?'

'I won't let you down, boss.' She was unexpectedly pretty when she smiled. 'And I only steal when I have to. I'll be a respectable citizen one day. You'll see. You'll ask me if I remember when I stole that fat Gestapo man's wallet, and I'll draw myself up and say, "How dare you?"'

When Lola woke, she was calmer.

'I'm sorry I lost my temper,' she said to him. 'Those poor women and children upset me so much.'

'I understand.' He kissed her hands. 'I'm sorry I shouted. We're all overwrought. And if I am condescending to you, scratch my face. I will try to be better to you, as I promised you under the old pear tree, long ago.'

Their train, which was due to set off at eight, did not depart until midnight. It was crowded to bursting, the air blue with cigarette smoke and the condensed breath of the passengers.

The three of them had been unable to get seats in a compartment, but managed to find a place in what had once been a First Class dining carriage. The tables and chairs had been stripped out and replaced with hard wooden benches, but odd touches of former luxury remained – walnut panelling, gilded art deco lamps, a carpet that had once been finest wool, now stained and torn. They wedged themselves in among the piles of suitcases at the end of the saloon.

Most of their fellow passengers in the overcrowded carriage were women with children. Max watched a mother change a nappy, the child's little bottom red with a rash. A woman opened a hamper and began to peel boiled eggs, another started to rant hysterically against the Allied bombers that had destroyed her home.

Two Mongolian soldiers had been sent to protect them. They added to the fug with cigarettes rolled out of newspaper, their eyes inscrutable.

The train had no sooner set off, at a very slow pace, when it stopped again. There was a long delay, and then it crept forward for another mile before stopping once again.

They were to learn that this was to be their rate of progress all night long. They tried to sleep as best they could, constantly jolted awake when the locomotive lurched forward, drifting into uneasy slumber when it stopped.

Max held Lola in his arms to shelter her from the hard suitcases all around them. Angelika smoked the whole packet of cigarettes she had stolen at Cologne. Max hoped she wouldn't try to steal a replacement from one of their fellow passengers.

The stops grew longer and longer, until there was a stop of almost an hour, during which they slept deeply. But they were torn out of their uneasy dreams by the shrilling of the alarm bell.

'Air attack!' somebody shouted.

The train jerked into movement, this time backwards. There were screams of dismay as passengers awoke, confused and frightened.

'There's a tunnel about a mile back,' someone said. 'He'll try and get us into it.'

They could hear aircraft now, not the distant drone of bombers, but the snarl of faster planes, flying low. It was still dark outside, and nothing could be seen.

The train picked up speed in its rearwards movement, jolting and swaying. Luggage slid around, thumping into the crouching passengers. Max held on tight to the women. Suddenly the world outside the train blazed into brilliant light, flooding the carriage through the slats.

'What's that?' Lola gasped.

'They've dropped a flare,' Max said. 'They can see us, now.'

They kept rattling backwards. Children were wailing, women crying out in fear.

An explosion rocked the carriage, shattering glass in the windows. The train stopped so suddenly that everything inside – adults, children and luggage – was thrown across the saloon. Dazed and bleeding, the passengers tried to disentangle themselves.

One of the Mongolian soldiers began shouting, 'Out of train! Out of train! Now! Now!'

Max had lost both Lola and Angelika in the melee. There was a mad rush for the exit, and it was impossible to find them. He was carried along in the crush of screaming women and children.

The door swung open, revealing a drop of ten feet or more to the ground outside the train. He was pushed forward and fell heavily into deep snow.

He looked up. The flare was directly over the train; it was of the multiple type that were called Christmas Trees, falling slowly in a dazzling group that lit up the virgin snow as if it were noon for a mile around. He reached up to help the women and children clamber down from the carriage.

'Hurry!' he shouted.

But it was impossible to get them down one by one. Passengers tumbled out in a panic-stricken jumble, limbs flailing, mouths screaming. Some jumped, others fell willy-nilly. Suddenly, he saw Lola appear in the doorway.

'Jump!' he yelled.

'I've lost our suitcases!' she shouted back.

'Never mind the suitcases. *Jump.*' He held out his arms and she leaped into them. He was knocked down again, but he held on to her tightly. They crawled out of the way of the others. 'Where's Angelika?' he asked.

'She was behind me. There she is!'

Angelika was now in the doorway. She had picked up somebody's baby. She sat on the edge of the step and then dropped neatly into the snow. The mother followed. Angelika gave her the child and floundered towards them. 'I'm okay,' she called.

Max could now hear the scream of an aeroplane growing louder. 'Get away from the train!' he shouted. He grabbed the girls' hands and they struggled through the snow. It was almost thigh-deep, and terribly difficult to get through.

The plane's machine guns began hammering. A storm of bullets tore into the train and the horde of passengers fleeing from it. Fountains of snow erupted around them. Human figures were cut down as if with a scythe. Max felt Angelika plucked from his hand; suddenly, she was gone. He turned to look for her, but she was nowhere to be seen. Their carriage was now blazing. The fighter was firing incendiary bullets.

It swept overhead with a shattering roar, and began to climb into the night sky. By the glare of the slowly descending flare, Max caught a glimpse of the Royal Air Force roundels on the wings. He couldn't see Angelika anywhere, but the snow was now dotted with dark bodies.

He dragged Lola onwards, panting. The air was icy-cold in their lungs, and they were both already soaked. But the fighter was preparing to return for another strafing run, and they hadn't got far enough away to be safe, yet. They threw themselves down in the snow as the fighter roared in for the kill.

This attack was longer, more accurate, and more deadly. The streams of tracer among the bullets raked the carriages, from which people were still trying to escape. By the time the plane was soaring up into the night sky, much of the train had erupted in orange flames. The fighter did not return this time. They heard the snarl of its engine receding.

Dazed and deafened, Lola and Max struggled back to the train to try to help the wounded. Most of those who had been struck by the fighter's bullets had no chance of survival. Massive holes had been torn in their bodies, broken and tossed aside.

They found Angelika, huddling in the snow, covering her cropped head. She had lost her hat. She was unharmed, but like all of them, in a state of shock.

'Everybody's dead,' she said, her teeth chattering, her eyes glazed as she stared around. 'All dead! All dead!'

They helped the injured as best they could. Many had died in the hail of bullets. Their warm blood had melted scarlet blotches in the snow, which were already starting to freeze and darken. An unknown number had been trapped in the burning carriages.

The survivors spent the best part of the day in the bleak landscape of woods and snow, huddled together, waiting for help. It was especially hard on the children. Much of the luggage in the carriages had been destroyed, or was impossible to get to, so there was little warm clothing to go around. The babies cried weakly in their mothers' arms, cheeks mottling in the icy air. Some of the injured died. A great silence settled.

The train continued to burn for some hours, some of the carriages partially derailed, its locomotive smashed beyond repair. The black smoke rose into a sky the colour of lead. They scanned the clouds fearfully for more attacks. A light snow fell, slowly blotting out the frozen, congealed pools where the dead had lain.

'Everyone around us dies,' Lola said in a thin, dry voice. 'How long can we keep on living, Max?'

'In the army we used to say, every bullet has its billet. When your number's up, you go. Not before.'

'I should have stayed in Cologne,' Angelika said, trembling. 'If I hadn't talked you into bringing me with you, I would be safe and warm in the cellar, now.'

'You can think what you like. But you did what you thought was best, kid.' Max put a hand upon her shoulder. 'It might have been worse for you if you'd stayed.'

She put her head in her hands.

Lola, too, was in shock, her movements slow and listless. The visions of death and mutilation had ripped her mind, even though her body was safe.

She saw Heidi's body again, lying among the rubble of the house in Düren. At least she had seemed at peace, not torn apart, not violated like the people around them in the snow.

She missed Heidi so terribly. Her death was unfair, a monstrous wrong. All those years fleeing, living in terror, but surviving, and then to be killed by the Allies – where was the logic in that? Where was the justice?

What had Heidi done to deserve having her life taken from her? She had been the purest, best person Lola had ever known. Self-sacrificing, protective, fundamentally good, her love had pervaded Lola's life. And now she was gone forever.

Lola thought back to all the times she had chafed under Heidi's gentle remonstrances, all the times she had been cruel when Heidi had tried to set her right. If only she could take them back! If only she'd had a chance to tell Heidi how much she loved her, how grateful she was for the years of care and nurturing.

She wept silently, rocking to and fro, lost in her grief.

Max put his arms around her, unable to say anything that would help. He recalled his own initial reactions to the violence of war, in his first months at the front. Things happened that you had only heard about before. Those first deaths were overwhelming. Later, you learned how to carry on. But it took time.

A goods train eventually slowly steamed into view. Three empty cattle trucks had been attached to the back of it, to carry them to Osnabrück. They packed into the trucks, which were furnished with nothing but straw, squeezing together in a miserable sardine tin of humanity. With a crashing jolt, the train set off.

But the train did not reach Osnabrück. In the early evening, it pulled into a siding some twenty miles short of the town. A makeshift sickbay had been set up in a tent to treat the wounded. It was already full. Other trains had been attacked that morning. One doctor and three young nurses, all in bloodstained uniforms, were struggling to cope with dozens of patients.

Those who could walk were steered into a goods shed, where a kitchen had been set up. A group of Nazi Welfare women ladled steaming soup into enamelled bowls. The soup was made from nothing more than Knorr cubes and noodles, but the frozen, starving passengers devoured it eagerly, huddling on long, wooden benches. There was a little formula milk available for the babies, and a few bowls of crumbled stale bread.

The hot liquid, and the feeling of being safe at last, started people talking, some even smiling and laughing a little as their spirits revived. Others were able to cry at last. Max made Lola take half his soup. 'We'll be in Dresden soon,' he promised her. She nodded without replying. Still in shock, she absorbed the food slowly.

He watched the contemptuous way the 'sisters' treated the refugees. How cheap life had become, he thought sadly. An elderly man, a mere shabby bundle of rags, his face seamed with wrinkles, reached out a knotty hand for a bowl of food. One of the sisters cursorily rapped him across the knuckles with the hot ladle. Human beings, especially the elderly, seemed to lose all the dignity they had in peacetime. They were treated as if they had no value to anyone, a drain on resources. In any war their lives were of little account, and at this stage of this terrible war their deaths were of none at all.

'You! Your papers!'

Jolted out of their exhausted sleep, they looked up to see that a group of SS storm troopers had arrived. One was towering over Angelika, his attention caught by her hair. Silently, she gave him her card. He inspected it. 'A juvenile delinquent, eh? On your feet. Come!'

Angelika stood up, looking very young and fragile.

'Who are you travelling with?' the storm trooper demanded.

Angelika didn't glance at Lola or Max. 'I'm on my own,' she said in a low voice.

'Outside, now. Move!' He grasped her arm and dragged her away. She didn't look back.

'What if she betrays us?' Lola whispered to Max in horror.

He shrugged grimly. 'There's nothing we can do.'

A *Hauptsturmführer* marched in, his boots thudding. His men took up positions at the exit. The men were in battledress, with steel helmets and sub-machine guns, as though ready for combat. The *Hauptsturmführer* was in an overcoat, with a peaked cap. He was middle-aged, with the expression of unassailable authority that appeared to be an SS hallmark.

Experienced at addressing large groups, he barely had to raise his voice to be heard all round the shed.

'Get on your feet, all of you. Your papers will be checked. Form two orderly lines. Women and children to the left, men to the right. Do not come forward until you are given the signal. Quickly, now.'

Max grasped Lola's hand as they got to their feet. 'Give me your identity card now,' he commanded in a low voice. White-faced, she passed it to him. He put it in his pocket. 'When they ask you for your papers, say that you gave them to me. And point me out to them. Understand?'

'Yes.'

'You are Heloise Wolff, my sister. Remember!'

'Yes.'

'If they ask you anything you can't answer, say you don't remember.'

There was no time for anything more. The storm troopers were already herding them into lines, their guns slung at the ready. Whether this was a random check, or something in particular, it was impossible to tell. Max just prayed that Lola would keep her nerve.

Lola was feeling numbed. The sight of SS uniforms had always filled her with terror. The day had been a dreadful one. Angelika's arrest was yet another violent shock. What if she gave them away to the SS? Now, yet again, their lives hung in the balance.

She shuffled forwards in the queue, her heart thudding heavily. Perhaps this was the end of the chase, at last. Perhaps it was best to just stop running, stop trying to stay alive, and let the vast monster of the state devour her. Then there would be no more pain, no more fear, no more weariness. She would be wherever Heidi had gone. With Mama and Papa, and all the rest who had gone before.

As if in a nightmare, she found herself standing in front of the SS officer. His face was clean-shaven, calm. His eyes were grey.

'Your papers, Fräulein.'

'I don't have them,' she heard her own voice say.

'Why not?'

'I gave them to my brother to keep safe.'

'Where is your brother?'

Lola turned and pointed to Max. 'He's over there.'

The SS officer beckoned to Max. 'This is your sister?'

'Yes, Herr *Hauptsturmführer*.'

'Both of your papers, please.' Max handed the cards over. The *Hauptsturmführer* flipped them open and examined them. He glanced up at Max with pale-grey eyes. 'You were discharged from the *Panzerkorps*?'

'Yes, *Hauptsturmführer*.'

'What was the precise nature of your wounds?'

'A fractured skull and lung damage.'

'You appear fit to me. You should be in the *Volkssturm*.'

'I am waiting for my call-up.'

The *Hauptsturmführer* held up Lola's card. 'This is a temporary document. Why is this?'

'The original was destroyed in the bombing of Düren. We're waiting for the new document to be issued.'

He continued to look at Max for a long time. Then he passed the papers to his adjutant. 'Checks will have to be made before you can proceed. You will remain with us until they are completed.'

'Why?' Max heard Lola ask in a sharp voice.

The *Hauptsturmführer* turned his gaze on her. 'Why what, Fräulein?'

'Why should checks have to be made?'

'To ensure that you are who you say you are. Move on, please.'

Lola held her ground. 'That may take days. Weeks. You are unnecessarily delaying us. We have to get to Dresden to take care of our uncle.' Her voice grew stronger. 'You don't need to check who my brother is. He is the holder of two Iron Crosses, like yourself. For that alone, he deserves to be treated with respect!'

'Lola—' Max said with trepidation.

'We have lost our mother and our sister in the bombing of Düren,' Lola went on, ignoring Max. 'We had to bury them ourselves, with the assistance of my brother's old war comrade, *Sturmbannführer* Peiper. We have lost our home, and everything in it. Today, we were bombed in our own country by the English. They killed our friends, and destroyed the last few possessions we managed to salvage. We have lost our family, everything we hold dear. We should not be subjected to any more! Have you no humanity?'

Her voice rang around the shed. There was a tense silence.

The *Hauptsturmführer* kept his eyes on her for some time. His face did not change in the slightest. Then he turned to his adjutant. 'Give them their papers back,' he said in his flat voice. 'You may go. Next, please.'

Max was shaking as they left the shed. 'Lola,' he muttered, 'you nearly gave me a heart attack, but you were magnificent!'

'I've had enough of these people, Max,' she replied tightly. 'I learned something with that official in Münster: the louder you yell, the more Nazis respect you. It's when you keep quiet that they trample you under their boots. I'll never be quiet again, I promise you that. If I have to die, I will die yelling.'

Outside the shed, they saw a wretched-looking group of people who had been detained by the SS, and were now being herded into

236

a truck. Among them was Angelika. She turned and looked over her shoulder at them for a moment. Her face was tense, white. Then she looked away. A moment later, she disappeared into the back of the truck.

'Is she going to talk?' Lola whispered.

'I don't know,' Max replied. 'It's up to her. But the sooner we get away from here, the better.'

'What will they do to her?'

Max just shook his head.

Chapter 14

Their onward journey was slow and painful. They had to take several trains, changing every few stops at times, sometimes making detours that were far out of their way, in order to connect with trains that were still running, or lines that were still open.

And everywhere they went, they found destruction. The towns and cities of the Rhineland lay in ruins, without shelter, water or power.

Osnabrück had been bombed.

Bielefeld, where they had to spend four nights, sleeping in a crowded air-raid shelter with other homeless people, had been bombed.

Hanover had been bombed to the extent that much of the city was no more than rubble. They were stuck here for another three days, sleeping in a basement near the station while they waited for tickets on trains that were jammed with soldiers, refugees, prisoners and forced labourers.

Max had managed to keep his army paybook. He was now drawing his *Wehrmacht* pension whenever they found a bank, and money was getting tight. They were also running short of food coupons, and would have to get another month's supply somehow. Although he had now lost both of his Iron Crosses, he still had the ribbon, which he wore on his coat. It served to get them a little extra consideration from time to time.

They ate in restaurants that were crowded with displaced persons like themselves, serving basic dishes at low prices. At least in these cities one could sometimes get potatoes without coupons. But Lola hated being in a restaurant, surrounded by people talking, listening, watching. She always felt afraid.

'You're an Aryan now,' Max said, trying to reassure her. 'Nobody will question you.'

'You don't know how it feels,' she replied. 'For a Jew to eat in a restaurant is punishable by death. So is travelling on a train. I keep feeling that someone is going to point a finger at me and shout, "She's a Jew! Arrest her!"'

'That will not happen,' he said firmly.

But she could not shake off so many years of fear easily. She was always glad when they had eaten, and were pushing their way out into the street.

Max called the telephone number he'd been given for his uncle at least once a day, whenever they found a telephone booth that worked. There was never any reply. As they travelled slowly eastward, they passed shattered railway stations, shattered towns, farmhouses, villages, even open fields that had been cratered. It was a picture of almost universal devastation.

Lola felt her heart wrenched by the destruction she saw. She had suffered much over the past ten years. Her family had been exterminated. She had lost the precious years of her girlhood to a crushing and overwhelming sense of fear. But she could not help but grieve to see the destruction of beautiful German cities and the degradation of German life.

Lola tried to explain her feelings to Max. 'I remember one day, when Mama and Papa were selling the house, a singer they worked with came round and offered to buy Mama's grand piano. It was a beautiful old Steinway, in rosewood. But Mama was so relieved, because it would bring in some extra money when we were desperate. Then we heard what she was offering – a pittance. When Mama protested, she replied, "Take it or leave it." She was a wealthy woman who had dined with us, visited us a dozen times. Mama looked at her and said, "I thought you were my friend." And do you know what she replied? "I am a German. I have never counted any Jews among my friends."'

'I'm so sorry, Lola,' Max said gently.

'You know what we felt? Not anger. Terror. We realised that we had no friends at all.' Lola stared out of the window of yet another train at the snow-covered hills. 'Nobody ever lifted a hand to help us. None of our neighbours tried to defend us. The people we knew just stood by and let it happen.' She grimaced in disgust. 'And so many were glad to have the excuse to spit on us. I've had no reason to love the German people, Max. I've prayed for the Allies to win the war.'

'I understand.'

She turned a sad face to him. 'But I am still a German, my dear. God help me, I'm still Lola Rosenstein from Berlin, and it breaks my heart to see the misery of Germans now.'

He put his hand on hers. 'One day I hope you can forgive me for my stupidity.'

'I don't think we Jews ever knew what we were. We wanted so badly to belong, but they wouldn't let us. I still don't know how I could rip the German out of me – any more than I could rip out the Jew.'

'I'll go where you want, Lola. If you'll have me. If you want to leave, I will leave with you. If you want to stay, and rebuild Germany once this is all over, then I'll rebuild with you.'

Her eyes were moist. 'That's a beautiful thing to say, Max.'

'I had my chance at building a Germany. You see how that turned out. Now we have to atone, and build a different kind of Germany.'

They finally came to Dresden. A glittering city on the River Elbe, it had been spared the thousand-bomber raids that had levelled other German centres, perhaps because Berlin, to the north, was a more important target.

Decked in snow, punctuated by the domes and spires of churches and palaces spanning the river with bridges, it seemed enchanted by its own baroque splendour as they arrived one December morning. They were worn out and cold. They trudged out of the grand station and into an icy wind. They still needed to get to Unterstein, the tiny village where Anselm and Ditte had a retreat. According to Max's map, it was deep in the countryside.

Enquiring with people in the square outside the station, they learned that getting there would be difficult. There were no buses going that way and no railway line.

'But they collect timber from the forest around Unterstein,' a man told them. 'If you go to the sawmill, you might be able to get a lift on one of the trucks.'

It was a long, cold walk to the sawmill, which was on the out-skirts of Dresden. But when they reached it, it seemed their luck had at last improved. The foreman told them that he had a truck going to the area the next day, and even offered them a place in the shelter of the mill that night. Several of his workers came from outlying districts, and at night they slept around the huge iron stove which was fed with offcuts from the timber.

The men shared their food with Max and Lola. They were for the most part Saxons, large, blond and pale-eyed. Despite the priva-tions they had suffered, they were kindly. In their soft accents, they told Max and Lola about the raids that had destroyed their homes.

'There are only bomb shelters for the Nazis,' the foreman said. 'The rest of us have to hide our heads where we can. And it's the same for the dead. When Gestapo or SS are killed, they come here wanting planks to build coffins for them. Everybody else is put in a paper sack, like garbage.'

Other than that, they did not complain about the war, or even discuss it much; instead, the conversation was about mundane things – football, the weather, their work. There was no hint of the imminent collapse of the Reich from these men.

Max and Lola were given a place close to the warmth of the stove, on a mattress stuffed with wood shavings. The large, open space of the mill, with its huge saws and piles of cut logs, was very different from the densely packed shelters where they had slept for the past week. The scent of freshly cut pine was all around them. Max had a sense of having left behind the darkness and horror of the war. Perhaps they had found peace at last.

Lola curled up in his arms, and he buried his face in her hair. Her scent had become part of his existence. He could no longer do without it, or her.

The truck set off early the next morning. As luck would have it, the driver, Horst, was a Nazi who boasted that he had joined the Party in 1931, 'not when it got fashionable, like all these others, but while we were still battling Bolsheviks in the street. I've got a low Party number, me. Nobody can take that away.'

As they rattled through the snow that had begun to fall, he favoured them with his analysis of the war. 'It was all the fault of the Jews from start to finish. Hitler saw it coming in the twenties. That's his genius. The Jews are our eternal enemy. Hitler understood this. Nobody would listen to him then, and now look where we are. If we'd liquidated them all when he warned us, we'd have peace and prosperity now, instead of war.'

There was much more of this, together with imprecations against 'the Jew Roosevelt and his Jew wife', repetitions of 'the Jews are our misfortune', and declarations that the final victory was certain, through the 'new secret wonder weapons' that the Führer was about to unleash on the enemy.

Max and Lola listened in silence. Much of it was recognisably the phraseology of Dr Goebbels' broadcasts and newspaper articles. It was puzzling to Max that anyone could still have faith in any of these wearisomely repeated ideas, given the catastrophic defeats of the past three years, and the vastness of the forces arrayed against Germany now. Had people like Horst lost the ability to recognise a monstrous lie? Or did they truly believe in the impossible?

'So what if we've lost all those territories we conquered?' Horst said cheerfully. 'We don't need them. And anyway, less territory to rule means less mouths to feed – and we can concentrate on building better weapons!'

The Elbe Valley through which they drove was a succession of rolling, wooded hills, with vistas of the winding river from time to time. On the far side of the river, the Elbe Mountains rose jagged and golden, marking the Czech border. Once again, Max had the feeling of having left the war behind. It was a relief to be away from the shattered industrial cities of the Ruhr, and to glide through this unsullied, snowy countryside – even with Horst pounding his steering wheel and spouting Nazi propaganda.

They reached Unterstein to find a picture-postcard village with a fortified church and a few streets of timbered houses. The sandstone outcrop that gave the place its name hung over the town, carved into fantastical towers and pillars by the millennia. Horst dropped them on the outskirts – his truck was too large to go through the narrow centre – and they walked into the church square.

'This is like a dream,' Lola murmured, looking around. The calm silence of the village was indeed almost surreal. Max realised that this was the first place they had been in weeks where there were no signs of war: no roofless houses, no stink of corpses and sewage from piles of rubble, no haze of burning in the air. Just the snow that drifted down on immemorial Saxon tranquillity.

There were three or four shops in the main street, including – almost incredibly – a bakery that was open and selling hot bread. They went in and bought a loaf with one of their last coupons.

'*Doktor* Wolff's nephew from Westphalia? The *Panzersoldat*? You are welcome in Unterstein,' the woman behind the counter said, when they made enquiries. 'Yes, their place is half an hour's walk from here. But I don't think there's anyone there. Let me ask my man.' She went into the back to speak to her husband, who was up to his armpits in the wooden dough bin. Their *Obersächsisch* accent, clogged as it was, was hard for Max and Lola to follow. She returned, shaking her head. 'The Herr *Doktor* sent word to say he was coming from Cologne, after the bombing. But we never heard if they arrived or not. They haven't come into the shop, and they usually come every three days to buy bread when they are staying here. You must go there and see for yourselves.'

They followed the directions they had been given, along the banks of the Elbe. The path to the house lay through the woods. The snow was smooth and virgin; no footprints were to be seen. Nobody had passed this way for days. And the woods themselves were silent, almost monochrome, black trunks and leafless branches austere against the white ground. A few birds flitted around the trees, but without making a sound. There was a breathless hush over the winter landscape.

Snow kept drifting down in the still air. There was hardly any wind to blow it, and it settled delicately, but with authority, on everything.

Frau Schubert, the baker's wife, had said it was half an hour's walk, but it seemed longer because it was all uphill, towards the mountain. They were hungry, and tore off pieces of the warm bread to devour as they walked. Max was rehearsing in his mind what he would say to his uncle. He would need to explain a great deal – about himself, about his mother – when they met.

It was going to be an imposition to arrive like this, with no warm clothes, no warning, and bringing danger with them. But he trusted in Anselm and Ditte's good nature to welcome them.

The house came into view through the trees. It was a woods-man's or hunter's lodge, part brick, part wood, apparently at least a century old, built close to the sandstone bluffs. There was no smoke from any of the chimneys. The snow lay on the roof in a thick layer, not melted in any part.

'There's nobody here,' Lola said.

They walked round the house, knocking on the doors and windows, looking for signs of life. There were none. Only silence. The snow everywhere was unsullied by footprints. The wooden shutters were all closed. Max was dismayed. The baker had been right. Anselm and his wife had never arrived from Cologne. Who knew what had happened to them on the journey to Unterstein? Lola began hunting under flowerpots, and within a few minutes held up what she had found: a large, heavy, brass key.

They unlocked the front door. The lodge showed no signs of having been inhabited for months. It was icy-cold inside, and they were frozen after their walk through the snow.

'What are we going to do?' Lola asked.

'We're here now,' Max said. 'It's pointless to keep wandering. We'll wait for them to arrive.'

'But where are they? And what if they don't arrive?'

'Then at least we're safe and sheltered for the time being.'

'Maybe our luck has changed at last.'

He put his arms around her and held her close. 'I hope so, my beloved.'

They explored the house. There were two bedrooms, each with a carved wooden double bed and a ceramic-tiled stove. The kitchen was primitive, but off it was a pantry that was stocked with basic provisions of various kinds – bottles, jars of preserves, sacks of rice, beans and flour.

An old, double-barrelled shotgun hung on the kitchen wall. Max took it down and broke it open. The barrels were rusty, but it seemed to be in decent condition, and there were a handful of shells in a drawer. After having lost Florentin's pistol, he felt better for being armed again.

There was a telephone, but when he picked it up, there was no line. Even if there had been someone here, the thing was useless.

The black, iron kitchen range surely dated to the construction of the house sometime in the nineteenth century, and had a multitude of doors and hatches which were difficult to work out. But they finally got the wood burning in it, and a slow warmth began to pervade the chill of the house. When the plates were hot enough, they made soup.

They chose a bedroom each, and found bed linen in a wardrobe, which they draped over chairs in front of the range to air.

'We're like those children from the Brothers Grimm,' Lola said. 'Hänsel and Gretel.'

'I hope not. Didn't they get eaten by a witch?'

'No, they pushed the witch into the fire and ran off with her treasure.'

'Are you sure about that?'

'Quite sure. Didn't your mother read you the Brothers Grimm when you were a boy?'

Max shook his head. 'My father regarded fairy tales as pagan. I was only allowed to read Bible stories.'

'Poor, deprived child. Never mind, I'll tell you them all. We'll start with Hänsel and Gretel.'

There was no electricity in the lodge, only paraffin lamps for lighting. They sat together by the warm, yellow light, talking quietly, until their eyelids were heavy, and then made their beds with the warmed quilts.

Max kissed Lola chastely goodnight, and they went to their respective bedrooms. Max lay in the darkness, listening to the silence. It was the first night for a long time that he had felt at peace, and free of fear. It was also the first night that they had not slept side by side, albeit fully clothed, and in a room full of strangers. He thought of Lola's sparkling black eyes and full lips, and yearned for her.

He was almost asleep when he heard Lola call his name from the other room.

He got up and padded across the icy corridor to her bedside. 'What is it?'

'I'm cold. Get in with me.'

He got into her bed and took her in his arms. Her body was supple against his, melting against him so there wasn't an inch separating them. 'There,' he whispered. 'You'll soon warm up.'

'I wasn't really cold,' she murmured after a while. 'I was just lonely.'

He kissed her brow, his heart singing. 'I'm here.'

'We can live here together,' Lola said dreamily. 'Until the war ends.'

'Until the war ends,' he replied.

Within a few minutes, she was fast asleep.

Chapter 15

It had snowed heavily in the night. The world outside the lodge was white; all traces of their footsteps had been obliterated. The silence of the place enveloped them. The past weeks had been filled with hideous noise – of war, of machines, of humanity. Coming into the forest was like sinking into a deep well of stillness.

They talked quietly about Magda and Heidi after they'd breakfasted, sitting on chairs close by the range. Grief, which had been crushed into a hard, tight ball by the necessity to survive after the catastrophes, now began to expand like a plant, producing dark leaves and sad blossoms. There was time to look back and reflect on two lives cut short.

'While I was listening to that truck driver yesterday,' Lola said, 'I thought I would be furious, and start hating him. But I didn't. I ended up feeling sorry for him. I pitied him for having such an empty life that he needed hate to give himself meaning. If he'd ever known someone like Heidi, he would have been a different man.'

'We had some like that in the *Wehrmacht*. They needed National Socialism to have a reason to live. They couldn't see the good in anything. They just needed someone to blame for everything that was wrong inside them.'

'I miss Heidi terribly. Do you miss your mother?'

'Yes,' Max replied. 'The day she died, I realised I'd never really known her. I understood so little about her. I was cruel to her, and I regret that very bitterly. I wish I could speak to her now, and tell her how sorry I am. But I can't.'

'I know she understood, Max,' Lola said gently. 'It happened to thousands of families. A whole generation. Hitler is like the Pied Piper of Hamelin. The only children who didn't follow him into the darkness were the lame, the deaf and the blind. And of course, the Jews. Shall I tell you a secret?'

'Please do.'

'I longed to be a Nazi when I was a girl.'

'You!'

'Yes. I was very young, of course. But it was so exciting – the flags, the marching, the rallies, the torchlight processions. Even the speeches, though I didn't understand what they were talking about. I wanted to be part of it. I felt proud to be a German. I was very upset when Heidi laughed at me and told me Jews couldn't belong. After that, I kept hoping Hitler would change his mind about the Jews. I used to dream that one day he'd decide he'd been wrong, and that we were good people after all.' She smiled ruefully at Max. 'I had a special fantasy: I would run up to Hitler at some parade, and present him with a bunch of flowers that I'd picked from the garden. And he would bend down and beam at me, and announce that he forgave us for whatever we'd done that was so bad. And then there would be no more persecution, and we could now belong.'

'Oh, Lola.'

'I was all of ten years old. Silly, I know. I soon developed a different outlook on the Nazi Party. Why are you looking at me like that?'

Max just shook his head.

'Tell me!'

'Well, if you want to know the truth, I'm trying to see what you will look like when you're fifty.'

She drew herself up. 'You wretch! Are you so eager for me to grow old?'

'No, but I want to grow old with you. So I'm trying to see what I'm in for.'

She turned to him, full face. 'And how will I be when I'm fifty?'

'Dazzling,' he replied simply. 'Just as you are now.'

'No grey hair or double chin?'

'Those will only make you more desirable.'

'So you admit there will be grey hair and a double chin! How dare you wish such misfortunes on me!'

'They aren't misfortunes. They are the enhancements of time.'

'You may find your own face scratched if you insist on prematurely ageing me.'

'Please don't scratch my face. I'm prepared to wait for the enhancements.'

Lola smiled wryly. 'How long has it been since we teased each other like this?'

'Too long,' he replied.

Since losing their luggage on the train, they were desperately short of warm clothes. Searching the wardrobes revealed a treasure trove of country wear – heavy coats, boots and hats. Suitably dressed, they went out for a walk in the woods.

Lola took a child's delight in the fresh snow, running on ahead of Max, ducking under the laden branches of the trees. The coat she had put on was patterned in red-and-black checks. Against the white of the snow she was a vivid figure, glowing with colour and movement.

This is what she does to my life, Max thought. *She gives all the wilderness meaning.*

Lola turned, her teeth flashing in a grin, and threw a snowball at him. It hit him on the heart. He chased after her. She bounded through the snow like a deer, her laughter echoing among the life-less trees. Finally, she stumbled in a deep drift, and he caught her. He held her tight in his arms, looking down into her merry face.

'Don't you know that snowballs are dangerous?' he said.

She stuck her tongue out. 'Nonsense!'

'I got my first wound from a snowball, in Russia.'

'You tell such stories!'

'It's true. We stopped in a field to read our maps and wait for the rest of our division to catch up with us. It all still seemed almost a game to us. We'd conquered such huge stretches of terri-tory. We were in high spirits, and the snow was so fresh and clean. We thought the enemy was miles away. So we got out of the panzers and started to throw snowballs.' He smiled. 'We were all just boys.'

'And then?'

'A Russian dive bomber came out of nowhere. He strafed us and launched a bomb. He must have been worried about the Messerschmitt fighters, because he flew off. We were lucky. Nobody was killed, but we had several injuries. My arm was broken in two places.'

She stared into his eyes for a while. Then, unexpectedly, she reached up and put her arm around his neck, pulling his mouth down on hers.

She'd never kissed him like this before, so hard, so demanding. Her tongue, warm and wet, probed his. He felt an electric shock jolt through his body. Their kisses had been like those of children up until now. This was something very different.

'Lola,' he whispered, his eyes widening.

'Don't talk. Kiss me.'

He could taste a fleck of blood as her sharp teeth crushed his lip. His head was spinning. He was gasping for breath when she finally released him.

'What was that for?' he whispered.

Her eyes were dark. 'I thought of all the times you could have been killed, and I would never have known you.'

'I have the same thoughts about you.'

'Do you really find me desirable?'

'What?' he stammered.

'You said grey hair and a double chin would make me even more desirable. Do you really desire me now?'

'Lola! You know that I do.'

She tilted her head to one side, her cheeks flushed pink. Her gaze was very direct. 'How does it feel, this desire of yours?'

He was even more taken aback. 'It feels like – I can't describe it.'

'Try.'

'It feels like standing in a river, and dying of thirst.' He laughed, a little embarrassed at his own words, but she was serious.

'You never show it to me.'

'I try to be affectionate.'

'Affection is one thing, Max. Desire is another. You hide your desire. You treat me like something that could break in your hands.'

'With all that has happened—'

'If I haven't broken yet, with all that has happened, why should I break because you show me you want me?'

Max was nonplussed. 'I know that you're a virgin—'

'Do you indeed! And how do you know that, pray?'

'Well, I assumed.'

'I see. You assumed. And you, of course, are so experienced!'

'I wouldn't say that,' he replied uneasily. She was in a very strange mood today.

'What *would* you say? Didn't you romp on the lake shore with the blonde when you were seventeen? The one with bosoms like a Valkyrie?'

'It was hardly romping. And she didn't have bosoms like a Valkyrie.'

252

'All true Aryan women have bosoms like Valkyries. The Party demands it. They must be able to produce at least a litre of milk from each one, daily. Did you go all the way?'

'No.'

'But you must have gone all the way with *somebody*.'

He searched for diplomatic phrases. 'There are always women, you know, when one is in the army.'

Lola folded her arms. 'Ready to throw themselves at your feet?'

'Hardly. One has to pay.'

'Oh, how shocking.' But her eyes sparkled. 'And what are they like, these women a soldier has to pay for?'

'I leave that to your imagination.'

'But I can't possibly imagine. As you say, I am a virgin, innocent as this driven snow all around us. You will have to explain. In detail, please.'

He felt himself flush. 'Well they're generally not very refined.'

'How ungallant you are!'

'It's not romantic. It's more of a – a business transaction.'

'Like having your boots polished?'

'I suppose so.'

She took his arm and they walked on through the snow. 'Well? Tell me everything.'

'Everything?'

'Yes! How do you begin?'

'Well, generally by asking the price.'

'Heavens! Don't tell me you're so unchivalrous as to haggle over the money!'

'It's usually a case of take it or leave it.'

'Ah. Like Mama's grand piano. And once you have decided to *take it*?'

'Well, then she leads you to her – to her – place of business.'

'Her bed?'

'If she has one.'

'And next?' Lola demanded. 'Do you kiss her?'

'Oh, no.'

'Why "oh no"?'

'Well—' He cleared his throat. 'You don't know who else she has kissed with that mouth.'

Lola burst out laughing. 'How squeamish! What about the rest of her body? What about her more intimate regions? Doesn't that worry you?'

'One takes precautions.'

'You mean—'

'I mean one wears protection. And in any case, it's different,' Max replied.

'In what way, different?'

'One only kisses a woman one loves.'

Lola snorted. 'But you can stick your *Schwanz* into a woman you despise?'

This time he was really taken aback. 'Lola!'

'Max!' she echoed. 'Have you never heard the word before?'

'Not from your lips.'

'I can say plenty more rude words.'

'Please don't,' he begged.

She was amused at his dismay. 'I wonder whether I'm really as virginal as you want to think I am. But pray continue my education. We had reached the part where you have retired to her bed, but you refuse steadfastly to kiss her, like the Aryan knight you are. What happens next? Do you just climb on top of her?'

'I refuse to discuss this any further,' Max retorted, half laughing, half angry.

'But I insist. And I will make your life a misery if you don't tell me every single detail. What happens next?'

He shrugged. 'You give her the money.'

'Before you've had your satisfaction?'

'Yes.'

'Isn't that rather risky?'

'They always insist.'

'Do they, indeed! So she takes your money. And now? Do you climb on top of her?'

'Or she climbs on top of you.'

Lola's eyes widened, and then grew speculative. 'How interesting. I never thought of that. Which do you prefer?'

'Depends on how drunk you are.'

'I am learning a lot,' she said dryly. 'And what does it feel like?'

'What does what feel like?'

'When you go inside her.'

'Like scratching an itch.'

'Not a paroxysm of delight?'

'*Certainly* not that.'

'And for them? Do they take any pleasure from it?'

'I very much doubt it,' he replied gravely. 'Although they usually pretend.'

'How do they pretend?'

'By making a lot of noise.'

'What sort of noise?'

'Moaning and – and so forth.'

'And they call you sweetheart, and treasure, and tell you how wonderful you are?'

He kicked moodily at the snow. 'I suppose so.'

'And do they wriggle around a lot? Or lie still, like dolls? Do they look up adoringly? Or do they close their eyes?'

'That really is enough,' Max said firmly. 'I refuse to say another word.'

'How am I supposed to learn, if you won't tell me?' Lola demanded.

'Why on earth do you want to learn about prostitutes?' he asked in exasperation.

'I'm not remotely interested in prostitutes,' she retorted. 'I'm interested in *you*. When the time comes, I don't want to disappoint you.'

'Oh, Lola!' He stopped dead, turning to her. 'How could you think you would disappoint me?'

'Because I'm so ignorant,' she said simply. 'I have absolutely no idea what's required.'

'Neither do I, come to that!'

'But you've been with all these soldiers' women.'

'A bare handful. And I was always drunk, and dragged along by comrades. Otherwise I would never have done it, I promise you. Darling Lola, going to a prostitute can't be anything like truly making love.'

'Well, I'm glad you have at least some experience, my dear. Because I wouldn't know where to start.'

'You are a very strange young lady,' he sighed. But his heart was beating fast.

'Look,' she breathed.

Max followed her gaze. Fifty yards away, through the trees, a stag was standing in the snow, staring at them. His powerful neck was erect, his spiked antlers arching upwards like a crown. He watched them for a minute or two, as they held their breath, and then turned and stalked away, lifting his slender legs high out of the snow. He was soon lost to sight.

Lola was exhilarated. 'What a magnificent creature! What was it?'

'A red deer. He had twelve points on his antlers, so he was a royal stag, about ten years old.'

'It's a sign,' she said.

Max didn't ask her what she meant. Hand in hand, they walked back to the lodge.

They spent the next days settling in. The house had been unused for a long time, perhaps a year or more. It was dusty and cobwebby, and Lola set them to work cleaning and dusting in every corner.

The cold was piercing. As they worked, their breath condensed on the glass panes of the windows, and then froze into lacy patterns. There was a stone fireplace in the main room of the house; and behind the house they found a shed that contained coal, firewood and various implements. They built a fire using fuel they gathered from there. The chimney was cold, and smoked at first, but after the first couple of days there was a constant, comforting glow, which brought the dark interior to life.

By mid-afternoon each day, the winter sun was already setting, but their new home looked and felt welcoming. When it grew dark, they lit an oil lamp and sat by the fire. The quiet of the house was so commanding that they instinctively spoke in hushed voices, as though not wanting to disturb it.

'What do you think has happened to Anselm and Ditte?' Lola asked.

'I don't know – but you saw what happened to our train. They may both be dead.'

'They were very kind to me and Heidi. We'd have been caught and sent to a camp if they hadn't helped us. What makes people risk their lives for strangers?'

'I don't know. But I'm ashamed of the way I treated you at first.'

Lola smiled. 'You should have seen your face. If you'd found a pair of crocodiles in your house, you couldn't have been more horrified.'

'Forgive me, Lola.'

'There's nothing to forgive. You were thinking of your mother's safety. I would have been the same.'

'Well I didn't know that I was going to—'

'Going to what?' she asked, as he stopped himself.

'Going to feel the way I do about you. You seemed so angry with me in Düren. As though you hated me.'

'Oh, Max! How could I ever hate you? I just hated the life I had to live. You were keeping me alive – but I came to think of you as my jailer. I know it was unreasonable of me. I just couldn't get my thoughts straight.'

'I should have understood you better.'

'What happened then was too terrible.' Lola covered her eyes. 'I wished I had died with Heidi and Magda.'

'Don't say that.' Max held her in his arms. They stayed like that in silence for a long while.

At last she spoke. 'We'll make love tonight.'

Max could smell the peppery scent of her hair, the faint, sweet smell of her skin. 'We're not married, yet.'

Lola raised her head. '*Married?* Max, we could be killed tomorrow. We can't wait to be married. Don't you want me?'

'I want you more than anything in the world, Lola. I want you to be mine forever. The thought of losing you is what terrifies me. More than the thought of losing my own life. I've learned something – grief isn't the most painful of all emotions. Love is.'

In the golden light of the oil lamp, her eyes were unfathomable. 'Do you really love me so much?'

'Yes. So much.'

'You should know something, Max. I don't know what love is. Any more than I know what sex is. I was sixteen when the war broke out. I've spent the last few years locked away in attics and cellars. All I know about people is what I've read in hundred-year-old books. You're the only man who's ever kissed me. The only man

I've ever been close to as an adult. I don't know whether what I feel for you is really love . . . or something I'm imagining.'

Max took her hands. 'Lola—'

'Let me finish. When this war is over, and if we both survive, my life will just be beginning. A normal life, I mean. I can't promise you that I won't fly away. Heidi always said that I was a wild bird. I don't want to wound you. But I fear that I shall. And you've been so good to me. You've saved my life. I want to give you something, in case later I can't give you anything at all. And this—' She raised his hand and put it on her breast. '—this is all I have to give.'

They went to the bigger of the two bedrooms, and for the first time, took all their clothes off before getting into bed together. He had never seen her naked. In the dim light, her skin was luminous, her curves unexpectedly voluptuous. He kissed the swell of her breasts and laid his cheek on the dark triangle between her thighs.

'The first time I saw you,' he said, 'you seemed to me like a dried leaf, blown into my life by a chance wind. Now you are a blossoming tree, full of scent and life.' He smiled. 'You've changed so much. You've changed me forever. I have loved you for a long time, Lola.'

'And I've loved you,' she whispered.

'If I ever have to let you go, it will break my heart. But I will let you go freely.'

Her fingers wove through his hair. 'What I am, I give to you now. I give it to you freely.'

Max was trembling as he took her in his arms. Her body was warm, her mouth soft. In its depths lay a sweetness that pierced him. He received her kiss with his soul, even if it was the last he would have from her.

Chapter 16

Love had made their house in the woods a magical kingdom. They had no electricity and no radio, and their shopping trips to Unterstein, which involved a half hour's walk each way, were few and far between. The war had left them behind. A week had passed in the blink of an eye, and then another, and another. Their first Christmas together came and went, and then the first weeks of the new year, which would surely be the last year of the war.

Max hardly knew how happy he was. Nothing before in his life could have prepared him for such joy. Whatever the future held for them, Lola gave herself to him now with all the treasures of her soul. She was his tree of life, replete with fruits and flowers. They were consecrated to one another.

She dazzled him in every way, with every word and gesture. Her mind was finer than his, more supple, richer in treasures that she had gathered by reading and listening and learning. Her vision captivated him. He learned to see the world through her eyes, not his own.

The weather was bad – bad for the rest of the world, with heavy snowfalls and icy rain – but perfect for lovers. The white drifts that built up around the lodge were insulation against the horrors and realities of a world that existed far away. Inside, they built fires and made love.

Making love was thrilling, divine. It was all-consuming, a new religion.

After the first few times, which had been strange, uncomfortable, even painful, each night became a new erotic adventure. On some nights, he led the way; on some nights, she did. On the best nights, they seemed to climb a mountain summit together, and reached a high, sublime peak that was above everything else.

She would lie in Max's arms, sated and exhausted, and already be thinking about next time, about new vistas to explore.

And each everyday ritual, no matter how humble it had been before, now became a ceremony in this new cult of love. Washing her hair was a rite of preparation, to be desired by Max. Cooking a simple meal was a holy offering. Making their bed, where the central mystery took place, was strewing a sacred glade with flowers. Lighting a fire in the ceramic-tiled stove in their bedroom was a preparation for the night to come.

Lola had discovered a new dimension to herself, one which she'd only had glimpses of before in her life. This new dimension grew more important daily, as she learned how intrinsic it was to her being. Without it, she had been incomplete. Whole areas of understanding had been shut off to her. Now they opened, one by one, doors leading to rich new chambers.

There was an inner voice whispering to her that the snow cloistering and protecting their lodge was a kind of wall. It reminded her that, even now, her only adult experiences of the outside world had been brief forays into unimaginable violence; and that, even now, she was still a prisoner. She had not yet known what it was to be free.

But for the time being, she accepted her imprisonment with joy.

One night in mid-February, as they lay half asleep and drugged with lovemaking, they became aware of a dull tremor that seemed to rise out of the floor.

'Is there somebody in the house?' Lola whispered to Max.

'Wait here.' Max arose and took the old shotgun off its place on the wall. He put two shells in the breech and prowled around the lodge; but there was no sign of anyone having broken in. He could feel the deep vibration under his feet, a continuous murmur, like a distant earthquake. The sound must be coming from outside.

He opened the door and went out. The weather had been harsh that week, but tonight the sky was clearing. It was very cold, his breath clouding around his face.

Baffled as to the source of the noise, he walked round the house, holding the shotgun at the ready. At the back of the house, facing to the north, he saw a dull, red glow in the sky. At first, he could not account for it. Then he saw dim flickering, and his heart sank. The sound was one that he had almost forgotten, but it was deeply familiar to him.

Lola had followed him out, and joined him now. 'What is it?' she asked, staring at the ominous glare on the horizon.

'Dresden,' he said tersely. 'They're bombing the city.'

They stood together, staring into the night. The concussions had turned into a constant tremor; and now, when the wind blew towards them, they caught the faint drone of the bombers in the sky, like the industrious hum of a hive of bees.

'How can we possibly hear it from here?' Lola asked.

'It's a huge raid,' Max replied. 'Hundreds of planes.'

Despite the bitter cold they remained there, transfixed by the distant tragedy. Thousands of lives were being lost, the patient craftsmanship of centuries was being destroyed. After a few minutes the thudding stopped, and the drone of the bombers faded into silence. Only the red glow was left in the night.

As they watched, the colour of the glow intensified, changing from red to orange, and finally to a glaring yellow that rose in a pillar, illuminating the vast cloud of smoke that had formed over the doomed city. It seemed to Max like the Biblical apocalypses his father had preached about, like one of the Doré Old Testament illustrations he'd been shown as a child. Dresden was being consumed.

'I can't watch any more,' Lola said. He knew she was thinking of Heidi and his mother.

They went back to their bed and lay in each other's arms, unable to sleep, the images burned on the retinas of their minds.

And then, at around 1.30 a.m., the thudding resumed. The bombers were back.

Lola could not bear to see it. Max went out alone to stand in the dark. The glow had become an incandescent white flare, lighting up the underside of the cloud that stretched from one side of the horizon to the other. This raid seemed longer and even more intense. Bombs were raining down on a city already ablaze. Conditions for the civilians and firefighters must be unimaginable.

Max felt the restless winds sweeping around him, as they had done at Düren; the firestorm was creating its own vortex, sucking oxygen into its fiery heart from miles around.

The next morning, the world was hushed. The silence lay heavy as lead on everything, and vast pillars of smoke hung in the blackened sky. An inky rain fell from time to time, streaking everything. The soot was the residue of the destroyed city and its carbonised inhabitants. It stained the hard-packed snow with strange hieroglyphs.

They could not eat or make love. They sat in silence all morning, listening.

And at noon, the bombers returned yet again. It was hard to imagine that there could be anything left to destroy by now, but fresh columns of smoke lifted to stain the sky, and once again they sensed the deep drumming of the high explosives through the earth.

The memory of Cologne haunted them both. They had seen Dresden almost untouched by war, a fairy-tale city of towers and palaces. It was appalling to think it might have been reduced to the same desolation as Cologne, thousands of its inhabitants immolated in firestorms. The thought depressed them both deeply.

'We can never get away from it,' Lola said emptily. It was as though all the happiness that she had built up over the past weeks together had drained away.

Max had the same sensation. The war, to which he had already given five years of his life, fighting for a Fatherland that had betrayed him, blindly following the orders of madmen and criminals, was inescapable. There was no refuge from it. It had taken so much from him already; he dreaded the day it would take Lola, who had become his reason for living.

There was a fourth raid the next day.

The ash fell in gusts of dirty rain, or drifted on the wind. By night, they could see the sky still glowing with the burning embers of Dresden. But the bombers did not return after that.

At the end of the week, they walked into Unterstein for provisions. The frost was packed as hard as stone beneath their feet. A light snow was falling. The sight that met their eyes at Unterstein was grim: the main street of the town was clogged with a long, grey line of refugees from Dresden, trudging to whatever shelter they could find.

As always, the majority were women, children, and the elderly. Wrapped in shawls, and in some cases dressing gowns, they pushed handcarts, prams, trolleys, anything with wheels, which they had loaded with bedding, or whatever else they had been able to salvage.

The children were suffering particularly badly in the freezing cold. Some, crammed between boxes and bundles, were being pushed on the carts. Others were having to walk through the snow, their eyes dull. It was a tragic, silent procession.

Some – but not all – of the villagers of Unterstein were offering food to the convoy. In any case, the line was endless, stretching out of sight; there was no way to feed such a huge exodus.

Max had seen similar columns of desperately fleeing civilians on the roads in France and Russia. To see them in Germany was a shock.

Lola, her heart wrenched by the sight of a young mother with three children, stopped her and held out the loaf of bread she had bought. The woman told them about the bombing in a hoarse voice. It had been one of the most fearsome air raids yet. The city was utterly destroyed, she said, the death toll in the tens of thousands. Nobody knew the figures. Nobody would ever know. People had been vaporised, not even leaving a corpse behind to show they had ever lived.

'I couldn't get to a shelter,' she said, tearing at the bread as she spoke, and giving out pieces to her exhausted children. 'But everyone in the shelters died, anyway. They were roasted alive. I took the children and ran to the cemetery. I thought, "They won't bomb that." But they were bombing everything. The roads were like rivers of boiling tar. People who tried to cross them got stuck and burst into flames.' The woman's eyes, swollen and inflamed with smoke, were wide, seeing nothing but her own terrible memories. 'The wind swept everything into the fire. I saw people flying through the air, their clothes and hair burning, until they were lifted up into the sky, and disappeared, like angels. Like burning angels.'

'You can come to our house,' Lola said. She turned to Max pleadingly. 'Can't they, Max?'

'Yes, of course.'

'No,' the woman said. 'We have to keep going.'

'Your children are freezing. You all need rest. It's safe there.'

'Safe? Don't you understand?' The woman seemed suddenly angry. 'The Russians are coming, girl! They will be here any day!'

'The Russians? Here in Saxony?'

'Yes! They are worse than the bombers. They loot every house. They butcher the men like pigs. And they rape every woman they see. Children, grandmothers, it doesn't matter to them. They rape them dozens of times, and then they come back again the next day, and rape them again. The women die – or they commit suicide.' She pointed to her children. 'I have two daughters.'

Lola was pale. In the autumn, the news had been full of stories of Russians raping and then murdering women at Nemmersdorf. 'Where will you go?'

'Anywhere west of here. The war is lost. The Russians are coming from the East, and the Americans from the West. It's a thousand times better to be under the Americans or the British than under the Russians.' She looked fearfully over her shoulder, as though the Red Army were already at hand. 'You are young and beautiful,' she said, turning back to Lola. 'They will destroy you. You have to get away from here, you and your husband.' She thanked them for the bread, and pulled her children back on to the road.

'Do you think it's true about what the Russians are doing?' Lola asked Max, as they watched the plodding stream of humanity.

'They are getting their own back,' Max said heavily, 'for Stalingrad.' He was thinking how terrible it would be if Lola had to pay for crimes committed by the SS.

They were silent and depressed as they made their way back home. For months, they had been sheltered from the war. Now, it was catching up with them, fast.

'I didn't think the Eastern Front would collapse so soon,' Max said when they reached the lodge. 'I thought they would have the sense to reinforce it, and hold the Russians back, even if it meant letting the British and Americans in the front door. As that woman said, they'll behave better than the Russians. Hitler must have put everything into the Ardennes offensive in the West. Another terrible mistake. That fanatic, Jochen Peiper, thought he could turn the war around with one campaign. By the sounds of it, the Russians will reach Berlin soon. It will be a bloodbath. They will fight to the last man to protect Hitler. It can only be a matter of weeks, now.'

'What are we going to do?'

'I think we should leave for the American zone, like all the others.'

'And leave our lovely, safe home?'

'It won't be safe for much longer.'

'But we have nowhere to go, Max! And I'm still a Jew, whatever my papers say! Marching back into the arms of the Gestapo doesn't make any sense. When the Russians know that I'm an enemy of the Nazis, and that you've been protecting me, surely they'll leave us alone?'

'There may not be time for all that explanation,' Max replied. 'All they want is to hurt and kill as many Germans as they can.'

'This house is hidden in the woods. Can't we just stay here until it's all over?'

'They'll find us.'

Lola took his hands. 'Max, you saw those people! They don't even know where they're going. They're just wandering blindly. They're going to die on the road by the thousand. Their children

267

will freeze, they will starve. It's too terrible. I don't want to end up like that.'

And she had a point, he had to admit. They had nowhere to go. Joining the endless flow of people trekking westwards, with no other objective than putting as much distance between themselves and the vengeful Russians as possible, was a grim prospect. The whole of eastern Germany would be on the move, soon. And the resources of the Reich were at breaking point already. There was neither food nor shelter for all these displaced persons.

The wave of rape and looting by the 'Mongol hordes' had been predicted by Goebbels in endless broadcasts designed to stiffen morale; and for once, he had been right. Stalin was exacting a savage retribution for Hitler's ill-conceived attempt to invade the Soviet Union, in which Max himself had participated. The savagery would surely burn itself out in time. Order would have to be restored.

But what kind of order?

His greater fear, even if they were to survive the initial onslaught of the Red Army, was to find themselves living under Russian occupation. They would be subjected to the harshest living conditions the occupiers could dream up. The Nazis had made slaves of the Russians. The Russians, in their turn, would surely enslave the Germans.

He tried to argue all this with Lola, but she was adamant. 'That's all in the future, Max. The point is surviving the present. We can't throw ourselves into the maelstrom when we have a roof over our heads here, and food in the larder, and enough wood and coal to keep warm until spring – *and* some safety from the Gestapo and the SS. We're not leaving!'

He had to bow to her reasoning. Protecting Lola had become his raison d'être. There was nothing more vital to him. All the way along, the choice had always been the lesser of two evils. Once again, he was having to choose a route that was not safe, only less dangerous.

Their luck had held so far, despite all the tragedies. Perhaps it would carry them safely to the end of the war.

But he took the old shotgun to the shed, and with the hacksaw he found there, sawed the barrel down to the stock, and then sawed off most of the butt, creating a stubby but lethal weapon that he could carry around under his coat. He took it with him wherever he went from now on.

The woods were still tranquil. Though anxiety never left Max, always lurking at the edge of his consciousness, he and Lola resumed their life together. They agreed that she would no longer venture out of the house until they knew it was safe. He would make the shopping trips to Unterstein alone – and they would be short. Not having a radio meant that this was the only way they could get information about the progress of the war.

The next time he went back to the town, he found the exodus of refugees even greater than before. And now, ominously, there were soldiers among the civilians. When he went into the baker's, he found an unkempt corporal trying to bully the baker's wife, Frau Schubert, into selling him bread without ration coupons.

'The war's over anyway,' the man said belligerently. 'We don't need coupons any more!'

'They are needed in my shop,' Frau Schubert snapped, 'or I will have to explain to the Gestapo. And the war is not over. Why aren't you at the front, keeping the Bolsheviks out?'

'With what? Sticks and stones? They don't send us tanks or guns any more, there's no Luftwaffe, and we haven't seen bread in weeks. We can't fight the Bolsheviks with empty bellies and empty magazines. I'm off home to my wife, me.'

'They'll hang you,' Frau Schubert said in disgust.

'They'll have to catch me, first. And by then, the war will be over.'

He managed to wheedle a heel of stale black bread from Frau Schubert, and left with his prize. Max followed him out into the street.

'What's happening at the front?' he asked the corporal.

'Front? There is no front,' the man retorted, gnawing at the crust. With a rodent face and long, narrow teeth, he was remarkably rat-like. 'The Russians are throwing division after division at us, and they don't care how many are killed. As fast as we knock them down, they send more. It's hopeless. We're being pushed back miles each day.'

'So it's not going to hold?'

'No chance.' He eyed the Iron Cross ribbon on Max's lapel. 'You in the army?'

'Panzer corps. Discharged.'

'I'm not ashamed of being a deserter. Hitler's ruined everything, the crazy bastard. You people live off the fat of the land out here in the country. The city folk are starving. But don't let the SS catch you. They'll drag you into the *Volkssturm*. Or hang you from a lamp post. They don't ask questions. You wouldn't happen to have a spare suit of clothes? I need to get rid of this uniform.'

'Sorry. How far away are the Russians?'

The man shrugged. 'Fifty miles, five, who knows? The Sudetenland is collapsing. You want to get away from here, mate. The Russkies are shooting young men like you out of hand. And what they do to the women doesn't bear repeating.'

The deserter re-joined the column. Max watched it passing, an endless stream of people and carts, tarpaulins flapping in the icy wind, here and there a bicycle or a horse. He stayed for a while, talking to the townspeople with whom he'd struck up an acquaintance, and sharing information.

Then he trudged back through the woods with the few provisions he'd managed to buy, including half a dozen eggs. The shops were almost bare now. They were better off than most, with their store of dry goods, but these would run out eventually, and they would have to forage.

With this in mind, he took a detour through the trees, and was rewarded with some early wild fodder – several of the velvety brown mushrooms he'd gathered as a boy from dead logs, a few stems of wild garlic, and some new nettle leaves that had just appeared from the snow.

Lola was waiting for him at the door. 'I don't like it when you're gone so long,' she said, throwing her arms around him.

'But I've got a tasty lunch for you.' He smiled.

As he prepared an omelette with the eggs and mushrooms, he told her about the corporal he'd met in the town. 'If soldiers are deserting, and getting away with it, then things are bad. And there are even more refugees on the roads, now. The Russians can't be far away any more. In Unterstein, they were telling me there are caves higher up in the mountain. The townsfolk have always hidden up there, since the Seven Years' War, in the time of Frederick the Great.'

Lola gave him a very dry look. 'A cave, Max?'

He smiled. 'We should try and find one, and maybe leave some food and water up there, just in case. Then if things get bad, we'll have somewhere to go, at least for a while, until the worst is over. You don't have to come. I'll go on my own and report back.'

'I don't like staying here alone. I'm coming.'

'It might be a stiff climb,' he warned.

Lola felt little enthusiasm for the venture, but the next day, she gritted her teeth and set off with Max to explore the mountain that rose above them. The climb began a few hundred yards from the house. Snow was falling lightly. The cold burned their faces as they climbed. There was a path of sorts, worn into the crumbly sandstone, but little vegetation. The mountain range towered above them, carved into bizarre shapes by rain and wind.

The climb was stiff, but so far not impossible. Where there were difficult places, Max took Lola's hand and helped her scramble up. She had changed into a pair of corduroy trousers and jumper from Ditte's wardrobe, clothes that enabled her to clamber unhindered. The exercise, challenging at first, became almost exhilarating. Her scepticism lifted, and when she looked back and saw how far they had climbed, her heart rose.

'I'm not such a weakling as you thought,' she panted, joining him on a flat boulder.

'I never thought of you as a weakling. Perhaps you thought of yourself as one.'

'Perhaps I did.' Lola shaded her eyes from the snow to look at the sprawling rockscape around them. 'I'm glad I came.'

But she was getting cold by the time they reached a natural ledge an hour or two later. They had now climbed something like six hundred feet, and the height had added drama to the view around them. They could see the distant spire of the church at Unterstein, rising above the trees. Max put his hand on her arm. 'Rest here. I'll go on ahead.'

He continued climbing while she settled in the shelter of the overhang to get out of the whirling snow. The silence all around was profound. She could hear the fall of every pebble, the whisper of every breath of wind across the rocks. Her legs and back ached from the unaccustomed exercise. Yet she felt oddly peaceful, as though she had disconnected – if only for a time – from all the tragedy in her life. Everything that had weighed on her, pressed in on her, seemed to have lifted away. Having to think about nothing but walking had cleared her mind.

She was just herself. She couldn't remember the last time she had been just herself. And despite everything that had happened, and all the uncertainty that surrounded her, she was conscious of a feeling that had become almost a stranger to her – happiness.

She sat in this tranquil state for about half an hour, disconnected, at peace, until Max came scrambling back. His face was bright with triumph. 'I've found a wonderful cave!' he said.

'I can't wait,' she replied ironically.

He grinned. 'You'll love it. It's not far. Come!'

The cave was not a long way up. It appeared as no more than a cleft in the rocks, almost imperceptible against the mountain face. They had to crouch to enter it. But once inside, the space opened up into a vaulted chamber. It was icy-cold, dark and dry inside. But people had used the cave, years ago. Max showed her the amenities. The floor had been strewn with rush mats. There was straw at the back of the cave, and a few clay water jars, some cracked. There was a crude, brick hearth near the entrance, blackened by ancient fires.

'It's not the Excelsior,' she commented.

'No, it's not the Excelsior. But we could stay up here for a week or two in an emergency – especially if we bring some provisions up here.'

Lola made a face. 'I hope we don't have to. It's freezing cold, and it'll be horribly uncomfortable.'

'Look at this.' He showed her a pile of stones and brushwood at the entrance that could be used to close the entrance of the cave, so it was practically invisible to the untrained eye. He was plainly delighted with his discovery. But it was getting very cold, and the snow was falling faster, now. They set off back down the rocks.

Chapter 17

At first, Lola thought it was distant thunder, but it went on all morning, a constant muttering, punctuated now and then by louder thuds that made the glass in the windows rattle slightly.

When Max returned from Unterstein, where he'd managed to buy some milk, he confirmed her fears.

'It's the Russian guns. They're shelling our lines.'

'How far away?'

'Maybe sixty miles. Maybe less. And I saw a Waffen-SS regiment passing through the town on their way to the front. That means the Russians are breaking through at the border.'

Lola felt her stomach dip disconcertingly. It was one thing to talk about the Russians approaching, another to actually hear their guns. Max had been going up the mountain every day or two, taking up blankets, food, firewood and other supplies. The cave no longer seemed so uninviting.

She heated the milk on the stove and made them both porridge. 'Do you think the army will try to negotiate?'

Max shook his head. 'When von Stauffenberg tried to blow up Hitler, he closed that door. The army has to fight to the last man to prove its loyalty to the Führer.'

'But it's the civilians who'll suffer most!'

'Hitler doesn't care about that. In fact, I think he's come to hate the German people. We let him down. We weren't the master race, after all.'

They made love slowly and gently in the evening, looking into each other's eyes. The drawing closeness of war made their time together all the more precious; each wanted to make every second matter. There was no need for words. Their bodies said everything that needed to be said.

Afterwards, they lay together in the darkness, listening to the distant rumbling. It did not pause, all through the night. There was no doubt in Max's mind that this was the final assault; the Russians would not stop now until they had reached Berlin and had locked Hitler in a cage, if he hadn't had the sense to put a bullet in his head first.

The atmosphere in Unterstein grew increasingly unsettled. People no longer spoke of *if* the Russians would arrive, but *when*. Each time Max went, he found that more of the townsfolk had left. Shops had closed, and those that remained open had little to offer.

But tight as the situation was in Unterstein, the news that people brought from Berlin was quite startlingly bad. The anti-aircraft defences that had ringed the city were now breaking down, and letting the enemy bombers through day and night. Gas and coal supplies were non-existent, and the electricity was only on for an hour or two each evening. The city stank of smashed drains and buried corpses. Water was cut off in many parts. Hospitals were unable to cope with the injured from air raids. Schools and universities had been shut. Some were being used as makeshift hospitals. The telephones were dead, and the trains were impossible. A mighty city was dying.

In the midst of the catastrophe, the last Jews in Germany were being rounded up and slaughtered, 'to stop them', as the baker's wife said, 'from gloating over our hardships.' If the Third Reich was going under, then none of its enemies must survive to witness the end and triumph in the Führer's downfall. An orgy of shootings, public hangings and deportations was in progress.

On one of his last visits to the town, Max saw a gang of prisoners being marched along by armed guards. They had clearly come from a concentration camp that had been cleared as the Russians advanced. Wearing striped cotton coats that were completely inadequate for the cruel winter conditions, the men stumbled blindly through the snow in wooden clogs, in the last stages of exhaustion and starvation. What work could be extracted from such living skeletons defied the imagination. They were clearly on a death march, and their hollow eyes were aware of it. The pitiless faces of the guards challenged anyone to show compassion. Not that anyone did. There was no violence meted out to the prisoners while they were in the town, but a few minutes after the tragic procession had passed through into the countryside, Max heard shots. Stragglers would be ruthlessly killed, their bodies rolled into ditches or left for the locals to bury.

He was grateful that Lola had not witnessed the dreadful scene. He remembered her bitter words, 'They'll be killing Jews until the last minute of the war.'

In the meantime, the radio broadcasts kept assuring Germans that the 'subhuman hordes' would never set foot on German soil, though it was obvious that most of Prussia was now under Red Army control. And the rumble of the Soviet artillery grew ever louder and more menacing. It shook the ground and lit up the horizon at night.

Luftwaffe planes – a rarity in German skies these days – occasionally flew over the area. Nobody waved to them, as they would once have done. The name of Göring, head of the Luftwaffe, had become a byword for betrayal. There was nothing to do but wait for the end. The end was near, and it promised to come with much suffering.

And finally, news of his uncle and aunt arrived. It was not the news he wanted to hear.

'The Herr *Doktor* Wolff and his wife were caught in an air raid on the way to Dresden,' Frau Schubert told him. 'I am very sorry. The news has just come. They were in a railway station, and a bomb fell directly on it. Nobody survived.'

'Thank you for telling me,' Max said sombrely.

'They were God-fearing people,' Frau Schubert said. 'Germany needed people like them.'

'Yes,' Max agreed. His heart was heavy. There was no chance now to apologise to Anselm for his behaviour as a boy. No chance to build a bridge back to his own family. Like so many other bridges in his life, he had burned it behind him.

The cave was now almost ready. They just needed a little more food up there so that their stay could be extended, if needs be. Max went into the woods with his forage bag each day, hunting for supplies. The woods were now full of the brown velvet mushrooms, which he sliced and dried on the old stove. They could be boiled in water to make soup, or at a pinch, chewed raw. They grew on dead logs, and a lucky find could yield two or three pounds of them.

He was carefully cutting a batch, making sure to leave the mycelium so that more would grow, when a plane flew low over the woods. The engine note, raw and uneven, made him look up quickly. He caught a glimpse of a mottled green fuselage, a red star. It was a Russian fighter.

His heart lurched. He straightened, and climbed on to the log to watch the aircraft's flight. It was swooping in the direction of Unterstein, its wings tilting. He was too deep in the woods to see the town, but the blast of high explosive shook snow out of the trees all around him, and he saw the black cloud roll into the sky. It was followed by the snarl of the plane returning and the rattle of its machine guns. It was strafing the line of refugees.

There was no more excuse for delay. They needed to get to the cave, now. He ran back to the lodge, ducking under the branches in his way.

Lola had heard the fighter plane, too. She'd assumed it was German, until she heard the explosion. She went outside, and saw the smoke in the sky over Unterstein. Panic filled her breast. The Russians were here already.

She went back inside and began packing the knapsack they would take to the cave. Where was Max? He had gone into the woods two hours ago. It was very bad timing. There were more explosions. The snarling of the Russian fighter down in the valley was like the buzz of an industrious bee, except that its yield was blood, not honey. She was shaking as she stuffed things into the knapsack. When would the fear ever be gone? Perhaps this was the end, at last. Perhaps this was the final act. Here, they would either die, and find peace at last, or see the end of the war, live free once again.

She heard Max's shout at last, and ran to open the door.

But it was not Max.

Standing at the bottom of the steps were two men in heavy overcoats. They wore round helmets of a shape she had never seen before, and carried machine guns with drum-shaped magazines.

Seeing her, one raised his weapon and pointed it at her. It was not until he shouted something at her in Russian that she realised they were Red Army soldiers.

The shock ran through her like electricity. She put her hands up, and tried to remember the Russian word for Jewess, which she had rehearsed so many times, but it had vanished from her mind, so she spoke in German.

'Not Nazi. Jewish. Jewish.'

They came up the stairs cautiously, pushing her back into the house at gunpoint. One of them spoke to her harshly in Russian.

'I don't understand,' she said. 'Not Nazi. Jewish!'

One was middle-aged, the other younger. They had hard, high-cheekboned faces, just like the Nazi propaganda images. The younger one held the machine gun pointed at her while the older one went into all the rooms of the house, kicking the doors open and looking into cupboards and under beds. Where was Max? If he arrived now, they would kill him at once. She couldn't face that. Let them do what they wanted with her, so long as they left her alive and went away again. Then she could pick up the pieces as best she could.

Satisfied there was nobody else in the house, the older man went into the kitchen and found the eggs and the bread. He barked a command at Lola, indicating the stove. They wanted her to cook food.

Suddenly, the Russian word that had eluded her came into her head. '*Yevreyka*,' she said, putting her hand on her breast, '*yevreyka*!'

The two men stared at her, then burst into derisive laughter, repeating the word scornfully. She realised that they didn't believe her. They had seen what German Jews looked like, in concentration camps, emaciated and degraded; and here she was, healthy and fit. They would never believe she was Jewish.

The younger soldier stepped close to her and swung his fist into her belly. Lola doubled over in agony, unable to breathe. He grasped her hair and yanked her upright again. *'Yevreyka?'* he said contemptuously. *'Nyet. Fashista.'* He spat in her face. He pushed her staggering towards the stove, shouting in Russian. With trembling hands, she started to crack the eggs.

The Russian who'd hit her stayed in the kitchen, staring at her as she cooked. He was grinning contemptuously, exposing the gleam of steel-capped teeth. The other went around the house a second time, sweeping things into a bag he had produced. He seemed to regard anything as worth stealing – the clock on the mantel, ornaments, candlesticks, even the useless telephone.

They found a bottle of schnapps, to her horror. They opened it gleefully and began swigging from the neck of the bottle. They pushed her into a corner of the kitchen while they ate, talking in low voices, staring at her. She tried to keep her composure, but the violence they'd shown her already had terrified her.

Every now and then, the sound of explosions would rattle the glasses, and one or the other would get up and look out of the window. But they seemed in no hurry to leave, or re-join whatever unit they belonged to. They emptied the bottle of schnapps.

There was no sign of Max. She had a sudden, sickening thought: what if they had come across him in the woods and shot him? What if he was lying out there, dead? She looked at their brutal faces. Soldiers like this killed without a second thought. Her own life was worth nothing if they took it into their heads to kill her.

If Max were dead, then she did not want to go on living. She would accept death. She was only afraid of what would come before it.

The Russians finished eating. The younger one swept all the plates on to the floor with a crash. The older smashed the empty schnapps bottle against the stove, and holding the jagged neck as a weapon, advanced on Lola.

She shrank back, trying to shield her eyes with her arms. He pulled her hands down and poised the dripping, broken glass over her face. He spoke sharply. She didn't understand the words, but his meaning was clear: if she resisted, he would use the bottle on her.

He pushed her towards the bedroom. The younger Russian stayed in the kitchen, with his gun at the ready, keeping watch on the doors. As though in a nightmare, Lola felt everything shrink around her to a dark place, in which she was trapped. She tried to tell herself not to resist. If she angered them, they would surely kill her.

The soldier jerked her arm with brutal strength, sending her spinning on to the bed. She couldn't help crying out in pain. He knelt on the bed, his eyes dark slits, and tore at her clothes. For all her resolve not to struggle, she did so now, trying to fight off his invading hands.

'No!' she screamed. 'No.'

He was far stronger than she. He struck her backhanded across the face, a casually vicious blow that almost knocked her unconscious. His knuckles felt like iron chain. Dazed, she felt him yank off her underwear. His knee was thrust between her thighs, forcing them apart. There was nothing she could do any longer.

The blast from the front room didn't register with her until the man on top of her jumped up, shouting in Russian. She saw Max appear in the doorway of the bedroom, holding the shotgun that he had shortened. He was aiming it at the Russian. The second blast was violent, deafening. Lola covered her eyes for a moment, then sat up, stunned. The Russian was lying on the carpet, clutching at his chest. Blood was gurgling between his fingers. His expression was one of astonishment.

'Max!' she gasped. She stumbled to him, too shocked to cry. He put his arms around her, dropping the shotgun.

The Russian on the floor had started kicking and writhing. She couldn't look at the terrible sight. She hid her face against Max's chest until the noises he made slowed into silence.

'Are you all right?' Max asked in a tight voice.

'Yes. Are you?'

'I'm hit.'

Lola drew back and saw that the front of his shirt was soaked crimson with blood. 'Max!'

'He got a shot off just as I pulled the trigger.'

Lola turned and saw that there was a pistol lying beside the dead Russian. 'Let me see.' With shaky fingers, she opened Max's shirt. The bullet had made a neat hole where it had entered his body below his ribs, but a long, ragged tear where it had emerged from his back. Blood was oozing thickly from the wounds on both sides. 'Oh, God. What can I do?'

His face was very pale, his eyes dark. 'Lola, I'm so sorry I wasn't here.'

'It's not your fault!'

'I should have been here. Forgive me.' He slumped back against the wall.

'You're not going to die.' She took his face in her hands. 'Open your eyes, Max. You're not going to die.'

'Don't stay here,' he whispered. 'Go up to the cave, now. Wait there until I come.'

'No! I'm not leaving you.' The blood from the bullet wound was dreadful to see. She pulled open one of the drawers and tore up a cotton shirt she found in there.

Max groaned as she wound the cloth around his waist, hoping she was doing more good than harm. She fastened it as tightly as she dared. Max, obviously in shock, was struggling to focus. 'Just let me rest a moment,' he said. She helped him to the kitchen.

'Don't look,' he said, but it was too late. She had seen the ruined head of the other Russian, who was sprawled under the table in a spreading pool of blood. She sat Max down and got him a cup of water. He sat with his eyes closed for a while, then opened them dully. 'It looks like a detachment of Russians broke through our lines. There's fighting going on all around Unterstein.' For the first time, Lola became aware of the noise from outside. The distant rumble of the past days was now a constant barrage of explosions and firing. Aircraft were snarling overhead. 'It's too small a group to be effective. They'll eventually be surrounded and eliminated by the Waffen-SS tank group.' Max jerked his thumb at the dead man on the floor. 'These two must have tried to get away. But others may follow them. And in the next few days, there'll be a lot more.'

'I'll help you get up to the cave. We'll do it together.'

Max looked at her with bleary eyes. He smiled tiredly. 'I'm not sure if I can make it, Lola.'

'You can! I'm not leaving you here! Come on, Max!'

They began climbing up the rocks. She led the way, stopping now and then to help him up the steeper sections. The snow was whirling down now, and the light was failing. The planes were no longer flying overhead, but from down in the valley came the sound of battle, the roar of tanks and the rattle of machine guns, with every now and then the blast of a shell.

Max was climbing very slowly, and seemed exhausted. She'd occasionally had to slap his face to make him wake up. He had lost a lot of blood, and she was terrified that she would turn around to find that he had died. They had to get to the cave before the night brought a deadly drop in temperature.

They made their painful way up through the desolate landscape of rock outcrops, interspersed with fields of sand and gravel, with the mountains looming up into the snow-clouds all around.

Wearily clambering over the next ridge, she heard the rattle of stones, and looked up. A figure was standing on a rock above them. She squinted through the snow. It was a German boy, no more than twelve or thirteen, armed with a stick. He stared at them in alarm, his eyes wide.

Lola called out. 'Help me! My husband is hurt. I must get him to shelter, or he'll die.'

'Is he Russian?'

'No. The Russians shot him.'

The boy scrambled down to them. Max had slumped against a rock. The boy helped Lola to pull Max upright. 'Where's your cave?' the boy asked.

'Just up there,' she said, pointing. 'Two hundred yards.'

'That's our cave!'

'It doesn't matter,' she said. 'Help me get him there.'

The last two hundred yards finished off the last of Lola's strength. It was almost dark by the time they reached the cave. There was only one person there, a very old woman, who emerged, pulling her shawl over her white hair, to peer at them with rheumy eyes.

Between them, they got Max into the shelter. He groaned as they moved him, his eyes fluttering open. The old woman brought an oil lamp and unwound the ribbon of torn fabric that Lola had tied on. It was stiff with blood. And blood was still seeping from the tear in his flesh. The old woman prodded Max with fingers that were swollen and crooked with arthritis, lowering her head to sniff the wound. Without a word, she shuffled off and returned with a Thermos flask and a small package that turned out to contain needles and spools of thread.

She gestured to Max's wound. 'You must sew him,' she said in a cracked voice.

'Oh no,' Lola said in horror. 'I can't.'

The old woman folded her deformed hands. 'Then he will die.'

It was a stark choice. She must either tend to Max as best she could – or with the constant flow of blood, he might not live out the night.

Lola gritted her teeth and set to work. Washing away the blood with the old woman's flask of warm water revealed that Max's torso was now covered with a huge bruise as the blood spread beneath his skin. Asking the old woman to hold the lamp close, she rinsed both the entrance and exit wounds as best she could. She didn't know what internal organs might have been damaged by the bullet. She would just have to trust to the healing power of Max's youth and strength.

As she pushed the needle through the ragged flesh, Max cried out. His eyes opened and met hers.

'I have to do this,' she said, 'or you won't stop bleeding.'

She didn't know whether he understood her or not, but his eyes closed again. She resumed work. The flickering oil lamp gave a poor light. She had not sewn anything since she'd been a girl; and in any case, sewing a man was a very different proposition from embroidering a handkerchief. She soon learned that the flesh would tear if she put the stitches too close to the edge of the wound. It was necessary to pull the gaping holes closed, and that made Max scream. Awful as it was, she had to shut her ears and her mind to his suffering.

Her fingers were slippery with his blood, and sometimes she lost the needle in the living tissue of his body and had to grope for it. The single wound at the front was easier; the one at the back was horrifying. The bullet had made a long, irregular opening as it erupted. She had to draw the skin up between her finger and thumb and push the needle through, looping the thread over in a blanket stitch, closing the lateral tears, working towards the middle.

At last the wounds were closed. She could hardly bear to look at what she had done. Her crude sewing had made a chaotic design, a hieroglyph of suffering in his body. But the bleeding had been reduced to a slow seep. The old woman gave her a relatively clean strip of cloth, and she bandaged Max up as best she could. He was now inert. At some stage during the operation, he had passed out. It was for the best.

'This is our cave.' The old woman had reappeared. 'It's been our family cave for a hundred years.'

'We didn't know.'

'You can stay.' She looked down at Max with her yellow eyes. 'But I think he will die.'

Too weary to think any longer, Lola curled up beside her patient. Someone – either the boy or the old woman – threw a blanket over them both, and she sank into the blackness.

She was awakened by the boy patting her cheek. She sat up, her heart pounding, and turned to Max. At first, she thought he was dead. Then she saw that he was breathing, though his face was drawn and deathly pale. Sweat was pooling in the hollows of his eyes and around his lips.

'He's sick,' the boy said. 'My grandmother says you must wash the wound with this.' The boy was offering her something. She peered at it. It was a small bottle of iodine. 'Use it all.'

'Thank you,' she said, taking it. 'What's your name?'

'Hans-Peter.'

'Where are the rest of your family?'

He had limpid blue eyes and a thatch of white-blond hair, with a simple, snub-nosed face. 'My father and my two brothers were killed in Italy. My sister got sick and died. My mother went to find work in Dresden, but we haven't heard from her since the bombing. I think she's dead, too,' he added, matter-of-factly.

Max stirred and groaned as she unwrapped his bandages. In the dim morning light, her crude stitching looked inflamed; some infection had set in. He was sweating because he had a fever. She forced herself to stay calm. She swabbed the wound with the boy's iodine. Max woke and stared at her with hollow eyes. 'Who are those people?' he whispered.

Her eyes filled with tears. 'I thought I'd never hear you speak again.' She lifted some water to his lips, and he drank a little. 'A boy and his grandmother. They say this is their cave. I had to sew your wounds closed last night.'

'I thought it was a nightmare.'

'I'm sorry. I had to do something.'

He struggled to lift his head, and looked down at himself. 'It doesn't look good.'

'It's going to be all right. Lie back down.'

He laid his head back obediently. 'Lola—'

'Hush. Don't talk.' She smoothed the sweat-soaked hair back from his brow. 'Sleep now, my darling.'

They could hear the battle going on down in the valley, but the bad weather meant they could see nothing. Snow and sleet whirled past the cave for hours at a time. The boy, Hans-Peter, told her that he and his grandmother, Oma Mathilde, had found the provisions that Max had brought up, so had been expecting them to arrive.

287

There were other families sheltering in other caves all around, as they had always done during unsettled times. A young woman, a relative of Hans-Peter and Oma Mathilde, clambered down to them and brought Lola a jar of wild honey, black, bitter and strong.

'Smear this on the wounds,' she said. 'It's better than iodine.'

Lola was sceptical, but the woman told her it was an old peasant remedy. In any case, it was all she had. She washed Max's wounds again and smeared the honey over them. Then she bandaged him again. He was restless, moaning from time to time in his sleep. Now there was nothing to do but wait.

The boy Hans-Peter kept watch outside the cave. The grand-mother spoke little. She largely ignored Lola, going about her slow daily tasks of preparing food and sweeping the earth floor. She and her grandson had also brought up provisions, packets of chickpeas and lentils, dried fruit, sacks of precious charcoal for cooking. The stone walls of the cave dripped with condensation, and the cold was intense, but at least they were sheltered from the fighting.

Lola sat next to Max for hours, watching him, and from time to time dribbling water between his lips. He had grown very hot and fevered, moving restlessly and muttering. She tried to talk to him, but he was deep in his own dreams. His words were indistinct. She could make nothing of them.

She thought about the Russians who had tried to rape her. They were brutes, but human brutes, who would never go back to whoever loved them in Russia. War had made them into brutes. In peacetime, their lives would have been ordinary, harmless. It was war that brought out the evil in men.

The explosions and firing in the valley gave her thoughts a backdrop. Her past life, with all its noise and movement and agita-tion, seemed unreal to her now, as though it had never taken place at all. Everything had shrunk to this cave, with its bare walls, where she watched over a wounded human being whose existence was strangely entwined with hers. Nothing else was real. The isolation was a strange, eerie feeling that she was unable to shake off. The hours rolled by.

Max's fever grew worse over the course of the next days. His face was gaunt, his youth now shadowed.

When Lola took off the bandages, it seemed to her that her honey treatment had done some good. The inflammation was at least no worse, and the area looked cleaner. She smeared on more honey.

But at the end of the week there was a bad night. Max became delirious, writhing so violently that he tore some of the stitches open. She would have to repair them when he was calmer. Lola couldn't bear to see him suffering like this. She gathered him in her arms and cradled his head on her breasts, stroking his face and murmuring to him.

'It's all right. Hush, my darling, hush. I know it hurts. It will be all right.'

He seemed to be aware of her embrace, and pressed close against her like a child, shuddering and whimpering. She kissed his burning forehead and rocked him. They held each other through the long night hours.

When she awoke the next morning, she found that she was propped up against the bare rock, Max's head in her lap. She touched his brow. He was cooler and seemed to be sleeping peacefully. But once again, her impromptu bandages were soaked in blood. She smoothed his hair until his eyes flickered open.

'I'm sorry,' she said, 'but I have to do some more mending. You've opened some of your stitches.'

He nodded slightly. 'Let me just lie here a little longer.'

She looked down at his face as she stroked his hair. 'You had a bad night.'

'I remember you comforting me.' His voice was little more than a rustle. His eyes held hers. 'Thank you.'

'I don't know whether I'm doing more harm than good.'

'I would have died without you.'

'You wouldn't have been shot but for me.'

'It wasn't your fault.' His eyes closed. 'I'm sticky. What have you put on me?'

'Honey. A peasant woman gave it to me. She said it was better than iodine. I think it works.'

He was silent while she repaired the stitches that had torn open, but she could see how much pain he was in. When she was done, she washed the wounds and dressed them again with honey. Oma Mathilde brought them a bowl of soup. Neither of them had eaten for days. They shared the soup, which was hot and good. Then, exhausted, they fell back into sleep.

They slept for a couple of hours in the same position, Max's head in Lola's lap. They were awoken by Hans-Peter.

'The fighting is over, Fräulein Lola,' he said. 'Listen.'

The valley was silent now. 'Have the Russians gone?' Lola asked.

'Yes,' the boy said, 'but they'll be back, soon. We are leaving.'

'Where will you go?'

'To Bavaria. To wait for the Americans. The Americans will take care of us. Under the Russians, we will starve and die. Come with us.'

Lola looked at Max. 'We can't. He won't survive a journey. We have to wait until he's better.'

The boy looked at them with clear young eyes that war had made old. 'Don't wait too long, Fräulein Lola. Or it will be too late.'

Chapter 18

Max awoke to the pain in his right side, which felt as though it had been crushed in a giant vice. He was almost too stiff to move. He had to take the shallowest possible breaths to reduce the pressure. The bullet had not punctured his bowel, or he would be dead by now; but it had broken at least one rib and damaged the muscles, and he had lost a lot of blood. He had been very lucky. Lola had saved his life with her care.

She lay beside him now, breathing evenly. He studied her face in the dim light of dawn. There had been many misunderstandings between them, at least half of them on his side. He had made assumptions about her that had been a long way off the mark. He'd thought her weak and in need of protection. But she had turned out to be something quite different: brave, resourceful and caring.

The realisation that he would not be alive now but for Lola was a sobering one. He wondered how he could ever show her his gratitude.

Her eyes opened and met his. She stared at him for a moment.

'I dreamed you were dead,' she whispered.

He smiled wryly. 'No such luck.'

'Don't make jokes about it.' She sat up and lifted her arms to pick loose straw out of her hair. The simple, womanly grace of the movement touched him deeply: the way her breasts lifted, the tilt of her head. 'We're alone. They all left last night.'

'We have to leave, too.'

'Not yet,' Lola said.

'Lola, we can't risk—'

'No,' she cut in firmly. 'You're not strong enough. We can stay here until you're better. They've left us food. And the weather is very bad. We'll have to sit it out. I'm going to make a fire.'

Max hauled himself to the entrance of the cave to look out. The storm was approaching fast. The sky was dark and turbulent. He used the branches and stones to block the cave as best he could, panting with the effort, until Lola stopped him.

She'd made a fire in the hearth. She heated water to make tea, which was consoling. The storm, when it came, was violent. The thunder was shatteringly close here among these peaks, the lightning blindingly bright in the gloom. They sat huddled in blankets by their fire, watching the sheets of snow and ice that whirled in strange dances at the mouth of the cave.

The next day, the weather was better. The young woman who had given Lola the wild honey came into the cave to tell them that they, too, were leaving the mountain, and heading west. Like Hans-Peter before her, she warned them not to delay.

When she'd left, Max said, 'She's right. We can't stay here, Lola. Even if they don't kill us, we'll end up under Bolshevik rule. And that might be worse than death.'

'Are the Russians really so cruel?' she asked.

He swallowed. 'We did terrible things to them, Lola.'

'What things?' she asked quietly.

'War is wicked,' he said. 'We do wicked things, and wicked things are done to us. All I see when I look back is destruction. We came to Russia in midsummer. The fields were golden. And wherever we passed, we left people's lives in ruins. We drove our tanks through the crops. So many farms destroyed, fields churned into mud by our panzers. Orchards devastated. We didn't care. After a battle there sometimes wasn't a tree left standing. Sometimes, at night, we would set fire to a whole village with incendiary shells, just so we could see whether there were Russian tanks in the surrounding area. We simply didn't care.'

Something huge, deeply buried inside him, was rising. He tried to fight it down, push it back into the dark place where it lived, where it had waited all these years. But he couldn't prevent it from surfacing, the thing he'd never wanted to look at: the small bodies scattered in their own blood. The sights and sounds overwhelmed him. They were as real as the day it had happened.

He covered his face with his hands and sobbed. He could barely articulate the words. 'I need to tell you this, Lola. I need to tell you who I was, who I am. We shelled a church once, because we thought it was occupied by soldiers. But they'd hidden all the children in there, because they thought a church would be safe. They all died.'

She was horrified, trying to comfort him. 'Oh, Max.'

'It was terrible. We got out of the panzers to look. So many dead children. So much . . . blood. They were all in pieces, like – like broken dolls. But they weren't dolls. We tried to see if any had survived. But we'd killed them all. Every one.'

They held each other for a long time in silence. He tried to stop crying, wiping his burning face with his hands. 'I've tried to forget it. But it's always there. Before we invaded, they told us we would be facing the Russian beasts. It was a noble war. But it wasn't like that. It wasn't like that at all. We were the beasts.'

'Poor children. Poor, innocent children, all of you.'

Max was shaking. 'We just had to go on,' he said, more evenly as he got his emotions under control. 'Our commanders told us it was an accident, that it was the Russians' fault, that we had to forget

293

it. But I couldn't. I've never told another human being about this. I was so ashamed. I will always be ashamed. I'm damned.'

'No, Max!'

'The Nazis corrupted me, but I made myself a murderer. I have the curse of Cain.'

She took his face in her hands. 'No. You're noble.'

'I don't suppose it matters either way,' he said wearily. 'I never had anyone I could tell, anyone who would understand. Until you.'

'Oh, Max.' She kissed him full on the mouth. He tasted the salt of her tears.

He felt as though some vital organ had been ripped out of his body. Confronting his memories had been harder, and had hurt worse, than being shot. He wondered how he was going to bear it, the weight of his guilt. 'I didn't mean to upset you. Forgive me.'

'You must learn to forgive yourself, Max.'

'I don't know how to do that.' They stared at one another. Her tears had smeared the dirt on her oval face.

Another storm was now approaching. The sun was being darkened. Buffets of cold wind eddied into their cave. There was a gleam of lightning, followed by a long grumble of thunder.

She dressed his wounds again while the storm petered out into a grey drizzle, and then he drifted into sleep with his head on her lap. He felt Lola's fingers stroking his hair. Their lives had contracted down to this moment, this place, this time. There was nothing else, no distractions, no outside world. Just the two of them, in this strange cave of time.

The next days passed with little intrusion from the outside world. From time to time they heard the distant sounds of battle and the drone of aeroplanes. Otherwise there was silence.

Day by day, Max's wounds healed. The bruising faded from black to purple, then to yellow. The angry red scars knitted together and tightened. Lola cared for him as best she could, given the limited means at her disposal.

He was able to walk unaided after a while and help with the simple tasks of their life – sweeping the floor of the cave or cooking their spartan meals, occasionally taking walks outside.

And then the spell of bad weather broke. They awoke to find that the blizzards had stopped. Max called Lola to come and see. They stood on the ledge and looked out over the valley. The air was clear enough for them to see that smoke was rising from various places. They could hear the growling of tanks.

'We should leave today,' he said.

'It's too soon.'

'It's almost too late.'

'But where will we go?'

'South,' he said. 'To Bavaria. It will all be under American control soon. The Russians are heading west, to Berlin. Going that way, or towards any of the big cities, is suicide. And in Bavaria there's food, and warmer weather.' He showed her the route on the map. 'Munich is only a hundred miles or so from here. We can be there in a week, if our luck holds.'

'And if it doesn't hold?'

'We have to try, my darling. We don't have much option.' He folded the map and looked into her eyes. They were the colour of the wild honey with which she had healed him. In their depths were flecks of gold. Under the powdering of ash and dust, her skin was fresh, her parted lips moist. He felt that he had never seen her beauty so clearly before. That he had never really looked at her properly until this moment. He was captured, held by her spell. 'I love you,' he said.

With her arms around his neck, she drew his head down until his forehead rested against hers. Her body was pressed lightly to his. He felt dizziness wash through him. 'I thought I would lose you,' she whispered.

'I've always been terrified I will lose you.'

Lola tilted her face so that her lips were almost touching his. He could feel her warm breath on his mouth. 'I'm here, now. That's all that matters.'

They packed their knapsacks as lightly as they could. Max's plan was that it was better to travel light and fast, to reach Bavaria as quickly as possible. Lingering on the road would expose them to more dangers of all kinds.

He took a staff to support himself. As they set off down the mountain, he realised how weak he really was. Every step was agony. He felt he could hardly breathe. But getting away from the Russian advance dominated everything else. He tried to ignore the pain and weakness, breathing slowly and shallowly, leaning on the staff.

The bottom of the mountain was misty and silent. As they reached the lodge, they saw that it had been burned to the ground. Only the few walls that had been built of stone were left standing – the rest was a pile of blackened timbers. It was impossible to tell who had done it, and why. The house where they had spent perhaps their happiest time together was now a ruin.

They walked towards Unterstein. The trees were so laden with snow that some of their branches had broken, or were drooping on to the ground. They could hear the roaring of engines up ahead, and slipped off the path into the trees. Moving forward cautiously, they made out the huge shapes of tanks manoeuvring up ahead. They were German tanks, painted white in winter camouflage, the black *Wehrmacht* crosses visible on their flanks. This was the Waffen-SS regiment that Max had seen earlier. They gave the machines a wide berth, and approached the town through a back street.

As they walked cautiously through the mist, they made out a figure ahead of them. Max stopped, waiting for it to move. But it remained motionless. He and Lola approached, and saw that it was a corpse, hanging by the neck from a lamp post, its boots a few inches off the ground. The dead man was in *Wehrmacht* uniform. Around his neck was a placard reading, 'I BETRAYED MY PEOPLE'.

'Don't look,' he said to Lola.

'I've seen dead people before, Max,' she replied grimly.

At the next lamp post, another corpse was suspended. The placard around this one's neck read, 'I ABANDONED GERMAN WOMEN AND CHILDREN LIKE A COWARD INSTEAD OF PROTECTING THEM LIKE A MAN'.

'Who is doing this?' Lola asked.

'They call it the flying court martial. Anyone who thinks he has the power. Party thugs, local fanatics. They do it to make people fight to the last.'

'What if they stop you, Max?'

That idea had also occurred to Max. 'Don't worry,' he said, 'I know how to deal with these people.'

There were more hanged corpses along the road. All bore a placard, some simply reading 'TRAITOR' or 'COWARD'. There were women among the men. The mist mercifully obscured some of the details, but it was evident that many of the dead had been badly beaten before being hanged.

The houses along the road all appeared deserted. There was evidence of some fighting – bullet holes in walls, shattered windows, here and there a wall knocked down.

They reached the centre of the town. The column of refugees was still moving slowly along it. They joined the stream of humanity.

This was where the fiercest fighting had taken place. The fortified church had been bombed, and lay partly in ruins. The market square, too, had borne the brunt of Russian bombing, and many of the stately old houses around it had been destroyed. Some were still burning.

The refugees had to navigate around deep bomb craters in the road. At one of these bottlenecks, a group of SS men had set up a roadblock. Their commander was on horseback, watching the trudging migrants from his vantage point. He spotted Max at once.

'You,' he barked. 'Come here.'

Max and Lola were driven out of the column by helmeted soldiers carrying sub-machine guns. Behind the roadblock, against a back wall, a small square had been formed, lined by soldiers. Three men were already standing with their faces to the wall, with their hands held above their heads.

'Papers,' the SS officer demanded. He studied their documents. With a sinking heart, Max wondered how many more times they would have to stand trembling before the SS, waiting to hear their fate. He did not look at Lola.

'Where are you going?' the SS officer demanded.

'I'm taking my sister to our parents at Chemnitz, Herr *Sturmbannführer*.'

'If you can walk to Chemnitz, you can fight the Russians,' the man retorted. 'You are a deserter.'

'He's not!' Lola's voice was fierce. 'He can't fight. He's been shot. I had to stitch him myself.'

'If you are lying, you will join those traitors.' He indicated the three men against the wall. 'Show me the wound.'

The soldiers seized Max and hauled off his coat. He grunted in pain as they jerked his shirt open. The *Sturmbannführer* leaned down. He wore gold-rimmed glasses, through which his pale eyes assessed Max without emotion. 'Take off the bandage.'

The exposed wound was livid in the icy light, the flesh puckered and inflamed.

'He can hold a rifle,' one of the soldiers said brusquely. 'Or throw a grenade.'

'He'll die,' Lola said. 'He needs to go to a hospital for proper treatment.'

'See if the wound is authentic,' the SS officer commanded.

Without warning, the soldier slammed the butt of his rifle into Max's side. Lola cried out in horror as Max crumpled to the ground. Her crude stitching had been torn open, and blood was pouring scarlet into the snow. The soldier kicked Max. 'Get up.'

Max tried to focus through dark veils of pain. He managed to get on to his hands and knees, but his strength failed him, and he remained there, his head hanging, unable to speak.

'Looks authentic,' the soldier said laconically. 'He's no use to anybody.'

'Max!' Lola cried. She tried to kneel down beside him, but one of the soldiers jerked her roughly back. 'Please let him go,' Lola begged, trying not to cry. 'He's bleeding!'

The SS officer was looking down at Max, his gloved hands folded on his horse's neck. 'Blood is a very special juice,' he said absently. 'Goethe was right. It condemns a Jew to be always a Jew, no matter how he hides. And it condemns an Aryan to be always an Aryan, and to fight until he dies.'

At first Lola thought the man had seen through her masquerade. Then she realised that he was half mad. 'Please let my brother go,' she repeated.

'Take him.'

'Thank you,' she whispered. They released her, and she helped Max get to his feet. Max could hardly walk, but she wanted to get him away from the SS men before they changed their minds. She supported him as best she could. Their progress was painfully slow. At any moment, she expected to hear a shot. Step after faltering step, they kept moving.

Once out of the town, the string of evacuees became looser, the gaps between the groups lengthening. The landscape was bleaker than she had imagined it would be, white fields of snow and ice stretching as far as the eye could see. The wind was in their faces, cutting like a knife, whirling snow into their eyes.

Numbly, Max was wondering how he was going to manage the hundred-mile walk to Bavaria. They would be lucky to do it in a week at the best of times, given they had little food and inadequate clothing. Now, with his injury made much worse, it did not seem possible to do it at all. His torso was one huge pain. He could feel the warm blood running down his skin, soaking his clothes. Each step he took was a gulf into which he had to lower himself, and then climb up the other side.

'I'm too slow,' he said to Lola through clenched teeth. 'You're going to have to leave me behind.'

'No, Max. I'll never do that. We'll just go little by little.'

'You don't understand. The Russians can cover twenty miles a day. They'll overtake us, long before we get to Bavaria.'

'Then let them overtake us,' Lola retorted. 'I'm not leaving you, so you can stop talking like that. As soon as we find somewhere, I'll put your bandages back on.'

A few miles out of Unterstein, they reached a barn in the middle of a field. They turned off the road and went into it. It was already full of refugees, taking shelter from the weather. Faces of the very old and the very young turned to them as they stumbled in together. They found a corner where Max could lie down. Lola opened his shirt, and drew in her breath. The wound was open again, and blood was oozing out constantly.

'I'll have to stitch it again, Max.'

He grimaced tiredly. 'No more stitching, my darling. This teddy bear has been played with enough. He is falling to pieces, and all his stuffing is coming out.'

'I can't leave you like this!'

He looked up at her with heavy eyes. 'The next town is Freiburg. There's bound to be a hospital there. We'll get help from a doctor.' His fingers closed around hers. 'Thank you, Lola. And I'm sorry.'

'What are you sorry for?'

He gestured briefly. 'All of it.'

'Don't be silly.'

She wrapped the cloth around him as tightly as he could bear, and they rested, with Max's head in her lap. They had come less than ten miles from the cave, but neither of them felt like going any further today.

The winter evening fell swiftly. They ate a little of their food. Max ate even less than Lola did. There were a hundred or so travellers packed into the barn, and they huddled together for warmth in the darkness. The wind was howling outside, making the rafters creak and the wooden walls rattle.

There was little sleep for any of them. It was too cold and too noisy – and the Russians were too close – for rest. Early the next morning, the party began to stir, coughing and groaning. Three or four hadn't made it through the night. Their bodies were already stiff, and had to be left in the position in which they had died.

One of the dead was an old woman. Her husband sat looking down at her face. When they tried to get him to leave, he shook his head. 'I'm not going. I will stay and wait.'

Nobody asked him what he was waiting for.

At first light, they were on the road once more. It had snowed again in the night, and the tracks of the previous travellers had already been almost obliterated. The fresh snow made walking difficult. Max plodded with painful slowness, leaning heavily on his staff, his head down. He would not let Lola support him. They soon fell behind the rest of the people in the group, and were overtaken by the group behind them, which included horse-drawn carts. Lola begged for a lift from these, but all were already packed to capacity with families and their possessions. One man lashed out at her with his horsewhip to drive her away. She gave up.

It was a barren, white world. The snow erased almost every detail of the landscape: trees were blurred into hills, villages were all but rubbed out. There was only the road that led south to Bavaria, and the dark figures that straggled along it.

At mid-morning, they heard the rumble of vehicles behind them. A long military convoy was approaching. With honking horns and revving engines, the *Wehrmacht* trucks pushed through the refugee column, forcing the carts and pedestrians off the road, and into the fields. There was no arguing with the huge vehicles. Each one was filled with soldiers or equipment. Half a regiment was on the move. The soldiers stared dully at the refugees as they passed, looking dirty and defeated, far from the proud German soldiers of the posters.

'Where are they going?' Lola asked Max over the roaring of the engines.

'They're retreating,' he replied tersely.

'But they were shooting deserters in Unterstein!'

'They want boys, old men and the wounded to die in their place while they get to safety,' he said bitterly.

And within an hour of being passed by the soldiers, a far greater danger appeared. They heard the drone of an aircraft in the sky. Panic-stricken, the travellers ahead of them began to flounder into the snow on either side of the road. But the enemy was coming fast. They saw it as a dot in the grey sky that swiftly became a cross, and then a dark-green Russian fighter that dropped to a few hundred feet above the ground to strafe the convoy.

Max and Lola threw themselves into the ditch. The machine-gun bullets churned up the snow yards from where they lay. With a boom, it passed overhead, then climbed back into the sky. It did not return, but there were bodies lying in the snow now, and wrecked carts, and the screams of the wounded and the bereaved.

'We have to get on to the smaller roads,' Max said, as they picked themselves up. 'They'll keep attacking the main roads from now on.'

'That's going to take us even longer,' Lola said. She was desperately concerned for Max. He looked exhausted, his face white and drained. Blood had frozen dark and hard on his clothes. She had banked on getting to a hospital today.

'I know,' he replied. 'But the Russians will use the main roads to move along, too. And soon there will be tanks, as well.' He was studying the worn map, which was by now torn in several pieces, and had to be arranged to make sense. 'Look, there are side roads that go through the farms. We can take those.'

They walked past the dead and wounded. There was nothing to be done for them. They had to keep moving. These sudden explosions of violence used to leave Lola shattered emotionally. Now, she took them in her stride. You just kept going. You just looked after yourself, and what was precious to you.

At the first junction, they took a side road. It seemed to be the one marked on their map, although all the signposts had by now been taken down by the *Wehrmacht* in a hopeless effort to make difficulties for the Russians. Narrower than the main road, this one was far quieter, but impeded by deeper drifts of snow. The landscape was even more desolate. The land was flat, its bleakness interrupted by woods here and there.

Coming over the hill to a small bridge over a frozen stream, they found the road was blocked by a pony trap that had over-turned, scattering its contents in the snow. The horse was on its side, thrashing and whinnying in the twisted traces. Sitting by the side of the road, with his head in his hands, was a boy. Seeing them, he came wading through the snow, shouting. It was Hans-Peter, their friend from the cave at Unterstein. His face was streaked with tears and dirt.

'Please help!' he begged. 'My grandmother is under the cart, but I can't lift it on my own!'

He had been waiting alone for hours. Lola and Max joined him, and managed to push the cart upright, by dint of unloading everything that remained on it to make it lighter. The horse stag-gered upright, exhausted and half frozen, but apparently uninjured. Oma Mathilde was buried in the snow beneath it. They dug her out, but she was already cold and stiff, her lined face smoothed out in death.

'I'm sorry, Hans-Peter,' Lola said, putting her arms around the boy. 'She's dead. But we have to keep going.'

'We must bury her, first,' the boy said, weeping.

'The ground is frozen,' Max said. He was all but drained with the effort of righting the cart. 'I'm sorry, Hans-Peter. We can take her with us or leave her here. But we can't bury her.'

The boy touched his grandmother's icy face. 'I will come back for you, Oma,' he promised.

They laid the old woman's body by the side of the road and started picking up the scattered bundles and boxes. Hans-Peter was crying tiredly, but with dignity. But the cart was the miracle Lola had prayed for.

They put Max in the cart, covered with blankets. 'Try to sleep, my darling,' she said, kissing him. She climbed on the seat beside Hans-Peter, and they set off.

Hans-Peter talked quietly, staring ahead. After leaving the cave, he and his grandmother had passed through Unterstein in the cart, and had come across the same SS officer and his thugs who had beaten Max. On finding out that Hans-Peter was thirteen, the SS man had declared the boy old enough to fight, and had marked him down as to be despatched to the front, on the Czechoslovakian border, along with a truckload of boys of the same age.

Luckily, the convoy of children had been intercepted by a *Wehrmacht* general, who had promptly sent them back. Hans-Peter had been able to find his grandmother, and continue their flight south, but by then they had lost over a week. But for that, and for the cart overturning in a drift, Lola and Max would never have met them again.

By mid-afternoon, as it grew dark, they reached a tiny village, no more than a row of houses. The place, almost untouched by the war, was abandoned. The farming community who had inhabited it had already fled.

They found an empty barn where they could shelter for the night. There was even hay for the pony. Hans-Peter boiled some potatoes in the billycan while Lola tried to make Max comfortable. He was very weak. He had bled heavily all day and his clothes were stiff with it. If only she could stop the bleeding that was slowly draining his life away. But she couldn't. She washed the wounds carefully with warm water. He smiled up at her. The heavy look around his eyes had intensified. 'You're so strong,' he said quietly. 'Much stronger than I am.'

She tried to laugh through the tears that had filled her eyes. 'Only because you've been wounded, my dear.'

He shook his head slowly. 'No. I could never have done what you've done. I couldn't have endured what you've endured.'

She fastened the bandages as best she could. 'Try and eat something now.'

'I'm not hungry. I just want to rest.' He closed his eyes.

Lola ate with Hans-Peter. 'Herr Max will die tomorrow if we keep going,' the boy said, keeping his voice low.

'Don't say that,' she replied fiercely. 'He's not going to die!'

'Sorry, Fräulein Lola,' the boy muttered.

'We'll be in Munich soon. And then we'll get him to a hospital.'

'Yes, of course,' Hans-Peter said.

Upset, she couldn't finish the humble meal; and when she took a plate to Max, he was asleep.

She sat with Hans-Peter, consoling him for the death of his grandmother, until he fell asleep where he sat by the fire. She laid him down and covered him with blankets. Then she went over and curled up next to Max.

She was awoken, she was not sure how many hours later, by Max touching her face. She turned to him in the darkness.

'What is it?' she whispered.

'I wanted to say goodbye,' he replied in a low voice.

'What?'

'I won't be here tomorrow.'

'Max, no!' She reached out to him, and found that he was lying in a pool of blood. '*Max!*'

'You once said that Hitler was the Pied Piper,' he said. 'It's time for me to go under the hill with all the others. But I want you to know that I love you, Lola. I think I loved you from the first moment I saw you. It just took me a long time to realise it.'

'Max, please don't die. Please don't leave me!'

'I must. But you will live. Live a good life, Lola. You deserve it. I don't.'

'Don't say that!'

'The only good I ever did was to help you a little. You've made me so much happier than I deserved.'

Lola was crying. 'Oh, Max, I can't see your face!'

'Don't cry, Lola.' His voice was growing weaker. 'Promise me you won't stay here. Don't let the Russians take you. Use my ration cards. When you get to Munich with Hans-Peter, wait for the Americans. Tell them everything. They will look after you.'

'I love you, Max. I can't go on without you.'

'You can. You saved my life so many times. You are the strong one. Not me.'

'Max!'

'Don't trust anyone. Don't give up. Don't forget me.'

He said nothing more after that. He sighed heavily from time to time. She cried helplessly as she listened to his breaths get slower and shallower, until at last they ceased completely.

Leaving Max's body behind was the hardest thing she'd yet had to do. She had no tears left by morning, but she felt desperately alone, desperately defenceless. The boy helped her arrange Max outside the barn. She put his identity card in his hands and crossed them on his breast, then wrapped him in a blanket. It was all she could do for him.

'Goodbye, Max,' she said, 'my brave knight.'

She and Hans-Peter huddled together on the cart. The boy held the reins; she followed the shredded map. This part of the country was all but deserted. Occasionally they saw a smudge of smoke over a remote farmstead, but the roads were empty, and the snow in places very deep. The signposts of the villages had all been taken down, but in any case, the map didn't mention their names either, so their progress was largely guesswork.

'I'm sorry about your brother, Fräulein Lola,' Hans-Peter said. 'He was very brave.'

'He died a soldier's death,' Lola replied after a while. 'He wasn't my brother. He was my friend. He lent me his name, because I am Jewish, and hiding from the Gestapo.'

The boy glanced at her curiously. 'I've never seen a Jew.'

'Haven't you? Well, here you have one before you.'

He studied her with innocent blue eyes. 'We learned about the Jews in school, but I didn't understand much. I still don't really know what a Jew is. I thought you would be different.'

'I am no different,' she said.

'Yes, you are,' he replied. 'You are very pretty.'

She grimaced. 'Thank you, Hans-Peter.'

'Would you have married him – Herr Max?'

'I don't know,' she replied. 'It doesn't matter, now. We loved each other. And that was enough.'

They spent the night in the open, because darkness fell before they could reach any shelter. Snow was drifting on the wind, and Lola was afraid they would freeze in the night. But Hans-Peter made the pony lie down, and they huddled up against the animal's belly, covered with a tarpaulin from the cart. The warm smell of horse enveloped them.

In the morning, the snow had piled up on their tarpaulin. It had provided a kind of insulation. The sky had cleared, and sun slanted down on the snowy fields, colouring them orange and gold.

Lola wept for Max, that he would not see this morning sun, that he would never be at her side again, that there would be no more time together. She felt broken. She had finally lost the last person who made life worth living. What remained was only survival.

She made herself stop crying. Crying did not help you survive. And there was a long way to go.

It took them a week to get to Chemnitz. The city had been recently bombed, its oil refineries still burning, pouring black smoke up into the winter sky. Their horse was worn out and half starved, so they rested in a deserted factory for two days, recovering from the gruelling trek.

Here they caught up with the war news. The Reich was crumbling, shrinking. Every day a city or a major town had surrendered to one or other of the Allied armies – sometimes with little loss of life, more often after a dreadful and pointless battle, insisted upon by the authorities, unnecessarily wasting tens of thousands more lives on both sides.

Dresden had fallen, and the Soviet troops were at Unterstein. The Americans had already begun advancing into Bavaria. She and Hans-Peter were in an enclave, sandwiched between two mighty armies. Lola didn't know whether it was better to stay put, and wait for the end, or press on to Bavaria.

Hans-Peter, like Max, had an ingrained dread of the Russians. 'If the Bolsheviks capture us,' he said, fixing her with his serious blue eyes, 'we will be slaves for the rest of our lives. They won't care that you're Jewish. Or that I am only thirteen. We'll never escape them. We have to go on.'

From Chemnitz, they kept to the smaller roads, even though their progress was slower. The weather was improving now, the

309

snow melting into slush and the first signs of spring appearing. The streams they crossed were no longer frozen hard. Water could be heard running under the thawing ice.

On the second evening after Chemnitz, they arrived at a village on the edge of a large wood. Here they stopped and heard more news: the war was continuing. There was to be no surrender. Goebbels was claiming new victories on the Eastern and Western Fronts. He was still promising a new wonder weapon that would give an instant, overwhelming victory to Germany. A ranting, rambling speech exhorted all Germans, old and young, to fight to the death to keep 'the barbarian hordes' from setting foot on the sacred soil of the Reich.

But the sacred soil of the Reich was already under the feet of the invaders.

A kindly couple, seeing their destitute condition, offered them a barn to stable the pony overnight, as well as a bedroom for the night. They didn't ask any questions, and invited Lola and Hans-Peter to eat supper with them. They had a daughter working in the Reich Chancellery in Berlin – 'just about your age, my dear' – who gave them news very different from Goebbels' claims. There was heavy fighting in the capital. The Russians were shelling the city night and day, causing terrible destruction; Berlin was a shambles, without water, electricity or gas. It could not possibly hold out much longer.

The couple, whose name was Hahn, were sick with worry about their daughter, but there was nothing to be done. The city was surrounded, and nobody could get in or out.

Being farming folk, they had astounding stocks of food: milk, eggs, bread, salami, macaroni, potatoes. They were generous, piling Lola's and Hans-Peter's plates. 'And we will give you something to take with you tomorrow,' they promised.

The Americans, they said, were now less than a hundred miles from Munich, the capital of the Nazi movement, where Hitler had made his first speeches and gathered his first followers. 'The Reich cannot last if Munich falls,' Herr Hahn said, shaking his head. 'The best thing for us all is if the Americans come quickly.'

Lola and Hans-Peter ate their first proper meal, and slept in their first proper bed, in weeks.

The next day, they set off early, with a sack of provisions given to them by the Hahns. The thaw was continuing. Fresh green patches were emerging from the white swathes of snow. The icy chill in the air had lessened. The pony, as though sensing spring in the air, broke into a trot despite his weariness, the harness jingling.

They reached the outskirts of Hof in the late afternoon.

It, too, had been recently bombed, its railway yard blazing, the blue sky overhead smeared with oily smoke. The roads were choked with thousands of refugees trying to get into the city. They had finally reached Bavaria.

Chapter 19

They slept in an overcrowded shelter in Hof for two nights. There were no rooms left for the bombed-out and the refugees. They wandered the town by day, and went back to the shelter in the evening. Their life had become one of waiting and uncertainty.

The food supplies that the Hahns had so generously given them had lasted a few days, but had now run out. The Welfare sisters at the shelter offered only thin soup three times a day, and noticed that Lola and Hans-Peter kept returning for meals, and were starting to make sharp comments. Lola had Max's food coupons as well as her own, but finding anywhere to shop in the town, which was filling every day with thousands more displaced and bombed-out people, proved impossible. The few shops that were open had nothing edible on the shelves.

So they ate in restaurants, congested canteens where one had to take a ticket and then queue to get in, and take whatever was on offer. These places were strict in demanding ration cards, too, and there was none of the kindly cheating that had made life easier earlier in the war. Each dish required so many meat coupons, so many fat coupons, so many egg coupons and so forth; and eventually, all of their coupons ran out.

She was forced to face the necessity of applying for new ones, something that terrified her. Any encounter with officialdom was potentially fatal – and she no longer had Max to help her. But unless they were to starve, she had to do it.

They asked for directions to the Food Office, which was close by the city hall. The offices were heavily crowded, with people queuing down the street. They got into the line and slowly edged forward.

While they were waiting, the air-raid sirens began moaning, and a policeman shouted to them to run for the shelter; but such was the desperation for food that hardly anyone left the line. They crouched where they were, looking up anxiously at the skies. Within a few minutes, they saw two Russian aircraft roar overhead, their red stars plainly visible. There was the sound of an explosion a few streets away, rattling the shutters and filling the air with smoke and dust. Some people flattened themselves on the ground, but still nobody left their place in the line.

As the droning of the engines faded away, they cautiously picked themselves up and dusted themselves off. Once again, Lola was struck by how calmly she accepted these irruptions of violence into her life. There were a few moments of terror, and then life simply went on. Her fear of bombs was still less than her fear of the Gestapo.

'When we get our coupons,' the boy said, 'I'm going to go to the restaurant and order *Weisswurst* and mashed potatoes and gravy. And a beer.'

'A beer?' Lola said, smiling. 'You're not even fourteen!'

He drew himself up. 'I'll be fourteen soon.'

'That's still too young to drink beer. You're just a boy.'

Hans-Peter frowned, and grew sulky at that.

They were separated by surname in the thronged building. Lola queued up the stairs to the ration-coupon office, her heart starting to beat fast. The line moved slowly, inching along, with much squabbling and ill temper. The encounter in the office was nerve-racking but brief. The harassed official made only a cursory examination of her papers. There were so many others in the same position, in any case, that she probably didn't seem unusual in any way.

The precious sheaf of yellow stamps, good for a month, were handed over the counter, and Lola jostled out of the office with her heart singing. She made her way down the stairs to find Hans-Peter.

She saw him standing near the entrance. She waved to him happily and pushed through the crowds towards him. As she reached him, she saw that he looked white and frightened. She paused; but it was too late. Strong hands grasped her arms on either side. Two men wearing leather coats had closed in on her. One showed her his metal badge.

'Gestapo,' he said curtly. 'Your papers, please.'

With trembling fingers, she handed over her identity card. The man gave it a hard look, and then put it in his pocket. 'Come with us.'

Blindly, she allowed them to push her out into the street. As they passed Hans-Peter, he called out in a shaky voice, 'I'm sorry, Fräulein Lola. I'm sorry!'

The interrogation room was small, and stank of stale sweat and terror. She had anticipated this moment so many times, preparing the lies she would tell, the excuses she would make; but now that it was here, there was an iron ball in her gullet that prevented any falsehood from coming out.

The Gestapo chief was fat enough to make the leather belts on his uniform creak when he moved. He was smoking a cigar, the possession of which – along with his obesity – marked out his power. 'You employed an innocent Aryan boy to disguise your identity. Have you no shame?'

One of the last things Max had said to her was to trust no one. But she had trusted a boy she hardly knew, foolishly revealing her secret. Hans-Peter, it seemed, had been offended by her telling him he was too young to drink beer. His boyish pride piqued, and perhaps not really having any idea what he was doing, he had betrayed her to the first Gestapo man he had seen.

'It was not my intention to use him,' she said in a low voice. 'It just happened like that.'

The Gestapo chief sneered. *'It just happened like that?* It just happened that you have been hiding from the authorities, living hidden like a maggot in the healthy lives of others?' He picked up his pen. 'Give me the names of all those who have sheltered you.'

'They are all dead,' she replied.

The blow across her face was so violent, and so unexpected, that she reeled back against the wall and slumped to the floor, numbly aware of blood flowing hotly from her nose.

The rough hands of the men behind her hauled her to her feet.

'The names. Or you will regret ever having been born.'

Lola spat the blood out of her mouth. She thought of Max, her brave knight. Of Magda. Of Anselm and Ditte. Of others before them who had risked everything to protect her from men like these. Revealing their names could hurt none of them, since none of them were in this dreadful world any more.

But revealing their names would be a betrayal, nevertheless. They had not betrayed her. She would not betray them.

She looked up slowly. 'They're all dead,' she repeated. 'They're not here for you to punish. But I won't tell you their names.'

This time the blow was even worse, crushingly brutal. Once again, they dragged Lola to her feet. They waited for the hurt to sink in, for her to feel it.

'Do you think you can resist us? The names.'

Lola couldn't speak, but she shook her head, her eyes closed against the pain.

They hit her again.

'The boy says there was a man with you. A panzer commander, called Max. Is this true?'

She simply shook her head again.

'Did you have sexual relations with this man?' They hit her again. 'Did you commit racial defilement? What was his name? What was his rank? What was his regiment?'

'She's bleeding all over the floor,' a voice said, as they picked her up yet again. 'The dirty bitch. Why are you bothering with her, Herr Köhler? Let's just take her out and shoot her.'

'I am not going to be beaten by a smart-mouth Jewess,' the man across the desk retorted. 'Not here. Not now. Give her a bath.'

They thrust her head under the water. And held her there until her lungs were bursting, and the terror was so great that every nerve in her body screamed out not to die. Then she had to take a breath, and the water rushed into her lungs with a pain that was beyond belief. Her mind went red and black and purple. There was a despair deeper and greater than she had ever known.

Only then did they haul her out of the basin. They watched her vomit up the water, choking and coughing desperately, trying not to die on the floor, under their boots.

The coughing was the torture. It saved them the effort of hitting her or kicking her. The pain of the water tearing at her lungs was worse than anything they could easily inflict. It felt like fire, though it was only water. It racked her and shook her and convulsed her, panic and pain doing all the work for them.

Then they picked her up and did it again.

At first it was more terrible than she had feared in her worst imaginings. Then she started to lose count of the number of times they did it. She forgot who she was. She forgot her name, and why this was being done to her. All she remembered was that she must not yield. That she must not give up this last secret.

Because whoever she was, and why ever they were doing this to her, there had to be that tiny core that remained unbroken.

There had to be something that was not going to be taken away from her.

They dragged in Hans-Peter. He had a swollen eye and cheek, and was crying bitterly.

'Fräulein Lola,' he sobbed. 'Tell them! Please! Tell them!'

Lola raised her head slowly. 'I am Heloise Rosenstein, of Spandauerstrasse, Berlin,' she said. 'I can tell you nothing more.'

'Tell them about Herr Max,' Hans-Peter begged. 'Just give them what they want!'

She shook her head.

The Gestapo chief, Köhler, unbuttoned his holster and took out his Luger pistol. 'Do you want me to shoot the boy in front of you?'

'Please, Fräulein Lola,' the boy blubbered. 'Don't let them kill me, *please*.'

'Don't hurt him,' Lola said. 'He did nothing.'

Köhler put the muzzle in the boy's ear. 'I will make a deal with you, Jewess. If you do not tell me the name and rank of the race traitor, I will blow this boy's brains out, here and now. And then we will resume the interrogation. Until you either speak or die. If you tell me, I will blow *your* brains out, here and now. And all your suffering will be at an end.'

Two tears slid down Lola's bruised cheeks. 'I cannot tell you,' she whispered.

There was an agonised silence. Then Köhler laughed shortly. 'You see, Hans-Peter? This is what you get for helping a Jew. She would rather see your brains all over the wall than give up the name of the race traitor, who is in any case dead. That is the nature of the Jew. She has defiled you, just as she defiled the man.'

Hans-Peter was hysterical. 'Please, Fräulein Lola, I beg you! I beg you!'

Köhler grunted. 'I have run out of patience. Hold her head over the drain.'

They forced Lola to her knees, and then on to her face on the wet, tiled floor. A boot kicked her head so that it lay over the iron drain that had been set into the floor. Other boots stood on her arms and legs, immobilising her.

She heard Köhler's dry, rather thin voice intoning, 'Heloise Rosenstein, you have been found guilty of crimes against the racial hygiene of the German state. The sentence is death, to be carried out immediately.'

Lola had been in a state of exhaustion, but now her heart raced into overdrive. She found herself gasping for oxygen. An image surged into her mind, of Max's face, Max's smile. *I am waiting for you, Lola. Not long, now.*

She heard Hans-Peter wailing in terror.

She heard Köhler rack the slide of the pistol, loading a bullet into the firing chamber. The cold muzzle of the weapon pressed against her skull.

'Do you wish to talk?' Köhler asked. 'Your last chance.'

One of the other men said something, but Lola couldn't hear it over the pounding in her ears.

318

'No,' she whispered.

'Then goodbye, Jewess.'

The silence yawned open. Lola felt herself falling, as though the ceramic tiles beneath her had emptied into a vast, black void.

Köhler pulled the trigger.

Lola heard the snap of the firing pin. But no bullet tore through her brain. The Luger was unloaded.

As the other Gestapo men dragged her to her feet, she became aware that her legs felt warm. In blind terror, she had emptied her bladder. She was crying, too, without realising it. Crying because she could no longer see Max in her mind. Crying because her heart had been wrenched all to pieces for too many years.

The men were laughing as they half walked, half carried her down the stairs to the basement. The corridor was lined with steel doors. They took her to a cell. They put chains on her wrists, and pushed her on to the bare floor. There she curled into a foetal ball, sobbing. The metal door slammed shut. There was no window in the cell. Only darkness.

She didn't know how long she lay in the darkness. Certainly days, perhaps three or four. For long periods, she wasn't sure whether she was alive or dead. Perhaps this was death, this eternal darkness, eternal pain. Perhaps this was Hell.

She suffered from raging thirst. The cellar dripped in places, and she was able to lap water from the floor, or she would have died.

She spent some of the time with Heidi, engaged in long conversations, which she couldn't remember when she woke up in tears. Sometimes Max was there, holding her in his arms and rocking her to and fro like a child. Sometimes they were both there. Once she was visited by Magda.

Otherwise, there was only darkness.

She was awoken by a touch. The touch was real, from a real hand. She stirred blindly, dazzled by the grey, subterranean light that came in from the door, dim as it was. The person kneeling beside her was a woman, wearing a Welfare sister's crisp, white apron and cap, her pale face framed by thick spectacles. Recalling that she smelled of her own vomit and urine, Lola was ashamed.

'Drink this.' The sister held the cup to Lola's mouth. She drank greedily, choking on the cold, ersatz coffee, and spattering the other woman. 'Slowly,' the sister warned.

'Sorry.'

The woman peered at her. 'I know what they did to you. It was wrong. They should not have done that. You made them angry.'

Lola's voice was just a croak, which came out with a painful effort. 'What's going to happen to me?'

'They're talking about you, now. They expected you to be weak. But you are strong. They feel very sorry for what they did.'

This must come from the Gestapo textbook, Lola thought. A mock execution, and then send in a kindly sister with a cup of coffee, and comfort, and flattery. 'I won't tell them what they want to know.'

The woman held the cup to Lola's lips again. 'I don't think they'll hurt you any more.' She paused. 'Things have changed.'

Lola gulped the rest of the bitter coffee. 'What has changed?'

'The Führer is dead.'

Lola was silent for a long time, wondering if this was a dream, after all. She shook her head wearily. 'You're lying to me. It can't be true.'

'It's true. Adolf Hitler is dead. The radio broadcast said he fell heroically in the battle for the Reich capital.' The sister lowered her voice. 'But people are saying that he shot himself in the Führerbunker. Goebbels is dead, too. And his wife, and all their children. Himmler and Göring have vanished.'

'When was this?'

'Two days ago. What will become of us? The Americans are almost here!' The woman began crying. Lola peered at her through her swollen eyes and realised that she was not crying from grief over Hitler's death, but from anxiety.

'Then – can I go?' Lola asked warily.

'They want to speak to you upstairs.' The sister wiped her eyes. 'Come.'

Lola could hardly walk. The sister had to help her up the stairs. She could only move with painful slowness, like a very old woman.

The Gestapo men were waiting for her, looking sombre. They made her sit at a table. Köhler had ordered food for her. They watched her attentively as a plate of fried eggs and fried potatoes was put in front of her. Her gorge rose at the smell of the greasy dish. In any case, two of her teeth had been loosened by the beating they'd given her, and her jaw ached abominably. She pushed the plate away. 'I can't eat.'

'You must be hungry,' Köhler said. 'You don't like the food? We can make you something else. We have chicken, if you don't want to eat pork.'

Lola almost laughed at the monstrous irony. A few days ago, these bullies had brutally tortured her. Now they hovered like anxious waiters. 'I would like some water, please.'

A carafe of water and a glass were swiftly put in front of her. 'Would you like to see a doctor? We can call one.'

'I don't need a doctor.'

'Good, good. That is better, not so?' Köhler cleared his throat. 'We were harsh with you. Perhaps we treated you roughly. We were only doing our duty. We were just doing our job. We kept law and order. Nothing more. We are different from the SS.' He frowned. 'The SS know what they have on their conscience. We never did anything like that. Never! You understand?'

Lola took painful sips of the water. She stared at the congealing eggs and potatoes, bemused. 'I understand.'

'Our enemies have never understood us. Especially American Jewry.' The Gestapo chief appeared to be searching for words. 'But perhaps if someone were to speak up for us – someone like you – they would see us in a better light? When the Americans arrive, I mean. So that there are no . . . reprisals.'

Lola had slowly finished the glass. They refilled it solicitously. She was starting to understand. They thought she could put in a good word for them with the Americans. The situation had its grotesque comedy, but she was still in deadly danger. If she gave the wrong answer now, they were capable of killing her without a second thought. 'I think the best thing,' she said carefully, 'is that you release me now. And when I meet the Americans, I will explain to them that you were only doing your duty.'

She saw the mingled doubt and relief in their faces. 'Good. This is a small town, you see. We don't do the things they do in bigger places. We try to be kind, here. Eat your food, Fräulein.' The men withdrew to confer in low voices in the corridor outside. It was clear that, while Köhler wanted to let her go, some of his men didn't.

The sister patted her shoulder. 'You said the right thing,' she whispered. 'We're relying on you. The SS will disappear overnight. You'll see. They've always been arrogant bastards. They have their own ways of escaping. But we – we have to stay. There's nowhere for us to go. And the Americans will need us after they arrive. Who else will keep order? You understand?'

Lola was still absorbing the news that Hitler was dead. She felt something like puzzlement. Adolf Hitler had been an all-powerful

322

figure in her life ever since she could remember – a cruel and vengeful tyrant, whose enmity had destroyed everything she held dear, omnipotent and all-consuming. Did his sudden death mean that Nazism, too, had suddenly died?

'Is the war over?' she asked cautiously.

'No. They're fighting on with old men and children. They send them against tanks with hand bombs.' The sister took out her handkerchief. 'There's nothing left of Germany any more,' she said through her tears. 'Just part of Berlin and upper Bavaria. But they haven't surrendered yet. Why don't they surrender? It's madness!'

She talked on while the Gestapo men discussed Lola's ultimate fate. She spoke of Hitler's death with neither jubilation nor grief. It was as though some distant and elderly relative, whose death had been anticipated for some time, had finally given up the ghost.

Admiral Dönitz had been appointed to succeed Hitler in the Führer's will. Nobody knew whether that gave him the power to sue for peace, or even to surrender. But now that Hitler was dead, people were saying the impossible – a German capitulation – was possible. The sister repeated a phrase that had evidently become current: 'Better an end with terror than an endless terror.'

The Gestapo men came back in. Köhler's fat face was wreathed in a saccharine smile.

'Good,' he said, rubbing his hands. 'You can wash, Fräulein. The sister will show you where. Then we will give you back your possessions. And new clothes.' His arm snapped up above his shoulder. 'Heil Hitler!'

Lola slowly raised her own hand. 'Heil Hitler,' she replied.

Lola limped out of the building. A long ladder was propped up over the door, and she had to duck to get under it. She looked up.

Two men were taking down the large metal swastika that had been fastened on the gable of the Gestapo headquarters.

They had given her knapsack back, with all her things in it, as well as clean clothes and a little money. She wandered through the streets, feeling that she was in a dream of some kind. Her body and spirit were battered, but it all seemed unreal – the crowded streets, the bombed buildings, the storm clouds overhead. There was a continuous rumble of artillery in the air. It never stopped. Fighting was going on in the outskirts of the town. But the people in the street, grey-faced and huddled against the cold, seemed unmoved. Perhaps hunger and cold were more pressing enemies than the Americans.

The deep drone of aircraft rose above the sound of the guns. A formation of silver-grey planes soared overhead. They were very low, seeming to skim the roofs of the buildings. She saw the red, white and blue stars on their fuselage. They were the first American planes she had seen since Münster.

They disappeared from view, and shortly afterwards, bomb blasts shook the street, rattling the windows. Lola hesitated, listening to the chatter of machine guns, the drumming of the cannon. Then she started walking again. She did not know where she was heading. There seemed nowhere to go. But her legs kept on moving, and she kept walking, just as everyone around her was walking, purposeful yet aimless, as though movement alone might provide safety, keep body and soul together, enable her not to be in the place where the bombs fell, or the shrapnel flew.

She passed a group of medics, hurrying along with stretchers, their faces taut. On each stretcher was a bloodstained heap with a helmet on its chest. An arm dangled, dripping. The front could not be far away. Around the corner, she came upon a party of soldiers, sitting on the kerb of the street, gnawing on loaves of bread. They looked up at her. She saw that they were all boys of thirteen or fourteen, with dirty faces and frightened eyes. Their weapons

– antiquated rifles and piles of stick grenade launchers – were scattered around them.

Suddenly the constant barrage of artillery fire turned into deafening blasts close by. The rattle of the machine gun was very loud and urgent. Bullets whistled through the air, careening off the brickwork. The boy-soldiers scattered, dropping everything. 'The Americans are here!' one of them screamed as he fled.

Lola came to a halt. She stood at the end of the street, too exhausted to put one foot in front of another any longer. She simply waited.

The sound of engines roaring and straining grew louder. More bullets screamed past her. More explosions shook the street.

And then, around the corner, an American tank rolled into view. It was squat and bulbous. It reminded her suddenly of the old-fashioned pressure cooker her mother had used, so long ago, to cook brisket on Sundays. She closed her eyes, and she could smell the fragrant steam that filled the kitchen, could taste the rich soup of beer, celery, onions, bay leaves, thyme, the tastes and smells of a world she could hardly remember, and would never forget.

Chapter 20

The Red Cross official was a Swiss, and spoke German with a gurgling *Schweizerdeutsch* accent that Lola found hard to follow. He had a supercilious manner, and stared at Lola with sceptical, slightly protuberant green eyes.

'And you admit that your papers are false?' he asked for the third time.

'No, they aren't false,' she replied, trying to keep her temper. 'They were issued by a government official in Münster. But the name and the address are not mine.'

'This,' he replied coldly, 'means that they are *ipso facto* false papers.'

'I am a Jew,' she retorted. 'If I had been travelling around the Reich with my own papers, I would have been killed a long time ago.'

'Quite,' he replied. 'But you have no proof of your Jewishness. Nor,' he cut in, raising a bony hand as she tried to reply, 'of what you claim is your *real* identity.'

'My real identity is Heloise Rosenstein of Spandauerstrasse, Berlin. But as far as I know, every member of my family is now dead. I've been told that my former address no longer exists. It was bombed to rubble by the Americans. And that part of the city is now under Russian control, in any case.' She drew a breath, trying to stay calm. 'As for my Jewishness, what would you like me to do? Recite the Torah?'

He raised an eyebrow. 'That would prove nothing.'

'Don't you think it's ironic that my Jewishness was a certain sentence of death during the war, and had to be concealed at any cost – and now that the war is finally over, I am unable to get help from you because you refuse to believe that I am a Jew?'

'It is not a question of belief,' he replied, unmoved. 'It is a question of proof. You must have some means of proving who you are in order to receive assistance.' He steepled his fingers, leaning forward across the desk. 'And quite frankly, Fräulein, your story is most—' He searched for the word. '—atypical.'

'You mean you think I am lying?'

'We deal with many displaced Jews,' he replied. 'They come to us from concentration camps and other prisons. Their authenticity is unquestionable. They have been ill-treated. They are malnourished. They bear tattoos. Other inmates can confirm their identity. You, on the other hand, come to us in perfect health—'

'Not exactly perfect health.'

'—with a tale that you have been in hiding since 1941, in the homes of various individuals who are now, conveniently, dead—'

'Their deaths were not very convenient to me,' Lola said in a low voice.

'—so that there is no corroboration of your story or your identity,' he concluded. 'You have no tattoo?'

'I was never in a concentration camp.'

'And the Jewish identity card, which under the Third Reich you were obliged to carry?'

'I destroyed that.'

'You should have kept it,' he said censoriously.

'What for? To ensure my death if I was to be captured?'

'It would have constituted at least some kind of proof. As it is, there is no evidence who you really are, or where you have spent the past six years. I cannot offer you assistance until these questions are answered.' He sighed, picking up his pen as though it were a great weight. 'Nevertheless, I will take your details. If you are truly who you say you are, you will receive accommodation, financial help, compensation for losses, and travel permits. Let us begin.'

Lola walked out into the mud and the rain. It was a change to be a nobody. Just another nobody. For most of her life she had been all too special, a somebody, different from others, and marked down for death because of it. How strange it felt to be free of that!

She went to her bicycle. She had found it in the street the day the Americans had entered the town, and it had been her constant transport and companion ever since. It had been painted sky blue by its previous owner, which she thought was a good omen.

As she was climbing on to it, she heard a voice calling her name.

'Lola! Is that you?'

She turned. For a moment she didn't recognise the young woman. Then she realised it was Angelika, the Edelweiss Pirate girl who'd attached herself to them in Cologne, and been arrested near Osnabrück. Her cropped hair had grown in the past months, and was now a flaming auburn mop. She wore lipstick, rouge and eyeshadow, and was in the company of two American soldiers.

She broke away from them, and ran over to Lola, throwing herself into Lola's arms with such force that she almost knocked her and her bicycle down.

'Oh, I'm so glad to see you! I thought you must be dead!'

'I thought the same about you,' Lola said, laughing as she hugged the girl in return.

'Where's Max?'

Lola shook her head, her smile fading. 'Max is dead.'

Angelika's face, still juvenile under the adult make-up, clouded over. 'Oh no! How?'

'First he was shot by a Russian, defending me. I thought he was going to recover. But then an SS soldier beat him and reopened the wound. He died in my arms two days later.'

'The bastards! And after he fought for them! Why did they have to do that?'

'Why did they have to do any of it?'

'What a shame. He was a good man.'

'Yes. He was a very good man.'

'You'll find someone else,' Angelika said, with a typically heartless pragmatism. She indicated the American soldiers proudly. 'Look. I've found two!'

'How do you manage two at the same time?'

'Oh, they're easy to manage. And very free with their money.' She hoisted her skirt to show Lola the stockings she was wearing. 'See? Real nylon. And the underwear, too! Get yourself an American as soon as you can.'

'I'm afraid I'm still grieving for Max,' Lola said gently.

'But he's dead.'

'It doesn't matter. I will always love him.'

Angelika shrugged incredulously. 'Love? Who's talking about *love*?'

'What happened to you after Osnabrück?' Lola asked, changing the subject.

'They threw me in jail with a bunch of other people. But I never betrayed you! They talked about hanging us, but never got around to it. Between the air raids and the invasion, they let us all go in the end. I got a ride here with three Gestapo men on the run. I learned a lot from them. And you?'

'Oh . . .' The impossibility of explaining what she and Max had been through took Lola's words away. 'We've been here and there. I came through. Max didn't.'

One of the American soldiers called out in English. 'Angie! Let's go!'

Angelika hugged Lola again. 'I'm so glad to see you. Let's meet up for a drink tonight, and catch up. Okay? There's a bar downtown where all the Americans go. It's called the Bayerischer Keller. See you there!'

Lola watched the girl run back to her friends and link her arms through theirs as they went on their way. She doubted she'd go to the Bayerischer Keller tonight. Or ever see Angelika again. Still, stranger things had happened. There was no telling what fate would bring. So many had died, so many good people. And Angelika, of all people, had survived.

Well, she thought, good luck to Angelika. She'd been glad to see her. Her survival was another good omen. A new world had to be made from the ruins of the old one, and it would take new people to make it.

She was very hungry. The ration cards were no longer valid, now that the Americans were in charge, and she had almost no money, and the shops were empty, in any case. She was lonelier than she had ever been in her life. She didn't have a friend in the world, unless you counted Angelika.

She was billeted in a cellar that was stuffed with refugees of all kinds, from former Dachau inmates to shifty German civilians who she was sure were SS or Gestapo thugs hiding their identities. There, bread and soup were occasionally handed out, but mealtimes were by no means reliable. You had to be lucky.

But despite all that, it was a joy to be alive. She had passed through storm, through fire, through the valley of darkness, and she had emerged at the other side. The shadow of death had been lifted.

For twelve years of her young life, the shadow of the swastika had loomed over her. She had lost count of the times she had thought she would die, and somehow, she had survived. She wouldn't be here but for all those who had helped her, many at the cost of their own lives. Above all, Max. She owed him a debt that she would now never be able to repay.

The shadow was lifting. The Thousand Year Reich, after barely a dozen unimaginably violent years, had crumbled into ash. It was as though she hadn't seen the sun in all that time, and now it had emerged from behind black clouds. She was scarred inside, but she had her youth and her strength. She had life.

She thought back to the interview she'd had with the Swiss Red Cross official. He had reminded her oddly of the various Nazi bureaucrats she had dealt with in her life, a man to whom a piece of paper meant far more than the warm, breathing human being sitting opposite him. Lola started laughing quietly.

There was no bitterness in her laughter. She had shed all bitterness by now. She had shed anger and regret. She no longer asked why, or wondered what for. She was free.

Yes, there was sorrow. There would always be grief, for as long as she lived, for those who were no longer with her, for those who had died so that she could live. She owed them each a life, what Max had called a 'good life' as he lay dying. Perhaps she would meet them again, somewhere, in some place beyond death. She missed them terribly. But her grief did not mean she couldn't laugh. They would have wanted her to laugh, the beloved departed. The past was alive within her. Only death and silence killed the past.

Mama and Papa's joy for living lived on in her. They had shone on the stage of life, spreading laughter and humanity. She would do her best to do the same. She would carry them, and Heidi, and Max, inside her forever.

She would have to decide what she was going to do with the rest of her life.

She was open to suggestions.

But whatever happened, she would live a good life. Somewhere, far away, she would have love again, would have a family, would have children of her own. There was evil in the world, but there was also good. There was tragedy, and there was also joy.

There were American soldiers everywhere. They were not military in the German sense of the word. They did not crash their boots down in orderly lines, or wear tight uniforms, or stare straight ahead like stern automata. No, these soldiers sped around in Jeeps, with their legs and arms hanging nonchalantly out, smoking cigarettes and tossing the butts, half smoked, on to the ground – where the Germans picked them up eagerly – wearing comfortable, loose overalls, with their helmets pushed to the backs of their heads, the straps swinging loose.

Swinging loose was what they did. Every movement was balletic, athletic, supple. At night she had heard the alluring strains of their jazz, 'debased jungle music' as the Nazis had called it, and that made her want to swing loose, too.

She could see the astonishment in the faces of the Germans that the mighty *Wehrmacht* had been crushed by such insouciant warriors as these. And they were tolerant, even kindly to the Germans who were now in their power. Smiles and chewing gum were handed out liberally.

Lola found that she rather liked this way of doing things. Kindness and grace were infinitely preferable to Prussian cruelty, any day. She felt she could get used to a life that was lived swinging loose.

A Sherman tank rolled past her. The soldiers catching a ride on it grinned at her and waved. She had never seen a black man before she'd met the Americans, although the Nazi propaganda had been full of lurid tales of their savagery and libidinousness. They seemed to be even kinder than the white soldiers. She waved back.

One of the soldiers called out to her, 'Hey! You speak English?'

She nodded. 'Yes.'

'Hungry?'

She nodded again. 'Yes!'

He hopped off the tank and ran over to her. How athletic he was! He was carrying a handful of American candy bars. 'Here. I hope you like these.' He tipped them into the basket of her bicycle.

Lola stared at the abundance: a Butterfinger, a Baby Ruth, a Hershey bar and one inexplicably called Mr. Goodbar. The wrappers were colourful, the gayest things in the grey day. She had almost forgotten what chocolate tasted like. The GI was already running back to catch up with his tank. 'Thank you!' she called. He turned and waved, prancing stylishly backwards with his knees high, like a circus performer. She laughed and applauded.

Today she would eat the Hershey bar. And tomorrow, one of the others. There would be a chocolate bar every day for four whole days!

She got on to her bicycle, and set off with a push. The roads were muddy and rutted from the tank tracks, but she steered skilfully between the potholes, which were filled with murky water of uncertain depth.

The day was changeable. A gust of rain swept over her, and then was gone. A rift opened in the grey clouds. Their lacy rims blazed silver. Beyond was the glowing doorway to some new world.

Suddenly, the potholes were all filled with blue sky. A pillar of vivid sunlight poured through the rift in the clouds. She leaned over the handlebars, and pedalled resolutely towards it.

Epilogue

The fire has burned low. My daughter looks cold. She hugs herself, shivering a little, in the semi-darkness.

'But Mom, I don't understand. The German soldier in this photograph – that's Max?'

'Yes,' I say. 'That is Max. The man who gave the photo to you was one of his cousins. He emigrated to America after the war, and always took an interest in you.'

'Took an interest in me? Why would some stranger take an interest in me? And why did Aunt Caroline say—' She breaks off, the truth slowly starting to dawn on her, at first unacceptable, and then irresistible. I see the glow of the dying flames illuminate the fine hairs rising on her forearms.

I nod slowly. 'I didn't realise I was pregnant until some weeks after Max died. I thought that the stress had stopped my periods. But it wasn't the stress. It was you.'

Maggie lays her hand on her mouth. 'Oh. Oh, my God.'

'I went for a check-up at an American army hospital, and they confirmed it. The doctor who saw me was a young obstetrician, so kind and warm that I just wanted to hide myself in his arms.'

'Dad?'

'Yes. Dad.'

Maggie stares at the fragile black-and-white image of the tall man in uniform, standing next to a woman in the clothing of the 1940s. 'But then this man, Max, is – was – my father?'

'Yes, my dear. And that is his mother, Magda. Your grandmother. You were named after her.'

Maggie is still trying to process it. 'Then Dad wasn't my real father!'

That makes me sit up. 'Never say that,' I rebuke her sharply. 'Never think it. Dad was your real father in every way that mattered. He was a wonderful father to you, your brothers and your sisters, and a wonderful husband to me. Never devalue what he was.'

'I always felt I was different from my siblings,' Maggie says slowly. 'I never knew why.' She is trembling. 'For God's sake!' Her voice chokes. 'Why didn't you *tell* me?'

I gather my thoughts to answer her. 'There were times, over the years, when I wanted to tell you,' I reply at length. 'But each time, I discussed it with your father – and each time, your father asked me to keep silent. He didn't want you to ever feel that you weren't fully his daughter. He felt it would damage your relationship with him. So each time, I said nothing. It wasn't my decision alone, Maggie. Today, for the first time, it is my decision alone. You asked. And now I've told you.'

'And if I hadn't asked?'

'But you did ask.'

'And if I hadn't?' she presses. 'If that old man hadn't given me this photo – and Caroline hadn't said anything – would you have kept it a secret?'

I am trying to be honest with her. 'Yes, I think so.'

Her face twists in pain. 'Mom – this is something I've felt inside me my whole life. I didn't know what the question was. I just knew there was a question.' Her voice rises. 'It's been so painful for me!'

'I've told you the truth, Maggie.'

'But your whole life, you've told me a lie!'

Without waiting for a reply, Maggie gets up abruptly, and walks outside into the garden.

After a while, I pull a cashmere wrap around my shoulders and follow her. She is standing on the terrace.

The sun is beginning to edge its crimson rim up over the hills. Long ago, my husband and I planted a Japanese garden of maples and conifers here, and their colours, in this Connecticut autumn, are glorious. I gaze at the immaculately manicured pines and azaleas, each leaf shimmering in the delicate grey light, as detailed as a painting, yet massed in uncountable numbers, a lifetime's labour of love.

A light rain washes over us. Two moorhens rise from the still water of the pond below, and flap away together like ghosts.

Maggie stands with folded arms, her back to me. I wonder what she is feeling. Anger? These days, women seem to be easily angry with their mothers. I never had that luxury. I saw my mother die before I was an adult. Does she feel relief, that she finally understands the subtle differences between herself and her brothers and sisters? Does she feel any compassion, for people who had to make difficult decisions, and did what they thought was for the best?

I doubt it.

I reach out and touch my daughter's arm lightly. 'There were other reasons, Maggie.'

'What reasons?' she demands. She is very angry.

'In those days, there was a lot of shame about these things.'

'Shame?'

'A child born out of marriage carried a stigma.'

She hunches her shoulders, rejecting such an antiquated notion. 'For God's sake!'

'Your father and I couldn't get married because he wasn't divorced yet. So you were born illegitimate. A war child. I couldn't register your father's name.'

'You cut him out of my life at birth!' she throws at me over her shoulder.

'The father has to be present to be registered,' I say quietly. 'And without him at my side, how was I to justify that I, a Jew, had been in love with a soldier of the Nazi state, and bore his child? How would I explain to my fellow Jews? It would not be easy. People wouldn't have understood. The few people who knew were shocked. They said hurtful things that could cast a shadow over a young life. Dad and I made a pact. We decided together, before you were born, that you would be *his* daughter. He knew about Max, of course. I told him everything, and he accepted it all. Dad delivered you with his own hands, in a military hospital in Germany. He held you before I did. He was ready to be your father. He was ready to love you all his days. And I hope you know that he did.'

Maggie is shivering. 'Of *course* I know that.'

'We weren't married until the following year, when we were in America together, and the way was clear. After that, the past was past. When the war ended, I told myself I would never have to hide again. Never tell another lie. But unfortunately, it wasn't as easy as that. Try to understand.'

'I *don't* understand.' She turns to me at last, blue eyes hot. She reminds me so much of Max when she is upset. 'You are very strange, Mom.'

'I suppose I am.'

'Whatever your reasons, you should not have kept this from me.'

'Perhaps not.'

She hunches her shoulders. 'Did you ever love Dad?'

'How can you ask that question?' I ask her. 'I think you know the answer.'

'The same way you loved Max?'

A difficult question. 'Love is not something you can weigh or count out like beans. I knew Max for a few months of war, while the world was falling to pieces. I spent the rest of my life in tranquillity, with your father. We had four children together, and we had you. I was very lucky to be loved by both of them. Both were very special, honourable, decent men.'

'Do you ever think of him – of my real father?'

'Of course. Not a day goes by that I do not think of him, and of all those I lost. I miss them all. They are in my dreams.'

'But you never said a damned word!'

'I'll tell you everything you want to know about him. He would have been so proud of you! But he left this world before he even knew that you were coming into it.'

'Mom—' For a moment I think she is going to reach out to me. Then she twists away once more. 'I'll never forgive you. Never.'

My heart drops. But I try again. 'You brought me so much joy, Maggie. When I had nothing left, to feel you growing inside me, waiting to live your own life, was a treasure beyond anything I could have imagined. You saved me. And you've never given me anything but joy, in all these sixty-five years since.'

There is nothing more I can say. Not right now. Later, perhaps, if she is not lost to me, she will have more questions. And I will try to find more answers.

I watch the moorhens return to the water, two spirits landing on their own reflected images, wings folding, gliding through the ripples that spread out and smooth back into silver. The sun has risen now, the red emblem of another day.

She says I am very strange. She's right. I am very strange. She is the flower, I am the roots, hidden deep, strange and tangled when dug up.

She says she will never forgive me. Never is a long time.

I fear she will soon get into her shiny American car, and drive away. And it may be months before I see her again. And I do not have so many months to spare.

My youth was lived in the shadows. I never wanted those shadows to fall on Maggie. I want to explain that to her. I wish I could talk fluently, like these American women do. I wish words came easily to me, words to tell her how much she means to me. I have tried to shed my German accent, but it clings on stubbornly. I am still a German. Though my limbs are stiff, and my hair white, God help me, I'm still Lola Rosenstein from Berlin.

I wait for my daughter's reaction.

How do I feel, now that I have given up my last secret? Not unburdened – because it was never a burden. It was a precious thing, that has enriched my life these sixty-five years.

And it was never my secret alone to keep. My husband was resolute that Maggie should not know the truth. 'Tell her when I'm dead, if you want,' he said to me once. 'Not before.'

So I kept silent. I owed him that.

But now, am I going to lose my daughter? I lost everyone I loved in Germany. Except Maggie. She was all that remained to me of Max. She was all I brought with me out of the Third Reich. I left everything else behind. I brought her to America. And here I made a new start. We've been blessed with happiness and love. For that – and for all the rest – I am grateful.

She asks me if I ever think of Max. A strange question. I think of them all, all. All of them who died, so that I could live.

I think of Mama and Papa. Of Heidi, and Magda. Of the friends of my childhood, whose faces come to me in dreams. And of Max. I talk to them all.

They are all up there, in the attic of my memory. I visit them there every day.

None of them grow old, as I have grown old.

I am older now than my parents were when they died. Max was not far off the age of my daughter's eldest son. Who, incidentally, looks like him.

They all suffered, but in exchange they were granted eternal youth.

I see that my daughter is crying, now. Perhaps that's a good sign. Perhaps she can forgive me. Though I don't know how she can ever understand.

To understand the past, you need to speak the language of the past. And the language of the past is a lost language.

Because the past is a foreign country. They do things differently there.

ACKNOWLEDGMENTS

I want to thank my wonderful editors, Sammia Hamer and Mike Jones, as well as all the team at Lake Union, who have been so unfailingly supportive and warm.

I also want to thank my readers. Many of you have been with me for thirty years and more. Your wise criticisms have educated me. Your compliments have encouraged me. Your companionship has made all the difference to a career that is necessarily solitary. You are always in my mind as I write. I am eternally grateful.

ABOUT THE AUTHOR

Marius Gabriel was accused by *Cosmopolitan* magazine of 'keeping you reading while your dinner burns'. He served his author apprenticeship as a student at Newcastle University, Britain, where, to finance his postgraduate research, he wrote thirty-three steamy romances under a pseudonym. Gabriel is the author of twelve historical novels, including the bestsellers *The Designer*, *The Ocean Liner* and *The Parisians*. Born in South Africa, he has travelled and worked in many countries, and now lives in Lincolnshire. He has three grown-up children.

Did you enjoy this book and would like to get informed when Marius Gabriel publishes his next work? Just follow the author on Amazon!

1) Search for the book you were just reading on Amazon or in the Amazon App.
2) Go to the Author Page by clicking on the Author's name.
3) Click the "Follow" button.

If you enjoyed this book on a Kindle eReader or in the Kindle App, you will be automatically offered to follow the author when arriving at the last page.

LAKE UNION
PUBLISHING